DATE DUE

THE

ULTRAVIOLET

SKY

THE

ULTRAVIOLET

SKY

ALMA LUZ VILLANUEVA

ANCHOR BOOKS
DOUBLEDAY

NEW YORK   LONDON   TORONTO   SYDNEY   AUCKLAND

To Bob Ross and Anna Marie Valle, my friends, and to my son, Marc Jason Goulet, who always lends me the bright side of his shadow, his huge courage like the heroes of old. Like the new hero—gentle, strong.

AN ANCHOR BOOK

PUBLISHED BY DOUBLEDAY

a division of Bantam Doubleday Dell Publishing Group, Inc.
1540 Broadway, New York, New York 10036

ANCHOR BOOKS, DOUBLEDAY, and the portrayal of an anchor
are trademarks of Doubleday, a division of Bantam Doubleday Dell
Publishing Group, Inc.

The Ultraviolet Sky was originally published by Bilingual Press/Editorial Bilingüe in 1988. The Anchor Books edition is published by arrangement with Bilingual Press/Editorial Bilingüe.

"The Sky" (p. 378) is published with the permission of its author, Wilfredo Q. Castaño.
"Dark Roots" (p. 79) by Alma Luz Villanueva is from *Life Span* (Austin, TX: Place of Herons Press, 1985). Printed with permission of the author.
"Of/To Man" (p. 170), "On Recognizing the Labor of Clarity/Sun to Sun, Moon to Moon" (p. 170), and "She Snake" (p. 362) by Alma Luz Villanueva are from *Third Chicano Literary Prize* (Irvine, CA: University of California, Irvine, 1977). Printed with permission of the author.
The quotation from Ursula K. LeGuin (p. 371) is from *The Beginning Place* (New York: Harper & Row, 1980), p. 129.
The quotation from Rosario Castellanos (p. 5) is from *Meditation on the Threshold*, trans. Julian Palley (Tempe, AZ: Bilingual Press, 1988), p. 79.

Library of Congress Cataloging-in-Publication Data

Villanueva, Alma, 1944–
The ultraviolet sky / Alma Luz Villanueva.—1st Anchor Books ed.
p.   cm.
1. Women artists—Fiction. I. Title.
[PS3572.I354U48   1993]
813'.54—dc20   92-42503
CIP

ISBN 0-385-42014-5
Copyright © 1988 by Alma Luz Villanueva

ALL RIGHTS RESERVED
PRINTED IN THE UNITED STATES OF AMERICA
FIRST ANCHOR BOOKS EDITION: MAY 1993

1   3   5   7   9   10   8   6   4   2

"I had what the mediocre envy, what
victors dispute and one alone snatches away.
I had it and it was like eating foam,
like passing one's hand over the back of the wind.

Supreme pride is supreme
renunciation. I didn't want
to be the dead star
that uses borrowed light to survive."

Rosario Castellanos (Mexico, 1925-1974)
From "Monologue of a Foreign Woman"

Part One

They were arguing again.

He was taking their child to visit his family for Thanksgiving. That was fine, she'd have time alone, and then her son, Sean, would be coming to stay for a while. But now it was the argument that preoccupied her, flared her up as though they'd never been separated this last year. What didn't go into love and passion went into hate and anger, and there never seemed to be a middle ground, a bridge, to simply stand on and speak, or to cross over in order to touch as friends. Yes, as friends.

"Can't you take my goddamned car and see what's happening to my starter? I've got to take off tomorrow. I have a flight, remember?" Julio began shouting.

"Then that means I have to drive you back and forth, twice. And then I have to drive back to the airport in a couple of days to get Sean." Rosa raised her voice as the old fury returned full force, in spite of her vow to remain calm, detached. "Isn't that a little selfish of you?"

"Should I call off my plans? Would that suit you, Rosa?"

"Why don't you take your car in right now? Why in the hell should I do it?" Rosa felt the tears behind her eyes, but she refused to give him that, her tears.

Julio stared at her, hard. There were no tears behind those eyes, just will, will, will. So they stood there, battle lines drawn. Rosa remembered the night, there in the same room, the front room, when they'd argued over the baby, Luzia. She wouldn't let Julio touch her and he nearly grabbed the baby out of her hands.

"Don't you dare touch her! Do you hear me?" Rosa ran for the bedroom, locking it behind her. Her breath came sharply, like an animal fighting for her young. Her lips pulled back, involuntarily, over her teeth.

As Rosa fed Luzia, his words kept repeating themselves in her ears, until she calmed herself in the darkness and her breath became human again.

After Luzia was fed and asleep, Rosa went out to the front room where Julio lay on the couch, in the dark, smoking a cigarette. He seemed to take delight, a silent one, in her great agitation and fury, lying there stretched out and maddeningly confident.

"Until you apologize to me for what you said, Julio, you may not touch her. Do you understand me?" Rosa repeated. "You may not touch her."

Julio remained stretched out on the couch, and with an unfeeling calm said, "I pay you two hundred a month for my child. You have nothing to complain about."

Sheer rage shot through Rosa, of a kind she'd never felt before. She grabbed the long, black, steel fire poker, its tip like a spear. She held it in both hands and, for a split second, she imagined herself plunging it right into his upturned belly.

"Why don't you do it? Why don't you kill me? Then you could really brag about something to your feminist friends." Julio's voice lost all control. There was anger, hatred, and a strange sorrow in it all at once.

Rosa could do it. He continued to lay there like a perfect target. Yes, she could certainly do it.

"I'd never forgive myself, Julio." Rosa slowly hung the black poker back up, steel for steel. The matter was finished in her self. She locked the bedroom door and passed out.

"They won't be able to fix it today. We could have dinner in Reno. My treat, and I'll pay for all your gas, of course. Can't we talk, Rosa?" Julio said, softly. Too softly.

"You still have time to go see if they can fix it today. Why do you insist I take it and then have to drive you to the airport tomorrow?" Rosa was calmer now but resolute. She wouldn't do it.

"I just called, Rosa." Julio's voice remained soft and insistent. "They have to keep it for a couple of days to order the part. We could take off early and have dinner in Reno, and I'll cover your gas." His eyes reached her, touching her with a sad, soft gentleness. I almost forgot, he told himself, again.

Rosa's body started when his words penetrated. She was prepared to hold her ground and not give an inch to his demands. And now Julio stood there with those words in his mouth, repeating them softly, as they reached her like a gentle wind.

Julio stood by the door still waiting for Rosa's reply. She walked a few steps and found herself across the room facing him. She felt no demand, but an opening, an unfamiliar opening. No, she'd felt it in the very beginning of being together before he thought he'd conquered her and she thought she'd submitted to him—to love, to what? As though it had to happen to have any dialogue at all as a man and a woman.

Rosa suddenly knew what she had to do, what she really wanted to do. She walked the few steps between them, quickly. Just as quickly Julio's face registered a minor shock, but he continued to stand facing her. Rosa, herself, was amazed at her inner command, as she placed her hands up toward him in front of her, palms toward him. His hands rose up in an instant touching hers, palm to palm. They smiled quick, embarrassed smiles, and an old wave of physical attraction shimmered between them.

"I'll take your car tomorrow. Wait a minute, why don't we take it right now so you can drive me back." Rosa shifted her body without denying the exchange.

"Good idea. I'll give them another call and let them know. Thanks, Rosa. Dinner's on me, wine included." Julio smiled like a suitor, with no intention of being a suitor. He shifted his body as subtly as Rosa's and a comfort passed between them.

The very earth underneath them seemed to have shifted, and that, too, was subtle, rare. And the house that stood on that piece of earth. Rosa had dreamt this place—that's what brought her to it, this place in the mountains. That and a friend's letter saying she was living in a remote place called Lupine Meadows. The map didn't mention it, but Rosa had guessed where it was by the largest town close by, the county seat.

It'd intrigued her, this invisible place where purple lupine must grow in dense, rich clusters. Lupine, the wolf. Were there wolves there? she'd wondered, seeing a running wolf in her mind's eye, strong, thin muzzle to the ground. Bears, mountain lions, rattlesnakes, coyotes, snow and ice—these would be there and she'd never lived within proximity to any of them.

It'd gotten so unbearable between Rosa and Julio that to hear him breathe unsettled her at times, and his eyes, whenever he looked at her, were full of dark reproach. He wanted to own her, to command her, entirely, she felt, and she was afraid he could.

One night when they still lived together by the ocean, close to the city, she took her sleeping bag out to the garden to a small wild spot of tall grasses, Queen Anne's lace, fern and wild mustard. A patch really, but enough.

Walking through the dark, barefoot, she felt exposed to prowlers, rapists, and the assorted teen-age drunks down the street. Not to speak of the neighbor's teen-age boys who were always alone and drinking, throwing their occasional deafening party. The father was a truck driver and gone most of the time, so they did as they pleased.

And so Rosa picked her way out to the back of the garden with all this in mind, laid her sleeping bag down in the long, dense grass and slipped into it with the usual delight sleeping bags gave her. The grass felt better than any bed ever could, and the smells of the earth and sleeping flowers began to soothe her, and she began to trust the cool, damp night. She knew she'd wake up a little wet, but she didn't care. Not really.

Then the stars began to draw closer, as they do when one sleeps under them. Their gentle lights, and the few fierce ones, began what she always felt to be a communication with her. They always, as she looked up at them, seemed to be trying to tell her something.

Rosa heard a low, growling sound behind her and her attention snapped awake to danger. She grabbed her Buck Knife from its black leather case in her right hand, and her dog in her left by his collar. Zack, an Alaskan malamute, lifted his head to watch her. Rosa noticed Zack wasn't snarling the way he should be to an approaching stranger, the way she'd seen him do on walks a couple of times when there had been danger. She looked at him closely and he seemed relaxed which calmed but also confused her.

Rosa heard the growling sound again, but closer, and she took the chance of speaking. "I have my dog here and I hear you coming." Rosa listened for movement and she stood up, slowly. A waning moon, to her startled eyes, revealed Julio crawling on his hands and knees toward her. The instant he saw her he leapt to his feet, in his underwear, with an ominous anger.

"You aren't safe out here, you know," he said with a threatening tone.

"Not with you around. What in the hell are you doing crawling around in the fucking bushes? Are you hungry or horny?" Rosa was livid. She felt like throwing a rock at him, maybe she could knock him out.

"I'm going back in, it's cold and damp out here. Back where the humans sleep," Julio responded sulkily. He hated her at this moment. Her submission had only been brief.

"If you try that shit again you're going to get it with whatever I've got in my hands. I won't ask next time who it is. You won't hear *me*. Do you hear me, Julio?" Rosa raised her voice. She wanted to push a button and make him disappear.

Apparently, Julio felt the same urge. He wanted to kill her and eat her she felt, and she was right.

Rosa returned to her sleeping bag sweating and trembling from anger and a strange fear. You would expect to protect yourself from an unknown man, but not your husband, she thought. Maybe he is an unknown man, she finally answered herself, letting Zack get comfortable next to her on the tall grass. She started to cry, silently, because some part of her still loved him, and she knew she would have to kill and eat that too. The last thing she remembered was a thin, quick shooting star, and clutching her knife beside her.

She'd been disappointed. The stars there were always watered down with too much city glare from the north, or fog as an almost constant feature on this part of the coast, so close to San Francisco where she'd been born and grown up.

The city, cities, brought back memories of unguarded violence, the possibility of human violence—sudden, unpredictable and somehow personal. And Julio, what memories did he carry . . . helicopters, automatic rifles, screams, night patrols. Human violence at its most unguarded. War. Vietnam. Her violence. His violence. To threaten. To retaliate.

It was a love story of their time. The love was hidden, a huge and constant pain threatening to explode and kill both sides. It was a dangerous blindness. Rosa had come to see only a man, an enemy—hadn't he gone to war? Julio had come to see only a woman, an enemy—hadn't she left, castrated, her last husband?

Twice Julio had goaded her into a frenzy, and she'd sprung on him hitting him with her fists. The first time they'd laughed later at her wildness. The next time it happened she saw it coming; she saw the smile begin to etch itself across his lips, slightly, and she realized he wanted her to do it. To *be* what he felt.

With an immense effort, like pulling open a jammed door, she pulled herself away from him and left the house. She felt aimless, insanely aimless, as she got into her car, but something dragged her toward the ocean; something always dragged her to the ocean. She parked her car in the dark, wondering what in the hell she was going to do there in the dark.

Rosa was still raging with the same energy, so she knew she had to get out and walk. And then she saw the cement pier stretching out into the night, dim lights halfway, then total darkness where kids had shot them out. She wanted to walk to the very end of the pier, and yet she was afraid to. Yes, Rosa admitted it to herself, she was really terrified to. And what was she afraid of—men. And what was she running from—a man.

Rosa's anger overwhelmed her and she jerked the car door open. She hadn't even thought to bring her dog or her knife. The night air was damp, a slight fog clung to her and everything else, but she could hear the ocean, steady and persistent, and it gave her a hollow feeling in the pit of her stomach. Rosa knew if she was going to take the walk out to the end of the pier—she could see it jutting out aggressively, its grey, manmade cement, to the sea—she was going to have to fill up the pit of her stomach with something, anything. Simple rage would do.

Rosa crossed the street to the largest lighted area of the pier where the hot dog stand was, now closed, and the bathrooms still threw a patch of light from open doors. Some teen-age boys watched her walk by—it would've made her feel a little better if some girls had been with them. But she knew what she must look like walking by them; determined, yes, a grim determination beyond cultural taboos of a lone woman in the night, the threat of violence, or perhaps just the reminder of possible violence, the imposition of masculine freedom, "Hey, sweet thing," or "Should you be out here by your lonesome?"

They said nothing as she passed.

As Rosa walked beyond the well-lit area the sight of the slender pier with its indirect lighting, and then the darkness beyond even that where all the lights were always out, terrified her and yet invited her at once.

She kept up her steady pace passing between scattered men on either side of her. How strange it is at night, she thought—a different world from the daytime walks of families, mothers with their children, kids bicycling by. This is the unspoken world of Men Only At Night—we are safe here, not you, alone. Alone—you must be very foolish or very crazy, Rosa felt their thoughts, their contempt. Or very, very dangerous, and in that instant she felt them turn away.

Now she was more than midway, and the dim lights gave way to absolute darkness, the night and the sheer presence of the surrounding sea. At this point, Rosa was well beyond the breakers where depth began and the waves prepared themselves to meet the shore.

A small, nagging part of her wanted to turn back, saying, "Okay, you've walked halfway, that's enough, don't be stupid." But a larger part of her commanded, "Walk the whole way."

Gradually, Rosa's eyes were becoming accustomed to the darkness and she could actually feel the pier tremble from the sea beneath her. Everything became sharper because she couldn't see as well, so she heard and felt acutely, and she welcomed it with a profound relief.

Here and there she began to see fishermen, their poles reaching out to the darkness. Some turned slightly to stare and some not at all. At the very end of the pier she saw a small fire burning directly on the concrete, a strange, suspended sight until she was closer and saw it was a small hibachi burning down to embers. There was an older man standing next to it, his two fishing poles flung out as they moved, subtly, to the tide.

As Rosa glanced down to the other side of her feet she saw movement and moved closer, and what she saw made her jump internally. A small silver fish was twisting itself among some now dead ones. Rosa flushed hot in spite of the wet, cold air.

She remembered, when she was a girl and she used to go fishing on the piers of the city, that when the men would kill the small fish because they didn't want to catch them over and over, she'd wanted to stop them, to rescue them, but she'd been afraid of ridicule, or worse not to belong to the world of the fishermen.

They'd usually take them by the tail and bash their heads, or more simply hold their bodies, tightly, to sever their heads. And though Rosa had never done it—only to those she brought home or sold—she felt a part of the horrible ritual because she watched mutely, ashamed—almost as though she'd wet her pants and at the same time thinking, I bet they think I'm a boy.

"Do you plan to eat that fish?" Rosa asked the old man, pointing to the small silver fish flopping angrily on the cement.

The old man looked up at her, an Oriental man with sharp, critical eyes. "What?"

"Do you plan to eat that fish?" Rosa asked him again.

"I don't understand," he dismissed her with his words and his eyes as though she'd ceased to exist at all.

Rosa drew closer to him, closer to his small fire. She could see he was dreading it. "What I mean is, do you mind if I throw that fish back if you're not going to eat it?"

He looked, momentarily, appalled, and then patiently amused. "No, no. You throw that back and I catch it again and again." Then irritation overtook him. "Why should I catch these again and again?"

Rosa felt a flash of anger and a great stubbornness, and she suddenly wanted to simply reach down and throw it back anyway. But she controlled herself, quickly, and said, "Maybe those fish give you good luck when you throw them back. Maybe they bring the big ones." She looked into his eyes all the while in the dark, the small fire giving her hints of his expression.

Then he smiled, just in his eyes, "Go on if you want. Maybe you're right. It could be."

She reached down and the small, slippery body felt repulsive to her bare hands for a moment, and then she realized the fish had razor-sharp gills as they grazed her. Should I just stand up and leave it? the thought came to her.

Rosa grabbed at its tail and finally held it, thrusting it over the side of the pier. It disappeared, and she imagined the sheer joy the small silver fish must feel, water all around her.

Rosa walked back to the old fisherman and stood beside him for a while, but there was nothing really to say anymore. If only a large fish would come now, she thought as she walked back towards her car, this time not terrified but alert, and a joy in the pit of her stomach.

When Rosa returned home Julio was asleep, or rather pretending to be asleep because when she entered the bed quietly—she'd purposely done everything quietly—he reached for her, to hold her, to take away the night walk. Their lovemaking would feel like an assault to her now, and the more she might enjoy it, the more he would make her pay. Later.

"Please don't touch me. I don't feel like being touched, at all, Julio," Rosa whispered, firmly, yet in the back of her mind the usual guilt lurked as though she had no right to say it.

"You always say that. Well, when *do* you feel like it?" He began to raise his voice, the bully routine.

Rosa remembered the small silver fish flopping on the pier. "Maybe never, who knows," her voice shot back. She began to leave the bed to sleep in the front room, her body almost upright, when Julio pulled her back down and pinned her under him.

"Where do you think you're going?" he exploded.

"Let go of me, you fucker!"

"Where in the hell do you think you're going?"

"I said let go of me right the fuck now!" Rosa's body erupted into a frenzy, slipping away from his hands.

"We aren't married, that's for fucking sure!" Julio shouted.

Rosa grabbed the sleeping bag from the closet. It felt like a bomb had gone off inside of her. If he tried to touch her again her skin would probably kill him. She understood murder, intimately.

She opened the front room drapes wide to an expanse of sea in the distance. A waning crescent moon was beginning to turn gold, and the island-rock, as she called it, commanded the dark. It was a presence she always imagined as holding its own against the sea, and the great white spray, constantly moving against it, in the daytime was a reassuring sight. Tonight the sea was relatively calm, and then she remembered the trembling of the pier even on a calm night. Rosa's breathing began to even out, and the radiation in her body to settle.

She listened to any sounds from the bedroom. She didn't believe Julio was giving up, completely, yet, so she waited with her ears cocked. Rosa focused the binoculars out on the water, skimming the moon's pale light, thinking of the silver fish, its strong, slim body. Then she focused on the silver moon, its now golden craters, and she was strangely sad thinking of how men could now walk on the moon, as though everything were within reach, the mystery touchable.

Yeah, but just try to live there, you idiots, she thought, and the thought consoled her.

Rosa got up without a sound and poured herself a glass of dry, red wine, earth-wine, almost granular. She thought of the reverse possibility of bothering Julio, and the thought made her laugh inwardly. She thought of the story of her grandmother pouring a pan of boiling water out the window on a daughter's—Rosa's mother's—unwanted suitor. Though the story had shocked her at first, she'd also understood her grandmother completely. She'd meant to say GO AWAY!, and she wasn't kidding. Now Rosa was sorry she hadn't asked, "Did you hit him? Did he scream? Did he jump around?"

That woman, Luz, her grandmother, with the legendary bad temper, how Rosa loved her memory. When Rosa was very ill one time her grandmother made a flour and dry mustard plaster for her chest because she could barely breathe, and the plaster threatened to take her chest off. It was almost unbearable. Her grandmother told her a story about her childhood in Mexico: "I was a young girl, your age I think, and my mother was with a man who I hated. He was a truly horrible man. I won't tell you why, you are too young. I ran away, my mother had no power with him. She would protect me, and he would punish her as well. Neighbors brought me home, they meant well, and my mother wasn't home. He took hot wood coals and burned my feet so that I would never run away again. My mother left that man soon after, and her other husbands would be kinder. In fact, Rosa, she had four husbands. The Indians in my old home had a good idea, if a man is cruel he is not your true husband. My feet, Rosa? Oh, yes, they blistered and swelled up so that I thought maybe he was right, that I would never walk again. But I did, of course. My mother healed my feet, I thought she would kill him with her eyes. But I don't think I ever ran again, as though my feet remembered their sorrow . . ." Rosa fell asleep, finally, with a larger pity for the other little girl of her own age, and in the morning she woke without a trace of congestion.

Now Rosa contemplated boiling a pan of water and sprinkling it on Julio. She wondered if her great-grandmother would stay with the likes of him. No, he didn't beat her, not on her body, but somewhere, somewhere deep inside of her, she felt beat up.

Then she heard Julio in the kitchen opening the wine bottle, and then she heard his voice, the charming one, "Do you want some wine, Rosa?"

"No, thank you," she returned stiffly.

"Why don't you come back to bed, I'll leave you alone. I promise." He sounded sorry, wounded, sincere.

"I have no desire to come to the bed, don't you understand? This is where I want to sleep, right here." She put no apology in her voice or he'd take it as weakness.

"What a bitch," Julio muttered, thudding into the bedroom like a bear, but he left the bedroom door open knowing how that would annoy her. He would curl up like a large, furry creature robbed of its prey, its warm-blooded sustenance. And yet within him was the man that knew better, who gave him no respite, "You fucking fool, you blew it, you blew it again. Who would love you anyway? You're ugly as sin and you know it," not knowing that Sinn was an ancient Babylonian Moon God, and that perhaps in some strange sense this God stirred in him, in the man.

Hadn't Sinn been invoked by his worshippers, "Mother Womb, begetter of all things, O Merciful Father who has taken into his care the whole world . . ." And hadn't Ishtar, the ancient Babylonian Moon Goddess, also been invoked, "O my Goddess and my God . . ." And even closer to their racial memories was Quetzalcoatl, Feathered Serpent, God and Goddess . . . and didn't Quetzalcoatl have an older sister, with the same qualities, who never stepped forth in the myth at all, who was never known at all . . .

If Quetzalcoatl is the morning star after his self-imposed sacrifice, then perhaps his older sister, Quetzalpetlatl, is the dark night, ever-present, infinite, ever-loving, holding her myth inside herself, holding the galaxies with a terrible love, and reaching out to place herself in the dreams of those who might remember her, Goddess and God, male and female. Was the real sin against Sinn, Ishtar, Quetzalcoatl, the sister Quetzalpetlatl: to not remember her?

Each era has had its abyss and its edge, but the one in which Rosa and Julio lived was particularly horrifying, and particularly beautiful. The major powers could exterminate an entire planet with ease, as easily as Rosa could've speared Julio belly up. And, yet, what a beautiful planet it was. What a jewel it was in the delicious darkness. World-wide, its people began to imagine this spinning globe, this immense, expanding crystal, the great intelligence of Earth, somewhere deeper than their dreams, so deep it resembled the delicious darkness, the infinite, ever-present Quetzalpetlatl. And when the Earth finally took its place spinning, spinning there in their minds, the beauty of the Earth woud stun them awake, and a voice would ask, How will *we* survive?

Rosa couldn't even ask this question yet, but she felt it daily, every single day, like a wild animal's mute desperation when it feels itself being hunted to its death, and the wild wisdom of the body, of the instinct, the cellular knowledge that also wailed an ancient warning of extinction. Extinction. How can they live with this persistent wail, this persistent warning? Rosa felt, but still she couldn't say it. Say it in words.

Extinction, not death. Sleep without dreams. Terror without beauty. Darkness without the jewel spinning, spinning. Ugly as sin? No, beautiful as Sinn becoming whole. Beautiful as Rosa reaching for a dream . . .

She stared into the darkness for a while. The moon had set, gently, into the sea's horizon, and the sea looked like an immense lake. Calm. She could hear Julio's breathing, even and peaceful as a child's, and now she began to feel that curious feeling of separation from the Earth, from the human—the only feeling that gave her peace like her painting. Through the plate glass window a small pinpoint of light welcomed her. A small, shimmering star in the delicious darkness.

Rosa sees herself standing on a blank terrain with a small, black dot miles and miles away from her. She knows she has to reach it. And then her arms begin to grow, causing her great, excruciating pain until she reaches the dot and stretches it open with her hands, until she sees where she is going. Where she has to go. A mountain, a forest, a meadow, a house. She sees it in great detail. She skims it carefully. She will remember it. She will remember.

The next morning Julio quietly showered and started the morning ritual pot of coffee. He made it exactly right; six scoops of French roast. Rosa suspected he tortured her sometimes by putting only five in which was too weak, or seven which was too strong—which was like eveything between them. Too weak or too strong. But this morning the coffee was just right.

"Do you want a chorizo omelette?" Julio asked, knowing it was her favorite. He said this with a certain care—not too weak, not too strong.

A part of Rosa sensed a trap—of indulgent affection (who says only women know this trick?)—but his chorizo omelettes were the best and she knew it. "Yes, thank you. I'll do the dishes."

Rosa's teen-age son was gone for the summer, or part of it, to work for the Forestry Service. She pictured him and she could see him darkened by the sun, his deep brown eyes a man's now. Sexual. Yes, definitely sexual. Weren't mothers supposed to notice? she wondered. She stopped bathing him when he was old enough to wash his own hair, around eight or so, and since then she'd respected his boyish privacy except for making sure he changed his socks and underwear.

Once Sean, yes she named him Sean because it was like the SEA, yet masculine with its N at the end. Sean decided to have an underwear contest, to see how long he could get away without changing it or taking a shower. This was when he was twelve, the hormones beginning to flow, she'd realized. His contest lasted almost six months, he later confessed. Rosa half-smiled at the memory of threatening to bathe him herself. His room smelled like the dirtiest sock imaginable as though Sean were proclaiming to Rosa his impending manhood by body odor alone.

Sean wasn't Julio's son, but from her first marriage, so he was mainly her son. She'd been mother and father, and friend.

"Are you getting in that shower, or do I personally have to

supervise this mess?" Rosa's eyes indicated her son. She knew if she started laughing he might try to go on for another six months.

"Come on, Mom, I was only kidding. It wasn't six months." Sean's eyes looked dark and cunning like her own.

"Bullshit, you stink! In! And when you get out I'm going to take a sniff!" Rosa replied harshly, with a playful edge. Sean balked. "Shall I bring in your ducky, too?" He gave her a final, searing glance and then she heard the shower running.

It seemed that every vital step of his growth demanded a kick in the ass, hardly ever a gentle nudge, from her. Now Rosa thought of this six-foot-two man, and the resemblance to her old lover was present in the man, her son. But, frankly, Sean was even more appealing. So there, she thought, it's true. So there.

She stood up to get another cup of coffee and walked right into Julio's arms as though he'd been waiting for the opportunity. The omelette simmered, gently, beneath the covered pan. He held her closely by the nape of her neck under her hair and around her waist pressing her into him, not too weak, not too strong. Just right. She flamed and he felt it. Her breath became shallow and her body opened up to him of its own accord. He rubbed her scalp firmly and gently circled her back, and she knew he would make love to her, perfectly. He could do that. She knew it, he knew it. She let him, she allowed him, responding and giving and taking when it was just right.

Rosa pulled away, gently, and poured another cup of coffee. "I can't wait to take a bite of that plump, little omelette. I really can't, Julio." Rosa looked into Julio's eyes, huntress to hunter. He got the point and smiled deep in his groin, his penis stiffening with anticipation.

As she sat by the kitchen window, sipping her coffee, she heard Julio clink the pan against a plate. He served her with a flourish. The omelette was neatly folded in half full of hot, spicy chorizo, sliced raw onion on the side like she loved it, a wet, green jalapeño pepper which she never tried to resist, and a folded tortilla to one side dripped with butter.

Rosa ate and Julio joined her. She looked at him, closely, without being obvious. Why do I love him? she asked herself. When he's on, he's on, she answered herself. Full Mexican lips, Mayan features, a strong, male body when he kept in shape, and an indiscriminate amount of energy poured through him at times to whatever he touched.

Julio was thinking in the same vein. What a bitch, why in the hell won't she give in to me, just give in and stop this foolish shit. He surveyed her face, proud, contained, dark, and sensual. She's almost in perfect proportion, he thought, except for when she smiles or laughs as she completely disarranges herself. No careful laugher, this one. I do love her. Could it be because she was herself, and in spite of him? Dangerous thoughts, but Julio knew in his most hidden silence that it was true.

His need of her, their struggle continuously out-shouted this clear, and fleeting, knowledge. And now he wanted her like breath. He would be patient. He would wait for the look in her eyes that always meant acceptance.

"From now on, Julio, when I want to sleep by myself you'd better leave me alone. Is that understood? Do you understand me?" Last night's memory rushed back making her angry again.

"Alright, take it easy. I promise you, it won't happen again. I freak out when your body's not next to me."

"Maybe you could rent a body for those occasions," Rosa retorted. "Also, don't count on me losing my noodle on your behalf again. You're going to have to figure out another form of self-justification."

"I don't know what you're talking about."

"I know you do. But whatever, I don't care. All I know is I feel like a psycho when I act like that, so that's it for me. Maybe you'll have to rent someone to beat you up, too."

They both started laughing at the absurdity of this hidden truth thrown out so nakedly between them.

Julio reached for her hand and tugged at her to follow him. He arranged the loose pillows in the front room in a comfortable pile and pulled her down, all the time holding onto her hand. She anticipated delight in the same room, on the same spot she'd fallen asleep last night dreading his presence. Now it was morning, a brilliant clarity engulfed the sea beyond. Not a shadow to be seen. She reached over and turned off the radio, the news: "Nuclear clouds threaten Japan . . ."

He began undressing her, covering her with his mouth almost sucking away her breath—she imagined the clouds, briefly, as the breath of the world deranged—and then she matched him, and they were wild as he took each part of her, and she took each part of him. Her orgasm came first to "I love you I love you I love you" deep from her belly, deep from her center. And then she wanted him inside of her, what she'd just held in her mouth she wanted inside of her feminine center. She often fantasized being filled at every opening—

mouth, eyes being kissed, neck licked, nipples, belly, everything—
vagina, clitoris, ass. Her body was an opening.

Now, with every thrust she told him, "Fuck me fuck me fuck me,"
arching her back to him, meaning it, only to him, the fantasies gone.
He and she remained.

And when he could no longer stand it he would tremble into her,
his sweet and salty life entering her, and some stubborn part of him
would mourn her, that she had given in to him, because he could not
receive her love. And it would begin again, and she would have to
understand, again.

And so would he, but he could not begin to know it yet. That this
battle was not about if they loved, but if they could each be weak
enough and strong enough to receive the other.

The room came back; pillows, the silky skin of intimacy; the
primacy of lovers, mothers and children. The other's skin was the
world—a shoulder, the chest, a belly. The shared pleasure a great
secret between them.

"What are you going to do today?" Julio asked.

"Work on that canvas that's been staring at me in the face, I
suppose. Tonight I want to go hear some flamenco guitar and see
Flora dance. Do you want to meet at La Casa?"

"What time?"

"How's eight?"

"How was your orgasm, was it good? Tell me, was it good?" He
caressed her possessively, making her moist again.

"You might say it was good," she laughed.

"Is that why you make all those noises?" and he mimicked her.

"Hey, I resent that! Why don't you make any noise? Are you
dead?" Rosa laughed, teasingly. "Let's see if you're dead!" and she
stroked the head of his penis. "You're alive!" Rosa screamed. "No,
no, that's enough. That's enough, Julio. I said, that's enough."

They made love again, and she straddled him, making him
moan, feeding him her finger and then her tongue. She knew she'd
have no energy left for painting that day.

As Rosa lay there entirely feminine, she felt—liquid, utterly liquid—she heard Julio showering. She wondered if he was in a hurry or
enjoying his body as privately as she was. For some reason she
thought of her aunt Maria who dutifully made tortillas every morning for her overweight husband as he sat waiting, impatient if not
regal. And the tortillas must be hot or she would jump up to warm
them if displeasure crossed his face after the third or fourth one.

Rosa had to admit it, Mexican Men had always turned her off, them and their fucking tortillas made by their mothers, their grand-mothers, and finally their slavelike wives. Yet when Julio had spoken Spanish in her ear the first time they'd made love, she felt herself drop into an old and necessary part of herself as though his words were linked to an intimacy she'd forgotten.

The words spoken to her as a child, her first words: *mesa, leche, hambre, por qué*: her first language. And at the same time she knew she had to watch it because he reached her there, and she'd forget her own warning and repeat the words, "*Te quiero*," without a thought to safety. Her own safety. Because it was inevitable, always it seemed inevitable that the overweight Mexican Man demanding a hot torti-lla would appear (not woman enough for this, not woman enough for that, not a proper woman anyway). However, Julio made a mistake in the scheme of things—he made love to her exactly as she needed to be made love to.

Rosa felt herself blossoming into a fullness that brought every-thing with it: pleasure, pain, joy, sorrow. The whole gamut, at last, and she instinctively dreaded it.

"Are you making coffee, Julio?" she tried to yell lovingly.

"There's only a cup left and I'm in a hurry." Julio sounded detached, businesslike.

Her heart shrunk with the sound of his voice. "Would you put the water on for me?"

"I cooked breakfast. Can't you get it, Rosa?"

She could see him—clean, combed, wet hair, his watch strapped onto is thick wrist. She didn't care what clothes he had on, she knew his penis was flaccid, self-satisifed, triumphant. Yet when he came in to kiss her goodbye, to make her kiss her own betrayal, she noticed his shirt, his pants, the scarf tied around his neck. She did love him.

Rosa brushed past him, locking the bathroom door.

"Okay, the water's on, Rosa. Do you hear me? The water's on," Julio repeated.

She was crying. The coffee would taste bitter. No, she'd sprinkle cinnamon on it. The pleasure she'd felt now drained out of her, leaving her with no vitality. No vitality of her own. She was silent, turning the shower on.

"Don't be angry, Rosa. Come on, open the door."

Rosa entered the shower with the water as hot as she could stand it. Yeah, he heats me a tortilla but he sure doesn't let me forget it. But nothing comforted her—not anger, self-pity, or anything else she could think of.

Putting her clothes on, a strange effort, she walked into the kitchen and found the coffee water half-boiled away. There was a note on the table in Spanish, "Querida . . ." It made her cry again, and she hated him as much as last night. "Querida, my ass," Rosa hissed and tore the paper into pieces to dispel her stupidity.

She made the coffee strong with a shot of brandy, cinnamon on top. One o'clock, the day half shot. Lifting a paint brush would be like lifting weights, and the colors didn't compel her, or the theme she thought she had. Rosa felt like painting a disintegrating, bleeding tortilla with overweight vultures surrounding it. And then she laughed because what she'd started was destined to be beautiful; a black, lace shawl suspended in a lilac sky with deep, purple orchids blooming in a circle, magically, without stems. That's how she saw it, and finally this thought gave her peace and she mixed the black.

Now, she asked herself, Why did his refusal to make me coffee, to put the water on for it, his harsh voice hurt me, wound me so damned deeply? She breathed evenly and slowly and answered herself in that calm voice inside of herself she'd come to recognize as truth. Because he gives so much and I take so much, and I give so much, and then he's able to take it *all* away.

As Rosa began to work on the lace, the floral design, inch by inch—it would be meticulous against its lilac sky—she began to clearly imagine the weblike lines becoming spirals of leaves, whole flowers, connecting one to the other. Lace. A black, lace shawl. And there would be one fold, one shadow within its darkness, the way there was one fold, one shadow within herself, she knew. Somehow she felt that within her private sorrow there was a global sorrow—the individual in touch with the whole. The hidden fold she would never fully see, in this painting, the way it had to be for now. And then Rosa imagined the beautiful finished shawl lifted from its canvas, large enough to cover the whole Earth. Only then, she realized, would it unfold itself.

The bleeding tortilla was feminine, the black shawl was feminine, the Earth was feminine, and everything that was feminine, she felt, was in danger of being destroyed by the masculine. She included herself. Tears came to her eyes but they didn't fall. Rosa was intent on completing at least one black flower. One black rose.

She'd painted the lilac sky already, the delicate, transparent, thin-washed color that could be seen at sunrise just as the sun began to rise, or sunset just as the sun set out of sight. So, in essence, this lilac was the color of beginnings and endings, of opposites merged momentarily before the night. And the shawl was the night that belonged to Quetzalpetlatl. Quetzalpetlatl longed to place it, the black, lace shawl, on the shoulders of the Earth.

Rosa painted four solid hours breaking once for coffee, more cinnamon on top, when an inner exhaustion hit her, and she began to remember food, time, the chill in her basement studio. A fog had rolled in making the pine needles framed in the window look immediate and important, as though nothing existed beyond their reach. The wind was blowing hard and there'd be no sunset tonight.

She looked forward to paella, dry, red Sangre de Toro wine, and flamenco, so she nibbled on cheese and leftover potato salad, searching out the shiny, black olives tucked into the whiteness, and she silently wondered, Have I always loved the darkness? . . . Yes. The pit? . . . Yes. The hidden? . . . Yes.

The phone rang. "I can't make it tonight, Rosa. I forgot an opening." She was silent. "Do you want to come?"

"Whose work is it?" Julio told her. "You know his stuff is awful. And then someone will ask me what I think. Forget it."

"He asked me weeks ago. I forgot about it. Sorry," Julio sounded genuinely sorry. "Are you still going to La Casa?"

"I sure am. If you change your mind I'll be there."

"Do you think it's safe to walk around there at night by yourself? Are you going with anyone?"

"No," Rosa answered, irritably. "Maybe I'll take Zack with me," and she laughed at the thought of her dog sitting upright opposite her in a chair, a candle between them. He could borrow Julio's clothes, and crunch the leftover chicken bones that he loved. "Do you mind if he borrows your burgundy turtle neck?" Rosa laughed out loud at the idea and added, "Anyway, I was there plenty of times by myself before I met you, Julio."

"Always the independent one."

Rosa heard the smirk. "Isn't the gallery in the gay district? Better watch your own ass," she couldn't resist.

"Always the funny one," and he laughed. "Okay, okay, pull in your thorns. If I don't get there I'll see you at home."

"The thorns, Julio, are *part* of the rose, not an added attraction. Haven't you learned that yet?" she prodded. "How was your class this afternoon; get any propositions from your fan club?" Rosa teased and especially enjoyed it because he was The Jealous One, à la macho, and she loved to turn the tables.

Julio was silent, then, "Are you through, Rosa?"

"Through with what?" she laughed.

"Being bad," he replied, soberly.

"Okay, well listen, if you show up with *her* I'll hear it from half the gathering. You could say it's your abuelita from Nogales—or was that nalgas?" Rosa exploded into peals of laughter.

"Yeah, well, you can say Zack's your daddy," and he finally joined her laughter.

"Your mama," Rosa gasped.

"Te quiero, cabrona," Julio said, softly.

"Te quiero, cabrón," Rosa murmured, and she meant it. The anger of the morning faded away, but she couldn't help but feel his change of plans was only an extension of the coffee incident, the withdrawal from her, and she sighed though the laughter felt good. She appreciated that part of herself that could laugh about anything given time enough. Time enough.

Rosa poured a half-glass of room temperature Pinot Noir, a thick vintage, one that reminded her of blood—like a transfusion, and she sipped it slowly as she dressed. Instinctively, she reached for the woolen black shawl, a gift a friend had given her one night on the spur of the moment saying, "It'll look better on you than me, take it." No flowers on this one, but a practical, yet beautiful, dark warmth. She reached for some elaborate, dangling earrings, a gift from another friend, and the simple star necklace from Mexico (she tried it on), a gift from still another friend, and she suddenly realized she musn't forget the love she'd drawn from others, still inside of her—hidden within her darkness, within her hard, hard pit. Because there were moments, like forever, when everything she was felt utterly exposed and worthless, as though no one had ever loved her, or could love her, and so these lovely gifts became more than gifts, but tangible proof in her hands.

And then Rosa thought of the empty fold in the black shawl she'd begun to paint, and she wondered how it would work. She tried to visualize it completed, hanging in the sky, but it still looked rather stiff, and then she knew the only thing to do was work on it bit by bit.

Rosa put the necklace back; the earrings were enough, and the shawl was as warm as her friend Clara had been. She'd died of cancer at twenty-eight, six years ago, and Rosa still missed her in the pit of her stomach. First she'd mourned her, then she'd gotten angry—wasn't it supposed to be the other way around?—and then the dreams began, the visits as Rosa thought of them. Others had died but she'd only dreamt them once or twice, but Clara was persistent, and Rosa laughed inwardly at the idea of Clara's strong, stubborn spirit and thought, Knowing Clara she probably doesn't want to incarnate into anything except perhaps the lilac sky. I think I'm becoming obsessed with that damned lilac sky.

Parking in San Francisco's North Beach was always a challenge, so when the parked car's back-up lights flashed on, Rosa killed her motor, stopping. She hugged the right with her turning signal on and slid in the moment the car cleared the space—and just four blocks to La Casa. The night was clear and cold, the stars tiny flickers over the lit-up city sky, and as she walked she was slightly afraid and very hungry which gave her an unusual sensory edge which she recognized and welcomed.

When she opened the worn, wooden door a soft guitar was playing and the dancer, Flora, was serving food and wine. Rosa chose a small table by the dance floor. The floor itself was extremely small, yet Flora forced it to the size of a stage, and Rosa was always amazed and loved to watch her do it.

"Welcome," Flora smiled.

"I look forward to your dancing," Rosa returned.

"You always come with someone. I like that you come alone again, like you used to," and they laughed together lightly.

Both of them had glimpsed a mirror of intensity in the other and had decided to acknowledge it and enjoy it over the years Rosa had come to watch Flora dance.

"Would you like your wine, a half-bottle?" Flora asked.

"That sounds good, and could I also have a salad as soon as you can. I'm starved."

"I'll bring you some salad and some bread. How's that? I'm due to dance pretty soon."

"Wonderful," Rosa answered. "That'll tide me over." She began to feel at home as she always did, and remembered that the half-bottles were house wine.

"Flora, I'll take a bottle of Sangre de Toro. I've been thinking of it all day."

"I understand," Flora laughed.

As Flora went to get her the bottle of wine Rosa watched Flora's husband play the guitar, slowly, with pleasure, a half-smile on his face; his eyes down, almost feminine, as a woman would show her pleasure with a newborn child. Everything felt so acute to Rosa, especially gentleness.

Carlos stopped playing to help with the serving of food and wine. He was Spanish, an older man in his fifties with white hair who possessed a short, stocky, and strong body. A peasant's body, with wide, flexible hands. His eyes were gentle—to mocking—to gentle.

Flora was in her thirties, Mexican, tall and amply hipped, her hair in a neat bun with a loose halo of hair that stuck up like an energy, filtering a firelike red in the muted light.

There was something frank and contained about each of them, their relationship, that Rosa liked. He egged his wife on sometimes as she danced, "Baila, niña!" Niña, child, Rosa thought and smiled to herself—hardly, with that knowledgeable woman's body. "Baila, niña!" a compliment to the first bloom of youth, but perhaps, also, his most intimate vision of her.

Flora opened the bottle and brought it to Rosa's table. "Take it home, the bottle I mean, if you can't finish it. Where's your son? I haven't seen him in a while."

"He's away, for the summer, working. I think this is how we do it, you know, bit by bit," and Rosa thought of him, his slow, dark looks. Sean. My deep, dark sea. She remembered him like liquid—her labor, now this man, and suddenly it didn't seem bit by bit. Just the present felt bit by bit. The years felt like a tidal wave. No, that's too lethal, she thought—a large, clear wave that I watched approach and couldn't resist its coolness and its light, and so I dove straight into it, and when I emerged for air seventeen years had passed.

The salad was in front of her with whole cherry tomatoes, and Flora had disappeared.

Carlos settled into his chair by the dance floor and began to play little trills and invitations. Flora emerged from the kitchen with a fuchsia shawl draped around her shoulders, and the costume she'd served dinner in—layers of black and purple at the skirt, and a skin-tight black sheath plunging deeply to her breasts. When Flora had served the food it seemed ordinary, she'd made it seem ordinary. But now she entered the room with a conscious command. Like a leopard, Rosa thought. Flora sat next to her husband tapping her feet, clapping, and singing in a clear, untrained voice, a love song, a sorrow, looking all the time, slyly, as though telling herself, You've enjoyed this, too.

Almost somberly, and shyly, a group of people entered; one young man in his twenties, and two older women perhaps in their fifties. He quickly grabbed a chair and took a guitar out of its case, and after a moment began to play a duet with Carlos as both men achnowledged each other with a look. Flora ignored everyone, singing the same compelling song again and again, until finally she rose like a flame, arched and tensed, yet completely graceful. One of the older women rose with Flora simultaneously. Sitting she'd looked entirely proper, dressed matronly in greys and browns, but when she rose she began to sing in a deep, husky voice, and it seemed her clothing fell away. When she stood, straight and rooted, her breasts became sensual and prominent, and it was as though her naked, feminine soul was fiercely, and finally, revealed. Then Flora met the woman's eyes as she began to dance.

Flora began slowly, circling the floor, creating her stage carefully. She snapped her fingers, a naked sound compared to the castanets, yet it seemed to signal something different, more personal, as though to say she was truly alone, although the singer was her midwife, her mother. The older woman's voice was strong and compelling as a mother's would be, yet no soft laments came from her mouth, but a persistent sort of full women's power encouraging her daughter to unleash herself to the dance. Carlos didn't call out to her this time as though he accepted his place as musician and witness to their feminine exchange. And Flora's dance that night was strangely disturbing to Rosa—it was fully sensual, only, to the woman in herself, in Flora. As Flora turned, turned, no part of her was not integrated with the rising music and the full feminine voice; this was where she would usually release her sensuality, the orgasm of her dance, outward, to the audience. Tonight she contained it in an excruciating, and almost unbearable, ecstacy. Tonight she gave birth to herself, hands raised toward an unseen sky. Yes, Rosa thought, that's what I must do.

Flora rested, sitting on a chair close to Carlos, and next to him the young man. She rested within their music and yet, at once, separate.

"May I share a bottle of wine with you?"

Rosa looked up. She'd been deep inside herself, the flamenco a turbulent chamber, but a familiar one she always welcomed. She looked up to a strikingly handsome, young man. Younger than herself, she noted. He was light-skinned, but tanned, blonde, with the bluest of eyes. His eyes were friendly and open to her searching gaze.

"That's very generous of you," she smiled.

He sat down, carefully, facing her, completely without pretense, and she instantly liked that.

"May I?" He indicated her glass.

"Let me finish this first. May I ask your name, Generous One?" Rosa laughed.

"Rolf. I'm visiting from Berlin on a grant. I'm a sculptor."

"I was wondering what accent you had. It sounds almost French to me."

"No, it is German," and he dazzled her with his boy/man smile—
open like a boy's and knowing like a man's. "And you, what is your
name, Lovely One?" he asked, laughing.

"Rosa, and I'm a painter and a teacher. I paint full-time and I
teach part-time." She looked into his summer-sky eyes and wondered
what they looked like when he was angry—still summer-sky in spite
of himself?

He reached over and poured her a glass of his wine. "This is good
wine, this Sangre de Toro. Blood of the Bull, no?" He looked at her
playfully, and she nodded yes. "I like that. It seems we both have
nearly full bottles of Blood of the Bull. I think we can drink it if we
give the matter our full concentration, yes?"

"I'll certainly try. Are you having dinner?"

"Yes. But I see you've already started your salad."

"That's no problem, Rolf. I'm the slowest eater on Earth."

As though on cue Flora brought Rosa's paella, and looked at
Rolf's new seating.

"Would you like your meal now?" Flora asked Rolf.

"Please. It's mandatory that we finish this wine."

"Right away," Flora laughed, giving Rosa a lingering look.

"What do you paint? I would love to see your work. What are
your persistent themes, shall we say?" he asked smiling, but with a
seriousness.

"I suppose my work is centered on what I consider feminine
themes with a, hopefully, universal message. Sometimes I'm not
aware, really, that they're feminine themes when I begin, for example, but it always becomes apparent. To me, anyway." Rosa looked
closely to see if he was really interested.

"What are you painting now?"

He was, she felt. "Well, I've just completed a view of Earth from
space, with the continents in the shape of a woman's body nursing
her child, laying on her side, the oceans surrounding them like blue
light. There's a dark sky, very dark, with brilliant stars that seem to
loom out of the painting, and a circle of clear, bright stars around the
Earth."

Rolf nodded silently, enjoying the intensity of the woman in front
of him, coupled with a focused force he usually saw only in men.

"And I've just begun another one—a black, lace shawl in space, a
lilac sky, a wonderful but a difficult sky. It keeps changing on me—
perhaps a lighter wash of lilac, I keep asking myself and all that. Not
to speak of the shawl. I want it to look soft and real. That's another

dilemma." Remembering the completed painting gave her a certain peace. Remembering the just-begun one gave her a peculiar anxiety, a familiar one but always a torture, an anxiety shot through with excitement like a mountain climber staring up at her new mountain. Could she reach it?

"I thought that's what they looked like," he teased. "Well, you sound properly obsessed by your work. I must see it. May I? I'll be here for a week more."

"I don't see why not. Do you have a car?"

"I'm renting one. It's so much easier, and it's less money by the week anyway."

Flora brought Rolf's salad and paella together with more hot bread.

"Flora, your dance was mesmerizing. It was different this time, and I loved it."

"You flatter me, but I like it. Gracias, Rosa." Flora smiled and went to see to another table.

Rolf watched the exchange with salad in his mouth, and finally said to Rosa, "Yes, she's very good, very good. As good, or better really, than any I've seen in Spain. I can see you love flamenco. So do I, but probably not as much as you, no?"

"Do you go to Spain often? I've never been to Europe—not enough money yet."

"Mainly in the summer when my classes are through."

"Are you a student?"

"No, I teach now like you, Rosa. Part-time but with a government stipend, and grants like this that help me travel."

"I do want to go to Europe eventually, but I've just peeked at Mexico and I've never gone to Central or Southern America, and I think I'd like to do that first. That is, if I can go somewhere where there's not a war zone. You have your own war zone over there in Berlin with the Berlin Wall, right?"

"At this point it's a wall I choose to ignore. Of course, I'm glad I'm in the West," Rolf answered with a slight irritation.

"Rolf, there's hardly anywhere left that's not in trouble—and really, globally, that's our collective situation. Why do you think I'm obssessed by in-space views of the Earth . . . at least that's the message I keep getting."

"I suppose—well, of course, you're right, it's just that it's not something one usually dwells on, no? But, yes, of course you do. And, of course, you're right—pay me no mind," Rolf smiled.

"Well, tell me about your work, your sculpting?" Rosa asked.

"I make temporary and travelling exhibitions. My pieces fly, Rosa. I'm afraid my pieces have very little to do with the Earth. I will bring slides to show you, no?" He looked full at her with his amused, frank face.

His blondeness startled her—somehow she wasn't accustomed to it, yet it added to her pleasure, visual and otherwise. She often brought students home to visit her studio, so why should she hesitate, she asked herself. And, in a sense, he almost felt like her student.

"How old are you?" she asked, surprising herself.

"Twenty-six. And you? he replied.

"Thirty-four."

He just smiled at her with an obvious approval and appreciation that made her blush. The difference is, she answered herself, is that he turns me on. So what, she further inquired inwardly.

Flora entered the room with her shawl tied to her hips, and this time Carlos and the young man called her out to dance. The older woman stayed seated, clapping her hands in a steady rhythm, adding her voice from time to time. As Flora stood, arms raised, this time with castanets, she turned her attention to Rolf acknowledging his masculine beauty, and then included every man in the room. Every woman in the room, including Rosa, agreed to her dance, to the explicit life in her dance.

Rolf divided the last of the wine between them. Flora's dancing for the night was completed, and she was taking a few minutes to wash her face, rearrange her hair up in a knot to cool herself. She would return to serve the strong, dark coffee and small, iced cakes with her skirt tucked into her side, a dark shawl loosely around her shoulders, swept clean by passion.

Flora's husband and the young man continued playing softly, then loudly, then softly, in a steady dialogue of hands and heart. The soft light surrounding them, and the timelessness of the flamenco made them friends and brothers, and it was restful, a lull, from the reality just outside the door: HEY BABY, GIMME YOUR WALLET, GIMME A DIME, GIMMIE YOUR LIFE—BITCH!

Rosa jarringly remembered, clearly, this morning's news of a nuclear cloud heading for Japan, the very winds of the Earth an enemy: an arms test out of control, not calculated, unforseen, and this, supposedly, was just a *small* test. *A small test*, Rosa thought. The news had come on briefly, before she and Julio began to make love.

She'd reached over and turned it off because it was turning her off. When they began making love it stuck to her like a grief her body had to consume, and she had: planetary and personal grief. For the moment. *Why do I connect my own heart to the Earth's heart? Why do I assume that because Julio must always sever himself from me, men must sever themselves from Earth? But it is how I feel, secretly,* Rosa thought.

"A friend of mine told me about this place," Rolf gently intruded. "It feels a little like home, like Europe. Even the coffee is good," he smiled.

"I've come here for years. I always feel at home here." Rosa paused. "Do you have a family, children? I'm just curious, it's one of my afflictions," she laughed.

"No children. I lived with my girlfriend for five years and now we're separate. She was a sculptor as well. We worked and lived together. We were also students then and took classes together. It was too much. We're still friends, though I think there's hurt on her part. And you?" Rolf asked.

Rosa briefly wondered why she was hurt and he wasn't—did he withdraw from her, the Earth? "I have an almost grown son who's preparing to leave me, and I have a husband," (who I'm preparing to leave, she thought suddenly as she remembered her dream) Rosa answered, watching his face closely to see if his interest in her work, in her, dimmed.

"You don't appear married," Rolf leaned forward. "I salute you," he proclaimed playfully. "And a son—do you get along?"

"Sometimes. I think that's a properly human response applied to any human relationship. Right?"

"Absolutely. I think I can't bear to go home because my mother always wants it to be perfect. But I admire her, she brought me up in spite of great obstacles. It was not easy. And I was a terrible child, running here, there. Do you know?" His eyes glittered.

"I can imagine. Actually, I was a brat myself. Maybe this is a meeting of the brats," Rosa laughed and Rolf joined her.

"No, I must say my relationship with Sean, my son, has hardly been perfect, and by that I mean I've literally choked him. When he was fifteen he had the courage to tell me, or rather try to tell me, to shut up. 'Shut up, Mom,' he said. I forgot my name and began choking him." Rosa started laughing at the memory. "Mind you, he was a full six feet and his voice had dropped. Anyway, he began saying 'Get a hold of yourself, Mom,' over and over. And I screamed, 'You apologize, you bastard,' and he did." Rolf's face registered a minor shock.

"Now I've shocked you." Rosa sipped her wine.

"Just a little. Please forgive me," Rolf smiled.

"Well, Sean and I have laughed about it. Anyway, that's one of the stories about my imperfect relationship with my son. And do you know what?"

"What," Rolf echoed.

"I think that's why I love him," Rosa realized. "I've been both his mother and father, like your mother—only, I suppose, I gave him a dose of father. I wanted him to love me but I also wanted him to respect me."

Rolf was listening and watching Rosa closely.

"The other side of the coin is we take long walks together, talk for hours and dance at parties."

"I'd never dream of dancing with my mother."

"That's why she should've choked you."

"It's never too late. I'll suggest it next we meet," Rolf started laughing and Rosa joined him pretending to choke the wine bottle.

"The truth is, Rolf, that Sean was already stronger than me, and I knew it, and he knew it, but he had to know he'd reached my limit. Anyway, look, here's my address and phone number."

The music had stopped and the clearing up process had begun, the tables being wiped. Flora approached the table, "Can I get you some coffee? You didn't have dessert, would you like some?"

"Yes, please, Flora."

Rosa indicated Rolf, and he said, "I'll take some coffee if there's still time."

"Sure," Flora answered.

"Flora, you were wonderful again," Rosa told her. "And that woman's singing was incredible."

"I'll tell her. She's an old friend of mine. She's taught me many old songs. She's actually Spanish from Spain—not like me, a Mexican from San Francisco," and Flora smiled.

"Your dancing was quite beautiful, and very moving. I'm a gringo—isn't that what you say here? A gringo from Berlin, and this place of yours makes me feel at home." Rolf laughed at himself good naturedly. "I don't mind this word 'gringo'—you must call me this so that I may really feel at home, here."

Rosa and Flora looked at each other and burst into laughter. Flora put her hand on his shoulder and said, "I'll get your coffee."

Carlos and the young man began to play again, softly. The older women were not to be seen; perhaps they were in the kitchen—yes, that's where they were—nibbling a bowl of steamed shrimp and a salad, and drinking red wine, talking quietly, on stools in the corner of the kitchen, a candle between them.

"Perhaps I could come tomorrow. Is that a good day for you?" Rolf asked.

"Tomorrow afternoon would be perfect, or should I say imperfectly perfect."

"What time is imperfectly perfect?"

"I would think two o'clock would save you from a strangling," Rosa's brat glared out at him.

"Then I will be there. But first give me directions, I can barely get from here to my friend's house," and suddenly Rolf seemed the older one.

Soberly, Rosa drew him a map, and gave it to him. "I have a morning class tomorrow, so I'd better go. I've enjoyed our talk, and I'll see you tomorrow."

"May I walk you to your car?" Rolf asked.

"If you don't mind—and since you ask, yes." She felt relief knowing she wouldn't have to portray her Total Bad Bitch performance at the end of the evening, knowing that the walk to the car, alone, late at night in the city required such a performance.

They finished their coffee, and as they stood to go, Rosa did so with reluctance and silently waved goodbye to Flora and Carlos, and the young man next to Carlos slightly bowed his head and smiled. Rolf tripped on a chair and quickly regained his composure; he was tall and gangly, but with grace.

Rosa opened the door, a different world, and it was cold. She wrapped her black, wool shawl tightly around herself, and Rolf buttoned his jacket against the clear, cold night. He walked beside her lightly, now and then showing his brat by jumping in front of her talking. At this rate, Rosa thought, I'll have to save him from a mugger. But no muggers appeared, and no one said "Hey, Baby" to her relief, and Rolf made her laugh all the way to the car.

As Rosa opened her car door she felt a stab of sadness, and as though Rolf sensed it asked, "May I kiss you on the cheek, Rosa? Just a friendly kiss."

She offered her cheek to him half-jokingly, and his lips parted, pressed against her skin like a flower, like a soft, hot flower. It gave her a sensation down the entire side of her body, the left side that he'd kissed. His breath was warm.

"Goodnight, Rolf," Rosa said softly. She shut the door, started the motor, and watched him walk away, his slim, light figure disappearing into the darkness. He stopped, once, and waved without smiling. He'd felt the flower too.

Would I make love to him if I weren't with Julio? she asked herself. I think so. It feels like I certainly want to, though his being German—Hitler, concentration camps, his blondeness—disturbs me. Yes, it does. But I like him, the boy/man—the self-proclaimed gringo, and Rosa smiled to herself. . . . But I just can't be unfaithful, whatever the hell that is. But it's true, and I know it. Why does Germany, Hitler, blondeness, this opposite of myself named Rolf appear right now? Why? Rosa turned on the radio, opened the window, erased the freshness of his kiss, and pointed the car toward the coast and home.

Julio sat on the rocking chair that faced the wall-sized window and the view of the sea. The fog had lifted and just dark bands of clouds streaked the sky, and the moon was preparing to set, half gone light to dark. He knew he should've gone to La Casa. He knew he could've said he'd forgotten the opening. He knew that being with Rosa, drinking wine, and watching her eyes take in the candlelight was what he'd really wanted to do. Now he was unhappy because he hadn't gone, and, in fact, he was somehow angry with her. You can bet she enjoyed herself, he thought darkly, and going on one. He'd brought the large alarm into the living room and it glowed in the dark making him angrier and angrier.

Why couldn't she have come with me, he countered and recountered, and deep inside of himself he shouted, Why can't she do everything I say? He remembered his grandmother—shy, stern, yielding, until he became a man. She'd shouted in Spanish, she'd accused him, "You're becoming a man like any other," and then the yielding door shut permanently. He knew his mother only by name, and he'd seen his father sporadically. Mother, father, distant planets he couldn't even gaze at because he'd been born without a telescope, and his grandmother was conveniently on Earth.

This watchfulness felt familiar, gazing out at the dark, the sea, the occasional traffic below—yes, he was watching for the enemy. They could assume any form—man, woman, child. They were silent and they were fast. This was the worst part, the watch. No, gathering the bodies had been the worst, but they transferred him to another unit because he could think, think like a white man, around the

corners into the bend where the thinkers hid, and out there somewhere the doers died.

The time he'd been out on patrol ordering people out of their
huts, searching for Viet Cong, and in one hut a young Vietnamese
woman was nursing her baby. He'd told her, "You can stay," and he
searched all around her. Not much to search, pretty simple—grass
mats, fire, utensils, sleeping roll. And the lieutenant walked in,
"What in the hell is she doing here? You lost your fucking mind?
You," he said, pointing at the woman, "get out."

He remembered their huts burning, and, again, he wondered
how the woman would gather her simple needs, as he remembered
her baby at her breast. It had been noted he wasn't to be relied on in
such matters, like a white man—no, he could think, but he remained
brown, brown like the enemy. A friend of his had said, "Hey, man, it
feels like I'm turning in my grandmother," when they'd rounded up
an old woman after curfew. But his friend couldn't *think*, and then
Julio was transferred, and the worst he did was to keep watch like
tonight for movement, for shadows, for the arrival of the enemy.

He began composing a photograph of his vigil—the clock glowing, he getting darker by the minute, the plant framing the window
on the right. He didn't realize that his face was the photograph that
he longed for, and that no matter how many times he extended his
arm and took a self-portrait, he would eventually have to trust
someone to show him what he really looked like. The photographs
taken of him in Vietnam made him look like a caricature of a soldier,
and the ones he took of his surroundings reminded him of the Twilight Zone. It *was* the Twilight Zone—everything was possible, everything was bizarre only as war is. Or as the world is before you
learn to focus.

Focus, he thought. Shoot it, keep it. A brown boy trying to see
himself wherever he can. The thought distressed Julio, but the magic
held him when he thought of the darkness and the image appearing
under his hands like creation. No matter how many times he taught
Beginning Photography he couldn't convey this. To do so would've
been like giving a war cry in the genteel, silent classroom.

"Shoot it," he muttered. Shoot it, you stupid bastards before it
escapes—before it gets you, before life gets you, he yelled in his mind,
a long, wild scream. I don't want to see the mother-fucking Golden
Gate Bridge one more time, or the Japanese Tea Garden, or close-
ups of a crack in buildings. I want to see a picture of all of you, every
one of you, waiting for your mother-fucking enemy.

The entire world, for an instant, loomed before Julio's eyes;

flashed like an exquisite hologram. Too many acid trips, Julio laughed to himself, and his breathing slowed, and he realized one of the most comforting thoughts he could have was of a woman's body seconds after making love. The illusion of complete surrender. That, too, he realized, was a hologram. The problem was he could only see it from one angle and there were many.

Headlights hit him right in the face as Rosa pulled into the driveway, and his mind riveted on the sound of her motor. Brakes, lights, car door, feet on the steps, key in the door—yes, let her open it and find me sitting here, waiting.

"Did you have a good time?" Julio asked.

Rosa stiffened at the sight of him by the window.

"Why are you waiting up like this, Julio?"

She was tired and relaxed. Deep down she'd let Rolf's light kiss go, but she'd carefully kept his laughter, so seeing Julio sitting in the darkness was particularly grim and somehow unbelievable.

"Do you realize what time it is? I've been sitting here since midnight! I got home at ten-thirty and expected you at eleven at the latest. It's one-thirty. Where the hell were you, and with *who*?" Julio shouted.

"You've got to be kidding. I'm not going to answer you. Good night, Julio," Rosa said between clenched teeth.

Julio leaped to his feet, grabbing the glowing clock.

"Where were you till this time, Rosa? Answer me!"

Rosa suddenly felt like laughing at the absurdity of the ghostly clock floating in his hand, the slight resemblance to cranky mothers and irate wives; an almost hysterical, feminine note to the gesture nearly made her laugh, but on the other hand the sight also frightened her. She walked quickly to the bedroom and locked the door.

"I'm not opening this door. The sleeping bag's in the closet. Now leave me alone—do you hear me? Leave me alone!"

The clock hit the door like an explosion. She waited for further dramatics but it was silent. She had to go to the bathroom but not that badly. Rosa changed, quickly, into a flannel nightgown, stretched herself end to end, and listening to her own breathing fell asleep thinking of dawn, the lilac sky.

She is being chased by a swarm of bees down the beach, and when she thinks she's safe they find her again, till at last she comes to the end of the beach, the very end of the beach where a cliff stands in front of her and to her right, the ocean to her left. When she turns to face the bees, a huge, black bull stands in front of her. His eyes are demanding but not murderous. The bull could kill her but it wouldn't be personal, not at all. She has to do something quickly. She puts a

garland of the most beautiful springtime flowers on his thick, black, muscled
neck. Rosa notes the pale-pink, baby roses.

Rosa woke clutched by terror and wonder, equally; the baby
roses were still vivid in her mind's eye—her dream-eye as her grandmother had called it—against the massive, muscled, pure black hide
of the sweating, young bull. And her mouth tasted awful—the meal,
the wine, and she hadn't brushed her teeth. Then she remembered
the clock splattering against the door. She wondered if the wood was
gouged.

She opened the door; chipped paint was all, and the clock lay
there glowing in the pre-dawn light. Peeing felt so wonderful sometimes, if not perfect, she thought. She brushed her teeth and ended
up washing her face as thin, delicate shafts of light began to strike the
cypress tree in back. It was five-thirty, and Rosa knew if she went
back to sleep she'd feel half-dead trying to really wake up at seven, so
she decided to stay up, get dressed and sneak out for a walk. Sneak
out because she had no desire to confront Julio—it would ruin her
day, and the desire to make love to him was absolutely absent. This
was when he liked it best, when she gave her body in spite of herself,
a kind of self-betrayal, and she despised herself for it. For pleasure,
for sensuality, for perhaps the most powerful part of herself, to hate
herself—to hate herself for surrendering to pleasure. Paradox. Rosa
remembered the bull's eyes. Nothing personal at all, not really. He
just wanted her. She gave him the garland instead.

She didn't flush the toilet. Quickly and quietly she got dressed—
jeans, parka, tennis shoes—and went though the basement taking
Zack. The sky was still grey but she could smell the ocean, fresh and
exciting, shrouded in mystery at this hour. At this hour there would
be no footprints on the tideline but her own, if she looked back. In
fact, no one was usually at this particular beach that dead-ended into
cliff and sea. The danger was that women didn't walk there alone,
only men did.

One night as Julio and Rosa had taken off down the beach with a
bottle of cognac, a clear night but windy, some teenagers sat huddled
at the bottom of the stairs talking in the enveloping darkness. When
they'd passed them to continue their walk down the beach there was
a silence as though two black belts passed by (though both of them
had silently dreaded passing the group), because they were obviously
going to walk to the end of the beach, at night, without even a
flashlight. Julio and Rosa had laughed once out of earshot at the

solemn greeting they'd received, making menacing karate shouts
that made them both feel very good. They'd collected driftwood and
made a warm fire, drinking all the cognac, talking about great subjects—yes, really, great subjects—and laughing to tears. This was
the real bond, when he made no effort to possess her. When they
were equals.

Rosa stopped to get coffee and a donut. The sky was still pale
with only the slightest hint of lilac, and the sun was steadily rising.
At the bottom of the steps Zack bounded ahead of her taking off for a
run, and Rosa took a careful sip of the slightly watery coffee, but the
chocolate donut helped. She looked up and down the beach, carefully, and as she'd thought she had the beach, the ocean, the early
morning, to herself.

Zack ran in the direction he knew she would walk, toward the
cliff, and a bee buzzed her. Rosa remembered her dream; it'd started
with bees, and she panicked for an instant. It circled her donut.
"Shit," she muttered, and walked quickly down the beach with the
lid to her coffee on tight, taking another bite of donut. The tide was
lower today, lower than she'd ever seen it. The ocean looked undressed.

The bee continued to follow her. She uncapped the coffee, took a
couple of steaming sips, then ate the donut, capped the coffee again,
half-full, and ran down the beach, looking up to the top of the cliffs
and down the beach to see if a man watched her. Once when a man
had approached her here Zack had circled back and been by her side
just as the man tried to speak to her. Rosa held his collar and Zack's
ears had stiffened, lips curled back to a beautiful snarl, his tail coiled
like the malamute he was, his wolf-face intent on her fear. "Okay,
okay, lady, just keep hold a that dog."

"Just keep moving, asshole," she'd said, with the asshole under
her breath. She'd never had to let go of Zack's collar so she never
knew exactly what he would've done, but she imagined him going for
the man's throat, instinctively, and a more beautiful sight she
couldn't imagine at the moment. And the other time she'd just
walked down the stairs when she saw a woman with the most delicate, flimsy summer dress pulled up to her knees enjoying herself in
the tide, and that guy seemed to come out of nowhere and started
tugging at her arm. Rosa could hear the woman protesting, softly,
with a lovely accent, a foreign accent, "Please, please, please let me
go." He clutched at her arm harder. Rosa grabbed Zack and
marched down saying in as threatening a manner as she could manage, "SHE SAID LET GO!" Then Rosa stood still as the man took her

and the dog in. Zack wasn't as roused as during a direct confrontation with his mistress, but he was alert. The man let go of the woman swearing at Rosa, and the woman continued to stand there to Rosa's surprise. She didn't run away, or walk away for that matter—well, it was her business, but it seemed to Rosa dense and foolish.

At the end of the beach where the cliffs constantly dripped water from an underground source, a tidal pool was completely exposed, and what seemed a grotto on the usually engulfed sea side of the cliff. Rosa drank the last of the coffee, took off her shoes and unzipped the parka. Zack was already out in the tidal pools sniffing and getting wet. As she walked carefully out among the sharp rocks, stooping to see what normally was hidden from view, it seemed a rare, rare miracle.

Large, pink anemones like open, exposed vaginas waved in the tide, and Rosa stuck her finger in for the usual, terrible thrill of their closing. Some of them were at least eight inches across and pussy-pink, their tentacles rising to transparency. They aroused her, definitely. Their delicacy depended on the tide, the hidden nature of their growth like the innermost labia, the menstral flow—the woman in woman.

She climbed into the grotto, the shallow, little cave, and sitting in it she imagined the sea day and night filling it, forming it, forever. She felt privileged to sit in such a place, and at the same time she felt strangely welcomed as though she truly belonged, fit. Rosa looked behind her, carefully, to a sunburst design, a perfect design. Not a flaw, Rosa thought, and she imagined the impact of the sea creating it millennia after millennia. She'd looked it up once out of curiosity, and the word had stuck in her mind, as the word *millennia* struck her with the force of the sunburst design: "A period of a thousand years—a period of great happiness—a period of freedom from imperfection in human existence." Yes, Rosa thought, this is the place, a small place, that proves this. This would be one of Quetzalpetlatl's thrones, her sea throne. She smiled to herself, and this is what you keep to yourself or they put you away. Yet the world faces daily annihilation and that is considered perfectly sane, and I sit in a little cave and call it Quetzalpetlatl's Sea Throne and if they knew they'd call me nuts. And suddenly Rosa realized, *This is the garland*, this is the garland I place on the young, bull's neck—this delicate, feminine place on the harsh, masculine neck of daily life.

And then, with a sharp clarity, Rosa remembered a similar grotto she'd seen as a girl in San Francisco by the General Hospital in the old barrio. It had given her a similar feeling, a longing, though of course she couldn't name it by any name. It was just an intense feeling like knowing something she'd forgotten. Once she had approached it closely and she was disappointed, and for some reason discouraged, to see broken bottles and cigarette butts inside of it. And, of course, it was man-made. Now Rosa knew why she'd loved it, why whenever she'd pass it, sometimes still stopping, it squeezed at her heart. Of course, of course, the Virgin should've been there, but they didn't know it was Quetzalpetlatl's throne. And, for that matter, even the Virgin was absent, and Rosa was too young to know, or dream, the truth. Her truth.

Rosa glanced at her watch. It was seven-thirty, almost time to get home and get to her class. Four classes a week kept her part-time at the junior college, and it was fine for now. It kept her out of the tenure position politics, and somewhere deep inside she was still a Spanish-speaking Mexican kid from a San Francisco barrio, one of the places the tourists didn't linger in; and for that reason—poverty, an inarticulateness in the face of White Authority, or an irresistibile urge (still) to scream FUCK YOU ALL, shame of the proverty, defiance of the poverty, the desire to embrace everyone, the inability to embrace everyone, the knowledge that they were poor, that they spoke Spanish, that they were Mexican, that they were different (from what?), that Mexican people lived only here or here or here, drove her crazy (still)—and for that reason she didn't see herself as a regular teacher, but as an escapee, and a woman-escapee, not too popular. In war she'd be raped, the final humiliation, and wasn't this war, she mused—am I not continually waiting for My Rapist, isn't the Earth continually struggling to survive Man?

She looked carefully down the beach and saw no movement. Zack was lying on the sand behind her, and Rosa faced the sea alone on Quetzalpetlatl's Sea Throne. She unzipped her jeans and exposed her own pussy to the sea, her pubis, her mound-of-Venus. Yes, Venus, a feminine divinity—Venus rising from the sea for a woman. Rosa remembered Flora's dance last night, her self-contained passion as though she made love to herself, as every woman there had known. Yes, to love one's self. She thought of Julio, briefly, like an obstacle, like a painful obstacle—and then she thought of Rolf's shy, soft kiss. Soft, soft like a muzzle, and the delicate sea anemone closing, caressing her curious fingers.

Rosa touched herself slowly, circling slowly, then rhythmically faster and faster, blending her body with the sea until the union was complete. A complete orgasm. A complete acceptance. Self-love without guilt. Peace, liquid peace, through her body, now, for the whole day, or at least for a while. But the acceptance, the self-acceptance, woman, sea, Venus, Quetzalpetlatl's Sea Throne, would stay no matter what. The girl died into the woman, once again, and she was born again.

Fresh wind played on her face like carresses, and under her nose it seemed a purity had gathered, again. The sea was sensually reaching for her, wave by wave, forever. She wished to remain with the sea, forever. And then, abruptly, Rosa thought of the day ahead, and tomorrow—she would paint all morning tomorrow, and her world seemed continuous again because of the black, lace shawl, still stiff but becoming.

Rosa gently squeezed her own soft breasts, and touched her face briefly and affectionately like a lover would, as lovers had, and then adjusted her clothing. Standing up to climb down now seemed almost aggressive somehow, but she had to leave, and besides the tide was coming in and she'd be late for her first class. She'd take coffee to sip today. And then she remembered Rolf, and that he was coming at two. Julio should be gone by now and not be back till four or so, she reasoned. Julio, it seemed, was completely unpredictable. He could be charming or a creep, and she knew she didn't want to deal with another episode like last night's surprise. And the charm, the charm she knew very well—she loved it, she dreaded it. It made her forget her mission in life, if there was one. Her own life.

What would the visit with Rolf be like in her place, away from the restaurant, the flamenco? For a second she forgot what he looked like but the memory of his high, feminine laugh made her remember, and she looked forward to his visit, his slides, his talk. His eyes. Would she have to explain him because she couldn't just say, "This is my student, Rolf." No, what she'd do was simply say, "Julio, this is Rolf, a sculptor from Berlin. Rolf, this is my husband, Julio, a photographer." And they would talk like three human beings.

When Julio woke up he expected the smell of coffee, or some sound at least of Rosa's presence—there was neither. He jumped to his feet and angrily walked into the bedroom to find the unmade bed. He looked out the window and the car was gone. A walk, alone. Sometimes he wished she'd get a good scare, maybe not raped exactly, but almost, to remind her not to stray too far from home, her place, me, Julio. Yes, not quite raped, but almost, and I'd comfort her, of course, and tell her how she shouldn't be out there alone, by herself, just her and that dog, and that pocket knife in her pocket.

Pathetic. Still, he had to concede, when she gets real pissed off I get pretty cautious—she's a trip. But what's a woman's strength next to a man's; what's a man's next to a bullet or strafing fire or napalm?

Rosa would handle it somehow, and he was proud of her confidence in spite of the persistent voice that told him to tell her, "You do what I say, you do what I say, you do what I say or I'll (you'll) die—Mama!" The abandoned boy on the battlefield who found out the enemy was all around him, and that there was no difference, no fucking difference between himself and *them*.

Julio made himself a big breakfast, a good pot of coffee. He made the bed, went downstairs and picked a freshly blossomed rose, a huge red one from the top of the bush. He placed it in water on the table with a note: "The clock still works. I love you too much, mi amor, mi Rosa. Let's go to dinner. See you at four or so. Te quiero."

As Rosa drove home she realized the lilac dawn had been extremely pale and brief, and that the dominant color of the morning was of vaginas, pussy-pink. The truly lilac mornings were mornings promising warmth, or sunsets promising change, but it was even more elusive than that. Maybe she'd seen three at the most, and they teased her because somehow she couldn't truly recall the shade, the exact shade, and she knew the lilac in her sky was not correct yet. It's the meeting, the exact meeting of night and day, she thought, with that damned, complicated, black, pure black, shawl hanging on it.

The sky was engulfed in blue, and the Sea Throne would soon be entirely hidden and filled with the tide.

Rosa's son, Sean, was having his first affair. Making love for the first time had been cataclysmic for him, not as awkward as he'd feared, but more intense than he'd imagined. And the girl loved his name, "Sean, Sean, Sean," she repeated, and he liked his name said that way, and he thought his lover was extraordinary and beautiful, intelligent and strong. He was picky about women; she was picky about men. She lived in Mendocino; he lived in Montara. It was his first time; it wasn't hers, but he didn't mind at all. He was glad she could guide him and show him what pleased her, and he did, he did.

Among the mail were two letters Rosa put to one side to read slowly with some tea and a roll—one from Sean and the other from Sierra, her best friend. It was one and she had an hour to herself till Rolf arrived, so she took everything downstairs into the garden. Spreading a blanket she sank into the grass, Zack beside her, and opened Sean's letter first.

Dear Mom,

It is I, your son, long lost, moskitto bitten, over worked,
under fed, but healthy and loyal son. (only kidding.) But if
you could send me a $10 I'd splurge on a Mexican restau-
rant near by. O.K.? I read the books you sent, pretty good,
but will read them again because I know you will grill me.
ha ha Met a pretty nice person here. She makes life worth
living. (oh no.) I think you would like her, she argues with
me all the time like you. (not kidding.) Well only a month
left here. Actually I've gotten to like it. Make chicken curry
for my Big Welcome Home Party. ha ha And buy me a
couple of beers. O.K.? You're O.K. Mom.

EVOL,

SEAN

Rosa laughed out loud at his usual insubordination and imagina-
tive appetite, and she sensed his passage sexually, from boy to man.
Not only the mention of the Nice Person, but that he'd signed his
letter EVOL/LOVE. It had been "sincerely" from the time he was nine
or ten every time he'd gone away, one letter per trip, two if really
anxious. He was easy-going and patient at bottom, and she imagined
him inexperienced, of course, but sensual and willing—and that
image curiously mixed with that of him starting to walk, coming
toward her. The enormity of life, simple life, was like that, she
thought—everything at once.

She sipped her tea and finished her cheddar cheese roll, laying
back on the blanket to stretch herself to the sun, the concentrated sun
of late July, rare here by the foggy sea and sweltering further north
and inland. Rosa imagined Sean swimming in the Eel River, jumping from rocks, and making love in the sand at night. She decided to
go camping next month after classes were over, up to the Eel but
away from Sean. This was their time of separation, and she knew it.
She wanted to be away from car noise, people, and be entirely ruled
by the sun and moon.

Sierra's letter began:

Rosa, Let's meet, I miss our bitch sessions, etc. . . . can you
come up for a couple of days—or perhaps I'll come down,
or perhaps we can meet in S.F. for dinner, sangría, and
more sangría. Life had me down for a while there—nothing
getting published it seemed, and then I got a book review in
the mail, a beautiful review (enclosed), and I do keep writ-

ing, and never a dull moment with "the man I live with",
though I would like to forget him a lot more often like a
vase of beautiful flowers, the painting(s) you gave me, and
then remember him again with sheer appreciation rather
than with this terrible apprehension that he's playing those
lousy games again, i.e. other women, or that when I do *see*
him again it feels like I'm a fresh convert, I must learn to
believe again—you know. However, my pottery sells, the
commonest things the best of all: bowls, platters, pitchers
. . . and my workshops go well, mixing poetry and pottery—why not—but mostly pottery, either the spout works
or it doesn't materialistically, for *real*—it drips instead of
pours. What kind of spout does Bob have, anyway? (He's a
drip—get it?) I'll give you a call (or call me) this week-end
about getting together. How's Julio, etc. Come up to the
farmlands and help me hoe corn, we'll eat fresh, steamed
yellow squash in butter (if not will bring a bag to S.F.). See
you soon, take care and all.

amor, Sierra La Peligrosa

And two poems were enclosed:

Eating

The blackberries call me
to bite, as life calls me
to bite—the sweet,

hot flesh from the
sun compels me to
reach in spite of the

fact that thorns will
tear me from time to
time. No matter—I,

for one, would never
let a ripe blackberry
live.

At the bottom of the page Sierra had written, "You know why I'm so
damned hungry." She was pregnant again, her third child—this
child and her four-year-old, Tomás, from Bob, and her oldest child
Marlin, who was fourteen, from her first husband. Rosa hadn't

thought the pregnancy wise, but what was wise when Sierra, after the first shock, accepted the unknown child she began to share blackberries with. And then this poem:

Narcissus

I keep learning how to love
you, and I keep wondering
if it's possible: but, of
course, I've loved you,

and, of course, it's possible
because we have in spite of
our weaknesses, and in spite of
our strengths. There is

something inevitable about
planting narcissus, the
way the shy, green tips
call you to love them

as soon as they poke
through the homely
bulb. How we've learned
to love ourselves, and,

finally, each other.
Then the long, slender
stalks, the tight,
defensive buds,

the surrender of
the flower, open,
open to all eyes—
and the scent

invisible and everywhere
at once. I keep learning
how to love you, from
shy, tender tip to the

extravagant flower, to
homely, brown bulb
again. In the form of
man, Narcissus.

For Bob, of course. Would he understand the subtlety of Sierra's heart displayed so starkly on the page, Rosa couldn't help wondering. He'd disappointed her so often. Like she and Julio exchanged images back and forth—painting and photography. His favorite medium black and white, hers the color of the spectrum. They understood, and then they seemed to forget. Mysteriously. It was as though they were unable to internalize the other's image, point of view, as a friend would. As friends.

The most brilliant, green hummingbird flew past her and began to hover in the Queen Anne's lace, flower to white flower—and then it turned in midair and held itself there as if to stare at her. What an intense creature, Rosa thought. If only I could have a fraction of its energy. The green head, the green body, the incessant, furious, little wings; the deep red on its throat suspended chronological time, and in that momentary silence she felt a fraction of its energy.

The bell was ringing, and her heart leapt. Rolf. She'd almost forgotten him.

Rosa opened the door to a man with sunlight in his hair, hair that reflected the sun in bursts of light rather than absorbing it like the moon, that clear, cool mirror. She couldn't help but laugh—he was all in grey with a white, silk scarf tied around his neck with well-made, white leather shoes. He looked as though he were going to a party. And from behind his back he produced a bottle of champagne.

"It is chilled and ready to disappear at once," Rolf announced.

"Come in, come in," Rosa laughed.

He touched her shoulder as he passed, lightly, in a friendly way.

"These are yours? Rolf asked of the paintings.

"Three of them are. These three."

"They are very wonderful. You use every color, no?" He indicated the rainbow she'd painted around the Earth in a clear, daytime sky, the rainbow tapering into a single stroke of color at one point, to a tip of black.

Rolf examined it.

"It is hard to tell, but is this not Mexico where your rainbow ends?" He pointed to the spot.

"Very observant—yes, southern Mexico," Rosa answered. "I think I'm going to enlarge this painting in a series of paintings. I think there's something there I want to see." She paused.

"Would you like to open the champagne?" Rolf asked, as she reached for some wine glasses.

Rolf showed her the label. "Do you think it is any good?"

"If it bubbles it's good. No, seriously, I think it'll be great. How much was it, if you don't mind my asking. I've never seen that brand."

"It was twelve dollars and highly recommended." He edged the cork off neatly in his hand without even a pop.

"That's pretty professional. My method is to see how far it flies," Rosa smiled at his deftness, and wondered what else he knew to do so well. The grey that he wore was actually in various shades of grey, all in soft cottons, even his jacket, giving him an appeal she wasn't accustomed to, but that she liked, very well.

Rolf poured the champagne to the brim.

"Do you have a slide viewer? I brought my slides to show you." He looked at her slowly, "I'd be curious to see what your paintings reveal of this spot where the rainbow ends."

"Yes, that's it, isn't it. That's where the rainbow ends, and perhaps begins. We shall see." Rosa returned his gaze. "I'll get the viewer."

Rolf felt an edge of worry from Rosa, but her welcome had offset it nearly entirely. He'd been nervous too, and had gotten lost twice taking the wrong turn-off once, and then over-shot it the next time. He finished his glass at once and refilled it, then her half-finished one and watched her return, her face full of color, like her paintings, he thought. He watched her body—slim, quick, strong, a curious blend for a woman. Married and with a grown son. I'm a visitor in her life, Rolf reminded himself.

Rosa plugged in the viewer and he stacked his slides in place. They showed his work in various stages of construction—huge metal, aerodynamic kites in brilliant colors, and Rolf made up as a clown in a white aviator's outfit. Then shots of a group of people struggling to launch one, and then some of the kites in flight against the sky.

"These are beautiful. I, for one, would've never imagined something like this. The colors and designs are extraordinary. Where did you do these?" Rosa asked.

"The largest metal one was constructed in a Volkswagen factory, the rest in my studio. You like them, no?" He looked very young.

"Very much. Sturdy yet delicate—definitely meant for flight. Who are all these people with you? And you, you're absolutely perfect as a clown."

"They are friends and artists who agreed to travel with me for very little money and very much fun. We slept in tents and ate outdoors. It would take all of us to get these up into flight."

The group ranged from children to an assortment of men and women, each face with an unmistakable vitality stamped on it. One of the young women edged close to Rolf and Rosa imagined she was his lover, or had been his lover.

"I love it. What an event your work is. How lonely my painting is in comparison," and she thought of the slow, painful process it had been to become disciplined. But then the joy. "Any more champagne?"

"But of course. If we run out I'll get more, never fear," Rolf laughed. "Now, show me your studio. Do you mind?"

"Follow me." Rosa reached for her glass and led the way downstairs. "There's really not enough natural light but it's big enough. I'd like either some sky lights or a fold-up roof."

"It is peaceful, or shall I say you've made it peaceful."

Rosa turned on a tape, piano music, Keith Jarrett.

"Now it's very peaceful. Do you like him?" Rosa turned to face him.

"Yes, especially his concert in Köln," Rolf smiled at her.

"Do you mind my asking—I've never spoken to anyone from Germany—how Hitler's era affected you? I ask because I was affected way over here. Do you see what I'm getting at?" she asked.

Rolf's face became almost stern, and his clothes suddenly seemed steely except for the playful, silk scarf at his neck. "It was before my time, actually. My mother didn't even know about it until after the war. It was not my fault—I was, in fact, unborn."

"I know that, Rolf. I'm just wondering how it affected you. Surely your own history did," Rosa said with an edge to her voice.

"Perhaps we could talk about this dreary subject another time. We're nearly out of champagne. Shall I get some more?"

The door upstairs opened and shut.

"Rosa!" Julio shouted. "I'm home! Rosa!"

"Down here, Julio, in my studio," Rosa answered him. She had no time to collect herself, he was down the stairs and walking toward them. She tried to touch his hand in greeting, but he pulled away looking quickly from Rosa to Rolf.

"Julio, this is Rolf, a sculptor from Berlin visiting for a while." She looked at him evenly, and, hopefully, without a trace of guilt. "Rolf, this is my husband, Julio, who's a photographer. Those photographs of the pyramids you saw upstairs are his." She hoped he'd noticed. It was hard to tell how Julio felt, he was composing himself, but Rolf reached out to shake his hand, gently, like a bird. Julio immediately pounced on it and gave Rolf a hard, firm shake, and gave Rosa a decidedly dirty look. Now she knew, but he looked like he'd be cordial.

Holding his own, Rolf didn't move forward or away from Julio, but almost as a woman would smiled into Julio's eyes, full of charm. "Actually, Rosa's paintings have claimed my attention. Her color, you know. I will go up and look again, no?"

Looking like a thunder cloud in a darkening sky, Julio answered, "I hope I didn't interrupt *anything*." He looked directly first at Rolf, then at Rosa without flinching, holding his lightning in at the gathering, dark edges.

"Rolf was about to go out for more champagne. Would you like some with us, Julio?" Rosa looked at him with what she hoped was understanding, but in truth she felt very little. She wasn't afraid of thunder, or lightning, but he wasn't thunder and lightning, he was a miserable man, a man that she loved who was trying to make her miserable.

"Save yourself a trip. I bought some wine on the way home, not champagne but a chardonnay," Julio said flatly. "Where did you two meet?" He directed his question at Rolf with a challenging air.

Rosa interjected, "We met last night at La Casa, Julio. Why don't we all go upstairs and have some wine, comfortably." She started up the stairs avoiding Julio's fuming eyes, and she knew what he felt: vindicated.

Everyone filed upstairs. Rolf and Julio went to the front room. Rolf examined the large black and white photographs of the Mexican pyramids. After an obvious silence that Julio was not going to fill, Rolf asked, "I assume you print these yourself?"

"Yes."

"These are quite fine. The shadow and light is so sharply contrasted, especially on the steps. And the clouds are lush, no?"

"Thanks."

"I do a little photography, black and white as well. Nothing quite this good."

"I took those on our honeymoon. We're married, in case you didn't know."

Now it was starting. Rolf could no longer ignore the situation, and he flashed his day-blue eyes into Julio's dark ones.

"Not only did Rosa tell me she is married, but that she is the mother of a grown son. He is your son as well, I assume?"

Julio got up, leaving the room, just as Rosa was bringing in the wine, some cheese and some sliced mango.

"Well, I can see you two are getting along," Rosa said guardedly.

Unable to suppress a smile, Rolf said, "I think he wants to hit me."

"Do you want to leave? You could call me later. I don't want you to be uncomfortable, Rolf."

"Is he always this jealous?"

Miserably, Rosa answered, "Usually only in private. This is a new one. I guess you pushed his button."

They looked at each other and smiled, and Rolf said, "I think he's acting like a fool, and I'd rather stay. Do you mind?"

"Only if you don't mind the fact that he wants to hit you," and they began to laugh quietly. Rosa noticed there was lightning in his eyes that came and went like a flickering energy. She wondered if he wept easily, or at all. She guessed he did. Poor Julio, his body would shake with a helplessness when he reached a pitch of anger. All thunder, no rain. Poor Julio, Rosa thought. Poor me.

"We should all go out to dinner." Rolf was dauntless. "I'm sure you know an excellent place close by, no?"

"Good idea," Rosa brightened, color returning to her features. "There's a really good Japanese restaurant with the most delicious sauces on everything. You know, I'm hungrier than I realized."

"Good, good. That's what I thought. I love Japanese food—with sake, no?"

"I think you're intent on getting me drunk," and they clinked glasses, drinking the chardonnay which was dry and very good. A pale, delicate color like collected tears. A lifetime of tears, beautiful tears, not bitter. The words *rain, grapes, wine* circled in Rosa's mind, each one a distinct image, and then blurring into one translucent color.

Julio returned. Reaching for his wine glass he asked, "What's the occasion, a new beginning of some kind?"

"Join us, Julio," Rolf answered him. "I thought we might all go to dinner. Rosa suggests a Japanese restaurant close by," and Rolf lifted his glass to Julio as though to include him.

Instantly, Julio threw his glass against the wall splattering Rosa's painting of the rainbow. "I can see what's going on. Do you think I'm blind?"

Rosa froze, staring at her painting, then at Julio.

Rolf didn't budge. "There is nothing going on, Julio. Nothing but the beginning of a friendship. I go back to Berlin next week."

"Just a quickie, huh?" Julio was exploding. The thunder without the rain.

"Julio, that's enough. Do you hear me, that's enough." She stood up to clean her painting. "Jesus Fucking Christ."

To her astonishment Julio began to stamp his feet like a child. "I'm not going to come home and put up with this cute little blondie from wherever-the-hell-he's-from trying to make it with my wife. I can read between the lines!" Julio yelled.

Everyone was silent, and then Julio turned his back on them, slammed the front door, got in his car and was gone.

Rosa began to clean her painting, slowly, and just as slowly she began to cry.

"Let me help you clean the wall. Where are your towels?"

Rosa pointed to the kitchen. Rolf returned and saw the misery in her face. "Rosa," Rolf touched her face and took her in his arms as she cried. Gently, he stroked her hair silently, and then she excused herself to go to the bathroom because suddenly she wanted to kiss him fully on the mouth, and feel his tongue fill her, and fill him with her tongue. She wanted, suddenly, to be filled with gentleness.

She washed her face, applied some make-up and returned. Rolf had refilled her glass.

"Are you still hungry?" he asked. "I am."

Rosa felt no pity for Julio anymore. If she felt pity for anyone it was for herself. Either way she moved, her instincts seemed thwarted. "Have you been through this before? You're sure better at it than I am."

"My girlfriend was jealous—and then I'm not directly involved here. She would frustrate me to tears at times, and then make fun of them, and then be angry that I wasn't jealous. An unhappy circle, no?"

"Yes. An unhappy circle. How about going for a walk, then dinner. I don't think I can eat right now." Julio's anger still clenched at her stomach, and now her own was beginning to rise. "We could walk at the beach."

"Excellent. Let's go."

Rosa took him down the coast to a beautiful, wide, sandy beach where a creek glittered into the sea. She usually didn't walk on this one because it was a twenty minute drive. Today she wanted the distance. The sky was a swirl of deepening colors—orange, red, purples—and the wind stilled as though for the occasion. The palette of the sky was almost violent; only at the edge, to the left, was there a hint of Rosa's lilac. Rosa kept looking for Julio's figure, but, finally, she relaxed as the sun set and the night began to cast itself like a net over the beach. Like Quetzalpetlatl's black, lace shawl.

They settled into the sand entirely hidden from view.

"Better?" Rolf looked at her.

"Much better. I'm starved. And you?" Rosa looked right into his eyes, and they almost seemed violet in the light.

"Yes, I'm starved too, Rosa." Rolf read himself in her eyes and leaned over the small space between them, kissing her delicately on the mouth, and Rosa responded, fully, without thinking, exquisite as it was.

She pressed his head to her, his shoulders to her, her mouth opening wide to him. His lips excited her almost beyond control, and he matched her hunger, beautifully, the night beginning to cover them like a secret, and though they'd ceased to hear the sea it sounded like the rushing blood in their veins creating a silence like the sea does when you surrender to her rhythm.

Desire. She could devour him whole. He wanted to lick her body till she screamed, every dark inch of her. He wanted to watch her convulse with an orgasm, and then he wanted to enter her softness, her strength, and submit to her. Entirely.

Rosa began to weep though she still moved against him, and he against her. She wanted to rip off her clothes and give him her breasts, she wanted to watch him suckle there making her swell and moisten. She knew he wanted to eat her up, and she wanted him to, but she couldn't do it, she just couldn't do it.

She didn't belong to herself, and she hated it. And that's why she wept.

"Rosa, Rosa," Rolf licked her tears and lay still. "Do you know your tears are delicious?"

"I want you, but I can't. Isn't that a bitch, I can't," and she cried as though something precious were being ripped away from her.

Rolf just lay there, his leg still around her, holding her.

A long while passed, as they stared up at the appearing clusters of stars. Rosa softly kissed his lips, holding him back with her hands at the same time. "If I kiss you again like before it'll be torture." Now the stars teased them with their illusion of closeness as they held themselves firmly to the vastness of space.

Rolf smiled. "You're right. Let's go eat," and he kissed her once and stood up. "Well, my scarf is thoroughly wrinkled." He started to laugh and stuffed it in his jacket pocket.

Rosa looked at him, "Do you know what?"

"What?"

"You're a lovely man. I mean it."

Rolf offered his hand to pull her up, and she got to her feet.

"Look. Venus." Rosa pointed to it. Desire engulfed her again looking at him in the star's light, but she made no gesture toward him.

"Beautiful. Are you sure it's Venus?"

"Yes," she said softly.

They ordered huge meals and ate all of it, every bit of it except the rice. A little tea, a lot of sake. They felt gentle with one another, and spoke lightly as though a loud voice would blow the candle out between them. It was an understanding Rosa felt with women, an intimacy and acceptance she rarely felt with men, if ever. They both felt it, as though a possibility were being defined in a very quiet way; as though to accept Rosa's limit made their meeting, now, possible.

"Can I see you again before I leave?"

"I'd like that. Absolutely. Would Friday be good for you?"

"Perfectly unperfect. Where shall we meet? I assume I won't pick you up." Rolf looked at Rosa wryly.

Rosa laughed. "Good thinking. We could meet at a restaurant, delicious Mexican food. We could have lunch and sangría. The most delicious sangría you've ever had I bet."

"Sangría, blood—of course. Like the Blood of the Bull, Sangre de Toro. I make sangría myself, you know."

"So do I," Rosa said.

"Then we'll meet at this restaurant and compare notes. I've been thinking, we are opposites, you and I, which relieves some tension in me. Do you know?" Rolf looked utterly relaxed and alert at once.

"That's exactly what I've been feeling, but if I think about it I get all worked up and want to ask you questions. You know, dreary subjects and such, and more. Maybe I'll save some questions for Friday. In any case, we've had enough profundity today," Rosa smiled at Rolf, letting him know she was still there with him.

"But, yes, your blondeness, if you must know, at first disturbed me—and your cultural signals, compared to this culture's signals, are different. You must know there's a whole social color gradation system here in the United States. I'm sure there's similar systems in Germany, but this is the one I've felt—and, globally, it's the Third World—brown, yellow, black—people who're suffering most now. Anyway, you're the color of the ruling class, and I'm the color of the other class." Rosa watched Rolf for withdrawal but he just smiled at her.

"Of course, you're right. And shall I add, I'm a man and you're a woman.

"Took the words right out of my mouth. And, in your case, you're a German from Germany. It seems somehow reassuringly uncomplicated. But, yes, anyway, culturally, and for real, right?" Rosa laughed, "I'm a woman and you're a man, and that's a whole history of inequalities right up to the present. I can't even walk on the beach alone without looking out for perverts."

"Don't blame the men entirely, Rosa—you're hard to resist," Rolf laughed.

"I know you're trying to joke, but it's not really funny. You should feel my experience to really understand it." Rosa touched Rolf's arm lightly.

"I think I know what you're talking about, our opposites I mean. We're opposite yet equal. However, that is not a relief to most men. In fact, it might become a pain in the ass for you in the long run if it were a daily reality."

They both burst into laughter.

"Now we're getting loud again. Would you like another sake?" Rolf wanted to know.

"You know, I dread it, but I should be going home. I'm getting sleepy and another sake's going to knock me out. It'll be good to see you in the daytime, early, Friday. Why don't we meet at eleven?"

"That's good. And where is this sangría at?"

Rosa wrote the directions for him. "If you want to call, call me in the morning. Oh, hell, call me anytime, this is stupid." She looked a little weary again. "Why don't you give me the number where you're staying, I never got it."

"I'll be there at eleven," Rolf said reaching for his fortune cookie, telling her the phone number.

Rosa cracked hers in half and read out loud, "The light of a hundred stars does not equal the light of the moon. Read me yours."

Rolf showed her his, "You will travel to many places."

"It seems more of a summation of our present. Here you are, and I am dealing with the dark side, my moon, in my painting, in my shawl." But, yes, the moon is also a great light, Rosa thought, and she carefully put hers away in her wallet.

In the car they were quiet, listening to music. Peace. The calm before the storm, she thought.

"Just drop me off in front of the house. I'm just going to get out and leave." Rosa kissed Rolf gently on the cheek. He pulled up to the curb and stopped. "See you Friday. Bye, and have fun." She shut the car door and he rolled down the window.

"Take care. Are you all right, Rosa?"

Rosa looked at him, and for a split second wanted to say "No." She felt trapped, that was the worst. "Yes, I'm okay." She smiled. "Bye."

"Good night, Rosa."

She waved him away and started up the stairs.

Rosa opened the door wide expecting Julio's voice to confront her, or to silently pounce on her, or a quiver of arrows to pierce her. This was silly; she stepped in and looked. Nothing. Sean's bedroom door was shut, and it was quiet, so he must be there. The unexpected. Julio's going to be apologetic, sorry, this time.

Julio had gone to a friend's with a bottle of brandy and drank that and some wine, and smoked some grass. With the first few shots he'd felt sorry for himself, the grass clinched it. "Fucking women," he'd said to his friend, "you know, you can't live with them, you can't live without them."

"Sounds like you blew it, man. Should a gone and kept an eye on em. Played it cool. When you hitched up with her you knew she wasn't the humble type," and he laughed at Julio openly.

"If you keep that up you can stay out a my brandy," and they both laughed, but Julio still felt constricted, like exploding, like crying if he could.

By the time the brandy was gone and the wine was being passed back and forth, he finally felt sorry for Rosa. The thought of the wine splattering her painting, and what he'd said, blared through his head. Everything fell into a strange perspective as though he were watching himself from far away, and he was ashamed of himself—and then the Vietnamese woman's face came sharply into focus, the photograph he would never take. Desperation. That was it. Rosa had never looked that way. Did he want her to? Did he? He blurred the focus with some more wine, and made it home on automatic pilot.

Sean's water bed. He passed out.

Rosa locked the bedroom door and got into bed. She decided to wear nothing, and opened the window wider. She wanted air. She thought of the dream of the house, the meadow, the forest. She wondered where the hell it was. She would have to sell this house. They'd agreed it was mainly her investment since the large down payment had come from the sale of her first house. She would have to go through with it if she meant it. Rosa had gotten no more hints, only the one dream. It had been clear, but it certainly didn't say take highway eighty north, and then take a left till you come to a meadow. But she knew what it would require of her—an emptiness, a silence, and a letting go to it. No matter what. She would let go of Julio. No matter what.

Rosa realized, suddenly, that this must be what happened to people who have nervous breakdowns. They knew what they had to do, but outwardly it looked crazy to everyone else, and since they couldn't go forward, or backward, they got stuck on the spot.

The one person since childhood who always understood exactly what she meant was Sierra. Not that everything was completely understood, they'd had their conflicts, but Sierra would understand, immediately, what she had to do. That helped, it had aways helped, but ultimately she would have to do it alone. Leave.

Like Rosa had understood Sierra's abortion years ago, though strangely Rosa had thought she should've had that baby and left Bob then, and now Sierra was having their baby and staying with him. Well, Rosa had gone with her to the clinic, Bob had preferred not to, but it was Sierra who walked in alone. This was, in essence, what they offered each other—understanding and separation. Friendship. Marriage. What each of them hadn't found yet with a man.

And then Rosa thought of Rolf, her opposite, and a feeling of peace and tiredness overcame her. She fell asleep.

Feelings of sharp horror and innocence mingle in the young girl, a young, dark-skinned girl. She is surrounded by other children like herself though she doesn't know them. They are naked. The heavy door opens and they're ordered inside a terrible room. They wait a long time to die. She cannot catch her breath, it stings to breathe, and instead of crying she is angry. At them. For an instant she longs to see the sky, and she does, in spite of the grey, thick walls. She sees the sky, clearly, perfectly, like a painting.

Rosa woke out of breath, sweating. Immediately, she sat upright. That girl, that young girl *is* me. She'd dreamt this twice before but never so clearly, to the end. This time it was nearly unbearable, and this time she knew, she knew it *was* her thirty-four years ago when she died in a concentration camp. The thought had crossed her mind, but she'd denied it. This time she couldn't. She knew it was true. Rolf. Germany. Concentration camps.

The sky, the sky. Perfect like a painting in the young girl's eyes. The sky the color of Rolf's eyes. A summer sky—a clear, deep blue covering everything like a safety, the promise of warmth, and as much fruit as a child could ever eat.

The sky changing into sunset, night, the darkest night, and then the sunrise. The sky she'd been born to paint.

She fell back to sleep, the dawn an hour away. The wind blowing through the open window gave her relief, and a star at its apex, a brilliant one, was the comfort she rushed to as she left the Earth, dreaming.

Julio was in the kitchen quietly eating as Rosa came in to pour a cup of coffee. Julio felt dismal and angry, and didn't trust himself to speak, so he sat and watched her enter the kitchen and leave without

a word. Rosa took her coffee downstairs to her studio, first standing
at the front room window. She watched the waves reach and spray
against the dark island-rock. She'd rather go for a walk but that
would have to wait till the afternoon, and she was wary of staying
upstairs. She didn't want to speak to Julio, at all.

Downstairs she turned on her Peruvian flute music tape—she
worked best with flute, piano or classical music. Rosa didn't want to
think of Julio or nuclear holocaust; the wars in Latin America; world
famine; kidnapped, abused, murdered children. It was a long list
and the flute rose and sang, piercing each thought until she arrived
at a place where sorrow and joy lived, in a harmony she could hear,
feel, see. Rosa could see them, utterly unable to add or subtract from
one another, and this was the music they made—this harmony of
wholeness. Rosa sighed remembering the girl of her dreams, her
acceptance of the girl—her horror, the power of her innocence. The
sky.

Rosa added a wash of turquoise to the canvas, the lilac sky was
too dark. She stood back and it was better, but she wanted it uniform, so she worked at it carefully for an hour and a half. The
beginning of the shawl looked like a small, black spider, and Rosa
silently asked it to help her weave itself, perfectly, whole—threaded
strength and trembling softness.

She heard Julio leave and went upstairs to cook chorizo and eggs.
She was extremely hungry when her consciousness returned to ev-
eryday matters, like her body and the rush the coffee and given her,
very strong that morning. It felt like it'd left a hole in the middle of
her forehead, and her stomach churned.

A rose lay on a photograph he'd taken of her on a camping trip,
nude with her backpack on. She remembered jumping into the river
immediately afterward. It was a good memory—their lovemaking in
the sand, the coyote who'd passed them not at all interested in the
human spectacle. The wild ducks at sunset, wine in the evening. The
talks threading themselves into unknown cocoons, their dreams large
and colorful. This was in the beginning, their first year, when Rosa
began to tell Julio of her dreams the way her grandmother had
taught her—to pay close attention to them. And so Julio began to
dream about something else besides mortar attacks and screams—
and he began to remember his dreams again.

She put the rose in water and ate in silence. A hummingbird
hovered flower to flower downstairs in the garden, and the sun was
out bringing everything gratefully to life. Color.

Soaking her dishes she made a note to call Sierra in the evening,
and went to assist her spider.

She wasn't angry at Julio anymore, but instead she felt a diffusiveness in its place. She wasn't angry at White People or the crazed masculinity that haunted her personally, and the world globally. She felt dull, a sort of dull acceptance of reality. A black and white reality. The black shawl occupied her until two complete spirals were done, and one black rose.

The spider had definitely done its work. Quetzalpetlatl's shawl grew larger.

Rosa looked up at the changing, lilac sky, and she felt exhilarated. The painting had begun to speak to her. The sky was now a sky, and she began to visualize the ring of orchids. She decided to let the spider worry about the shawl—she, the spider, had been weaving since the beginning of time, Rosa reasoned, and laughed out loud at the idea.

At the same time she wanted to enlarge the rainbow painting. Rosa rarely worked on two paintings at once, but she might try it because she felt that the lilac sky was going to occupy her for a while. The rainbow sky was the color of the simplest blue ozone intended only to convey breath, not transformation as this lilac persistently insisted of her, as though it were a color she'd never seen or could ever see.

Rosa heard the front door shut, and she realized it was after four. The dull acceptance vanished and she was alert. She grabbed her parka and took Zack through the garage. They walked to the sea's cliff and back without incident, high tide reigned on the shore. The grotto was completely inaccessible, the pussy-pink anenomes ate to their fill fluttering back and forth beneath the sea, and Quetzalpetlatl sat on her throne for a thousand years.

Rosa found one treasure on the beach; she always seemed to find at least one, a rock with a circle surrounding it. A completely joined circle. Rosa secured it in her pocket and ran all the way back up the stairs without stopping.

When she got home Julio had fixed a meal. "I made a baked chicken. It'll be ready pretty soon. You hungry?"

"Do you want me to make a salad?"

"I already did it," Julio responded.

Rosa went in the bedroom to call Sierra, and briefly they made plans to get together. Rosa would go up to Sonoma county for the weekend, and she looked forward to it. It was fertile farm country, dark and rich earth. Her first house, one that she'd owned, had been there on five acres of apple orchard, some walnut, cherry and pear trees, a wild grape arbor, a young stand of redwoods, and more. The animals she'd raised—she who'd been born in a city—her first fresh eggs, pigs and steers for the table. It had been a life within a life. There she'd softened the harshest memories of her childhood's hunger. The days she and her grandmother had nothing to eat in the crowded, noisy city.

She and a lover, Sean, and another couple had shared in it. There'd been many friends, Sierra who'd lived nearby, Sean's friends who were allowed to build forts and play football in one of the fields, even in the rain. Consequently, Rosa was always aware of a consistent flow of people. But it was there her work really began to flower as though her paintings were finally able to take root, blossom and ripen to maturity. And it was there her paintings began to sell, one here, one there.

They'd been six years of hard work, physically hard work, pruning and harvesting the orchard, canning, freezing the garden harvests, learning to care for animals she'd only seen in pieces wrapped in cellophane, and then she'd had to face their slaughter. She began to teach two classes at the junior college, and to paint in a completely unknown way as though someone had spun her around, and her view of the world was simply not the same.

Her lover, Dan, who was a poet and a carpenter, lived with her for three of those years. Intense, dark, Portuguese-English mixture—intense and self-centered. It was good for a while, and then he began to drink. His poetry was very fine, and Rosa'd respected that, but then Dan began to neglect his poetry, and worked only when absolutely necessary. She'd lost respect for him, and Rosa already had a son to raise. She didn't need two angry adolescents.

"Rosa, it's ready whenever you are," Julio yelled through the door.

She bounced back to the present and opened the door. Whatever it was it smelled delicious. He'd set the table, a bunch of slender, purple iris in the center, two red candles, and the food.

"It looks great, Julio," Rosa told him without looking into his face. To break some of the stiffness she put flamenco and classical guitar on the stereo, and some Joni Mitchell because she felt like it.

He'd baked a chicken in honey-orange sauce, steamed broccoli and a salad. He'd chosen the six purple iris on the way home. Julio lit the two red candles and breathed softly.

They ate in silence listening to the music, and their own thoughts, wondering what the other was really thinking.

Rosa thought of Sierra's words, "I'm like a fresh convert that must learn to believe again," only she felt no desire to "believe again," but the signals were all around her, inside of her, to start that weary process. Rosa thought of the poem "Narcissus"—to love one's self. To blossom. Did the iris love their own beauty?

"I'm going to Sierra's this weekend. I want to leave early Saturday morning. Don't look uptight, Julio. You know we need a breather, and I'm going to see Sierra. Period."

"Nothing pleases you, does it? There aren't a lot of men who'd put up with this shit."

Rosa just stared at him.

"Look, I'm sorry about yesterday."

"Julio, you're telling me, in essence, that I can't bring who I want here, and that I also can't go where I want. I'm sick to death of this double bind. I want out of this relationship, that's what I want."

"You don't mean it. You're pissed right now. Rosa, I love you."

"Like you love a pet poodle—a nice, obedient pet poodle. I'll tell you, I can't think about *love* anymore. When I married you I was aware of the mortal danger, but I didn't care. I loved you. We talked about the Mexican Man syndrome—when are you going to give it up?"

"You're exaggerating now," Julio replied.

"I am the wrong woman for this script, and the tragedy is you are the wrong man as well. You've shown me parts of yourself that I'll never forget, like that time at the river camping. But it's got to keep happening, a whole gallery of photographs, connected and changing."

Julio was silent and refilled his wine glass sullenly.

"Julio, love yourself so I can. You won't let me love you," Rosa quietly said.

"Oh Christ, a psychology lesson."

Her eyes flared, "No, just an obvious perception. I'm wading through my own psychic shit, believe me, and right now I feel totally exhausted of optimism as far as we're concerned. It feels like any energy I emit you suck up without a trace, and only want more." She began to cry.

"Look, I'm sorry. What else can I say?" Julio sounded miserable.

"Julio, I'm going to sell the house. I'm going to leave. I need to live by myself, that's all I know." Tears were falling steadily from her eyes. They just kept coming.

"Look, why don't you go to Sierra's. Go ahead, and then come back and we'll talk about it," he said, trying to sound calm. She'd threatened this before in anger, but now he really believed her and it frightened him. She meant it.

Rosa stood up and began doing the dishes as Joni Mitchell sang,

"I had a king in a tenement castle, lately he's taken to saying I'm crazy and blind—he lives in another time . . . and I in my leather and lace can never become that kind . . . I can't go back there anymore, you know my key won't fit the door . . . beware of the power of moons."

She heard Julio slam his darkroom door. He hated this record, and she knew it. Should I play it only when he's gone, she thought, and she had, but not tonight.

The last of the sunset was visible, streaks of purples, pinks. Only the first minutes of the sunset seemed to be a uniform lilac before the dark. The sun had been an orange fire-globe, stubbornly setting. Persistence was definitely a quality of the universe.

Rosa took some tea into the bedroom, and a map of California. She looked at the county she'd never seen—Plumas. Feathers. Wild geese, hawks, and yes, eagles. She'd seen hawks—red-tailed, sparrow, peregrine, but never eagles. Hawks took her breath away, their silence in the sky.

Julio, too, loved hawks, the desert, small quick lizards. He'd grown up in New Mexico surrounded by brown people, an Indian culture, the only small male in a family of women. His uncles initiated him into the world of men, the world of hunting, and once he'd shot a hawk and killed it. The mass of feathers was not the bird that'd flown. He'd taken the tail feathers, the longest ones, and never spoken of it to anyone but Rosa. He'd told her of the desert's silence and she'd understood that, and his love for his grandmother, his sorrow and longing for parents he'd never known, the old hunter, a friend of his uncles, who ate what he killed. A dark, old Indian man who'd given Julio his first taste of deer's liver hot from the fire—yes, she'd understood that.

That's why she penciled her way up highway eighty north, and into a thin, dark vein that ran into the mountains. She circled the county seat and could only guess where Lupine Meadows was. The thought terrified her, but now Rosa knew she had to go where she'd never been, where winter was, a beautiful harshness she couldn't yet imagine, and she knew she had to go alone. She had to trust her instincts . . . beware of the power of moons.

Sierra is about to give birth. She's terrified, and Rosa holds onto her. They walk together down a long, dark tunnel until they come to the end of it, and an edge appears. An unmistakable edge of nothingness. The complete unknown, and nothing can ever fill it. They sense it is bottomless, fathomless, as death is. Rosa realizes she can go no further, and Sierra will have to go alone. Rosa feels

Sierra's terror, and then the release of her spirit as she flies into the face of it, as it turns into wonder.

Julio slept in Sean's room again after working in the darkroom till around three in the morning. For some reason he'd printed up the stark mountain—desert shots he'd taken on his last visit home when his grandmother died. They were filled with a stark and beautiful longing, and at once they held the image of contained wholeness. Was it only here where the hunter knew his place—he ate what he killed. In one of the photographs he'd chosen a small cactus and surrounded it with stones, some of the longer, larger ones spraying out from it like a mandala. The grand, imposing mountain shots were for himself, only for himself. There was no enemy in those mountains, only death as it exists in lonely places. The small, sturdy cactus was for his grandmother, and his gesture was complete.

Rosa woke slowly with smaller dreams clutching at her, till she fully woke and remembered Sierra's birth. It was seventeen years since she'd given birth, and now the memory clung to her vividly like an old wound. She realized this was exactly what she felt at the thought of leaving, this feeling of arriving at the edge, alone.

She got up and quietly began the coffee, jumped in the shower, and came out to find Julio drinking coffee by the kitchen window.

"I worked in the darkroom pretty late. Some of the prints look pretty good if you want to take a look."

He wants me to pretend our talk never happened, but it did. "Sure." And then Rosa began frying bacon. "I'll be taking off tomorrow morning as early as I can."

"How about going out for dinner tonight?"

A frown crossed Rosa's face.

"Come on, Rosa, just dinner, wherever you want."

He looked tired this morning, and the word *husband* echoed in her mind, and what she most resented in him rested itself within her.

"Okay, Julio. I'll meet you here at five."

He gave her a slight smile. "Great. Are you going to paint today?"

"Maybe. I have some business to take care of. Anyway, I'll be here at five." Rosa thought of Rolf and wished she didn't have to lie, but she really didn't care. Not anymore.

"Today I have a shoot and then I'll be in the darkroom till it's time to go." Julio looked like he wanted to nail down exactly where she'd be going, but as Rosa didn't ask him where his job would be he'd look pushy again. Instead, he got up to get ready to go. He also knew better than to try to kiss her—she'd flare up, and dinner would be down the drain.

Rosa took her bacon and eggs down to her studio, turned on classical guitar, and stared at her lilac sky, her sleeping spider. She took out a fresh canvas, one of her larger ones, primed and taut. She placed the lilac sky to the left, and the fresh canvas to the right, and she decided, firmly, to begin the enlargement of the rainbow painting. Rosa began to imagine the Earth on the canvas, magnified, and where the rainbow tapered off to a single stroke. She couldn't understand it yet, but it was as though her lilac sky wanted her only to look at it, to see it for now, and the sleeping spider reassured Rosa with her appearance. A painting had never demanded this of her, to simply let it exist, unfinished, for a while. In fact, just sitting and staring at the lilac sky made her want to alter it again.

No, she'd begin the new canvas, the blue ozone, the Earth with its encircling, vivid rainbow, a living rainbow—and, of course, the continents would become clear and recognizable. Would she show dogs and cats walking around? Rosa laughed at the idea. No, but there was something in particular she wanted to see, she could feel it.

As Rosa got dressed to meet Rolf she remembered Sean's letter, and sat down to write him a brief, humorous letter with a twenty dollar check inside, also reminding him of college registration, and that if he wanted there was time enough to stay two more weeks. Rosa realized all of this was up to him, and it felt like a relief, yet foreign, like an unfamiliar distance was beginning to grow between them.

Sean's first love affair would also make a difference too, she thought with a pang of possessiveness, but hadn't he written "EVOL, Sean"?

A friend of Sean's had offered to share with him the separate downstairs apartment his parents maintained for free. They'd be on their own. Rosa had been reluctant, and they'd argued about it in indirect ways, like the time he stumbled in drunk banging pots trying to cook something to eat at four in the morning. She hadn't allowed him to, which was exactly what he'd wanted.

"If I want to cook a hamburger, why the hell shouldn't I?"

"Because you don't know how to do it quietly, and because you're drunk."

"I'm tired of being told 'No, Sean this, and no, Sean that.' Shit!" And he'd lurched to his room.

Rosa never saw him drunk like that again, but he'd said it. Now, if she was leaving, his way would be clear. Yet she sensed it wouldn't be easy, for either of them.

She ended her letter, "I'd love to meet this mysterious Nice Person, if possible. Take care, EVOL, M."

Rosa wore purple, well-fitting but comfortable pants, and a light cream sweater with a woven scarf of various shades of fuchsia. She slipped on her dark brown boots and tucked her pants inside, and then she grabbed her warm black and purple poncho with a hood in case it was foggy and cold.

Rolf was sitting by the indoor fountain, a simple one that dripped water continuously. Two enormous gold carp swam back and forth through bright green vegetation, and a multi-colored parrot perched on a stand, in a cage, and whistled. Rolf had a pitcher of sangría in front of him, and he looked utterly at ease. Pouring her a glass he said, "I won't even ask if you'd like some, no? We're both on time, how nice!" He was wearing jeans and a delicately made sweater of a pale blue color, leather sandals and a lovely turquoise bracelet.

"You should wear an earring, Rolf. It would definitely suit you."

He frowned.

"I mean it as a compliment. It would look great on you."

"Do you mean as a sailor would?" he laughed.

"Kind of. But I also just mean it would suit you, and perhaps you have earned it like a sailor. Have you ordered yet?"

"No, I've waited. What's your favorite, Rosa? The sangría is everything you said, delicious."

Each glass was decorated with fresh pineapple, a slice of orange and strawberries, and in the pitcher there was more fresh fruit and ice.

"My favorites are flautas and chimichangas, but I'll tell you, everything here is good."

"Order for me. Do you mind?"

"Sure," Rosa laughed. "Is that sweater hand-made?"

"Yes, my mother made it. She also knits me socks, beautiful socks," Rolf smiled delightedly.

"I don't knit. If a sock develops holes we throw it away. How lucky you are."

"I don't knit either, Rosa, but if I did I'd make you some. How is your husband?"

"He apolgized, but it's very tense. Actually, I've told him I'm leaving, but I don't think he really believes me. Maybe I don't really believe me. Anyway, it'll work out. When are you going back?"

Rolf reached over and smoothed her hair. "Sunday. Early Sunday morning."

"Well then, this is it. I'm going to a friend's this weekend."

"I'll be back here again, Rosa, and maybe you'll come to Berlin, no?"

"Of course. But I want you to write me."

"Of course."

Rosa ordered flautas for both of them.

"Do you know that Golden Gate Park is close by? Have you gone?"

"I've driven through. It looks beautiful."

"Why don't we go there after this and take a good look?"

"How perfectly unperfect. Oh, I did go to the museum and the aquarium one afternoon."

"Do you roller skate?"

"I think so. Why?"

"Do you want to go roller skating? They rent skates in the park."

"You don't care if I fall and make a fool of myself?" Rolf asked in a serious tone.

"Only if I can laugh. Hey, I'm not that hot anymore either, so you can laugh too," she added reassuringly.

"Do you have your list of questions today?" Rolf teased her.

Rosa laughed, and then looked at him intently. "Actually, I have answers. I think knowing you has given me some answers, and now I'm left with a very good feeling about you, and a somehow better feeling about blue eyes in general. Okay, I have a question—do you worry about our planet surviving this century?"

"I believe I will now, now that I've known you. You make me think of it as something distinct and alive. Your work certainly does. I've always dealt with abstractions, symbols, flight. So, though I've thought of nuclear war, it's always seemed extremely remote and troublesome as though it had nothing, really, to do with me. I sound rather selfish, don't I?"

Rosa shifted in her seat and said, "Maybe that was what people felt in the face of the reality of the concentration camps." As though to herself, she added, "What horrible dreams they must've had."

Rolf's face darkened. "Touché."

"What I'm trying to say is we're all in that position, globally. To not accept our common reality, as potentially destructive as it is, is to deny our awareness, our part in it, as a part of it. The whole damn thing."

"It is difficult, isn't it? Consciousness is difficult, but then what else is there?" Rolf half-smiled. "This room demands my attention, for example, this obnoxious, brilliant parrot, the colored tissue on the ceiling, the murals on the walls. I feel that I should have balloons attached to my wrists to truly belong here, no?" He smiled fully.

"But, yes, we must include as much as we possibly can. One can't fly forever—one must come back to earth, no?" His eyes were gentle, a gentle, summer-blue like her dream, like the sky of her dream. Its pain and its promise.

Rosa felt like weeping but instead she laughed, "Well, it seems I've included you in my consciousness, Gringo, that's for sure. It seems I've had enough trouble with men, and now I include a gringo, and I'll tell you, it's been a pleasure."

When they parted at the end of the day, they cried, then they laughed. Rosa had never seen a man with tears on his face, a man that made no effort to hide them.

"I like your tears. I like the rain in your summer-sky eyes," she'd said with the unsaid image, in her mind, of fruit getting fatter. Ripe. Yes, ripening.

And they'd laughed as he picked her up off the ground in a joyful hug, a quick kiss. She'd felt his features with her hands, and had kissed his eyes, one by one.

Rolf had watched her drive away, her dark hair a bit wild after the crazy day of skating and talking and wind, and he'd said her name once under his breath, gathering her memory like a flower.

Rosa stopped at a bathroom, looked at herself in a mirror and brushed her hair. She would compose herself for the evening—could she burst into the house looking this happy? He'd know. She put Rolf, her tender secret, away for another time. Does happiness have to be a secret? she wondered. Not only Rolf, but happiness in general, joy. My joy seems to offend Julio. Julio. My dark husband.

Julio was downstairs working, and the house was very quiet, so she poured herself a half glass of chilled chardonnay and decided to shower. She took a long, hot shower, and then dressed slowly, applying her spare make-up slowly. She needed this interlude of silence. Rosa looked at herself in the mirror in her black dress with a full skirt, a slightly scooped neck, the silver star necklace, opal earrings, slender shell bracelets, and decided she'd wear the warm, black shawl. Now, she felt somewhat separated from the afternoon.

Julio was in the front room. "Well, for once you're dressed before I am. You were in there long enough," Julio surveyed her. "Have you thought of where you'd like to go?"

"Actually, I'm pretty hungry. How about the Greek Taverna?" Rosa thought of Greek music, the dancing, retsina.

"You're looking pretty good. I like that dress on you. Sure. Why not? Have you been there before, I'm sure?" Julio asked in a slightly accusatory voice.

Rosa ignored it. "We've never been there together, have we? I think you'll like it. The food's great, really spicy, and there's music and dancing. Do you like retsina?"

"It's okay if it's very chilled. Did you get everything done today?"

"Yes, I did, Julio. Look, why don't you get dressed so we can go. Are you hungry?"

"Yeah. Be right out." He turned and left the room abruptly, sensing a secret because of her brief reply.

Rosa put her shawl around her and sat by the window watching the sea and sky clash and merge, and in this painting she had nothing to do but watch the color and light change of its own accord. She thought of her lilac sky downstairs and how restless it made her feel, how compelled she felt to endlessly alter it, how she hadn't found the exact shade yet, the exact light—and yet a certain conversation had begun between her and the lilac sky. It began to exist in spite of her, like this changing sky she loved. Like Rolf going out tonight with friends, enjoying himself. He'd been disappointed she couldn't come, but Rosa knew he'd enjoy himself. Rosa felt even now he was changing, as she was changing, as the sky was changing, as everything alive was changing whether they welcomed it or not, whether they accepted it or not. This sky was forever changing.

"I'm ready, Rosa." Julio's voice sounded loud after the silence and she started. "Let's take my car, it's got a full tank. Do I look Greek enough?" He turned around.

Julio wore a white Mexican shirt of a thick cotton material that did look Greek, and it looked very good against his darkness, unbuttoned to show his chest.

"You should wear that shirt more often, it looks good on you." Rosa stood up to go and saw that her compliment caught him off guard. She opened the door and he followed her to the car. The air sharpened Rosa's hunger and she picked a few ripe strawberries from the bed she planted instead of a lawn. She offered some to Julio and he took two, touching her hand as he did.

"To tell you the truth I never thought the strawberries would grow there. These are so juicy." Julio smiled at her intimately, but she didn't trust it, she didn't want to trust it because it meant another turn around the wheel of intense pleasure, and intense pain.

They were seated at a table by the dance floor. A candle lit in a red container glowed, and the food from the kitchen smelled absolutely enticing. Rosa ordered retsina immediately, and the Greek salad special of the house. She urged Julio to as well, and he did. The salads arrived glistening with olive oil, feta cheese, fat black olives, and the retsina was tart and perfectly cold.

Julio felt a little out of place in a Greek restaurant, but the first bite of his salad was delicious. The band started playing, and though the music was unfamiliar it was moving and beautiful, passionate. One man stood up to dance to Julio's surprise—defiant, alone, at the center of the floor, and when it seemed as though he'd made his authority clear by the command in his body, he began to bend to the music as the tempo rose. Yes, that's how it feels to be a man, Julio thought—that's how it feels to be alone. Then other men joined him until four men danced shoulder to shoulder.

"Do men and women dance together?" Julio asked Rosa.

"Usually only in a line or circle dance as far as I know. Do you like it?"

"They're pretty good. Actually, I was a little worried there when that one guy got up by himself. I kept expecting someone to tell him to sit down, or that he'd fall on his face. Don't ask me why," Julio laughed.

Rosa enjoyed the men's dancing; she liked looking at them. But their bodies looked strict and controlled, their masculinity honed to a hardness, and the men dancing together looked like a barrier against her. If only one of them would lose control and simply dance, Rosa thought—but then, maybe, they only danced like that for each other. Flora acknowledged the men in the room as she danced, but these men didn't look at any of the women, just each other or straight ahead. And in Flora's dance there was an edge of uncontrolled ecstasy constantly moving her to the limits of her dance. Rosa didn't see this ecstasy in their movements.

As the music reached a pitch of intensity, what could only be described as unleashed joy, a woman from the audience jumped out of her seat and put her arm around the man at the end of the line, and joined their dancing. With his free hand he pushed her away from him. It was too embarrassing to be true, but the woman persisted, she seemed to know the steps very well. She grabbed hold of the man's shirt and continued to dance with a burst of energy and an unbelievable smile on her face. A waiter walked out on the dance floor and took hold of her arm. They exchanged words, briefly, anger sizzling on both sides. The men in the line next to them danced on stoically with traces of smiles on their faces, except for one man who obviously felt ashamed. The woman jerked her arm free from the waiter's hold and stalked to her seat in tears, and then she fled to the bathroom.

The band stopped playing, and the men sat down. One of them, a waiter, came and took their dinner orders.

Rosa asked the waiter, "May I ask why that woman wasn't allowed to dance?"

The waiter glared at her. "That dance is only for men. It's not permitted. That's all," he said with a finality.

Rosa raised her voice. "I think that little scene was unnecessary and rude."

With a forced charm he responded, "We're all entitled to our opinions." He quickly walked away.

Bar drinks were sent to the musicians as they sat and laughed among themselves. Rosa was livid. The people who'd been with the woman were gone, and the woman with them.

"I don't think it was very polite, but it is their culture. Don't get all worked up," Julio tried to laugh. "We came here for dinner, right?"

"I think it sucks. That's what I think."

"Come on, take it easy, Rosa," Julio said, getting uncomfortable.

"I like their food, and I also like their music, but it doesn't mean I have to swallow that kind of behavior. Culture, my ass. This is San Francisco, not ancient Greece," Rosa flared.

"Do you plan to make a scene?" Julio asked edgily, darting his eyes left to right.

"So you don't like public scenes? Just semi-public ones with an audience of two." And then she added, "Maybe I can throw my wine glass against the wall for added effect. A little drama to the drama." She stared at him without flinching.

Julio rolled his eyes up in painful exasperation. "Come on. Christ! We ordered our dinners, and the woman's gone. She had her big moment, now can't you forget it?"

The waiter brought bread and soup, saying, "Eat it while it's hot." Then turning to Julio he said, "Sir."

"Thanks for the great advice," Rosa said without a trace of manners, and the waiter stiffened and walked away.

Rosa felt better now, her pulse evening out. She blocked out Julio's face and tasted and seasoned her soup. They ate in silence. When the waiter came to clear the soup plates Rosa ordered another retsina. The waiter nodded his head and left. Julio thought, Thank God, and said, "I liked that soup. Tangy. Just right. Anyway, when do the men and women dance?"

"Later, I suppose," Rosa answered icily, finishing her glass of wine.

"We can't do anything anymore without ending in a fight, can we?"

"Well, speaking of big moments, you certainly had one the other night at my expense. Look, forget it. If that waiter has the brains to be quiet, I'll attempt to enjoy my meal."

The band began to play a kind of slow, circling tune. The music was beautiful, exquisitely rich and full with a strange vitality.

At a crowded table across the room, obviously an entire family, a disagreement was going on. An older man, who sat at the head of the table, was trying to persuade a young man to his left to join him in a dance. The young man refused, shaking his head hesitantly, the rest of the family was quiet and tense. The older man insisted loudly, "Come on. It's for my birthday." Someone at the table said, "He just doesn't feel like it," in a cautious, feminine voice. Now the older man grew louder, he'd had a lot to drink, "What is he, some kind of sissy?"

The young man sprang to his feet and walked to the center of the floor. The older man finished his drink, keeping a cigar in his mouth, and the music grew louder holding its slow, circling tempo.

The older man swaggered over to the young man in time to the music—he'd already begun to dance. This crucial victory also seemed to be part of it, the rhythmic swagger.

Rosa glanced up at Julio and he said, "Is this a regular feature, or what?" in a tone of disbelief.

"This show must be for us, Julio. I've never seen anything like it," and like everyone else in the room she was riveted to the old man's dance. She felt sorry for the young man, he looked like he was condemned to death, standing there holding a dangling, white table napkin up in the air, his eyes averted.

The old man grabbed the napkin and pulled with all his weight, arching back to the music, and the young man had to sustain him. It was an effort, but he didn't move an inch. He stood absolutely still. The music kept its circling quality but the music grew faster, and the old man arched back again and again, each time coming up to the young man's face to smile. The young man never looked at him, and though there was an unmistakable disgrace in his face there was a dignity in his bearing. He refused to meet the old man's gaze.

The music was becoming wild, and the old man was sweating with his efforts, the white napkin still between them. The old man arched his body entirely backwards, puffed on his cigar till it glowed, then he slid the lit cigar into his mouth and held it there, slapping the floor loudly with his free hand. He pulled himself up, slowly, and produced the still glowing cigar on his tongue. The young man was slightly trembling with sweat on his face, but he still refused to meet the old man's eyes.

The old man raised his arms in triumph and the band ended on an upward note like a thrust. The young man dropped the white napkin on the floor and silently went to his seat, as the old man took a round of applause and whistles of appreciation from the other, presumably, real men in the audience.

Julio's face was a blend of horror and fascination. "Well, that was my camera's loss." He went on, slowly, "You have to admire the old man's spirit, but I sure wouldn't want him to be my father." The word *domination* echoed in his mind: *conqueror, conquered.* The enemy. To dance with your enemy. Another man? Your own father? Of course. That's focusing everything down to basics, keeping it on a personal level. Was the old man's dance necessary, he wondered, and if so, why? A peculiar sadness engulfed him as he looked at the white napkin, still spotless, on the floor.

Rosa snapped, "I think the young man's spirit was to be admired, that he endured the ordeal at all. All he had to do was let go of the damned napkin. The cigar was a bit phallic, wouldn't you say? Took the whole thing in his mouth." She went on, "That kind of power's terrible. It preys on the vulnerability of others, not to speak of innocence, sensitivity, the feminine the old man denies in himself and still sees in the young man. The feminine he hates and uses in his wife, I bet, he's used in his son, if that is his son—but I think you're right. That's his son." Rosa looked over at the young man. He was talking quietly to a young woman next to him, shoulder to shoulder, walled off from the rest of the table, the constant, loud talking, the family's relief of survival. They chose intimacy. Rosa wondered if he'd force his son, years from now, to endure that dance.

"Rosa," Julio looked at her closely, "do you see the feminine in me?"

Their food arrived, an assortment of spicy meats and sauces on earthenware platters, seasoned rice and fresh vegetables. The intensity of the evening extended even to the food.

Rosa filled their wine glasses with retsina and took a sip.

"Yes, but you don't like her yet, you don't trust her yet, so she turns on you." And then she added, quietly but clearly, "You won't let her love you."

Julio felt a part of himself reach out to merge with Rosa, to agree and mourn with her. Her words were so clear they bypassed his reason, and he felt an acute and sharp despair because he knew the clarity would pass; that he would forget he and the enemy were one. He looked at Rosa, across the table as she began to serve herself in the silence, and he knew she loved him, but he couldn't, he just couldn't trust it. Her. Rosa. It. Her. Himself.

He felt his eyes fill with tears and his mouth jerked into a funny shape—I'm certainly not going to cry here, he thought with alarm. "What are we going to do, Rosa?" Julio asked in a strangled voice.

Startled, Rosa looked up at Julio, at the pain in his face, and she said, "Let me love you," almost involuntarily. She reached over with her fork and put a piece of the rich, pungent meat into his mouth, and they both burst into laughter. He took a piece of meat from the platter, with his fingers, and placed it into hers. One, long tear rolled down his left eye and settled into his neck, and it seemed everything he looked at was fresh and vivid, heightened by an unknown light.

The band began to play again, a slow, passionate music that embraced every human emotion; each instrument was a master of its realm: hate, love, sorrow, joy. Together, they were inexplicably beautiful. The music made Rosa's body yearn to dance, as one man stood to dance alone. He was the man, she noticed, who'd looked ashamed when the woman had been forced to leave the floor. His movements were sweeping and strong, yet graceful. His face was sombre but not sad as he clenched the music to himself, and instead of a rigid control of his body there was a joy. The music grew faster, and his body turned with it, and as the music rose she saw the ecstacy overtake him. His surrender to the music was his release. His dance was exquisite, virile, sensual. He was a man dancing, alone, for everyone. Rosa felt included, embraced, exultant; a deep part of her exulted with his masculinity, a masculinity she longed for. Sheer masculine joy.

The music slowed again, and the man's dark skin was covered in sweat. He smiled widely as he reached over to a nearby table and grabbed a woman's hand to join him, saying something to her and the man with her. Embarrassed, she refused. Without missing a beat he approached Rosa, grabbed her hand and said to her and Julio, "Both of you join me! Come on!"

Rosa took Julio's hand. "Come on, Julio, let's try it. Hurry!"

Julio refused, shaking his head. "Not me."

The man hesitated for a moment and, on impulse, without looking at Julio, she took his hand and followed him. They went table to table until a line of men and women was finally formed like a long, living snake. Rosa watched the man's feet closely; his hand was firm in her own. The music began to repeat itself as though announcing a beginning of a new phase. Everyone in the line quieted down in their laughter—none of them believed they were actually going to dance. The man's feet began to move deliberately to the even rhythms in a perceptible pattern, over and over, and each person watched the other's feet next to them. They began to move through the room awkwardly, then a little more smoothly, and they began to laugh again. Rosa was silent as she watched the man's feet, and then she began to smile as her own feet became confident. His free hand rose in the air, waving grandly, snapping his fingers from time to time, and the snake moved to the music, slowly, in unison, men and women. They moved in and out of tables, around the room, laughing at their daring, a curious joy running through them, through their hands. Their bodies felt fully alive, each one separate, yet consciously joined to the others as they moved like liquid, like slow, thick honey, through the pulsing hands of the music. More people joined the line and it became harder to move, and the snake came to a halt.

As the music came to an end everyone shouted, and Rosa looked at the man next to her—his eyes were on fire. She would remember his fire.

The line began to break as the huge snake dismembered itself. "Next time you lead," he said jokingly to Rosa. "I loved your dance, and thank you!" she shouted through all the noise.

"You're almost done. Wait for me," Rosa said as she sat down laughing. "It wasn't that hard—next time join in."

"It looked like a regular orgy," Julio said with an edge to his voice. He caught himself. "Sorry, I'm just a grouch. It looked like fun. Who knows, maybe next time I'll give it a try. I can only break my neck, right?"

She looked at him cautiously and asked, "What did you think of his dance?"

"I've never seen a man dance like that. There was a real freedom in his movements."

"Joy."

"Yes, definitely, joy. It made me jealous," Julio laughed.

"I wish you would've danced."

"I do too. Now. Are you still going to Sierra's tomorrow?"

"Yes, as early as I can get out."

"Are you still going to leave me, Rosa?"

There was a sudden tight pain her chest, and the recent joy fled. "I don't know. I really don't. All I know is, I can't stand the miserable cycles we seem to get stuck in. And something tells me I should live by myself. I just don't know."

They made love that night with candles lit so they could see each other in the darkness. Julio put a mirror next to them to watch themselves like they had in the beginning. In the mirror the candles gave the illusion of ancient ritual to their joined bodies, and it worked. They felt like they had in the beginning, but this time the lust, and the love, was fully human as they each memorized the other's face. As their bodies memorized each other, skin to skin, cell to cell.

The last thing Rosa remembered was her desire to blow out the four candles, and that she hadn't used her diaphragm. It was close enough to her menstrual, and it'd been seventeen years since a child had lodged itself inside of her body.

She never blew out the candles. Each one burned, slowly, down to the last of its wick until darkness recovered itself.

There is a child between them, a dark-haired little girl. She's just beginning to walk and Rosa helps her stand. Rosa lets her go and she walks, haltingly, without falling, to Julio.

Rosa woke, sweating, in Julio's arms, his legs wrapped around her. Turning away from him she looked into the mirror flinging the blankets away from herself. The child, she dreamt the child again. The first time she'd dreamt giving birth to a dark-haired daughter surrounded by women. The second time she'd dreamt holding a soft, sweet-smelling baby, and staring at her delicate, perfect features with absolute concentration. A beautiful Indian child with thick, dark hair.

Apprehension clutched at her as she looked into the mirror. I've skipped a diaphragm before, she thought. Maybe someday I'll have a child, but not now. Certainly not now.

Julio turned toward her, his eyes meeting hers in the mirror. "Morning," he muttered and kissed the inside of her neck as he cupped her breast and coiled himself into her, his penis hardening.

"I'm getting up, Julio. Right now. I'll make some coffee." She turned and quickly kissed his lips lightly, playfully, and jumped out of bed before he could grab hold of her.

He moaned, "No, stay here with me. Shit!"

By the time Rosa showered, made the coffee, some bacon, Julio came into the kitchen. "So you're really going to Sierra's?"

"I told you I was, Julio. Do you want an egg?"

"I kind of thought after last night we could use the weekend together. When is Sean coming back?"

"In a couple of weeks, I think. I told Sierra I was coming up today, and besides I want to see her. Do you want an egg? Speak now or forever hold your peace. The coffee's made." She turned her back to him.

"Yeah, I'll take an egg," Julio answered sulkily. "How long are you staying?"

"I'll be back Monday."

"I thought you were just staying the weekend."

"I am. The whole weekend. I'll be back Monday afternoon. Big deal." She began frying the eggs, watching the edges become firm in the yellow margarine, and she took a sip of coffee.

"Are you sure you aren't meeting your blonde cutie somewhere?" He was intent on making her angry.

Rosa felt like throwing her coffee in his face. "Okay, Julio, that's enough." She turned off the stove, put her poncho on, grabbed her bag, tears streaming down her face.

Julio tried to stop her in the front room. "Hey, I'm sorry. Rosa, I'm sorry. Stay and have breakfast with me. Do you want an omelette?"

"Shove your omelette, you fucking asshole!" she shouted as she slammed the door behind her. Rosa thought of last night and an unutterable sorrow filled her. She felt utterly betrayed, desolate. She kept to the coast route, time to think, and stopped for a sandwich. He just doesn't believe me—that I really love him, or that I'll really leave. She looked out at the relentless ocean, the endless movement of all beginnings. Life.

Then she knew she would sell the house and leave. It was necessary that she believe in herself. Yes, this time, now or never, she had to believe herself at least. It wasn't enough to love anyone else if this wasn't true.

The scattered afternoon fog looked like a mind trying to speak to itself, patches of clarity constantly threatened by doubt. Rosa knew her desire to live in the mountains, in the forest, in snow, by herself, where she'd never lived before, was not rational. There was no promise of a job, she only felt herself going toward it like her dream—and that place within the black dot of her mind that was solitude. Her solitude. A wholeness she had to know like a fire, a small, circular fire, in the fog, in the damp fog. Her mind warmed itself against that small, circular knowledge.

Sierra was in the kitchen washing vegetables for dinner, her dress splattered with dry clay, her long dark hair held back by an abalone clip. She ran to the back porch when she heard Rosa's car. She felt pretty good—finished a poem, four large bowls to be fired, and the child moved within her.

"Hey, bitch!" Sierra yelled as Rosa got out of her car.

Rosa yelled back, "Where's the wine?"

"Chilling for hours and hours. Where were you?"

They hugged and kissed each other, looking slowly, as they always did when they met, into each other's eyes. It was difficult, if not impossible, to hide anything. They were childhood, girlhood, friends.

"I stopped at the beach for a while to think things through. Otherwise I'd of gotten here with swollen, red eyes and snot dripping down my nose." They broke into laughter. "Give me a glass of that chilled wine. I could use it."

Sierra put her hand on Rosa's shoulder. It felt like a butterfly, reassuring and light, unexpected. "Are you hungry?" Sierra asked.

"Starved. Let me help you get it together." They prepared the food, quickly, to a lively Renaissance music on the stereo that gave a tone of celebration to everything—their meeting, the fresh vegetables frying in oil with onions and tofu, the rainbow of sweet peas crowding a clay pitcher in the center of the table, grown in a secret, shaded spot in back of the barn throughout the summer, and so fragrant they made your senses blur on command.

Sierra was tan and healthy, rounder, more ample than Rosa, and the child made her look like a blossoming garden rose. Sierra looked like she'd had time to herself.

"Where are the kids?" Rosa asked.

"Bob took Tomás to his mother's for a couple of days, and Marlin's with her father for a few weeks. She's even thinking of living with José for her senior year. I'm not too thrilled about her idea, but we're fighting more than ever. Anyway, I worked straight through yesterday and finished some good bowls. I'm also thinking of a series of poems. I want to get some real work done before I'm too big to think."

Rosa looked at her expectantly, "How would you like to drive up to the Eel and camp tomorrow night? I need to lay on rocks and swim. I'm glad Sean hasn't been around for a while. It would've been a lot harder. You know, everyone tells me daughters are harder than boys, for the mother that is. I know Marlin loves you, that's obvious. Maybe it's because you two are so close it's like drawing blood now that she's separating. I think, too, it's that we don't believe they'll actually leave us. Though, of course, we think of that day whenever they drive us crazy. It's a bind, love is. With Sean and I it's not that intense. I only have to go crazy once every six months or so."

"It feels like I'm going crazy every six hours with that girl. That camping idea sounds good. Let's take off at sunrise, coffee on the road. We could be there by eleven. So, why the dripping snots?" Sierra looked concerned.

"I'm leaving Julio. I'm going to live by myself somewhere. Don't ask me where. I don't know yet," Rosa blurted out.

Sierra's face registered disbelief. "You're kidding. No, I can see you aren't. But where?"

Rosa's eyes filled with tears, but they stayed there clouding her vision. "First I'm selling the house, and then I'll go find it. Sounds logical, doesn't it?"

"Of course, I know what you mean—all the times I've almost left Bob, and a part of me still thinks I ought to, and here I am," Sierra said, holding her stomach.

The music came to an end, a solo flute held its last note like one long breath, and the last light of the day floated on the peaceful dust between them. They felt the peace, and the tension, of its passing like any alert consciousness watching itself live.

"All I know is, I've got to live by myself. I don't even know what *I* think anymore. Everytime I start this crying I feel like a lost puppy, not a woman with a brain. Anyway, I dreamt a place in the mountains, so I'm going to look in the mountains in a place called Plumas."

"You've never lived in snow."

"I know."

"What about a job?"

"If I have to I can get unemployment for a while, and besides I should have some money left over from the house. I know, I'll eat snow and dig roots." They laughed at the idea.

"Rock bottom, right?" Sierra managed to keep a straight face. They calmed down. "Seriously, I've always, secretly, wanted to live in the mountains too. You know that. I think everyone wants to live in the mountains, secretly, from time to time. The eternal spiritual journey, but not everyone does it, that's all. Besides, can't we spics do it too? In fact, I had a dream that definitely reminded me of mountain energy. Here, let me get it for you." She handed it to Rosa.

> *Dark Roots*
> Child,
> you are being born into
> the most beautiful planet
> I know of (the
> > sun would scorch
> > your feet: the
> > air would strangle
> > you on
> Mars): this
> planet of water, earth
> and fire—O
> the beauty waits
> for your new
> eyes (can
> > you imagine moon
> > sets, earth tilting redder
> > than blood: skies
> > full of wonder,
> > for
> ever): you are so
> new—you've just
> imagined yourself
> there in the
> dark; I
> ask you to look
> toward a sunrise
> on a field of
> ice, an

ancient eyelid
melting in
the snow,
the ocean
heaving naked
foam, the
trees gathering
dark roots.

Child,
I dreamt the seashore—the
beauty darkened
to all black—
a destroying
light began
to pulse in
the distance (we
 ran, quickly,
 many dying on the
 way—to a ladder,
 to a safe world still
there): my
daughter, your
sister dreamt me
crying by the
sea: "They're
killing the
children."
again and again.

Child,
you come among
dreams, tides,
stones and
dark blood—
but you come,
like the earth,
perfect and pure
at the center
of the
heart.

 "This is it," Rosa finally said. "This is the feeling I'm dealing
with. You actually dreamt this, this pulsing light?"

"It kind of crept into the poem by itself. But, yes, I dreamt running with a whole bunch of people and trying to climb to what felt like safety. A high, separate place—definitely like mountains. It was, well, like a terrible dream tinged with a sort of wonder. I was scared shitless when I woke up."

Rosa was always amazed at their synchronicity, and she silently thanked Sierra for adding to her sense of sanity.

"You know, this child of yours is going to come of age at the turn of the century. A child of the next century. That's brave. Of you, I mean. What I mean is, is that Sean is grown up now. He's lived seventeen years, and I wonder if the new ones will have as much of a chance. I don't mean to depress you, but it's how I feel. It's how I really feel."

Sierra lit some candles in the dusk rather than turn on the lights. The house was silent and they could hear the crickets beginning to announce the appearance of the first stars in the evening sky. In that moment they could've been in any time stretching back for centuries. Yet the pulsing light, nuclear destruction, belonged to their century, to their time.

"It's how I feel, too, sometimes, and I cry or rush out and yank weeds for hours. And I dream these dreams, and write these poems. Do you want some more squash?"

"How about a walk? We can clean up later," Rosa asked her friend.

The next morning they rushed through showers, packed, put coffee in a thermos, and were on the road by seven. The morning light was clear, and the sky was a uniform blue, a pale blue, and the early morning scents promised a very hot day. As Rosa's car topped a hill, the wine vineyards below spread themselves to the horizon in a luxury of green-leafed growth, to the subtle streaks of a lilac-orange sunrise—the reddish sun rising with a hiss.

Sierra sliced bread, cheese and fruit, and they passed the coffee back and forth, silently. The windows were wide open, and they felt like little girls at the beginning of summer vacation. They could already hear the river surging through their minds.

They climbed down the trail, took their shoes and socks off, slung them over their shoulders, and waded through the river to the other side. They lowered their packs through an opening that Rosa discovered, accidently, years ago, following a shaft of light. It was large enough for a body, but awkward for a body with a pack. The opening led to a wide, sandy beach, and beyond that a twelve foot stone wall with hand holds that led to a smaller, sandy beach. A ring of stones, blackened by fire, were piled on the far end of the little beach. It was perfect, as usual. Whoever camped there last had picked up after themselves, leaving no trace besides the ring of stones which was more like a welcome, a thoughtful remnant.

"Well, I'm sure not going to make that climb in a couple of months," Sierra gently laughed. "However, I could bring the little critter strapped to my back next summer."

"You can visit me in the mountains next summer," Rosa reminded her. "There's a river up there called the Feather—and who knows how many creeks and lakes. Imagine camping by a lake accessible only in summer?" Rosa imagined deep snow.

"I'll come."

"You could carry the baby, and I could carry everything else. First I have to sell my house, tell Sean I'm leaving, have him look at me like I'm crazy, and who knows what Julio will really do. Then, find this place." She felt like crying again.

"You will, Rosa."

"Keep saying that whenever I sound like this," Rosa said, breathing out. "Let's strip. Look at that water."

They drank straight from the river, figuring, as they always did, it was safe this far up on the Eel. They dunked entirely and floated in the clear, shallow pool that trembled with the late morning's light. Their bodies were comfortable and familiar with the other as women are, alone, away from male eyes. Not only had they taken off their clothing, but self-consciousness as well. Naked. They were, finally, naked.

Across the pool Sierra submerged smoothly as a seal, and when she surfaced and smiled at Rosa, Rosa recognized the twelve-year-old still alive in her eyes, sparkling with a boundless energy, and an unmistakable mischief.

They got out to dry on smooth, warm rocks facing each other. Rosa was amazed at the fast changes in Sierra's body in the relatively short amount of time. The slight but definite swell of her belly, the darkening nipples of her full breasts, and her skin fairly glowed. Her face had a light of its own as though something had been switched on inside her, deep inside her.

Rosa looked down at the angles of her body, her flat belly, her small breasts. Certainly it was strong and not unattractive, but it seemed to her uninteresting. She could see little pools of rainbows on her skin where the water still clung to her. She remembered the patient swelling of her own body, and the feeling of having swallowed the moon—new to full. She could say that now, but she couldn't have said it then. She'd been so young then, and afraid. Not yet married to her first husband, and absolutely belligerent. City kid. Ghetto kid. Unmarried, Mexican mother. Blind, belligerent courage had seen her through—innocence, she now realized.

Sierra sat up and looked at Rosa, and her eyes had changed. They were peaceful, but an old sorrow looked Rosa plainly in the eye.

"You know, sometimes I think Bob's still seeing someone, and the one time I brought it up he made me feel like I was crazy for even thinking it. I actually had to apologize he got so pissed off. Fuck." Tears rolled down Sierra's face, and suddenly her body looked heavy as though she were trapped inside of it.

"Well, fuck him! What does he expect after his last episode, total forgiveness? You had the abortion, not him. He should still be apologizing to *you*—and then you turn around and decide to have this baby. That, my dear, is enough forgiveness as far as I'm concerned." Just the thought of Sierra apologizing to Bob made the sunlight darken. "That man can kiss my brown ass."

Sierra laughed and splashed water on her face, smoothing her hair back.

"Come on, let's go to the whirlpools," Rosa said, unaware of the twelve-year-old tone to her voice.

They sat in the center on rock ledges, the sound almost deafening, and white foam hid the bottom.

Rosa looked at Sierra, "You okay?" She had to shout it again. Sierra nodded her head yes with a slight smile.

They took turns going to the bottom of the whirlpool. Holding the sides of the rocks, they pushed themselves down to the bottom, about six feet. Looking up, the turbulence looked far away, and only the countless, gentle bubbles caressed their skin. It was like a journey to the bottom of something they couldn't name: fear, chaos, raw power. One, or all of them, perhaps. And at the bottom of it was the softest sand, like silk. It was always a shock to touch it, that softness. And then they remembered why they had to go to the bottom, again—what impelled them to surrender and struggle down past the powerful flow of water, the deafening vortex of water. That softness, that secret softness, at the bottom of the whirlpool, and, yes, at the bottom of themselves.

Rosa took a walk up the creek and left Sierra by herself, and also to be alone. If she'd been with Julio she'd have to explain she wanted to be alone for a while, and she was relieved to just glance at Sierra like a signal, and just leave.

She got to a spot where the river provided a kind of stone chair, and she sat in it feeling the river touch her and leave, touch her and leave, and the sun made her forget everything. Almost. Rosa dunked her head to cool herself, and she genuinely wished she were a fish, a salmon, strong and muscular, good to eat. Now she was getting hungry, but it was good to be hungry.

A quick movement in the water made her start. A small, thin water snake flashed towards the bank. Even a few years ago she would have jumped out of the water, but she stayed where she was with a sharp eye for movement, though she knew they were really harmless.

Why was it such a struggle to come to this place in herself, this softness that she knew, in that moment, was actually her deepest strength. Feminine strength. Because, because, because, she told herself, it takes all the strength I've got to push down through my fear, and you never really know if you're going to make it. But when you make it again, it's always enough. Why do I forget this powerful softness? Rosa asked herself—and the image of the black, lace shawl hung, whole, in her mind, complete.

She climbed onto a flat rock and slept on her stomach, with her hand dangling in the moving water.

A small, thin snake struggles with desperation to shed its skin, as though it will die if it doesn't. And it does, finally, leaving the shape of itself behind. The skin is covered with rainbows. Empty.

Immediately, Rosa looked to the bank where the snake had gone. Nothing. The strange skin, alien and beautiful, was so vivid to her, her own skin felt unfamiliar as though she, herself, weren't human.

Rosa swam in a little pool, and then started back to the campsite. She looked at the back of her legs. They weren't burned, and her back and shoulders didn't feel burned, so she guessed she must've slept maybe thirty minutes. The sun was just about the same. Just about the same position, but definitely afternoon.

Sierra was cooking beans and chopping onions, chilis and a tomato. She looked up and said, "It came from beneath the sea! You look like shit! Are you hungry?" Sierra laughed. "I'm just kidding. Actually, I'm jealous, except for that hair."

"Thanks," Rosa laughed. "That smells great. What is it?"

"Leftover beans. I couldn't resist bringing this here tomato," Sierra held it up triumphantly, "and it made it unsquashed. Also, some extra-thick tortillas, jalapeños, avocado. Do you want a piece of raw garlic? We'll gross out any intruders, human or otherwise."

Rosa took a piece and heated up a tortilla with a slice of cheese in the middle. "This is fantastic. Look what I brought. My contribution." She unpacked two bottles of wine. "The only thing is I forgot to chill the white. How about the zinfandel?"

"Let me at it. These beans are just about ready. How was your walk?"

"Perfect. I fell asleep and dreamt a snake shedding its skin—an incredibly beautiful rainbow skin."

"I fell asleep too. What a beautiful dream. I dreamt Marlin, a very unresolved dream. Frustrating. And then I dreamt her as a baby, briefly. When I woke up I almost thought I was pregnant with Marlin." Sierra's face looked tender, diffuse.

Rosa poured the wine and offered a salute, "Here's to renewal, birth, and rainbow snake skins."

"I second that," Sierra added.

They put some clothes on and finished the meal preparation. Rosa sliced cheese into the simmering beans, and fresh onion and avocado slices to the side. They scooped the beans into their tortillas, devoured jalapeños, homemade from Sierra's garden, and washed it down with wine and cool water from the river. Their concentration on the food was absolute until they heard some voices and a dog barking.

Three men in waders, with fishing poles and packs, came into view. Each one was drinking a beer, and their dog spotted the women. It promptly rushed over and shook itself on their sleeping bags. The men laughed, and one of them threw his empty beer can onto the bank. The men made no gesture of recognition, but just kept staring, mutely, with highly amused looks on their faces. One of them burped, and they all laughed again.

Sierra and Rosa looked at each other, and silently got up to stretch their sleeping bags in the sun.

"Spending the night, ladies?" one of them asked in a mocking tone.

"That's what it looks like, gentlemen!" Rosa yelled back at them, standing up straight and looking the speaker in the face. He looked away and then back at her, challenging her with his eyes.

Sierra yelled, "Hey that damned dog's in our food! Call your dog, damn it!"

They all burst into laughter again at the sight of their dog taking over the campsite.

Rosa grabbed a stick just as the dog swallowed a tortilla and smacked it hard against its side, yelling, "Go on! Go on! You bad dog! Go on!"

The dog yelped and ran for the river.

"Hey man, that's not very nice," one of the men yelled. They were all pretty young, but he seemed to be the youngest, about nineteen.

Rosa looked at him and saw a trace of Sean. Her body felt absolutely rigid and tense. Her shoulders seemed to burn. She yelled right back, looking at him, "Look—if that were my dog I'd of done the same, and so would've you! Why in the hell didn't you call your dog? He's your responsibility, not mine! I have a dog at home, and I'd never allow him to act like that!"

One of the other men shouted, "You ain't got no right ta be hittin my dog! Bitch!"

Rosa's body twitched into readiness, and she glanced over at Sierra. She had one hand on her belly. Now Rosa's shoulders were on fire, as though all her energy were gathered there.

"Hey, she's right, man. The dog was acting like a turd. You'd a kicked his ass, Joel. Come on, man, let's get outta here. I wanna do some fishin," the younger man said.

The other men grumbled, and the dog had gone ahead. Rosa heard one of them say, "That's a real bitch, man." She could read Sierra's mind—she didn't want to be raped by three men, pregnant. Neither did she, but she wasn't as vulnerable as Sierra.

The men started walking off, slowly, and they burst out laughing again. As they climbed around some rocks and out of sight, the younger man turned and gave Rosa a quick wave of his hand, and a quick, shy smile.

"Fuck," Sierra exhaled. "That was more excitement than I asked for. What a bunch of bastards! Do you think we should spend the night with them up the river?"

"I think that young guy is our secret ally. Did you see him wave?"

"No, I didn't. Did he?" Sierra sounded slightly relieved.

"Yeah, he turned around and waved. I think they're going up there to get so drunk they'll be out till morning. But if you want to go I don't blame you. If I hadn't seen that little wave, I think I'd want to leave, too."

"He was the only decent one, for sure. Hey, thanks for taking over. I felt rooted to the spot." Sierra's face looked terribly tense.

Rosa poured some wine and handed Sierra a cup. "Do you want to finish eating or pack up?"

"Have you had any warning dreams about rape?"

"No. Have you?"

"No, me either."

"We could sleep with knives over behind the rocks instead of in the open. But I think that guy is okay. Plus, as I said, I think they're here mainly to get wasted."

Sierra waded over and got the beer can. "Fucking slobs," she muttered. She bent down and splashed water on her face, and lingered, looking down the river as it disappeared around a curve. She looked up at the sun and figured it was going on four. Neither of them had brought a watch.

"I think you're right about that guy. We could sleep behind the rock, I suppose. What a bunch of shit to be worried about being raped every moment of your life. I kept thinking about what they do to women in El Salvador." Sierra looked at Rosa. "Pregnant women. They cut their babies right out of their wombs. And then I'd make myself stop thinking it. I didn't want to give them any latent ideas." The thought of babies lying exposed and dying beside their dead mothers came vividly to her now, and she cried, crouched over, with her head in her hands.

Rosa walked over and knelt down beside her. "Hey, we could go. We could sleep in your back field for that matter. Come on, let's pack up."

Sierra wiped her face on her hem and looked at Rosa. "No, really, let's stay. It's just that I've never felt that vulnerable, pregnant, and those women kept coming to my mind between visions of being raped. You know, it's funny, we don't worry about mountain lions or snakes, or any wild animal, really—just men. Civilized, in quotes, men." Sierra's voice became dark with anger.

"Are you sure, Sierra? I mean, you are pregnant," Rosa looked at her friend closely.

"I think you're right; the worst is over. Besides, we'll knife them." Sierra managed a laugh. "Holy shit! Where's my wine?"

"Here it is. Do you want some more beans? I'll heat some tortillas. The dog left us some. Did you bring a bathing suit? I don't think we should go nude anymore in case they pass this way again." Rosa looked at the rock they disappeared around, and she thought of the whirlpool a little farther on. How dare they, she thought to herself—how dare they threaten us. And then she thought of the young man's shy smile.

"I brought a leotard, Rosa. How about you?" Sierra answered her.

"Yeah, I brought my in-case bikini."

Rosa brought the plates to the edge of the water, next to Sierra, and they finished their meal with their feet dangling into its shallows. They ate slowly as the sun began to disappear from the little beach, and the afternoon shadows were soothing to look at—deep purples in the rocks, and the deep green of the river became even more pronounced and tangible. Not the silky stuff they'd plunged into in the morning—now it seemed a robe, a dress to wrap themselves up with. Encompassing, protective, warm.

Rosa told Sierra about the lilac sky painting, describing it in detail. "It's the elusiveness of that color that's so distracting. I mean, the sky *is* always changing, moment to moment, as is the light, and the rest of it. So, what it seems to be demanding of me is to leave it alone for a while—to just *look* at it. What do you think?"

"It sounds like you're onto something. It sounds a little like your meeting with Rolf. Kind of like an unknown you had to accept and just look at. Blue eyes and all." Sierra laughed.

An old warmth passed between them.

Sierra scooped a drink from the river. "I've often wondered why I beat my brains out with Latin men. Maybe the secret's with opposites," Sierra said, laughing. "Julio is the, shall we say, typical possessive macho, and Bob is the typical chingadero macho. There, I've said it. I think he's having one of his cute little flings. His father did it, his brother does it. His brother has two different families in the same town. What a bastard!" she spit out, scornfully.

"What are you going to do?" Rosa gently asked.

"I don't know. A part of me wants to believe he's telling me the truth. I just don't know." She sounded miserable. "Like him taking Tomás to his mother's this weekend, to give me some time, was thoughtful and sweet. I almost wanted to go with them at the very last moment. Well, I'm glad I didn't." Sierra sighed. "Tomás' little face—'Bye, mommy, I miss you.' That's what he said."

"What are you working on in your poetry?" Rosa asked instead, unable to stand the sheer misery in her friend's face.

"Actually, I want to work on a series of poems having to do with powerful women as witches—you know, brujas," Sierra smiled. "The witch/goddess set on fire because of her power."

"Their fear of the feminine," Rosa echoed, "and so they kill it." Rosa thought of Quetzalpetlatl, Feathered Serpent Woman, but kept it to herself, as though she had no choice. As though Quetzalpetlatl had survived the fire and couldn't be spoken about. As though her presence were evident and secret at once.

"It's the fire image that's got me going. It stirs me up, definitely stirs my shit, and gets me angry. So, this has got to be one powerful image, right?" Sierra took the plates and rinsed them in the river, turning them over to dry.

"I guess! That's exactly what I read—women were burned as witches, and not just a few thousand, but over a million, for their belief in the Goddess. Reading some of those things brought back one of my most vivid memories as a little girl. Of a journey at night, once, in my uncle's car, and laying in the back seat watching the moon. I felt it was following me, literally following me, and it gave me a feeling of absolute comfort, like a mother."

"I used to feel like that in the old willow tree, the only tree, in our backyard. Only, come to think of it, the fact that it seemed stationary was what I liked," Sierra remembered.

"Isn't that the tree we used to climb in and sing?" Rosa asked.

"That's the one. I was always braver in the dark when you were there."

They both laughed at the memory of two little girls sitting in a willow tree dangling their legs into the air.

"And, you know, in spite of all the church stuff I did as a kid, all those hymns," Rosa laughed. "The only one I ever liked was Jesus, the baby, the boy. I was always impatient with that crucifixion bit, and I was always mad at his so-called father. *God.*"

"You're bad, girl. You wanna spend the rest of your eeeterniteee with the guy that has a tail?"

"In fire, of course."

Sierra hooted, "That's right! Another witch for the flames! Now I'm getting inspired. You know, when you're hot, you're hot. I purposely didn't bring pen or paper. Oh well, I wouldn't write anyway. Too much wine and sun. Not to speak of assholes and their dogs."

"You know, my grandmother mainly prayed to the Virgin, and, in fact, she told me the Virgin appeared to her in dreams, and once, she said, in a vision. I think she secretly didn't like that God guy either. In fact, if anything, it was as though she emotionally lumped God and the Devil together. Distant, threatening—one threatened if you did, one threatened if you didn't. Both masculine, isolated entities."

"Holy shit!" Sierra yelled. She was pretending to take notes, and then she stopped. "We didn't go to church that much. Just mass once in a while. And my mother was embarrassed because my father was such a drunk. What a sob story, really."

Rosa felt like she'd come back from a brief, intense journey. "Well, you know, I think that's why we're threatening to blow ourselves up. That God guy has us in a bind. Too isolated, not enough joy. He needs a lover, that's what I think."

Sierra smiled. "Well spoken. You should try some poetry. Really, I think you should."

"No, not me. I freeze up when I know my words will be formal or permanent. Color gives me room to breathe, imagery can mean something else. Besides, you're the poet." Rosa looked at the water moving, moving away, and at the same time coming toward her.

"The Great Goddess, like Isis, had lovers and children." Then softly Sierra said, "You know what?"

"What?" Rosa asked.

"I've prayed to Isis," Sierra giggled with a trace of embarrassment. "I imagine she lives in the budding plants and flowers. Especially the corn. Yeah, I think God needs some pussy. You know, help hoe the corn and all."

"Talk about me being bad. Maybe you could fix Isis up with God," Rosa laughed. "Now, that would be hot. Very hot. Maybe this little, dinky planet would have a chance. God needs to fall in love with an equal like Isis. Definitely."

"I'll work on it," Sierra said with great seriousness. "Do you want to climb over to the big beach? I bet the sun's still there. I feel like swimming."

"That sounds good. But first we should put all this stuff away in case Rin Tin Tin comes back for dessert. And put our packs and bags up on rocks. Dogs just love to piss on things for revenge."

After they put everything away they climbed over the rock cliff. The last of the sun sprayed wide golden shafts of heat, and the rocks looked red. The water rippled with gold.

There was a deep side, and they swam over to it, glad for the silence except for the sound of birds preparing to help with the daily ritual of sunset.

Sierra pushed off from the rock face of a cliff and swam at a confident, lazy pace, diving down and surfacing.

Rosa jumped from the rock ledge of the cliff about twenty feet up. She always had to talk herself into it, but she loved the ripple in her stomach. Then she floated on her back. Sierra looked covered in liquid gold. A shadow crossed Rosa and she looked up. An immense hawk was scanning the water.

"Sierra, look at that!" Rosa yelled.

Sierra flipped over and caught sight of it gliding away. A great, winged, hungry hawk, she thought, and it made her heart clench with a strange longing. What am I going to do? she asked herself, and she dove to the bottom, and then lunged back up to the air. Rosa was watching her.

"It was beautiful!" Sierra yelled.

They wrapped themselves in towels and watched the sun pulse and disappear behind the distant ridge of trees to the horizon. The birds seemed to echo that pulse, that last burst of energy.

Rosa thought of her grandmother's song to the setting sun. She couldn't remember all the words, but she remembered that her grandmother had sung to the sun as though it were her child about to go to sleep. A tender song of dreams.

"Well, it's three nights to the full moon, so there'll be some light," Sierra said.

Rosa remembered their situation—the men up the river. "We should get back and make a fire. I brought some instant chocolate, with marshmallows even."

The moon wasn't up yet, and the twilight was deepening into night. They climbed back over the cliff wet and beginning to shiver. Rosa was first and she looked for any movements. She swore at herself for not bringing her knife. But it looked still and peaceful, exactly as they'd left it.

Rosa jumped down and added kindling to the embers. It blazed, and caught fire to the larger wood. She went and got her knife and strapped it to her waist. It was a Buck Knife Sean had given her for her birthday. She was glad it was big and sharp. When she first got it she felt a little awkward strapping it on—now she was used to it.

"Good idea," Sierra said. "Only mine goes in my pocket. My old, trusty Swiss Army Knife. You can kill them, and I can carve our names on their chests. Now, that's gross, isn't it?"

"Definitely. Let's not think about them. Let's just be prepared. Do you want some chocolate?"

"Two or three cups at least. And guess what I brought?" Sierra paused by the fire. "Banana-walnut bread."

"Bring it out! The water's almost ready."

The night brought the seriousness of their situation home to them; they were alone. They talked quietly, listening for anything, attuned to the darkness.

Sierra stretched out in the sand, away from the fire, and looked up at the sky crowded with stars, brilliant with light.

"They seem so cool and distant," Sierra whispered.

A shooting star streaked, briefly, and disappeared.

"Did you see that one?" Sierra asked. "They say when we see one, here on Earth, it's actually been dead a million years or so." And then she realized what she'd said—that stars died. Into what? she wondered. The child inside of her gave a little thump, and she couldn't help thinking, A human soul. And the sadness she always felt when she saw a shooting star lifted from her as though she'd remembered something she used to know.

"They also say the stars are actually pretty hot. On fire. The baby just moved, just a tiny bit."

Rosa was on her back now looking up at the sky. "It must be nice to watch shooting stars while your baby moves." She sat up and looked at Sierra. "Look, I'm going to spread the sleeping bags out and climb in. Do you feel like it?"

"Here, I'll help you."

"No, just stay there. I'll get it."

Sierra brushed her teeth and changed into a flannel nightgown.

"You look like Ma Kettle," Rosa laughed.

"Thanks a lot, Olive Oyl."

Rosa brushed her teeth standing by the river, straining her hearing to any sound. Nothing. She climbed into her sleeping bag, leaving it half unzipped. It was a warm night, though it'd probably drop in temperature toward dawn.

Sierra looked like she was falling asleep, and then she reached for Rosa's hand. "Here feel this," she said, putting Rosa's hand on her belly. "Did you feel it?"

"No, I didn't. Probably just missed it."

"Keep your hand there. He'll probably strike again," Sierra said.

"He?"

"I think it's a boy. I feel something extra."

They laughed.

"Do you have your knife, Sierra?"

"Under my bag, to my right. Open."

"Good night. I think we're okay. Try and have some good dreams."

"You, too, Davy Crockett. You have the real knife. Good night, Rosa."

Rosa kept her ears alert and her hand on Sierra's belly for quite a while. She thought of the young man's smile again, and it calmed her. She imagined them passed out, and she wished them all, except for the one, monster hangovers.

The glow of an almost full moon began to apepar on the ridge in front of them. They were sleeping, sheltered, behind a massive stone, so the light wouldn't necessarily expose them.

Rosa felt the tiniest flutter under her hand, and she almost started to tell Sierra, but she'd gone to sleep. Inexplicably, she began to cry. For an instant it felt like the child's movement travelled through her arm to her own womb, and that she'd felt the flutter inside herself.

She took her hand off Sierra's belly and covered her. She could barely keep her eyes open, and she gave one more glance to the night sky. She saw what must've been a shooting star, but it was so slow. It was so slow it seemed to leave a trail behind itself, and the tail was red like blood. That's got to mean something, she thought, and the thought comforted her.

Rosa touched her knife and fell asleep.

Rosa wanders through an empty house, room to room. Each room has a fireplace that bursts into a bright, hot flame. As she enters each room the same thing happens, and it feels wonderful, incredible. Suddenly, a wild ball of fire, an uncontained fire, rolls past her and her first impulse is to try to divert it into the fireplace, when a voice says, "Some for the hearth, some for the heart." An immense, fluorescent—brilliant green with a ruby head—hummingbird, as large as a hawk, is hovering by the front door and banging it with its furious wings. The sound is deafening. Rosa hesitates, and then opens it. The bird flies free.

She opened her eyes to the absolute stillness of the night and she saw the moon had passed over them. She looked at Sierra turned on her side facing away from her. What was it the voice said? She forced herself to remember: "Some for the hearth, some for the heart." She touched her knife, and, as though she'd never woken up, fell back to sleep.

Sierra sees Rosa in a terrible wind that wants to take her away. She can see the pain on Rosa's face as she struggles against it. Just as she begins to feel sorry for Rosa, the wind turns on her. The wind seems to be tearing at her flesh. The more she resists, the harsher it is. And then Sierra is angry at Rosa for the wind, as though she'd created it. Rosa is gone, and Sierra is alone with the wind, in pain.

Sierra woke with her bladder about to burst. The first hint of dawn was in the air, and it was chilly. She looked at Rosa, on her stomach, her own favorite position, but out of the question now. She forced her feet to the sand and threw her jacket around her. It was beginning to be light. At least she didn't have to pee in the dark.

She didn't want to wipe her eyes because she might wake up, so she kept them half-open. Well, we survived the night, she thought. Sierra looked at Rosa sleeping peacefully, and resentment filled her. It's the dream. Jesus. Go to sleep, she told herself.

Sierra settled into her sleeping bag, zipping it up. Her bladder felt wonderful, and she almost forgot she was pregnant. She thought of Tomás' little face, and she felt an indescribable sorrow as though she'd never see him again. And then she realized Tomás looked so damned much like Bob. Bob, that bastard, she loved him. Sierra felt utterly protective toward, and sorry for, the faceless one still inside her, as though it were going to be born only to her sorrow.

She turned over to her other side and cupped her belly in her hands. She would make it work; he would change. He had to because she loved him. She needed him. He would realize that. He loved me once, didn't he? Of course, he did. She would not imagine him with another woman. No, she wouldn't. She was very tired, still. How tired she was. Tired.

Rosa got up, quietly, and started the morning fire. The sun had risen and it was already beginning to be hot. She walked off to pee, and she wondered if Sierra had gotten up in the night—she hadn't heard her. Rosa was so glad they'd stayed; the early morning silence filled her senses. There was no canvas here, no inner compulsion at the moment—but, then, everything else fell away, and she could simply exist. Exist to exist. Rosa imagined her cells replenishing themselves in the early light and silence. It was so still.

She took her coffee to a flat stone to watch the quick, sparkling lights of the water. With a jolt, she remembered the men, and the limits their presence gave her. If she'd wanted to stay another night, she'd have to consider them. Rosa dismissed them and went to see what Sierra had packed for breakfast.

They cleaned up, leaving the ring of blackened stones intact, and hiked over to the larger beach.

Sierra took the pack off her back. "I hate to leave," she moaned. "When do you have to be back?"

"Tonight. My last classes are this week. I'm going to go back and see about a leave of absence, or really, I suppose, something more permanent. And I want a good letter of recommendation from the department head."

"So, you're really going to do it?"

Rosa's face clenched, "Yes, I am. Or I'll never respect myself again. It's crazy, but that's how I feel."

"Well, at least you don't have any kids to consider," Sierra said with a strange tone.

Rosa looked up at her. "It's still not easy, Sierra. I still have to leave Julio, and probably Sean." She sensed something had changed between them. Something so subtle, it seemed silly to dwell on it. "I'm going in for a final fix."

Rosa leaped out from the rock ledge giving a yell that hurt her throat.

Sierra decided to stay dry, and as she watched Rosa leap, the yell she gave was so full of defiance, and an unmasked pain, she felt her body tremble. Sierra took her shoes and clothes off, changed into her leotard, and walked into the water.

The drive back felt sombre, like the last day of vacation. Neither could find the right words to express it, so they stayed largely silent. Rosa and Sierra had always welcomed silence between them as something meaningful and comfortable when it happened, but this felt unfamiliar to them both.

As they turned into Sierra's driveway Bob's car was parked ahead of them.

"Well, I'll be damned!" Sierra exclaimed with excitement. "He's back early. He was supposed to come back tomorrow night."

Tomás ran out and started waving both of his arms. Sierra scooped him up in her arms and asked him, "Where's daddy?"

"In the house."

"Did you miss me?"

"Yeah, I sure did."

Sierra carried Tomás into the house, and Rosa followed her. Bob was in the front room lying down.

"Hi, Bob. How was your visit?" Sierra smiled at him hopefully.

"It was getting claustrophobic, so I decided to get back, and Tomás was turning into a little whiner. I was going to take him to the zoo, but he blew it. Didn't you, Tomás?"

Tomás glared at him, and his lips twitched into a cry. He buried himself in Sierra's neck.

Rosa hung back in the kitchen trying to avoid Bob for the time being. She'd witnessed his browbeating scenes before, and she hated it. She'd also noticed that he liked to lay it on thick for her benefit, because he knew it got to her.

"Do you mean you promised to take him, and then you didn't?" Sierra asked him with a trace of a plead.

"Yeah, he promised me, Mommy," and Tomás began to cry loudly.

"Oh, shut up, Tomás. Little cry baby. That's why I didn't take you. So you amazons went camping, huh? Where is La Rosa, anyway?" he asked in a mocking tone. "What's for dinner? We drove straight through."

Tomás whimpered, "I'm hungry, Mommy."

Rosa wondered how the hell Sierra worked at all, listening to the demands in stereo.

"Well, couldn't you have started something, Bob?" She was beginning to sound angry. "I just got in myself."

"You just had a few days to yourself, and I never know what's stashed away for later, or what." Bob's voice was loud and demanding.

"Jesus F. Christ," Sierra said in absolute exasperation.

Tomás still clung to her. Rosa wondered how she held him that long, he was getting so big.

Rosa had to pass through to get her things which were in the back bedroom. She just wanted to leave. She walked through the front room with a curt, "Hi, Bob," shut the door and packed her things. She could hear Bob's voice.

"What's with her? Seems like you guys should be relaxed after camping. All I heard was my mother complain about my father. What a drag. Come on, Sierra, cook something up." His voice sounded matter-of-fact, as though he'd seen her face surrender.

Rosa heard the refrigerator door open and shut, and a pan banging the stove. Rosa gathered her things and walked out to the front room where Bob was still lying down with a sly look of satisfaction on his dark, handsome face. The handsomeness melted away into the layers of a cunning, and stronger, animal victimizing its prey. She tried to dispel that impression, and, instead, tried to remember the man she'd liked as a friend from time to time. Those times he'd called her to go to a movie with him when Sierra hadn't felt like it, or a beer, and they'd talked. They'd come to terms with the boundary of friendship and sexuality, and they'd had a friendship of sorts for a while during the years Rosa lived nearby.

She spoke first. "Why don't you go out and get some take-out food? Surprise her, Bob. Have you considered she's pregnant and tires easily."

"Are you leaving so soon?" Bob dismissed her suggestion. "Why don't you stay for dinner?" He smiled slyly.

"Why don't you get up and help her cook it? What the hell's the matter with you? You're getting a little nasty, aren't you, Bob?"

"I don't think this is any of your business, Rosa. What's always given you the idea our relationship is your business? Anyway, how is poor old Julio? Old, ever-faithful Julio." Bob's face looked bitter.

"I thought, Bob, that we all were friends." Rosa paused looking for a response and saw none, and then came to the point. "Don't you feel like a hypocrite out at the college counseling all those feminist hippie chicks like the last of the great hero liberals, and then treating your wife like a barefoot, pregnant Panchita?"

Bob's face darkened so that the whites of his eyes stood out prominently, and the dark pupils stabbed her like sharp darts. He leaped from the pillows and slammed out of the house, the harsh sound echoed in the silence. A dark smoke seemed to trail him. Rosa had never seen him so livid.

Tomás was sitting at the kitchen table with wide-open eyes, and Sierra looked shaken and angry, a wooden spoon in her hand. Rosa felt her face flaming, and her breath felt shallow.

"If I were you, Sierra, I'd turn off that stove and take Tomás out to dinner. Bob'll get over it, maybe he'll even think about it. Besides, now he's mad at me."

"Rosa," Sierra turned to look at her with a hardness, an anger, she couldn't hide, "you've got to stop protecting me. It just makes it worse for us. For me. I don't want you to do that again." Sierra began to cry.

Rosa felt like she'd been slapped in the face. Tomás ran to his room.

"Sierra, do you mean you're willing to accept your suspicions of what he's pulling on you, and also allow him to treat you like this?"

"I just can't let you do that again," Sierra said in one breath.

"You're going to let him treat you this way, then. Is that it?" Rosa began to cry. "It won't happen again."

She flung the screen door open and walked to her car. She could see Bob out in the field, moping, plucking at the waist-high oats—feeling sorry for himself, no doubt.

Sierra didn't come to the porch. They didn't hug goodbye. They didn't wave or joke or laugh. It was different now. Rosa knew, in that instant, it would always be different, and that they were saying goodbye to more than summer. Their souls had been severed.

Rosa stopped at a bar in Point Reyes, a small seashore town, to get a drink; a real drink. She hadn't noticed there wasn't one woman at the bar, and that she was being stared at, intensely. The bartender passed her once, then twice.

"Is there a magic password here to get a drink?" she almost yelled.

The bartender turned, looked at her, and laughed. "Open-sesame. What'll ya have?"

"A very strong margarita. Easy on the ice, please."

"Do ya want salt on the rim?"

She calmed down. "Yes." She gathered herself in the darkness, and took a look in the mirror over the bar. Rosa had to laugh; she looked frenzied. She wondered when the ache in her heart would pass. She wondered if this was what was meant by being alone in your soul. She wondered this without these words, because these words weren't available to her yet, and, yet, she wondered like a wolf howls to the moon, alone, with her own, endless longing. She didn't know, yet, that this was the price of freedom.

The bartender was standing in front of her. "This here's from the gentleman at the other end of the bar," he said indicating a man who was lifting his glass in a friendly salute.

This had never happened to her. No one had ever sent her a drink; in fact she'd never sat at a bar by herself, and it felt embarrassing. And then she had an image of the man walking over and trying to join her. It was the last thing she wanted. She just wanted to sit in the dark, without speaking to anyone.

"Oh, I can't take that."

"He already paid for it." The bartender lowered his voice, "I'd take it if I were you. Tell me if it's what ya had in mind."

Rosa looked at the man across the bar and he was talking to someone next to him. She took a sip, and it was strong. She looked at the bartender. "Damn! What's in it?"

"Double shots," he said, and walked away.

There was hardly any ice. It was perfect.

She would go to the real estate office tomorrow after classes and see about selling the house. Rosa tried to imagine Julio's face, and she got such a jolt of anxiety it almost made her sick to her stomach. She sipped the margarita, and it blurred the edges. But the wolf, the wolf inside of her would not stop howling, but that was anguish and not despair. Was there a differnce?

She finished her drink, and caught the man's eye at the end of the bar, lifted the empty glass toward him. And then she left.

It was ten when Rosa got home, and there were no lights on in the house. A note was on the dining room table. "Welcome home, I guess. Went out to see friends," and signed, simply, J. A very large, imposing J.

She was relieved. No scenes tonight. Her head felt fuzzy from pressure. She locked the bedroom door and got in bed. The words *Lupine Meadows* came to mind, and she commanded the wolf to run. To run through the night, stretching herself farther and farther, feeling her muscles move, and the wind in her eyes, and ears, the taste of her tongue, until the howl was eased with panting, sleep.

Julio left the next morning without even making coffee; his pride was hurt, injured, insulted. He was angry. Hadn't he always been faithful to her, which was more than he could say about Sierra's old man. Not that he didn't like Bob—in fact, he secretly admired his style. He sure wouldn't put up with this shit. Julio looked at the locked bedroom door, and, for an instant, he felt like breaking it down and raping her. Yeah, raping her. But once the thought had release he felt a tinge of shame. Well, fuck her, he thought, if she thinks I'm going to hang out for some left-over affection, she's got another think coming. Then, unexpectedly, he felt like crying, like getting on his knees and banging at the door until she opened it. Rosa, Rosa, his mind screamed, please don't leave me—I'm such an asshole, but I need you, I need you. I love you. I love you, Rosa.

Instead, he slammed the front door shut.

The door jarred her awake. Her head felt stuffed with misery, and she had to remember why. And then she remembered. Rosa held her breath and listened for the wolf's howling, but what rose up was a surge of anger, so much anger it threatened to overwhelm her.

In class everything went like film played at high speed, hardly the slow, careful process she was always aware of when she dealt with students. It was the last week, maybe they felt the same. She'd give them evaluations Thursday, and that would be it.

After the last class an older woman came up to speak to her as she was gathering her things to leave.

"I hate to bother you, but I'm so worried about the evaluations. I dread public criticism, to be honest."

Rosa looked at her, and the usually very composed older woman looked absolutely terrified. "There's no pass or fail in the evaluations. You might just consider it good advice, and if you don't like my advice, forget it," Rosa laughed.

"Well, that's a relief. Sorry to keep you. Thank you very much," and she walked away.

Thank you, Rosa said to herself, for making me feel human. Rosa still felt angry, but somehow the woman's eyes had softened its blows.

The real estate people would be out the next day to look the house over and draw up a contract. She'd felt so nervous and shaky, she almost felt like she was asking them to do something illegal—to sell her house. She would give Julio some of the money, of course. Yet, she couldn't deny it—she felt guilty. She was leaving her husband— her Mexican husband, she reminded herself—and for no good reason, the voice echoed in her mind. She'd had good reason with Sean's father; she hadn't married Don. She was leaving because she *wanted* to. Now, Rosa felt so human she felt as terrified as the older woman had been. There is no pass or fail, she told herself—just good advice, and the terror passed.

There was no food in the house, so she made a list, and for some reason, at the bottom of the list, she wrote the word *tattoo*.

She'd passed a tattoo studio in the city a few times, and once she'd stopped to see photographs of the tattoos the man did. They were very good, not at all ships or anchors, or hearts with "MOM" in the middle. Some were quite huge and complicated, and some delicate and simple, like a woman's whose left breast had a spread fan tattooed on it with a banquet of flowers filling it. Bright, vivid flowers, full colors, not cartoonlike at all. That's when she'd begun to think of a tattoo for herself. But she couldn't imagine what or where.

Rosa put the grocery list in her pocket and got onto the freeway.

Her heart pounded as she walked into the tattoo studio, and she wondered if she looked silly and out of place. Who the hell's watching, she reprimanded herself. She stood looking at some photographs on the walls when the man came out, the one she'd seen before.

"Can I do anything for you?" he smiled.

He was maybe thirty with long hair tied in a ponytail, with a direct gaze. Rosa liked him.

"Well, I was thinking of torturing myself for beauty," she said.

He laughed. "It's not a torture anymore. I hate to disappoint you. They used to do it a stab at a time," he looked at her with amusement. "But now we've got these contraptions." He showed her a little instrument that looked like a miniature dentist's drill. "It makes the design with so many pricks per second, it's just about painless."

"Well, that sounds like an improvement. I like your colors, too. I always thought tattoo colors looked kind of corny."

"Everything's improved," he smiled. "Do you have anything in mind? Any particular design?"

"How about flowers?"

"Take a look in this printout and see if you see something you like. We could work from there." He left her alone.

She hadn't even asked him how much they were, she realized. Would he take a check? Was she really going to do it? The thought of two crossed swords tattooed across her chest came to mind, and she wanted to run out the door. And that little drill is most likely an improvement, but it still has to pierce the skin, she thought. Rosa looked at the flowers.

Many were ornate and gorgeous, like the orchid design in purple—but where? A big purple orchid on my abdomen, a garden on my breast. Breasts are too sensitive—forget it. Then a simple, blossomed rose, with the words "Wild Rose" under it, made her stop. The other roses surrounding it were much more lush, more mysterious, in their budding promise. The petals of the "Wild Rose" were sprayed wide open, with its stamens and pistils exposed. A burst of small, seemingly sharp, thorns trailed its curved stem. And then she knew where she'd put it—on her womb. Not her stomach, not her belly. Her womb. Let's see, where, exactly, where would the womb be—and she stared at a blank spot of the white wall, and she saw it lower than her belly button, and to the left. She'd put it to the left. It'd look a little silly right under the belly button, like an extra.

Rosa walked back to where he'd gone, and he was bent over a book. He looked up at her.

"So, have you decided?"

"How much would the 'Wild Rose' be?"

"Oh, that's thirty dollars."

"Do you take checks?"

"Sure."

Some people came into the studio, and he excused himself. Rosa wondered about exposing her lower belly area to him. She didn't

even know him, and, obviously, his hands would have to touch her.
Intimately, she thought, and she reddened. Rosa, the sophisticate,
and artist, she reminded herself, took over, and she told herself, You
wear a bikini and show it all the time—He's done plenty of other
women's tattoos, probably even on their asses—He looks like a nice
guy—He really does—How about the fan on the breast?

He walked in. "Someone's going to be after you. Do you mind if
they watch?" He smiled reassuringly.

"I was just wondering if I could let you watch, so I don't think
so." Rosa said without smiling.

He burst out laughing. "Hey, that's okay. I just thought it might
make you feel more comfortable with other people around." He
walked over to the door and said, "Sorry, she isn't into it. Make
yourself at home, or come back in around a half hour." He shut the
door.

A half hour, Rosa thought—a half hour; and now that the door
was shut, she was sure she was in the early stages of insanity.

He reached into a drawer and pulled out a replica of the "Wild
Rose" she'd chosen, and asked her, "Where do you want it? Would
you like a glass of wine?"

"Whatever it is, I'll take it," Rosa finally laughed.

He opened a little refrigerator and poured her a glass of chablis.
"Hey, seriously, this won't hurt that much." He hurried on. "What I
mean is, the skin actually numbs after a minute or so, this little thing
goes so fast. Watch." And he showed her by turning it on.

"May I ask why you're doing it?" He looked at her, mildly
curious.

Should I answer him? Why not? "Because, I'm moving to the
mountains, and I want Big Foot to recognize me."

He laughed. "Where are you going?"

"Plumas County area."

"Beautiful country up there. You'll like it. You ever live in the
snow?"

"Not yet."

"It depends on where you live, but you can count on needing a
fair share of wood for the winters. Now, where would you like your
wild rose?" he said matter-of-factly.

Rosa hesitated. Then in a louder voice than she intended, she
said, "On my lower belly, to the left side."

"There's a bathroom there, if you want."

"Okay, be right out." She adjusted herself and returned to the
room.

"Here's a pillow. Just lay down here, and get comfortable. But first, any colors you prefer? Red's obvious, but there's these fuchsias and purples."

"I'm a painter, by the way," Rosa smiled.

He smiled back. "Well, then, help yourself. Any preferences? What's your name?"

"Rosa Lujan."

"I see. Rose. I'm Jeff Russell." He pulled up his sleeves and showed her his arms. They were each a portable, living canvas—color and form merged harmoniously. Deep, rich color covered his arms to nearly his shoulders. Flowers, animals, vibrant suns, came to life when she focused on them.

"Very beautiful. Did it hurt?" she asked.

"Something like this takes years. These took about eight years, and I plan to start on my back next. So, you don't do it all at once."

"I assume someone's doing these for you."

"Yeah. A good friend. An artist."

"From the photographs of your work, I'd say your style is more etched, Oriental. I love the dragon you did on that man's back—but I, for one, am not that brave," Rosa laughed. "How about that fuchsia, this one, for the petals, and then outlining each petal in this pale lilac—the stem this dark green."

"It's your rose, Rosa. Okay, just lay back and relax. I'll do a line to show you what it feels like, and like I said, it'll numb up in a minute or so, this little tool goes so fast." His face became business-like, detached. "Show me, exactly, where you want it."

Rosa edged up on her elbow and took a good look at her lower belly, imagined the small oval of her womb, and moved her finger to the left. "Right here," she pointed to the blank flesh. Fresh canvas, she thought and laughed to herself.

She felt the first line, staring up at a wildlife poster. Just like the gynecologist's office, she thought. It was uncomfortable but it cer-tainly didn't sting.

"Do you mind if I prop myself up and watch?"

"Try it. I don't want any skin to wrinkle though."

She propped herself on her elbows.

"I guess that's okay. Just don't go any further. If you want to lay down again, let me know first. Any mistake here's permanent."

Jeff outlined the rose, quickly, carefully, and then began to fill in its petals with fuchsia. It began to come to life. The last time she'd been propped this way, she remembered clearly, was when she'd given birth to Sean. When she'd propped herself up on her elbows to watch his head emerge between her open legs. Her breath caught at the thought, and tears stung her eyes. Well, little rose, I pull you from my womb, to expose you to air, forever. She corrected herself. As long as this body lasts.

The lilac outline gave the petals what Rosa had wanted—an aura of light, a living quality. Her lilac sky.

"What about the center?" Jeff asked. "I'd say the yellowish gold would be the best."

"I think you're right," Rosa answered him. "I'm going to lay down, Jeff." As he continued working, she closed her eyes. Her belly was entirely numb. The tattoo had sprung to life.

"Well, that's it. Here, take a look. I like it—that lilac was a good idea."

It was beautiful. Jeff had covered the tattoo with oil, and it glistened on her flesh. The yellow-gold center pulsed like a sun: life, birth, life, until death. The death of the body, the naked canvas. Now, not so naked with one wild rose. Sierra came sharply to mind—she'd always imagined being old women together. Rosa realized she never imagined being old with a man.

"Jeff, it's exactly what I wanted. It really is."

He beamed. "Glad you like it. Great. Keep it oiled. It's going to scab. That's how it heals."

"It'll scab? I didn't know that. It's hard to believe it'll scab, it looks so smooth."

"Here's some cards in case friends get inspired after they see yours."

Rosa took them. She paid him, and walked toward the door.

"Don't forget, keep it oiled. Good luck in the mountains, Rosa."

"It was almost painless, Jeff. Thanks for putting up with me," she smiled back at him. "Good luck to the rest of your tattoo."

The sun was bright and warm, nearly blinding after the false light of the back room, but she instinctively put her face toward it, and shut her eyes for a moment. Her secret was hidden, and it throbbed, lightly, in its newborn state. Little rose, wild rose, you are *mine*, she thought with a shudder of delight.

Julio's car was in the driveway when she got home. Rosa wondered what mood he was in. She carried two grocery bags, and he was at the door, opening it for her before her key fit into the lock.

"Anymore bags?" he asked.

"There's a couple more," she answered.

Zack was in front of her wagging his tail, and smiling breathlessly. Somehow, his malamute mask never looked ominous to her, at all. In fact, it'd always struck her as playful, cheerful. Rosa put the groceries down and petted him.

Julio came back in. "I took him for a walk this afternoon. How was your visit?"

"A thrill a minute," Rosa muttered, and then looked up at Julio's wounded face. "Sierra and I went camping on the Eel River for the night, and it was worth it in spite of a nasty encounter with three young men (Rosa silently acknowledged the one young man, but kept it to herself—his shy smile), and their equally nasty little dog. Actually, he wasn't so little; he was a German shepherd." Rosa put her head to Zack's. "If you would've been there, Zack, you would've eaten that twerp for dinner. Right, Zack?"

Zack panted excitedly and pushed his huge head into her chest. "Good old dog. Good dog, Zack," Rosa laughed.

"What happened?" Julio sounded concerned.

Rosa told him, and then added, "And then we came home to find Bob The Slob waiting for his din-din."

Julio laughed, wondering, at the same time, what turn her humor took when she described him. "Did you and Bob get into it?" Julio asked, trying not to sound too enthusiastic.

Rosa sensed it anyway, and her midsection clenched though tears also threatened to expose her. She didn't want to give Julio any satisfaction in this matter. He knew, only too well, what Sierra meant to her. Rosa looked closely at Julio's face and found a moment he'd left unguarded, and she knew her words to Sierra had been true. That she loved him, still, in a half-assed way. Her own half-assed way.

"We exchanged a few words, that's all. How was your weekend?"

Both nights Julio had drunk enough brandy, and smoked enough grass, to put himself to sleep. Once with friends, and once by himself. "It was okay. I got some darkroom work done. It was quiet around here." He looked at her with a mixture of anger and self-pity: reproach.

"Julio, I'm putting the house up for sale. The realtors are coming tomorrow to take a look at it." He didn't answer. "Did you hear me?"

"Yeah, I heard you," Julio's voice sounded strangled, though she knew he wasn't crying. But the pain in his voice turned on her like an exquisite secret weapon she had no defense for.

"They're coming tomorrow, and I'm going to do it," Rosa said softly.

He turned and faced her squarely. "Where do you think you're going, anyway?" His face looked fierce.

"To the mountains."

Julio forced himself to laugh. "You're kidding, of course."

"No, I'm not, Julio."

"What in the hell do you plan to do *in the mountains*? What mountains? What mountains are you talking about?" He was shouting.

Rosa rallied herself. "I'll do what I want in the goddamned mountains! I'll pick wild flowers, or pick my goddamned nose! I'll become van Gogh in the goddamned mountains! That's what! And where I'm going's none of your damned business!" she yelled back.

"So you're just going to pick up all your marbles and go away. Is that it?" Julio lowered his voice, but the edge of his anger still sliced at her.

"I was trying to let you know in a civilized way, I suppose, what I'm doing. I've told you, repeatedly, that I'm leaving. You, obviously, never believed me. What does it matter where I *go*, anyway?" Rosa kept her voice firm, and she stared at Julio evenly.

Julio turned away and looked out the window to the sea. His mind was on fire—what a flaming bitch! She'd actually do it. She'd actually leave me. With more control than he knew he had, he said in a calm tone, a deadly tone, "Do what you want, Rosa."

Rosa's tattoo itched, and she remembered it. I already have, she thought. Suddenly, she felt like talking to someone, and the thought of staying in the house with Julio was more than she could bear. Without a word she left.

Julio had a brief vision of dragging her back in the house by the hair and tying her up in a chair. She means it, she really means it, his mind echoed. He took a sip of brandy, and it nauseated him. He poured it down the sink. He wanted to cry, but he couldn't. He just couldn't. Julio closed his eyes, and the darkness trembled with his rage, and he wondered what he'd do with it. What was he to do with it? Was this war going to end? Ever?

Rosa decided to go to Rob's place. He'd been a student of hers for a couple of semesters. She remembered his intensity, and his talent for black and white drawings; his obvious dislike for color. At first, his complexity repulsed her, instinctively, and then in brief exchanges she sensed a deep intelligence. He always came to class in what she later, teasingly, called his hiking gear: flannel shirt, worn jeans, boots.

Julio's angry face was superseded with Rob's ironic one, and it helped. She hoped he'd be home. Rosa thought of the time he'd asked her for dinner, and she'd explained to him that she was married. He'd answered, "I assumed you were from the ring on your left hand. I didn't think it was against the law to go to dinner." He'd smiled; his dark, intense eyes never leaving hers. "I just want to see what makes the teacher tick." And that's what she liked about him— the churning complexity translated into disarming directness. When he told her he was a doctor, a director at a ghetto clinic in the city, his black and white intensity fell into place somehow.

Rob's van was there, but it didn't mean anything because he usually used his motorcycle in the city. At first she'd been a little surprised to see the motorcycle he drove, and later when she saw the funky but functional van she had to laugh. It seemed to be his insignia, these eccentricities. Of course, she'd kept these meetings to herself, but they hadn't really bothered her—though once in a while a flash of guilt would overtake her for being with a man, secretly— probably because sex hadn't been such an instant, burning issue like it had with Rolf. So, when he invited her to his house after their second meeting to make a fire and have a drink, she accepted. When she entered, to her left, was an immense grand piano. Rob had seen her admiring look and said, "My twenty-six-thousand-dollar Porsche."

His house was on the edge of the neighborhood he served, and it was rented. Rosa went up to his door, and his bell was still taped, so she knocked. She could hear his bounding steps, and she felt relief. Good, she thought.

Rob opened the door with a quizzical look; his piercing, dark eyes with the bushy eyebrows seemed poised to expect whatever came to his door. He was tall and slender, and unlike Rolf, a bit gangly and awkward. It was as though his sheer intensity kept him lean, and he had no time, or patience, for a cultured, personal gracefulness. Just the thought of him in an over-large—it had to be over-large—white doctor's coat, plunging ahead to patient after patient, with his quizzical look of intensity, always made her smile. His irony was another matter. Another thing—Rob was Jewish, and Rosa had never known any Jewish men, though she had two Jewish women friends, both married to Gentiles.

His face exploded into a smile, and he yelled, "Welcome! Welcome to my cave! Come on in! Are you hungry?"

Rob stood there looking at her full of frank affection, and it made Rosa blush.

"What're you having, for Christ's sake, hot dogs?" Rosa laughed.

"No, but you're close. Frozen won-tons. I'll put some more on if you want some. I even bought French colombard yesterday. I must've known you were coming! It's chilled—I swear it!" He was yelling with exaggerated enthusiasm, enjoying himself.

Rosa went into the kitchen and peeked at the miserable, little won-tons baking in the oven, and she laughed. "Okay, okay. Only if you have some vegetables and rice, Dr. Simon."

Rob rushed to the refrigerator and searched through the crisper pulling out carrots and green beans, a little aged but still edible.

"Look, there's some frozen vegetables in the freezer, too." He opened the freezer and brought out a bag of Mixed Chinese Vegetables, Safeway brand. Holding all this, he gave Rosa a hug, the frozen vegetables falling across her back.

Rosa screamed. "Are you trying to greet me or torture me?" she laughed. "Here, give me those and put on some more of that won-ton stuff. Do you have any hot mustard and soy sauce? Are you on-call tonight?"

Rob was calming down, and the soft jazz playing on the stereo was becoming audible.

"I'm off-duty tonight, Rosa. In fact, I was tempted to call you. Every time I've called and your husband's answered, I've felt like hanging up. That guy's uptight."

"Don't remind me, please. I guess I came here for a number of reasons. One, to tell you I'm selling my place and leaving, and before you ask, I'll tell you. To the mountains, somewhere in Plumas County. Do you know where that's at?"

Rob started yelling again, "TO THE MOUNTAINS? TO THE MOUNTAINS? Great! I'll have someone to visit in Plumas County!"

Rosa was chopping the vegetables. "Well, I'm glad someone's excited. Do you have any tofu?" she said, laughing.

"What is tofu? But wait a minute, I'm going to miss you." He stopped and looked at her. "Yeah, I'll definitely miss you, Rosa."

"Tofu, Dr. Simon, is healthy stuff, unlike frozen won-tons. Are you kidding me?" Rosa looked at his eyes which looked terribly soft. "Hey, look, it's okay if you don't have any tofu." And then she added, "Imagine how I feel—I don't even know where the place is."

Rob smiled, then glared at her. "Then why are you going?"

"Because I've got to. May I have some of that chilled wine? Maybe I could explain while we eat this gourmet meal. You really don't even know what tofu is? I'm a Mexican and *I* know."

"I know, I know. I just don't have any. Sometimes I eat tofu and hot dogs," Rob said with an air of offense.

"I wouldn't doubt it," Rosa laughed. She sipped the colombard. "Number two, is that I just got a tattoo."

"Where, for God's sake? Does it say 'MOM'?"

"As a matter of fact, it does, and it's on my womb, Dr. Simon." Rosa began to giggle and couldn't stop. She poured Rob some wine, handing it to him.

"Okay, why are you going to the mountains, and why do you now have a tattoo, for God's sake?"

"For Goddess' sake," she corrected him.

Rob laughed. "You and these obscure religions. Okay, for Goddess' sake. Why?"

Rosa pulled herself together for a serious reply, and answered with a seriousness bordering on Rob's own intensity. "Rob, I'm going to the mountains, so I need this tattoo so that Big Foot will recognize me, just in case," and she began to howl again until she could barely catch her breath.

"Are you through? If I didn't know you better I'd say you were hysterical."

"I am hysterical, but it sure feels great. To laugh, I mean," Rosa said, wiping her eyes.

Rob looked directly at her with his quizzical look, the one he faced the unknown with, and said, "It's your husband, isn't it? You still love the guy, and you don't know if you're coming or going. In fact, you *don't* know where you're going. Am I right or not, Ms. Luján?" Now his face switched to irony, and he added, "Show me the tattoo. That is, if you really did this distasteful thing to yourself. 'MOM'?" The irony deepened.

Rob's mention of Julio sobered her, but the tattoo almost sent her over the brink of laughter again. She stopped herself and said, "A perceptive diagnosis, Dr. Simon. I believe I'm nearing collapse, or in more accurate terms, a nervous breakdown, but I do have a further belief that this tattoo will save me." Rosa laughed.

"Do you realize this 'MOM' will be on you till you leave this particular body?" Rob looked genuinely disgusted.

Rosa laughed again. "Rob, it doesn't say 'MOM.' Here, I'll show you. You've seen plenty of bellies in your time, I'm sure. Wait a minute." Rosa went into the bathroom to take another look at it, and kept her jeans at a decent angle.

She emerged from the bathroom without a word and just stood there in front of him. "Well?" Rosa finally asked.

The quizzical look again. "Well, to be very honest, it's a sight, a damn sight better than 'MOM.' That's for sure. No, I like it, but I can't help thinking not on you."

"Why?"

Rob was silent for a minute and finally said, "I can't say why. Maybe because I've never known a woman with a tattoo. Maybe because I can't help but think of The Tattooed Lady in the circus. Have you shown Julio?"

"No way."

"He's bound to see it."

"Maybe. Remember, I'm going to the mountains. Anyway, do you like my tattoo or not?" Rosa demanded to know.

"Yes. Yes, I do. At least it's not conspicuous. Whoever did it, did a good job. Did it hurt?"

"I'll give you his card in case you get the urge to sneak on down. And, no, surprisingly it didn't hurt. It actually numbed up. The rice is about done. How's the won-tons coming?"

They took their plates to the front room and settled on the couch.

"How've you been, Rob? Actually, I haven't seen you for a month."

"A little lonely. No special woman yet. My son was just here last weekend. You know, if it weren't for him I'd feel entirely alone in the world." Rob looked down at his food, then took a bite.

"Also, a patient of mine died. He was old; it was coming. I advised him to cut out his daily walks to and from the store because he lives on a pretty steep hill, and his house has a lot of steps. Anyway, he died climbing the steps. For the first time I went to the funeral—I was invited. I sat by his body for a while without thinking, there is a dead body, but rather thinking here is Mr. Rodríguez. I can't explain it, but it was good for me. I liked that old man, a lot. In some funny way he treated me like a son." Rob looked at Rosa for response, saw her understanding and looked away.

"I'm starting to think all life's a parting. Like when you're really young, you think all life's a kind of constant greeting—a waiting to be joined. Yet your sitting with Mr. Rodríguez was a parting, and a joining. It's like you had to teach yourself that part of it, isn't that it? They didn't teach you that in med school I assume."

"That's for damned sure," Rob said, looking up at her and smiling. "Then, I was invited to a wedding last week, and I went. A big, beautiful family, lots of food, drink, the couple in love. I got so drunk they helped me get home. Me, the doctor. They just laughed and picked me up. Someone drove my motorcycle back for me." He laughed. "I haven't had a hangover like that since I was a teenager. You know, Rosa, I want to fall in love like that. I want to have a big wedding. Silly, isn't it? Me, a grown man."

"It isn't silly. At all. Sounds to me like you're ready. If you're acting like a teenager, you must be." Rosa laughed. "How's your son?"

"Oh, Jake's okay. I just hate to see him go, and yet I know I couldn't take care of him every day and do what I do. And sometimes I wonder if he hates me because I spend more time with other people. It's like I can't imagine that he really loves me. It sounds crazy, doesn't it?"

"Jake's only eight, and eight-year-olds are usually self-centered and ruthlessly tuned into the next possible toy. I know if you were with him every day you'd see more evidence, little things, of his love." Rosa sat back, comfortably, and tired, into the old, worn couch.

"Maybe you're right—but it's almost as though Jake senses my choice in the matter, about my not wanting to take care of him every day." Rob felt the familiar anguish he got whenever he thought of Jake so soon after a visit. He paused to let it subside, and then he thought of his ex-wife. Would she really have let me have him? I just couldn't do it, Rob remembered his choice, clearly, again. What's important? What's really important, he wanted to ask Rosa, but when he looked at her she seemed to be melting into the couch.

"You look pretty tired. I've got some new sheet music. How would you like a tune or two?"

Rosa smiled and said, "You read my mind, Dr. Simon."

Rob wiped his hands on his jeans thoroughly, but then decided that wasn't enough and went to wash his hands. "Sorry for the delay, madam," he said smiling, and then he carefully opened the keyboard, did some scales, adjusted the sheet music and began to play. His playing wasn't flawless, but the feeling he poured into it, shyly at first, and then, finally, unselfconsciously was strangely moving as though this were the one thing about himself he wished were beautiful.

Rosa leaned her head to one side, and the music felt like it was pulling out her wolf's howl, her long, slow sorrow. She cried, and he didn't look at her, not once, and it was better than words. Rosa watched his fingers, his long, slim fingers, gracefully moving. Beautifully. Rosa wondered if anyone really believed they were loved, or that they really loved anyone else. What was the evidence? What would make Rob believe that Jake loved him, or that Jake believed he was loved? What would make Julio believe he was loved? Did she really love anyone? Did she? What was the evidence? she asked herself.

Rob kept playing and she began to get sleepy. Wasn't it the music? Wasn't that enough? Rob, she wanted to say, it's the music, but she fell asleep.

Rosa woke up on the couch covered by a blanket. A small fire still burned in the fireplace, and Rob was asleep next to her on the floor, his arms flung over his head. She got up, quietly, and checked the time: two-thirty. She wrote Rob a note: "Rob, It's the music. See you soon, as soon as I get back. con amor, Rosa." She covered him with the blanket and went home.

The house sold within two weeks, and the new owners wanted to move in by October. Sean was due home in a week. Julio fluctuated between seduction and rape, tenderness and fury. He saw Rosa becoming more and more distant; soon she should disappear altogether like a ship on the edge of the world. He wished to seize her before she discovered the world was round, but he knew that was impossible. She was in the wind.

He and Rosa are in the desert, walking. The day is clear and hot. Saguaro surrounds them, and they sit at the foot of an immense one. Two small lizards appear in front of them, one male, one female. The lizards face each other, waiting. Rosa says, "They're waiting for blood. They're thirsty." Julio hands Rosa water and tells her, "Drink, slowly." Rosa takes a sip, turns into a hawk and flies away. I must lose this weight, he tells himself, and he begins to cry. Julio licks his tears, and he feels full. Satisfied.

Julio woke himself up sobbing out loud. This was the clearest dream he'd had since he was a child. His face was dry, and his heart felt wrenched of all blood. Dry and dead it felt. But it couldn't be, could it? He breathed, in and out.

Rosa was gone to a place called Plumas to find her house. Was this a dream? he nearly asked himself out loud. If this is love, I'm lost, absolutely lost. He remembered the two small lizards facing each other. The words, "They're waiting for blood," came sharply to mind, the taste of his tears, and inexplicably he was comforted. Just a small edge of comfort in the vastness of the unfamiliar terrain he stumbled through, parched and thirsty. Wait, he told himself, I know this country. I know these saguaros. I know these mountains. I must watch the sun, carefully, rest often, and drink water, sip by sip, like gold. First, I'll become a mountain lion—yes, I've seen his tracks. Strong, lean, muscled . . . hadn't Rosa turned into a hawk? The hawk of his boyhood. ROSA! He almost cried, but he didn't.

Rosa found the cabin as it had been in her dream. The real estate agent took her there first, the first place within her price range, and with her down payment she'd be able to assume the loan without qualifying. It was two miles up a dirt road, the only cabin on its unnamed street. As they drove up thick mountain dust, waves of dust, flew into the air behind them. There was the cabin, there was the meadow, there was the forest. The forest was all around for millions of acres, ridge after ridge. A person could spend her entire life walking it and never see it all. Fly it and they'd miss the subtlety of the fresh spider's web, the tiny wild roses, wind rippling the forgotten lakes. Rosa didn't think of all this. She felt sick to her stomach with recognition, and insisted on seeing the other cabins on the agent's list. She refused to surrender to her recognition without a ritual test. The air was so rich, it smelled only of the forest, and clouds, she inhaled. Fertile and potent at once.

The drive through the canyon had been a mystery. She'd never seen anything like it in her life—a road dynamited through granite. Bridges, tunnels, sheer drops to the river below, granite shooting up on every side of her as though the only reality permissible were stone. She felt altered, passed through the eye of a needle held by some great, unknown hand—as though she'd passed into an entirely different world. So far away, it felt, from everything.

After seeing the other cabins, Rosa made a bid for the first one, and wrote a check for the deposit. She'd have to move in by October or the snows would make it impossible. She was advised to get a four-wheel-drive car, and get rid of her Volvo. She thought of Sean, Julio, Sierra, Rob, her other scattered friends, and she suddenly felt like she was committing suicide. But Rosa noticed in the motel that night, as she got into bed, that the wolf was silent.

The cabin was in Lupine Meadows, population ninety. She hadn't seen her friend, though she found out Julie worked at a guest ranch down the road as a wrangler. The only woman wrangler, she was told. It figured. Julie had always ridden horses even in the bay area where she'd been a second grade teacher for years. Rosa'd met Julie through a mutual friend, and it'd been at least three years since they'd seen each other.

No, the wolf was silent. Was she waiting for Rosa in the endless forest, trotting down by the creek, staking out her new territory, sniffing the edge of the warm wind, perhaps searching for her own kind? Would she be waiting there in the front patch of scraggly grass, stiff-legged, shoulders poised, eyes burning directly into her own?

All Rosa knew was that the wolf was silent, and it gave her an absolute clarity of her situation. She would go back to the house, prepare to move, speak to Sean. Sean could come with her if he wanted. There was a junior college close by, twenty miles to the county seat. Town, as everyone called it. Yes, he could come; he had a choice. She could use his company, and his help. There was the winter wood to get, that was evident. But it would be up to him.

She would put her application in at the college. She had a good letter of recommendation. It hadn't looked promising, though. Personnel told her, straight out, that there was no current hiring in the Art Department. Well, she could type—she'd done that before, hadn't she? Rosa was so exhausted she fell asleep with the lamp on in the little room, and turned it off when she woke up the next morning.

She decided not to have breakfast, it took too much time, and she wanted to get back by dark. She also wanted to drive down the mountains in the early morning, so she bought coffee, a roll, and some yogurt. As Rosa walked out to the car she realized the sky, in every direction she looked, was a uniform lilac. The most subtle lilac she'd ever seen. She stood still and tried to memorize it, taking it in through a kind of osmosis. The air was absolutely still, and prisms of light played on everything as the sun began to rise. Rosa thought of her lilac sky painting at home, and how she hadn't touched it for weeks, only staring at it from time to time as she began to work on the series of rainbow paintings. Perhaps, here, I'll finish the lilac sky, she told herself.

Rosa stopped two more times going down the canyon. Once to swim among some giant, grey boulders; the water felt so alive rushing all around her, and so fast it carried her downstream a couple of times. The first time it scared her, and the second time she enjoyed it allowing the current to take her for a ride past the somber presence of the immense boulders. The last, brief stop was to take in the dimensions of an enormous rock slate dripping a wide, sweeping waterfall. This beauty was everywhere—would she ever get used to it? It felt as though her eyes were jerking hungrily in every driection, and it almost overwhemed her. How desolate it seemed; how inhumanly beautiful. It ached in her, and the silence, the vastness of the silence, frightened her. She was still too human.

The drive back was so long Rosa felt glued to her seat. What a drive—and where is that place—did I really see it—she asked herself. When she opened the door Julio was sitting in the dark drinking a glass of wine.

"You missed a good sunset," Julio said, quietly.

"I saw it crossing the Bay Bridge," Rosa answered him.

"Well, did you find it?" Julio asked, keeping his voice as neutral as possible.

"I put a deposit on a house," she answered him in a tired voice. "I think this is it."

"When are you leaving?"

"Mid-September at the latest. I'll know for sure by the end of next week." Rosa looked at Julio as her eyes grew accustomed to the darkness. She saw that his face was drawn with a painful look of acceptance. A harsh acceptance, and her heart turned over with a sudden pain.

"I'll help you move, of course." His voice was gentle.

"You don't have to, Julio."

"I want to."

They were silent in the darkness. The sound of a motor worked its way up the hill. She looked at Julio, and he was crying. Tears rolled down his face. She walked over to him and held his head like a child, like a child to her breasts.

"What are we going to do, Julio?" Rosa asked, her sorrow naked in her voice. It was unbearable. She hadn't realized it would be unbearable.

He didn't answer. He didn't ask her to stay. He didn't say, "Don't leave me." He never said those words. And she never said the words "I love you"—it would've split her right in two, right there.

"Make love to me, Rosa. Dame tu cuerpo, tu alma," Julio asked thickly. He hadn't expected to want her—not this way. He did want her, body and soul. Watch the sun, he told himself, rest often, drink the water, sip by sip, like gold.

Rosa spread the Indian blanket from the couch onto the floor, and they faced each other for a minute before coming together with soft moans of mourning. Not cries of joy or desire, but gentle sounds like a mourning of separation, death, beforehand. And it was like death, one of the few times it's allowed to mourn the separation of body and soul.

"Dame tu cuerpo, tu alma," Rosa whispered as his tongue drew her orgasm out, spreading out to every corner, each extremity of her body, radiating from the central pulse of her sexual sun, her moon in her womb. She moaned into his neck, "Please." She wanted him inside of her, to feel the moon that pulled at her, blind and wise at once. They were wet with tears, and it felt as though he entered her, completely, and that she entered him, completely. For a long, long moment they were transparent. They felt transparent with pleasure and pain, joy and sorrow, life and death. They fell asleep breathing close against the other—not clutching, but touching with open palms the chest, the breast, the face of the other.

Julio's hand closed on Rosa's shoulder, involuntarily, in a grip, and Rosa turned away. And then his hand fell open across her thick, dark hair catching itself in a million strands, like living roots, grow-ing into the flowing blood of her body.

Rosa's dream had been vague like a series of fast film, except for one clear image of the cabin, brief and clear, as though to remind her of its reality—and a large, dark bird hovering, and then spiralling away. Larger than a hawk. Eagle. A brief, clear command.

She woke toward dawn, chilled on the front room floor. The blanket was wrapped around Julio, and his face was turned up toward her. All the misery erased itself, and his face had a baby's gentle quality. His tears. Rosa began to shiver and got up, carefully, to get a glass of juice, go to the bathroom, and then she got into bed under the warm quilt. Her body shivered, once, with delight as last night's memory overtook her—but then a sadness took its place. Their separation had begun.

When she got up the house was quiet, and Julio was gone. The fog was in, and the sea was blocked from her view, entirely, by its grey, dense wall. He'd left a note: "Coffee made, just heat. Fresh pan dulce in cupboard. Your body didn't lie last night, it told the truth. I wait for you at the foot of the mountains where it's safe. Will be back by four. J."

Where it's safe, Rosa said to herself. How well put, how percep-tive. No, my body didn't lie, but my soul is trying to leave, and death is dangerous. Tears came and eased her though they burned her eyes, but they burned with clarity. Her mind was clear; the wolf was free, ahead of her.

Rosa looked in the full length mirror just before she got in the shower, and the rose was still in place. Julio hadn't seen it in the dark. Good, she thought, it's still my secret. Maybe this is so I'll recognize *me* in the mountains. Now, what would Rob think of that, she wondered and laughed to herself. No more crying today; my eyeballs will fall out. Period. She oiled her tattoo, carefully, looking for scab formation. Still nothing—and still so beautiful and fresh against her womb. Rose of the womb, she thought—blood of the moon, she didn't think. Yet.

Rosa heated coffee and scrambled some eggs, taking them downstairs to her studio. She ate facing the paintings—the lilac sky and the magnified Earth. She hadn't begun the wide circle of the rainbow, but she imagined it so well she could almost see it on the canvas already. The Earth was closer, and it began to assume a living quality. The oceans and the land masses began to emerge distinctly, with depth. Rosa wanted to give this Earth a shimmering quality of light and energy. Life. A living being breathing in the oxygen-filled sky, the blue-ozone sky. It had begun to assume a living quality, but she couldn't see it yet. Involuntarily, Rosa pin-pointed current and past wars. The whole globe a target. But in space, far away, or in a river's whirlpool, up close, the Earth's natural sense of peace—a harmony of the dying and the living—became evident. And if this should disappear, who would imagine it into being, she wondered.

Rosa imagined Julio bringing his camera into focus, leaning forward, stepping back, moving toward his subject—his heart pounding as it always did, but his hand absolutely steady. She saw his face registering doubt, then certainty, then a brief, intense pleasure. A man's face. He'd cried. Would the man remember? Would he be ashamed? Rosa imagined the ocean, shafts of sunlight beginning to pierce the fog, but the battle would be difficult, and today the fog might win. The ocean doesn't care, grey is necessary and beautiful, I suppose—it's I who resists the fog, she thought finally. She tried to imagine the ocean, the grey ocean, playing with the shifting fog, and blending as far as the eye could see.

Rosa finished her coffee, and instead of working on the Earth as she'd planned she prepared a small amount of black, and, calling on the sleeping spider, she began an intricate, spiral rose on the shawl hanging in the lilac sky.

Sean would be home today. She'd pick him up in San Francisco at five. How will I even begin to explain it all to him, Rosa wondered.

Rosa stood back from the completed rose, and the sharp contrast of the lacy black against the pale, uniform lilac surrounding it pleased and startled her at the same time. The sky seemed too pale, and then as she concentrated only on the rose it seemed too vivid. No, she refused to touch that sky. She'd changed it three times already, and she knew it'd make no difference to make it four. Just keep looking at it, and work on the rest of the painting, she told herself.

The shawl began to soften itself in her mind, and Rosa began to see its fold, its single fold. Its shadow. I won't complete these paintings here, she realized, and the realization terrorized her. It's too stark—it's too isolated—it's too damned vast, she told herself. Maybe I won't be able to paint there at all; and then I've got to find a job. The realtor said to count on four cords of wood at least. Where's that going to come from? And the snow—do people really get cabin fever? Will I get snowbound? Will the solitude drive me crazy? Crazy. Yes, that's really it, isn't it? Is that what's in the shawl's single fold? Its shadow.

Rosa's mouth felt dry, and her head reeled from her sense of aloneness—the choice she was making. She cleaned up and took one last look at the paintings, lilac sky to blue sky. There's more where that came from, she told herself. Rosa remembered the brief image of the cabin in her dream, and the solitary eagle flying over it. "There'd better be," she said out loud.

Sean's bus had already arrived, and baggage was being distributed. Everyone looked the same to her—a little tired, a little dirty, and about the same age. Rosa gave up looking for him and just stood in an obvious place. A loud, piercing wolf whistle that sounded almost in her ear made her spin around angrily.

"Don't get uptight, Mom," Sean was laughing.

"You asshole!" Rosa hit him on the arm, and then grabbed him and hugged him.

Sean reddened and pulled away. "Everyone's staring, for Christ's sake."

"You're the one who made the scene, kiddo," Rosa laughed. But she let him go, and then she took a good look at him. He was very tan and lean. He'd lost some weight. And his dark eyes looked as she'd imagined them. Sensual.

"You look very good, Sean. Is The Special Person here? I'd love to meet her."

"She got bussed to Mendocino. Look, my bags are over here. Come on, let's go."

Sean walked over to a group of people, yelled goodbye, grabbed his bags and walked back toward her.

"The car's this way. Here, I'll take this little one, Sean. I'm taking you to dinner. Are you hungry?" Rosa asked. "You notice I'm taking you to dinner whether you're hungry or not," she teased.

Sean broke into a grin. "I'm starving, Mother dear. Where's Julio?"

Rosa stiffened, but tried to keep her voice even. "He's probably home. Look, there's a lot we have to talk about, believe me."

"I could tell by your eyes. They're a little swollen. What's going on?"

"Well, thanks. That's just what I needed. Do I have a red nose, too? Do I look that bad or what?" Rosa demanded to know.

"Nah. I just know the difference."

"That's okay, Sean. I'm just being sensitive. The wolf whistle helped," she laughed, opening the car door.

"Really, Mom, you look great." And under his breath he added, "For thirty-four."

Rosa socked him again, laughing. "All right, Sean—you're really asking for it, aren't you?"

He put his arm around her. "You must be okay if you can sock me with the old gusto. What's going on? It's you and Julio, right?"

Rosa got in the car and started the motor. "I sold the house, Sean. I'm planning to move to the mountains, about six hours north. You can come with me—there's a junior college close by, or you can stay here with your friends."

"You actually sold the house?"

"Yes."

"How's Julio taking all this?" Sean couldn't keep the disbelief out of his voice.

"It's working out, I suppose. It's not going to be easy for either of us, but I guess that's our business, Sean. You don't have to decide about coming or not coming right now. I'll probably be leaving in two or three weeks. But like I said, there's a junior college there. You could learn to ski and cut wood with a chain saw." Rosa smiled at him.

"I did some chain saw cutting on the work crews, so that's no problem. What's this place in the mountains like? You sound like it's there waiting for you." Sean's face was serious, but he was doing his best to not look too upset or alarmed. In two weeks he'd be eighteen, he reminded himself.

"Well, it's in the Plumas National Forest, about five thousand feet up, so there'll be snow. The cabin I put a deposit on is small but adequate, and you can't see or hear anyone. It's the only house on the road, a dirt road. There are neighbors within walking distance, and there's a guest ranch a few miles down the main road. It closes during the winter. Do you remember Julie?"

"The blonde? The one with the crazy laugh?"

"Yeah, that's her. I found out she works at the ranch as the only woman wrangler. Do you believe it?" Rosa laughed.

"I think I'll believe anything from here on out," Sean said edgily.

"Are you pissed off?" Rosa looked at him sideways as she kept an eye out for traffic.

"Well, I sure didn't expect to come back and find the house sold, and you moving to the Yukon." He was angry.

"It's not the Yukon. It's about six hours from here, Sean. Besides, weren't you talking, in fact demanding, to live with your friends this semester? Weren't you the one who said he wanted to be on his own?"

Sean was silent.

"Look, what I'm saying is that you're welcome to come with me, or you can stay and do what you planned to do. That's got to be up to you. But I'm going, Sean," Rosa said gently.

"What're you going to do up there, anyway?" he asked in a resigned voice.

"Paint, shovel snow, and get used to silence."

"I mean for money."

"I'm putting an application in at the college. I'll keep selling my paintings, and see what else there is. Office work, whatever." Rosa was always surprised at how confident she sounded when these were the issues that caused her such bouts of terror. The silence, solitude, money, snow, and madness.

"How much wood do you need up there?"

"The realtor told me at least four cords for the winter." Rosa pulled into a parking space.

"Goddamn! That'd fill our living room floor to ceiling. How much you going to pay me, Mother dear?" Sean looked at Rosa shrewdly.

"I *was* thinking about a graduation gift, like a car. Not new, obviously. But something that'll run without too many hassles."

He shot her a look of surprise and excitement, and then tried to sound matter-of-fact. "Sounds fair to me."

"Do you still have that job lined up at the restaurant part-time?" Rosa asked. "That is, if you stay. Also, there's grants and financial aid, you know. I'll go with you to the financial aid office if you want."

"I think I can handle it, Mom." I'm going to be eighteen—shit, I am eighteen, he told himself. The motor was silent, and Rosa was watching him. "Yeah, the guy promised it to me. No problem. Let me think about all this startling information for a while. When can I start looking for a car?"

"Scout some out and we can take a look day after tomorrow. I think you'd like it up there, Sean—though you'd probably have to get used to it. Hell, I'm going to have to get used to it. But it is really beautiful. Those mountains are stunning," Rosa said remembering the expanse of rock slate shooting up toward the sky, as her head bent backwards.

Now it was Sean's turn to watch her closely, and he began to imagine a roomful of cut wood, floor to ceiling.

They got out of the car and started toward the restaurant.

"Tomorrow I'll make that curry. Have you been running?" Rosa asked.

"Six to eight miles every day. Track starts pretty soon. I have to call the coach, I guess. Lisa is a runner, too." Sean's eyes softened at her name. "Pretty good, too. She surprised me."

"I bet she did," Rosa laughed.

They sat down at a table, and all they could think about was food, so they snatched up menus and decided to order as quickly as possible. The waitress took their order and smiled invitingly at Sean.

"These older women like you, I see."

"She wasn't that old, Mom."

Rosa laughed. "Just kidding, dear boy. So, what was Lisa like? Do you have any pictures, if you don't mind me being so nosy."

Sean looked up at her with an intensity that startled her. "Sometimes I wonder if it's possible to really love someone. Do you know what I mean? I mean, didn't you and Julio love each other? So what happened? Sometimes things don't seem too real somehow."

"I love you, Sean, if that counts," Rosa said softly, and he looked away. "And I still love Julio, but I just can't live with him. But I know what you mean. I know exactly what you mean, Sean. Maybe that's what I'm trying to work out, and here I am thirty-four. Maybe that's why I've got to go away to this place in the mountains."

"Yeah." Sean's voice was low, and he still wouldn't look at her.

"Do you have a picture of Lisa?"

He took out his wallet and handed her a photograph of a dark-haired girl—woman, Rosa corrected herself—with what looked like green eyes in a dark, healthy face, long tanned legs in shorts, and a t-shirt well defined by her femininity. She was standing in a bold pose, smiling, surrounded by trees.

"Well, she's gorgeous, and I think I'd like her. She argued with you a lot, right?"

Sean smiled. "That's for sure."

Their food arrived, and his combination plate was truly enormous—tacos, enchiladas, chile relleno, and a side of carne asada. She had flautas topped with guacamole, generously.

"Do you plan to eat all that, Conan?"

Sean grinned. "Yeah. Wish I could have a beer."

"Take a sip of mine. Do you plan to see Lisa again?"

Sean darted his eyes up at Rosa to see if he should talk about it, and then decided not to. "I don't know. Both of us want to go to a university with running scholarships—you know. I think she's a great person. Anyway, I don't know."

"Did you have a fight?"

"Kind of." He was evasive and final.

They ate in silence for a while.

"Any interesting dreams while you were gone? Anything you feel like sharing?" Rosa trod carefully, though the subject of dreams was usual and routine between them as it had been between her and her grandmother, and, to an extent, her aunt. Rosa rarely thought of her mother. It'd been over a year since she'd seen her. She'd left Rosa with her grandmother when she was four and never came back. Only brief, emotionally distant visits with the Beautiful Lady. Rosa had no idea who her father was—only that he was a man her mother had run away with against her grandmother's wishes, and that he was a gringo. No one had ever spoken to Rosa of him. Ever.

Sean looked up at Rosa with his mouth full and swallowed. "You know, I did dream I was moving. Yeah, I sure did. I thought it was just me moving, not everyone else at the same time. Does that college up there have a track team? This is the only year I want to go to a junior college. Next year I want a scholarship to a university, so I intend to bust my ass this year."

"I could find out about the track team. I didn't think to ask. Think of it this way—you aren't paying for your required subjects." As Rosa looked at the dark intent on her son's face, her first husband's face became clear again. Sean's father, Gene, was sixteen when they'd met, and it startled Rosa to realize she'd fallen in love with a boy younger than Sean. Her pregnancy, their marriage two years later. Gene was Italian and Russian (his father Italian and his mother Russian), and his parents were appalled that she was Mexican, though they lived in a predominately Mexican neighborhood. Their worst fears had come true. She remembered Gene's mother's first words to her when they met: "You're lighter than I thought." "Lighter than what?" Rosa responded. Gene's mother tip-toed around her after that.

Rosa looked at Sean becoming a man, a beautiful man, and she knew it—her life had been worth it. Her heart felt like it swelled huge with love, and then it calmed down and resumed its usual task of simply keeping her alive. She thought of Sean and Lisa with a fresh wave of tenderness. And then she thought of her own determination, when she finished her masters degree after she separated from Gene, the three years on food stamps, scholarships, grants.

"Do you remember when I was finishing school? Did it seem hard to you, your father gone and all?" Rosa wanted to know.

"Do you know what I really remember?" Sean asked.

"What?"

"Those first camping trips we took after he left. The ones by ourselves, even though they were kind of scary at first. You didn't even know how to make a fire." He started laughing.

"I learned fast though, didn't I?"

"Yeah, they were fun. Anyway, we always had enough to eat. It was kind of exciting being on your own after a while. You know, my favorite place will always be the farm. No one could believe I could have all those forts."

"I remember well. Also the presence of bunches of little boys. So, you don't have any major complaints I take it?"

Sean smiled. "Nah. You pass my test. So far, anyway."

Rosa flashed him The Finger and started laughing.

"God, Mom—cool it," he said, but he couldn't help laughing.

They got home and Rosa found a message on the table: "Rosa— ROB called. J." Julio's car was in the driveway, so he was around somewhere.

Sean went to his room. "Do you mind if I take the TV in here? Where's Zack?"

"Go ahead. Just keep it low. Zack's probably in the back. Why don't you bring him in?" She went to the bedroom to call Rob.

"Rob, it's me, Rosa."

"So you're back. I assume El Groucho gave you my message."

Rosa laughed. "Don't get nasty, Rob. Yes, he did. What's up?"

"So, did you find it?"

"I did, and I'm excited and terrified. Equally."

"When are you taking off for the wild blue yonder?" Rob's voice was absolutely serious; not a hint of a joke.

"Jesus, Rob, lighten up. How about some friendly support? Anyway, probably two or three weeks."

"Okay, okay. How about dinner, on me, this Sunday?" he asked, his voice softening.

"How's five?"

"Fine."

"It'd better be expensive!"

"Did anyone ever spank you?"

"Just once, but then I had my revenge."

"Tell me all about it Sunday night. Also, the wild blue yonder. See you at five, right?"

Julio opened the bedroom door. His face was dark and angry.

"Right." Rosa hung up the phone and waited.

"Well, who the hell is *Rob*? Or is it Robby? And where the hell have you been? With Robby?"

"Lower your voice, Julio. Sean is here, in case you didn't know. You obviously forgot I was picking him up," Rosa said as she contained her anger.

"Four hours to pick him up?" Julio lowered his voice only slightly.

She was ready to explode, but she was aware of Sean in the next room—and hadn't he gone through this before, twice? Poor Sean, she thought. "Look, we had dinner, Julio—and I haven't seen my son for over a month."

"Okay, who's Robby?" He wasn't going to let up.

Rosa felt like killing him, again. "*Rob*, Julio, is a student of mine."

"Why's he calling you here?" He was going to be relentless.

"Why shouldn't he?"

"He had a snotty tone. I don't have to deal with that shit," Julio yelled.

"Maybe you had a snotty tone when he said his name was Rob. Why am I explaining this? Really, I'd like to know," Rosa began to raise her voice.

"Maybe because we're supposed to be married or something like that."

Rosa stood up to face Julio, and in a low, angry voice she told him, "Okay, look, Rob was a student of mine. Now he's a friend. If you weren't so damned ridiculous I'd probably introduce you. He's a fine man. He happens to be a doctor. I've known him for over a year, and, and, no, we aren't lovers. Also, I'm going to dinner with him Sunday. Does that answer your question as to who *Rob* is, Julio?"

They stood there facing each other, and without a word Julio turned and left. Rosa heard him slam the front door and leave.

She felt relieved; she'd said it. She wasn't going to let him bully her again. Hot, cold, hot, cold. She was glad she was leaving. The thought of the cabin being alone and remote made her glad. And she wasn't going to cry. The thought of tears—her tears, his tears—absolutely repulsed her. If anyone's going to cry from now on, he can, Rosa thought. He can learn to cry for both of us. I refuse to.

Rosa got ready for bed, and as she turned off the light her calm surprised her. Sean went to the bathroom, and passing her door knocked once, saying, "Goodnight, Mom." He sounded young, as though she'd forgotten to read him a bedtime story. But she was relieved he only knocked once. She didn't feel like talking at all.

Rosa and Sean walk out to the darkness. A fine, steady snow is falling all around them. Everywhere. The snowflakes are light, so light. It seems a miracle in the absolute darkness of the night. "Sean," Rosa says, "they're falling stars. Look. They're falling stars." Sean holds out his hand and laughs, catching them as they melt and disappear in his warm palm. "Make a wish, Mom. Quick!" Then Sean is gone, and the silence is deep but not terrible.

When she woke up, her eyes focusing on her surroundings, Rosa had the feeling of an immense cyclone putting her down. Everything seemed to be whirling around in chaos. Her life felt like a cyclone. Rosa thought of Sierra and a jolt of sheer sorrow went through her. Her friend, her sister, her mother, her daughter. Can you lose all that and still be whole, she wondered. Maybe it would be different now, but after twenty-two years what would that mean? The sorrow stayed. It refused to budge. But Rosa knew she wouldn't contact Sierra first, and if Sierra never did, then that would be it. She had her limits, and she seemed to be reaching all of them at once. Rosa thought of Sierra's pregnancy, and, then, the dream she'd had of Sierra's birth. Well, my friend, perhaps we will meet again, and the thought comforted her, but an old primary part of herself would not be comforted.

The dream of Sean and the snow overtook Rosa with its visual wonder. I'm leaving everything known for the unknown. My unknown. And this is the price, Rosa, she told herself.

Rosa took her coffee down to the studio, quietly. Sean was sleeping in, so she let Zack out of the room and took him to the yard. Either Julio left early or stayed out all night. Fine. She had no desire to discuss anything with him. It was hopeless, so she blotted him out.

The day was clear and sunny, and as Zack made the rounds of the fencing, Rosa noticed the blackberries were ripening. If there were enough she'd make a cobbler, buy some cream and whip it for topping. Sean would love it.

On the farm the back fields were bordered with blackberry bushes, and she'd canned blackberry jam and syrup for the entire year with enough to give away. Cobblers had been her specialty, with a nutty whole wheat crust. Some friends brought fresh milk, daily, with its wide band of dark cream at the top. Rosa would skim most of it off for whipping and stir in the rest for richness. Sean had loved that milk, drinking as much as he'd wanted, and for free. Rosa thought of her grandmother—the image of the dark-skinned, Indian-looking, old woman with a small child by the hand, taking a much-folded shopping bag to the the place where free canned goods were handed out, and sometimes, rarely, fresh milk.

That was it, wasn't it? The abundance on the farm had revealed its secret to Rosa. The Earth was there—fertile, yielding, nurturing—and so many people had forgotten. They'd forgotten the Earth was under them—spinning, breathing, dreaming, sustaining them. Wasn't that when her paintings began to mirror the Earth, the whole Earth, as she saw it? Of course.

How many times she'd wanted to show her grandmother the budding tomato plants, the shiny-leafed jalapeños, the immense squash of every variety, the rows and rows of tassling corn. Rosa's grandmother told her that she'd ground corn for the tortillas with a metate as a girl, and that her mother had grown her own corn. Everywhere her grandmother lived her box of cilantro, basil and oregano followed her—and flowers, how she'd loved flowers. Her herbal teas and plasters for stickness. People had once come to her, she'd said, for her medicines.

Rosa reached for a watering pot and began to pick the ripened blackberries, eating one now and then. They were warm from the morning sun, firm and sweet. No, her grandmother hadn't forgotten the Earth, but she'd believed them. She'd come to believe she was poor, that she, somehow, deserved poverty. That she didn't belong here in this country, but then she'd refused to go back to Mexico with her brothers. Hadn't her husband been thrown out like a criminal for his politics, taken to the border with only what they could carry. No, she never went back. Then, her grandmother's anger flashed out at her, clear as the morning sun. "Do you make the blackberries grow, Mamacita?" Rosa asked the warm air.

Rosa continued picking the ripe ones, the air swirling around her. She brought the blackberries in. There'd be enough for a cobbler. Just enough. She left the back door open for gusts of warm wind and more light, so Zack followed her in and curled up in a corner on a throw rug. He looked at her expectantly, asking, she felt, for a walk. "I'll take you later, Zack. I promise." He made a grumbling sound and settled in. "Go on outside, grouch," Rosa laughed.

"Hey, Mom! You down there?" Sean yelled.

"Me and the dog," Rosa answered him.

"How about if I line up some car possibilities and we can take a look tomorrow?"

"That's fine. Go ahead. I'm going to be down here for a few hours. Do you want to go for a walk later?"

"Okay. Do you want some scrambled eggs?"

"No, thanks. I picked enough blackberries for a cobbler tonight."

"All right!"

Sean slammed the door and Rosa could hear him start the shower. She put on a tape, piano music, and worked on the continents, defining them further. She wanted that quality of a living light surrounding the entire Earth, and yet that light coming up from the Earth as well. Rosa glanced at the shawl, Quetzalpetlatl's shawl, and the little spider was there, waiting, and she knew, then, she'd finish it in Lupine Meadows. She refused to look at the lilac sky; it never failed to disturb her with its spectral fluctuations. Today she would work on the rainbow painting, wrestle with the light surrounding the Earth, and see if she could get that right. And where, she asked herself, where was that rainbow ending, and why?

When Rosa went upstairs Sean was lying on the rug with ear phones on listening to music. She made a cheese and onion sandwich, and ate it with some milk.

Sean took off the ear phones. "There's four good possibilities. Good prices and years. They're all fairly close by, too."

"Okay. Well, anything that looks real good has to have a compression check, the brakes and all that."

Sean was smiling. "I know that, Mom."

"Are you ready to go for a walk?"

"I should really go for a run, but I'll go early tomorrow morning. Do you mind if I run a little right now?" he asked.

"Go ahead. We'll go to the long stretch beach, and I'll meet you at the end when you're done. Come on, let's go."

Zack didn't know whether to go with Rosa or Sean, but when Sean started running in the opposite direction, and Rosa started walking away, Zack ran with Sean for a quarter mile and then doubled back to Rosa. She grabbed him by the ears and snout. "It's Hector The Protector. Hi, old Zack. Do you know where we're going to live, old Zack? In the mountains with the wolves. You'll have your own territory up there. You sure will." Rosa looked around to see if anyone was witnessing her conversation. No one she could see. "Let's go, Zack," she said as she began to run.

The day was still sunny and the spray from the sea was delicious. A fine mist hung in the air by the tideline. A couple of joggers went by, and each time she thought it was Sean. At the end she sat down in the warm sand and took off her shoes. The tide was too high and the Sea Throne was covered. That day of the low tide had been rare, she realized.

In the distance Rosa saw a runner coming toward her, and she knew it was Sean. She called to Zack, "Hey Zack, there's Sean! Go on! Go on, Zack!" Rosa pointed toward the runner and Zack took off.

Sean started winding down and let out a big yell. He came up to Rosa. "You know, I missed the ocean!" He grabbed Zack and tumbled around with him like he had as a kid, Zack and he growling at each other.

"Someday Zack's going to forget you're a human," Rosa laughed. "Remember that time you were pretending to eat his food and he almost bit you?"

"He wouldn't bite me. Would you, Zack? Would you? He knows I'm the alpha wolf. Right, Zack boy?" Sean pinned Zack to the sand.

"If Lisa could see you now."

"Come on, Zack. Three licks and you're up. Three little kisses, Zack."

"She'd never kiss you again, that's for sure."

Sean let Zack up, and he sat up facing the sea to Rosa's left.

In a sombre tone he said, "That's the truth."

"I was just kidding, Sean," Rosa said.

"I'm not."

"Is something wrong? You look so serious."

Sean steeled himself and said, "Lisa thinks she might be pregnant."

Astonished—foolishly astonished, she told herself—she asked, "Why?"

"Her period was over two weeks late."

"Did she say if that's ever happened before? It does happen, you know."

"She said it's never happened to her, and, plus, she felt funny." Sean continued to stare at the ocean.

"Have you called her to see how she is?"

"I called this morning. She's going to the doctor next week."

Rosa asked softly, "Did you guys use anything?"

"I thought she did, and she thought it was okay. She seemed to know what she was doing, so I thought she did." Sean put his face in his hands.

"How do you feel about it? That is, if she's pregnant."

"I feel pretty damned stupid, and lousy, that she has to go through all this. Lisa wants to have an abortion. We talked about getting married, but then we realized how stupid that'd be. Both of us want to go to university and run track." Sean looked up at Rosa. "You were my age when I was born, weren't you?"

"Yes, I was." Rosa saw the boy and the man taking turns right in front of her eyes. Had she looked that transparently vulnerable when she'd carried Sean in her body seventeen years ago?

"So you both decided an abortion would be best?"

"Yeah."

"How will her parents take this? Did she say?"

"She said they wouldn't be thrilled or anything, but that she was sure they'd understand. Her mother made sure she took the pill when she told her she was seeing someone, but the pill made her feel lousy, so she stopped taking it."

"So you don't think you should be up there?" Rosa asked him.

"Lisa said it's better if she takes care of things by herself. But what gets me is that she's pissed at me. I can tell. Well, shit, I can't blame her. We should've talked about it. Birth control, I mean." Sean paused, and then said, "This will never happen again, that's for sure. It's just not worth it." He sounded miserable, but not whiney, and the boy and the man fused for the moment.

"I wouldn't go that far, Sean. I think it's worth it—love's worth it. Six weeks, six months, sixty years—it's worth it." Rosa stopped to gather her thoughts, and a seagull screeched overhead. "You're learning about love. That's the one they don't give any degrees in, right? Because it never stops, the learning. Next time you'll know something new. Next time you'll know half of it's your responsibility, and if you don't forget you're ahead of the game."

"I guess you're right. You're the expert."

Rosa laughed, "Hardly. Did you hear last night?"

"Kind of." Sean smiled.

"I loved him, Sean, and it was worth it, but I just can't stay anymore. It's like we're outgrowing each other. I'm changing, he's changing, and the differences are too great. That happens, that's all I know."

"Are you going to make that cobbler? I'll help you cut and stuff. I'm feeling pretty hungry."

Rosa got up and touched his shoulder for a moment, lightly she hoped. "Come on. Do you still want that curry?"

"For sure," Sean answered her.

"Then you can piece the chicken."

"I thought so."

Zack ran ahead, and a wave caught them once up to their knees. Rosa felt Sean's reserve return, and the new distance between them. She wondered how much of what she'd said he'd really heard; but then she realized she couldn't worry about that. Not really. She'd said what she'd said because she loved him, and that would have to be enough. Because it was, it *was* worth it. Wasn't it?

Just as Rosa was getting ready for bed with a glass of brandy, Carmen called.

"Rosa! Where have you been, girl? I haven't heard from you in over two months!"

"You wouldn't believe me if I told you. My life's gotten crazy again. Look, why don't we get together tomorrow night. I could drop over."

Carmen was laughing. "Okay. I guess I can wait for the juicy details. You all right?" she asked.

"I'm okay. Would six be okay? Tomorrow night." Rosa's voice sounded tired. It'd been another long day.

"Sure. See you tomorrow. Don't take anything too seriously, mujer. Bye, Rosa."

"Good night, Carmen."

Rosa got up to get another brandy when the front door opened. Julio came in. Rosa poured the brandy and walked, quickly, to the bedroom, and shut the door behind her.

Julio knocked on the door, softly. "Rosa, can I speak to you? Please?"

She didn't answer.

He knocked again. "I just want to talk to you for a few minutes, Rosa."

Rosa had no real desire to, but she was aware of Sean in the next room, and she dreaded another scene. "Okay, come in," she said in a guarded way.

Julio came in looking the prototype of apology, and he carefully sat down by the bed. "I just want to tell you that I'm sorry about your friend Rob, and that it won't happen again. I'll try to let the remaining time here be, at least, peaceful."

Rosa was silent.

"I found a place close by, and there's plenty of room for Sean if he wants to stay with me. Is he going with you?"

"He doesn't know yet."

"Well, he's welcome to stay with me. In fact, I'd kind of like it," Julio tried to catch her eye and smile.

"I'll tell him. I'm pretty tired. Listen, if you want we can take turns sleeping here and the front room. That's only fair," Rosa said avoiding his eyes.

"No, you take the bedroom. I'll be working in the darkroom finishing some things up for the next couple of weeks."

"Okay, thanks," she said shortly. "Do you mind turning off the light? I'm very tired, Julio."

Julio's face flickered between hurt and anger, but he got up and turned off the light. At the door he said, "Good night, Rosa."

She didn't answer him. She finished the brandy in the dark. As she opened the window wider for the night she caught sight of a brief, shooting star, and she thought of Lisa's pregnancy, Sean's first child. Rosa knew it was the only thing they could do besides Lisa having the baby, and then giving the child up for adoption. Clearly, Lisa didn't want to do that, and Rosa didn't blame her. How inhuman it would be to carry a child for nine months and never see it again, ever. Rosa understood Lisa's passion—all or nothing. She saw the bold dark-haired woman in the photo, and she loved her though she didn't know her. She wished her strength and luck and love; and to the child she carried she wished another time, another chance, another star.

Julio went out to the backyard and paced. There was nothing he could do anymore. Nothing. He finally sat and watched the fog creep in, blotting the stars out. It made him even lonelier to see the stars disappear, but even if he could have a choice in the matter he'd prefer it that way. No stars. Nothing. He'd forgotten the simplest rule of the desert: patience. The sun had claimed him, and nothing could quench his thirst. No, he wouldn't drink anything tonight— he'd had enough. Julio went upstairs and filled a large glass with ice and water. He drank it all at once, and then lay flat on the living room floor. Unyielding as it was, it comforted him with the painful knowledge of its hardness, its lack, that so perfectly matched his own. There were no tears; that implied a softening, and he felt that if he softened he might disintegrate. Die. No, he wouldn't die. He would fall in love with nothing. Look how beautiful nothing could be, he thought, imagining perfect darkness. Perfect darkness. He fell asleep.

Sean wondered if he'd ever be able to go to sleep as the boring movie kept right on going. Flick, flick, flick—the light changes projected onto the walls made him feel like he was in outer space. Yeah, that's what I am, he told himself, a fucking Space Cadet. Boy's pee-pee goes in girl's pussy, little people come out—and you don't even have to be married. He groaned and turned the TV off. He was starting to feel like his mind had turned to mush the way Rosa always said it would—and there he was in space without Captain Kirk, without Spock. Without Lisa.

The drone of the senseless dialogue was gone, and Sean pushed his window open behind him. The ocean, at this time of night, could usually be heard. There it was. He turned onto his stomach and passed out.

They're by the river. Lisa is nude and bent over examining something by the water's edge. "Look, Sean. Here." She hands him something. The sun is bright, but he can't feel it. He sees her with her hand outstretched, saying, "Look, Sean. Here," but it's so hard to move. It's impossible to move toward her. He's helpless, entirely helpless, and he just can't move. He tries to speak to her, and that, too, is impossible. Lisa looks calm, unsmiling, with her hand, outstretched, holding something.

Julio woke toward one o'clock surrounded by cold and realized he was on the floor without covers. He stumbled to the bathroom, to the closet for the sleeping bag and threw it down, stripped, and climbed in.

His old hunting teacher, Gonzales, is standing in front of him, smiling. Behind him the mountains become clear, and then the desert around them. Without a word Gonzales points to the mountain lion tracks, and he looks up at Julio, again, and smiles.

Rosa couldn't get comfortable. Every position made her sweat as though she were running a fever, and if she took off the covers she felt chilled.

She enters an emptiness, and simply stands there. Something is placed in her arms. A baby, her grandchild. For a moment, a brief moment, she feels his weight. Then a sharp, endless sorrow.

The next morning Julio was up first and prepared coffee. He began frying strips of bacon.

Sean walked into the kitchen finding Julio at the stove. "Hey, how's it going, Julio? Any coffee yet?"

"Just made. Pour yourself a cup. How was your vacation?"

"A lot of work, believe me. But I had a good time. So, we're moving, I hear. Where're you going?" Sean asked.

"I told Rosa last night that I found an apartment close by, and that if you want to stay with me, you're welcome. It's one bedroom, but you could take over the front room. Kind of a nice place. A weight room and sauna downstairs, and a view of the ocean." Julio struggled to keep the depression out of his voice. "If you could chip in a hundred a month, that'd do it. And share the food."

"Is it in one of those apartment complex places by the school?"

"Yeah. The big one behind the shopping center. Do you want an egg? I just fried up plenty of bacon. Is your mother up?"

Sean sipped his coffee. "Yeah, I'll take an egg. Thanks." He walked over to Rosa's door and knocked.

"Yes?" Rosa answered.

"Do you want some bacon and eggs, Mom?"

Rosa hesitated but then said, "Okay, be right out."

Sean went back to the kitchen. "She'll be right out. It looks like we're going to look at cars today. Maybe a Karmann Ghia."

"Good, you'll need one. How do you feel about your mother going to this place in the mountains?" Julio carefully asked.

Sean felt a trap, but, then, he wasn't really on anyone's side. Not really. "Well, I think it's her business. Though moving to the mountains seems a little radical, and I sure didn't expect the house to be sold when I got back. Shit, I don't know."

Julio smiled, "Me either, Sean. I wonder how she's going to take those winters by herself?"

Rosa walked in. "Good morning," she said and poured herself a cup of coffee. "I'll get my own egg. You two go ahead."

"Do you want to take off to see about the cars after breakfast? I got three lined up." Sean looked at her.

"I said I would. Sure. But if we see anything good, it gets a compression check and all," Rosa reminded him. She poured the scrambled eggs into a pan with garlic and onions.

"I told Sean about the apartment, Rosa," Julio said with a tinge of I-beat-you-to-it in his voice.

Rosa shot him an angry look. "Well, I said it's up to Sean. Entirely." She looked at Sean and then turned her back on both of them, stirring her eggs.

"Hey, look, I'll think about it. Mom, do you mind frying me another egg?"

"I'll put it on for you." Rosa took her breakfast to the kitchen window and ate alone. "No offense intended. I just want some air," she said opening the window. Fog clung to everything. She wondered what it was like in the mountains, at her cabin right then. Were the oak trees in front losing their leaves? Were there deer tracks in the meadow? Where was her wolf?

Rosa could hear Sean and Julio laughing, and it made her feel defensive. She washed her dishes, quickly. "Sean, I'll be ready in a minute," she said and left the room.

As she got dressed she looked in the mirror, closely, and told herself, No more crying, at least not for petty shit like that. Would it hurt her if Sean sided against her? Of course, it would. But why should he? Just thinking about it stabbed her with pain, but she knew Sean had to decide his life from now on. Even if he went to live with Julio it didn't necessarily mean he'd be against her, or turn against her, she reminded herself. Rosa sat on the edge of the bath tub and visualized her wolf laying in the sun without a master. No one had ever mastered her, not even Rosa. Rosa smiled.

Her belly itched. She lowered her pants to take a good look at her tattoo. It was a little inflamed at the edges, and a hint of a scab was forming. It itched and felt tender, sore. It would heal now, but first it had to disappear behind the dark, dead skin. Entirely.

The Karmann Ghia worked out, and it was exactly what Sean wanted. Almost, anyway. It was a sports car, got good gas mileage, had good compression and brakes. In fact, new brakes. And it was a bright yellow. Rosa paid for it by check, and as Sean put the key into the ignition, Rosa said, "Don't forget the wood pile, my son."

Sean looked up and laughed. "No way! Thanks, Mom. What can I say? I don't believe it!"

"I know it's tempting to drive around, but you're not insured yet, so drive straight home."

"Are you kidding?" he almost moaned.

"No, I'm serious. Really, Sean. You're not insured. I'll add you to my insurance, and I'll pay the first six months, then you take over. But go straight home. I'll add you Monday."

He just glared at her.

"I'm going to Carmen's, so I'll see you back at the house. Drive safely, if at all possible," she teased.

"Right," Sean muttered.

Rosa had a fleeting urge to tail him home to make sure, and instantly dismissed it. She had to trust him sometime, starting now.

"The car looks good. I think we got a good one. See you later," Rosa said without smiling.

Sean pulled away without a wave.

Fucking brat, she thought to herself. Rosa walked to her car and calmed down—it was his first car. Calm down, Rosa, she told herself.

She stopped to get a bottle of champagne to take to Carmen's. They'd lived next door to each other when their kids were little, and their two families were like one big family. They'd shared food, children, much laughter, and the kind of day to day friendship that's wearing and wonderful at once. Rosa thought of Carmen's face. There was such a strength in it, in her dark, Indian face. She and her husband, Alejandro, were from Guatemala, though Carmen had grown up in San Francisco. They were still together after eighteen years. Both Carmen and Alejandro hadn't really understood when Rosa left Sean's father. Yes, yes, he'd hit her, but didn't that happen in marriages sometimes, she could hear them thinking—though Alejandro would've never, in his wildest dreams, hit Carmen.

Rosa loved them both, but she wondered how this turn in her life would effect them. And, of course, there were things she'd told Carmen that she couldn't tell Alejandro. Maybe Carmen would understand.

Now Rosa almost dreaded the visit, but she was pulling up to the house and turning off the motor. Rosa rang the bell and knocked, but no one came to the door. Carmen's car was there, so she tried the door and it was open. She walked through the house and started downstairs yelling, "Carmen, where are you?"

"Down here! I didn't hear the bell, damn it!" Carmen appeared and, with an immense smile, hugged Rosa. "What is that? Booze? Right up my alley. I'm pooped. I love those little kids, but sometimes thirty-five preschoolers can get me talking to myself," she laughed.

"I still don't understand how you can teach preschoolers after your own four kids. After our combined kids, I got the message," Rosa laughed.

"I know. I know. I don't know how long I'll last. Here, I'll get some glasses. Now, why haven't I heard from you in so long?"

"I was in the mountains buying a house."

"Buying a what?" Carmen almost yelled.

"I'm going to live in the mountains," Rosa said, popping the champagne cork.

"Girl, have you lost your mind? What about Julio? And Sean?"

"I'm leaving Julio, and Sean has the choice to come if he wants." Rosa realized she was getting somewhat used to the idea. It didn't sound as crazy anymore—at least to her.

Rosa poured the champagne. Carmen was clearly shocked.

"Rosa, why are you leaving? Are you sure you're doing the right thing?" Carmen modulated her voice to a register of calm.

Rosa looked at Carmen, her old friend, and said, "No, but I've got to do it. The why isn't clear, but the must is. And part of the truth is, I can't stand Julio anymore. Do you know how jealous he is?"

"That's very Latino. You know that," Carmen said.

"Well, I'm sick to death of it. Fed up to the eyeballs with possessiveness masquerading as love—whatever the hell that is." Rosa's face flushed with the mention of the word "Latino," Latino men— what she'd tried to avoid, until Julio. Both of them brought up by their grandmothers, both of them Mexican—her twin, her nemesis. Both of their families from Sonora—both of them Yaqui Indian.

"Okay, okay, but why go all the way to the mountains, mujer?"

"Do you really want to know?"

Carmen just stared at her.

Rosa returned her gaze and said, "I dreamt it, and then I found it, and I've never lived in a place like it, so silent and separate, and I feel like the idiots of the world are going to blow us up and I'm losing some kind of basic faith, in myself I suppose, but also the kind of faith that believes the Earth is round, and the sun will come up, and that all this shit is really, truly worth it." Rosa took a swallow of champagne, and her hand was trembling as she lifted the glass.

"My God, a seeker of truth! *You* should be the Catholic, or whatever. Pass the booze."

Rosa couldn't help but laugh, but it was half-hearted, and Carmen heard it. Whenever Carmen became serious she averted her face to one side, so that her eyes took on the intensity of a very wise, old woman.

Carmen did this now. "Rosa, I can't pretend to understand what you're doing, but as long as I've known you, in many ways, you've done what I've wanted to do."

They were silent. Rosa poured the remainder of the wine.

"Thank you," Rosa finally said.

"For what? Some truth, Truth Seeker? Have you eaten, mujer?"

"I sure haven't."

"If we don't get out of here, right now, the entire gang is going to show up. I told them we were going somewhere, so they won't miss me. Let's get out of here. Quick!"

Carmen started up the stairs, motioning Rosa to follow.

"After something to eat, we could go dancing. Shall we sneak a dance or two?" Rosa felt like laughing or crying, or laughing and crying. Dancing always seemed to solve the riddle.

"Now you're thinking! Have you actually bought the house yet?" Carmen asked, grabbing a jacket.

"It's in escrow."

"You could still change your mind, you know."

Rosa began to laugh. "I also got a tattoo."

"Don't tell me! Don't tell me! Where, in God's name?"

"Where in Goddess' name, mujer."

"Where in the hell did you put a tattoo?" Carmen began to laugh, and they were out the door.

When Rosa got home there was no sign of Sean's car, anywhere. Her heart began to pound and her face flushed red with anger—and she had just settled so much with her visit with Carmen somehow. She'd felt so light. Rosa slammed the car door and ran up the steps. There were no lights in Sean's room. She went in anyway and noticed one of his bags was gone. He hadn't unpacked yet, and both of them had been right by the closet. She looked in the closet. His sleeping bag was gone, too. Rosa ran downstairs and knocked on Julio's darkroom door.

"Just a minute," he yelled.

Where in the hell is he—where is he? Rosa repeated to herself.

Julio opened the door. "What's up?"

"Have you seen Sean?" The words came out like bullets.

"He came in for a minute and said he'd be gone for the weekend, and that he'd be back Monday. Is something wrong?" he asked, a little too innocently.

"Did he say where he was going?"

"All he said was somewhere up the coast to see a friend," Julio answered smoothly, taking a secret pleasure in her apparent rage.

Fucking wonderful, she thought—take a little ride, why don't you! "Didn't you think it was a bit strange for Sean to be taking off for the weekend right after he gets his car? That maybe he didn't have any insurance? Did you ask him where up the coast he was going?"

"All he said was somewhere up the coast, and besides it seems like everyone here's doing just what they want when they want to. I'm not about to ask questions," Julio said with obvious pleasure.

No, she would not answer that. Rosa turned to leave without speaking. She didn't trust herself to speak.

Julio didn't want her to leave. An argument was better than nothing, but she wasn't even going to fight. Quickly, he flipped the coin.

"Rosa, would you like a hot brandy? He'll be okay. He isn't stupid—you know that," he said in a comforting tone.

Rosa didn't even stop. "No, thanks, Julio. Good night. I'm not stupid either."

She took off her clothes and got in bed. There was still a hangover of laughter, the dancing, which took some of the edge off her rage. Damn it to hell! I don't even know Lisa's last name! Of course, that's where he is! Somewhere in Mendocino County. Then, she thought of the dream she'd had of the child, Sean's child. The pregnancy, the abortion. Oh, Sean, she realized, of course you had to go. Of course.

Rosa turned off the light and opened her window. A light rain was falling. To soften the Earth, she thought. Suddenly, she felt like being held, so intensely, that she imagined going downstairs to Julio, but the memory of the pleasure on his face stopped her.

Her wolf drew near and curled herself at the foot of the bed, silently. Will you show me the way home? Rosa thought, and the thought comforted her. Home? What home? She saw the cold, empty cabin in the vast darkness of the forest, and it was not a comfort. But the wolf didn't howl, or move. She just rested, quietly, alert. She would leave the instant Rosa fell asleep. She would go home.

Rosa thought of Zack. Tomorrow morning a good run, then paint, do not argue with Julio. Do not. See about dropping in on

Erica, a friend and a painter. If everything worked out, the realtor said, since Rosa was assuming a loan, she could move in within two weeks. Rosa realized there were some people she wanted to see before she left. Then Rob Sunday. Lighten up, she told herself, you can always drive back down. But somehow the journey, not so much the six hours, seemed so far away.

The last thing she thought of was Sean, somewhere up the coast, and Julio's words: "Everyone's doing what they want when they want . . ." Sean had snatched his freedom.

Julio continued to work until exhaustion promised a night's sleep, but this was good. He was getting caught up on a backlog of developing. Why did I persist in angering her, he asked himself—why? The image of Gonzales pointing to the mountain lion's tracks came clearly to mind, his slow, patient smile. Patience, Julio, he told himself. Yes, it was time to see about getting a new show together. He felt like shit, but so what? And the war, the soldier, the enemy, was fading with only flashes of the old terror, random death. But the hunt, and the hunter, was exacting and necessary, and, mysteriously, equitable. Yes, he would learn to hunt again—the photo show, the mountain lion, and Rosa.

The next morning Rosa drove down to the beach where she'd taken Rolf. It was an immense, white stretch of beach, and the early morning invited her to run. She ran to the end and back with Zack and sat down to watch the water beginning to reflect the sun's light. It was still cloudy, but the sun shone through in streams of clear, cool light. And the air was so fresh after the light rain; everything was slightly damp. She thought of Rolf and smiled, and she wondered if she'd hear his laugh again.

After Rosa called Erica she worked on the rainbow painting, leaving the shawl alone. She'd definitely decided to save that for the mountains. Rosa glanced at the lilac sky and began to work.

Julio came down about two o'clock, approaching her carefully.

"Am I bothering you?" he asked.

"It's okay. What is it?" Rosa looked at him.

"Do you want a taco? I'm making some. Have you heard from Sean?"

"I have an idea where he's at. Anyway, I'll just wait till he comes back at this point."

"Do you want a taco?"

"I'll take it down here if you don't mind. Thanks. Or I'll come and get it, just give a yell when it's done." She kept a distance in her voice.

"Are you going to be home tonight?" Julio asked.

"I'm going to Erica's. Why?"

Julio hid his disappointment. "I thought I might make something for dinner, that's all." He looked at the painting she was working on. "Looks pretty good. I like that light. It's very much like the one upstairs, right?"

"It's next in a series. Kind of a close-up."

He could see she wanted to work, so he went upstairs.

"I'll bring the taco. Just one?"

"Just call me, Julio. Two would be great."

When he turned to leave she glanced at his back and felt such a wave of pity it surprised her. Jesus Christ, not again, she thought. No, I won't. I won't do it. And then she thought of Sean. He could at least call, damn it.

It was good to see Erica and talk about their work. There was something refreshingly impersonal, and at the same time intensely personal, about their friendship. Impersonal because their work bridged a difficult understanding, and a respect, an earned respect, between them. Intensely personal because their revelations came not all at once, as she usually felt with women friends, but a little at a time, almost painfully conscious.

"Obviously, that lilac sky is telling you something. When I hear you talk like that I'm glad my work is of a more abstract nature. But I love the clear ideas you always seem to work with." Erica looked at her with cool, green eyes—the eyes of a lioness. Her full mane of gold-brown hair completed the effect. Erica conveyed a beautiful balance of instinct and intellect, and it was that quality that drew them together in their comparatively new friendship.

Rosa laughed. "They may be clear to you, Erica, but not to me. That's why I'm just looking at the lilac sky, and that's why I'm enlarging the rainbow painting."

"What I'm saying, I think, is that even in your process there's a certain clarity. From what you tell me, even your dreams are clear. Like this house you dreamt, and now you're buying it. I think that's fantastic, really. If I were to follow my dreams as closely as you do, I might trade my daughter in for a calico cat. The other night I dreamt she turned into a calico cat. What a feeling of relief that was, in the dream." Erica laughed.

"Well, she is three years old. Do you think maybe your dream was giving you some needed relief? I mean, I have those kinds of dreams too, you know. Then, these other kinds. It was my grandmother who brought me up and taught me this way of dreaming, as she called it."

"You don't talk very much about your mother." Erica became uncomfortable. "In fact, not at all."

"No, my grandmother raised me, but actually my mother does live close by. I haven't seen her in quite a while. I just feel a lot of anger toward her. Hey, look it's okay. I don't mind saying it; she's a bitch."

"I see my mother about three or four times a year now, but living in the same city with her and that big Jewish family would drive me nuts. We always have a shouting match, my mother and I, when we first get together. Then, and only then, is everything stabilized."

Rosa was amazed that Erica and her mother shouted at each other at all; Erica seemed so reasonable, and her mother so conservative and calm.

Erica continued. "It's kind of an old power struggle, I suppose, but we love each other. Like my not wanting to get married nearly drove her crazy, but she's finally started to get used to it. In fact, I think she understands."

"Power struggle, of course. That's exactly what Julio and I have been locked into, but no amount of shouting seems to resolve a thing. Now, Sean and I seem to reach more of a resolution. Maybe." Rosa laughed.

"But aren't lovers different?"

"I'd say so."

They both laughed.

"Sometimes Chris and I can barely stand each other. You know, all that stuff. It's definitely a power struggle, but more of a balancing of power without a winner. Yes, I don't know if I could take all that macho stuff, that possessiveness. Chris definitely has his macho side, shall we say—The Male. But he does leave me alone in my person, and in my most personal choices."

Balancing of power—the words echoed in Rosa's mind. "It sounds like it. The fact that you've chosen not to be married, I think, sets the tone. I think it's an excellent idea. You know, I vowed to not get married again, but the man swept me off my feet with the outdoor wedding, a fellow artist, his Spanish in my ear." Rosa laughed. "No, I think you're both very wise to keep it open like this."

"When I went to New York last year I had a lover. It's been over four years since I made love to anyone else. Why should I leave Chris to check someone out if I'm really curious?"

"Did you tell Chris?" Rosa thought of Rolf and agreed.

"We've talked about that option in our relationship, but as an option, not as an abuse. You know, like a weapon."

Rosa thought of Sierra and said, "Yes, I know." Then she felt the depth of her conflict with Julio so sharply she nearly moaned out loud. "It seems like war, doesn't it?" Rosa asked almost in a whisper.

"In a way it is, isn't it? The old balance of power—will we kill each other or accept each other? And between lovers, men and women in this case—thought I'd clarify that," Erica smiled and went on. "Between lovers it's will we fight each other or fuck each other. Anyway, no I didn't tell him because it really had nothing to do with him."

"Erica, what do you think—do you think we're going to survive the century? What is the fucking balance of power?"

"Whenever I look at Dawn's face I think we will, but when I hear the news I think we won't. And when I think of all the kids that died in the concentration camps, I feel like clutching Dawn until she can't breathe, until she's safe inside me again. You know?" Erica asked.

"I sure do," Rosa answered, thinking of her own dream of dying in Germany thirty-four years ago. It was startling to think of it in the middle of their conversation, but she decided to keep it to herself.

"I'm sure that's why I waited to have a child so late, but even I couldn't hold out. Maybe the balance of power is love, whatever that is."

"It seems so obvious sometimes, doesn't it? But then it, love that is, goes and hides. Or at least, I sure can't see it. When I think of the people I've loved, and now they're gone, it makes me almost physically sick. Like the world could disappear in a moment."

"Maybe that's why we paint," Erica said softly, knowing in that moment she answered herself as well.

As Rosa drove home she thought of her mother, and of what she'd said to Erica—"She's a bitch." And it was true. The few times Rosa had attempted any intimacy with her, she'd regretted it. Her mother, Dolores, knew how to open the door just a crack and then slam it right in Rosa's expectant face. Perhaps that was my mistake, she thought, to expect or want anything from that woman. It'd been over a year since Rosa's last attempt to know her, and a persistent inner voice told her to take another look at this woman she could barely stand. Her mother.

There was a note on the kitchen table: "Sean called, said he was in Mendocino, that everything was okay, and that he'd be home Tuesday. Good night, Julio." At last, Rosa thought with relief.

Julio was in Sean's room, so Rosa took the good sleeping bag and a tarp to the backyard. Zack was asleep on his rug in the basement until he sensed Rosa, and excitedly followed her outside. Rosa got into the bag, placed her Buck Knife to her right, and Zack curled next to her, his snout on his paws. The sky was overcast, not a single star was visible, but the night was all around her. She remembered when she left Gene, how she'd opened the curtains one night instead of keeping them closed as she'd always done in the city. How frightened she'd felt, as though by opening the curtains she'd let in the night, the darkness—what she tried to keep out, lock out, especially in the city. How the distant stars seemed to greet her, especially one, and Rosa never shut her curtains again.

Luz, her grandmother's name: Light. Rosa imagined her grandmother's face, and then she heard the words—"Los estoy juntando" (I am gathering). Her grandmother would say that when she was angry, like a threat: "Los estoy juntando." The look, the threat, had always worked with Rosa till the next time, and Rosa had never been spanked. Now, like her grandmother, she was gathering, gathering darkness for the difficult time ahead. Perhaps that's the way to coax a star to shine, she thought. "Estoy juntando la noche. . . ."

Rosa was damp the next morning when she woke up, but she still felt like laughing. Zack was laying in a patch of sun and he wagged his tail when she opened her eyes. She'd dreamt she was shopping in an expensive store. She'd snatched a beautiful, purple leather belt when the salesperson wasn't looking and took it into the dressing room with her. The belt was wide, supple and soft. Rosa'd put it in her purse, and bought a sweater, walking out with it. She hadn't felt the old thrill of stealing since she was a girl, and it made her feel wonderful to remember it. She'd stolen as a girl from necessity and daring, and she'd never been caught. Now, Rosa wanted a beautiful, purple leather belt. Maybe. Maybe not. But now she remembered that old daring.

After breakfast Rosa called her mother. It was early Sunday morning so she was likely to be there unless she was on a church jag, which she periodically did until she got bored with it again. At least, there, she respected her mother's honesty—it bored her. Period.

"Hullo," a voice answered. It was her stepfather. Louie.

"Hi, Louie. Don't faint. It's me, Rosa."

Louie laughed. "Well, I'll be damned. Do ya wanna talk ta yr old lady? Haven't seen ya for a while. Come on by! I'll fix ya some stew." He laughed again.

"I was thinking of coming over today if it doesn't cause World War Three."

Louie laughed louder. "Well, here's yr old lady, Rosa."

"Rosa, honey, where have you been? I've thought of you, you know." Dolores' voice was smooth and sweet, tinged ever-so-slightly with motherly hurt.

"Then why didn't you call me or drop me a line? Anyway, I called to see about dropping by, if that's all right," Rosa said, keeping her voice neutral. It was only when Dolores sensed a caring in Rosa's voice that the door slammed shut.

"Well, sure. You're my daughter, aren't you?"

Rosa didn't answer that but said, "I was thinking of noon. I'll see you at noon."

"We'll have a little something for you to eat, honey."

"Goodbye, Dolores," Rosa said, hanging up with her usual fury at Dolores' pretense of motherly concern. A caricature, Rosa thought. At least in the rejection phase there was a semblance of honesty. What in the hell happened to that woman, Rosa asked herself for the millionth time, and she wondered what possessed her to call Dolores at all.

Erica's talk about her mother, probably. But it seemed they yelled first, then accepted each other. Rosa's mother had always seemed backwards to her. The one cake she could make with any success was a pineapple-upside-down cake. Rosa remembered eating it, still warm, one visit, and then wanting to throw the rest of it on the ceiling as Dolores began a nasty tirade, without any apparent purpose, toward Louie. He took all this in stride—he was largely patient with Dolores' fluctuations. He was retired now, and did all the cooking, which he enjoyed anyway, and kept a garden, a dog and a cat. Louie fed stray dogs and flocks of sparrows, and any kid that really wanted an ice cream could get the money from Louie. He also drank. Then he would rant and rave at everything, including Dolores, though when Rosa had looked closely it looked like he was crying. Rosa'd seen him drunk a couple of times and that was enough. But she liked Louie, very much.

"Did you get Sean's message?" Julio asked, coming into the kitchen.

"Yes, I did. Thanks." Rosa said, pouring herself another cup of coffee.

Julio looked disheveled as though he hadn't wiped the sleep from his eyes yet.

"Did you work in the darkroom again?" she asked.

"Till two. How's Erica? Got any plans today? That is, if you don't mind my asking. Oh, I forgot, you're meeting Rob tonight. Right?" His voice was getting nasty.

"That's right, Julio," Rosa said, leaving the room. She could hear him in the bathroom. She got dressed as quickly as she could, putting a dress and some shoes in a bag. She'd go straight from Dolores' to Rob's. Julio was obviously gearing up for a fit of jealousy.

Julio washed his face, telling himself, breathe, breathe, breathe. What else is there to do but breathe, you idiot. Don't push. He brushed his teeth and combed his hair, and opened the bathroom door, catching Rosa in the hallway.

"Hey, look, my apologies. I didn't have my head on straight yet."

"Forget it, Julio. I've got to go."

"Sean sounded okay. I asked him for a phone number, but he wouldn't give me one. Said he was camping out. He said you'd understand."

"I guess I do. Look, I've got to go," Rosa said, starting for the door.

He was trying, damn it. Why couldn't she at least respond? "Where are you going?" Julio asked in an angry tone.

"None of your damned business," Rosa said, slamming the door.

Before following the temptation to follow her out the door, he made himself stop. He turned around and hit the sofa as hard as he could making a sound of utter exasperation. "Goddam bitch!" he yelled—she's probably going to meet Dr. Robby for a day at the beach. So what am I supposed to do, stay here and take messages? Fuck patience! He decided to get a six pack of good, dark beer and visit someone. Maybe he should visit his woman friend, Joan. They'd been lovers first, though he hadn't told Rosa that part. Yeah, maybe Joan. He'd work in the darkroom tonight. Maybe. He could hardly believe he'd be packing in a week. "Rosa," he said out loud, and the wave of exasperation returned full force.

Rosa rang the bell. She could hear Louie's cocker spaniel barking, then a slight commotion, and then the door opened.

"Beware of the man-eater. The dog, I mean," Louie laughed. His face was flushed in a good natured grin. "Yr mother's in back takin down her underwear. Don't ask me why—it was like she suddenly remembered a roast or somethin. Can't figger that woman out. Come on in!"

"How've you been, Louie?" Rosa laughed. "You look in top

health. You really do. The flowers in front are quite a show. Are the tomatoes and squash in yet?"

"Yeah. I'll cut ya up some for yr steak. Garden onions, too. Like I said, she's out back. I'm goin to pull them onions," he said, and then he was gone.

Louie was a Scot from Texas, as he put it, with steady, blue eyes always on the verge of a joke. He'd been with Dolores for twenty years, and he'd always liked Rosa, giving her a much needed check from time to time in her student years.

Dolores burst into the room. "Sorry to take so long. Had to get some things together for work tomorrow. You've cut your hair. I like it. It makes your hair look fuller. You always were such a pretty little girl."

"I just trimmed it, actually," Rosa answered.

Dolores got the-wistful-mother-look in her eyes and stepped forward to give Rosa a hug. Rosa dreaded it. Why did I come? she asked herself. She let Dolores hug her, but not with the warmth she usually tried to convey.

"Would you like a glass of wine? I just opened some chablis." Dolores started for the kitchen as though Rosa had said yes.

Rosa walked out to the garden and watched Louie pull the onions and rinse them with the hose.

"Do you want me to pick some tomatoes?" she asked.

"Go head. They're all pretty ripe."

"You should can these, Louie."

"Nah, I just give em away. Take some home with ya. Take as much as ya want. Where's Sean?"

"Up in Mendocino County, seeing a girlfriend. What else?"

"How'd he like the woods? I worked up that way myself while back."

Dolores came to the back porch. "I'll say it was a while back. Biblical times, wasn't it?" She gave a loud laugh. "I poured the wine. It's too hot out here for me." She went inside.

"That don't bother me none. In fact, she was carryin on before ya called. So yr comin put her in a good mood."

"Mind your own business, Louie!" Dolores yelled from the kitchen. "There's plenty I could say about you! That's for sure!" She came to the back porch again. "You should've seen him last week. Drunk and locked himself out. Nearly killed himself climbing through the window, and damn near broke his TV set. You old fool!" she yelled.

Louie just laughed. "Entertainment for the neighbors. You don't need no TV with her round. Better go on in fore she starts in on my sex life."

"What sex life?" Dolores yelled, and started laughing. "You must know something I don't know! That's a laugh! His sex life!" She gave a harsh laugh and went inside.

"That's a good mood? No wonder I haven't been here for over a year. Fuck!" Rosa stood up with an arm load of tomatoes.

"That's a good mood," Louie laughed. "She hasn't called me an old bastard yet. She can be charm itself, ya know. I'm sure she's got the big smiles at work." He laughed some more. "It's a good thing she works so I can rest up in the day."

"Oh, shut up, Louie. You old bastard!" Dolores yelled.

Rosa looked at Louie, and he just waved her away.

"She must have her ear next to the window."

"Probly does. Go on in. I'll be there in a minite. I don't pay her no mind unless it comes to knives." He chuckled to himself.

"I heard that, Louie," Dolores said, back on the porch.

"Look, I'm coming in for a while. If you don't calm down I'm going to leave. Maybe he can take it, but I can't," Rosa said with an edge to her voice.

"Louie knows I love him! Don't you, you old bastard!" Dolores laughed, but stopped when she looked at Rosa. "You don't know what he's like when no one's around," she said, trying to justify herself.

"A real monster, I bet," Rosa said stiffly.

Rosa took the chablis into the front room and Dolores followed her.

"How's your painting, honey? Are you still doing that?" Dolores smiled at Rosa, but there was a feeling of panic between them.

"I'm still painting. I'll always be painting. I guess I came to say a kind of goodbye. I'm moving away."

"Where are you and Julio going?" Dolores asked, keeping a thin smile on her face.

"I'm moving to the mountains, six hundred or so miles away, north of here, and Julio's staying here." Rosa was sorry she'd come.

Then Dolores' face changed to genuine concern. "You don't have to go all the way up there because it didn't work out."

"I'm not going to the mountains because of Julio. I'm going because I want to."

"I see," Dolores said almost softly. "Does it snow there?"

"That's what I've been told."

"A real adventure, is that it?" Dolores' face lit up.

"I suppose."

"That's how I felt when I went to work on the army base where I met your father. All those men, and on my own for the first time."

Rosa nearly leaped out of her seat, but she forced herself to stay calm. Dolores had never talked about her father, as though she'd sliced him out of her memory.

"What was he like?" Rosa asked in a calm voice.

Dolores' face darkened. "Grandma told you he was a gringo, right? Well, he was sweet, but lazy, and a real push-over for his family. They got rid of me and you right away." Dolores stood up. "Do you want some more wine or some corn chips with it?"

Rosa could see she wanted to change the subject, but she asked anyway. "What do you mean, got rid of you?"

"I was Mexican and he was blonde, and they couldn't stand that. Look, these are bad memories. We were married. Isn't that what you really want to know?"

"I knew that. Grandma told me," Rosa said, but what she really wanted to say was, Why did you get rid of me?

"Is Sean going with you?" Dolores sat back down and took a sip of her wine.

"He doesn't know yet. So, you went by yourself to Santa Barbara? I thought your sister went with you."

"No, she came later after I had you. Maria helped me take care of you and I went back to work. But I spent over a year there by myself. I had men coming and going," Dolores laughed. "Yes, I had my pick. It was nice, too. They treated me very nice. I even went with a colonel, but he was too stuffy. All self-important. Enough of this yakking. You must be hungry."

Before Rosa could say another word, Dolores got up and left the room.

"Louie! Are the steaks still frozen or what? What are you doing back there, talking to the birds like Saint Francis or something?"

"Hold yr horses. What's the hurry?" Louie said, coming into the kitchen.

"I'll make the salad, old man. You can't make a salad worth a shit. And none of that home made dressing stuff. I'll use mine. It's from the health food store. Keep using that stuff and you're going to keel over. I'll be at your funeral, that's for sure."

Dolores put the radio on, and Rosa could hear what sounded like everything in the kitchen being used.

Louie came in and sat down on the arm of the couch as though prepared to flee at any moment—but, really, he looked poised on the edge of the couch. Rosa realized she'd never seen him actually sit on the couch or in one of the arm chairs, but always on the edge of an arm. These are his terms, she thought—he would not be trapped. He was a big man, thick chested, and his forearms were still powerful, and she thought, as she looked at him framed solidly for the moment, for some inexplicable reason, instead of the usual "This is Louie, this has always been Louie. . . . ," that his skull and face looked Neanderthal. Neanderthal. She'd read somewhere that these ancient Homo sapiens had been extraordinarily gentle, and she'd gotten the feeling from the text that they'd invented love.

"What brings ya ta these neck of the woods?" Louie asked, lighting a cigarette and opening the front door. "Ya know the old lady. Can't stand no cigarette smoke, so I humor her." He laughed.

"Better keep your voice down," Rosa glanced toward the kitchen where the radio blared away. "It looks like I'm moving to the mountains, up in Plumas County. Do you know where that is?"

Surprise and amusement spread over his face like sunshine. He shifted his feet and flicked the cigarette ash into his left hand. "Shor do! Up by Reno, ain't it? Used ta ride the rails through there. Beautiful country. Hard to relax though with all them bears and rattlesnakes." Louie chuckled. "Up in Butte County, where I was loggin, went to the privy, and was coming out when I bumped into this brown bear. Well, he raised up taller an any man, so I decided I had to go to the privy again. Why the hell ya goin up there? Not enough ta fight yr old man, got ta fight the bears too?" He laughed.

"That's about it. I'm dying to fight a bear. The realtor told me that when they were building my cabin they spotted one of the largest mountain lions sighted in a long time one morning when they came to start work. He knew one of the work men, a deputy he said, who does construction on the side. Supposedly, the deputy almost bought the place himself. Anyway, I'm moving in about two weeks, I think."

"Is that boy of yrs, Sean, going with ya? Could put im to work shovellin snow an fightin bears." Louie's face never faltered—the amusement was a permanent condition. "Well, ya must know what yr doin, a smart person like yrself." He laughed loudly.

"What's so damned funny, Louie?" Dolores yelled from the kitchen.

"Nothin much. Jes sittin here talkin ta yr daughter bout shovellin snow an fightin bears," he yelled back, and then lowered his voice.

"Now, there's the one ta fight the bears. Take er with ya, free a charge. Can't git meaner an that!" Louie said and began to laugh loudly again.

Dolores came into the front room flushed from her kitchen exertions. "Sounds like a regular party in here. That kitchen's hotter than hell! We need an air conditioner back there. It traps every beam of sunlight, I bet," she said, eyeing Louie, then Rosa.

"Most folks'd like that, ya know. Keeps the place temperate, as they say. I'll toss on a steak fr ya too, d'ya want one?" he asked Dolores, and then winking at Rosa he said, "Got ta feed the ornery bears."

"Oh, shut up, Louie. Can you manage to broil a steak without putting any of that A-1 Sauce, or whatever you put on it that kills the taste of what you're eating? Just a few onions on top, no garlic or garlic powder—and no salt!"

Louie started walking back to the kitchen.

"I said no salt, Louie! Do you hear me?" Dolores yelled.

"I could give it ta ya raw. Now, that'd be real natral," he said in a guileless tone.

"You're not funny, Louie!" she yelled, and then said in a normal talking voice to Rosa, "Do you want all that A-1 stuff he puts on his steaks?"

"I don't care. I kind of like the way his steaks taste. Instant bar-b-que," Rosa answered as neutrally as possible.

"Do you think it's a good idea to leave Sean on his own down here? He is only seventeen. Men are little boys till they're at least twenty-one."

"He's eighteen, or will be next week," Rosa looked Dolores right in the eye, "and I've been with him all his life. It's up to him if he wants to go with me or stay here."

"Well, if he were my son, I don't think I could leave him to go to any mountains. Girls can take better care of themselves earlier than boys, you know," Dolores said with obvious satisfaction. She knew she was getting to Rosa, and in some dim, blind way she wanted to get the best of her or be gotten the best of. She had no idea how irreparable the words she'd spoken were. To Rosa.

Rosa was enraged. She felt like slapping her right across her foolish face. So she's done it again—snuck right up behind me, clobbered me where it really hurts, Rosa's thoughts burned.

"Is that your personal philosophy on child rearing? Dump the girls at four, and the boys at twenty-one? Your ignorance is astounding. I'm not asking for your damned advice. Is that clear?" Rosa said in a tone so loaded with anger that each word hung in the air for a while pushing itself into her mother's consciousness.

"Well, you don't have to get so angry," Dolores said, and her voice trailed off. She went to her bedroom and slammed the door.

For an instant Rosa felt like crying, the old hurt rose up in her so quickly. And then she thought, No, let her cry. Let her cry. The bitch. Rosa just wanted to leave, but she could hear Louie in the kitchen.

Rosa walked into the kitchen. There was no sound from Dolores' room.

"What's all that bout?" Louie indicated Dolores with a cock of his head.

"She can't take her own medicine," Rosa said in a low voice. "Actually, I was thinking of going, to tell you the truth. I didn't finish my last meal either, did I?"

"Well, it's jes bout done. Seems like a shame ta waste it. I don understand it, she can't wait fr ya ta show, an then all the trouble starts. Women!" Louie picked the steaks out of the broiler in a couple of swift, bumpy gestures.

"What do you mean women? You haven't got a chance in hell when she starts in on you. Anyway, Louie, I'm tired of trying to get to know someone who's supposed to be my mother. Do you know what I mean, damn it!"

"Ya ain't goin ta have no trouble with them bears, I cn see that." Louie smiled. "Now, them wolves is another matter. Yr goin ta hafta outsmart them wolves, ya know? D'ya want mashed tatos an gravy? Yr skin an bones, that's fr sure."

"Sure. I may as well get a layer of fat for the winter," Rosa laughed, relaxing just a little. She realized how much she'd come to love this strange man. The wolves. How did he know about the wolves, her wolf? Rosa looked at his bright, humorous eyes—he just knew, that's all.

Rosa took her plate to the table. "Are you going to eat, Louie?"

"Nah, but I'll take a front row seat ta make sure ya do the eatin," he laughed.

"You know, you've never eaten your own meals, as far as I know," Rosa said.

"Oh, I'll probly have somethin later. Jes not hungry yet is all."

Dolores went into the kitchen. "Is this my steak in the tin foil?"

"Shor is, all yrs. Help yrself."

Rosa waited for her "Shut up, Louie," but she was silent.

Dolores came into the dining room, visibly subdued. She'd put

an attractive auburn wig on—Rosa could remember when her hair
was black and thick and long to her shoulders—and fresh, red lipstick. She was still an attractive woman with clear, healthy skin, light
skin. Dolores never sat in the sun. Without the harsh laughter and
anger, Rosa could see a fresh young woman still there, even younger
than her memories of the dark-haired pretty lady. But this is a tight
rope act, Rosa reminded herself. Just get through the meal, your
annual visit. And leave. Leave. The thought gave her relief.

"Oh, my salad," Dolores remembered. She brought it in, placing
it on the table.

Louie got up saying he was out of cigarettes and that he'd be
back. "D'ya want s'more wine, winos?" he asked Rosa.

"This is enough for me, Louie. Thanks."

Dolores served out two bowls of salad. "Forgot the dressing," she
muttered, going back to the kitchen. She placed the salad dressing on
the table. "How's your steak?" Dolores asked in a pleasant tone.

"Pretty good."

"Do you want some more onions? I'll get you some."

"No, this is fine," Rosa answered, but the stiffness in her voice
wouldn't leave.

"When are you leaving?" Dolores asked in a careful voice.

"Probably two weeks at the most."

Dolores turned the radio off, so the silence between them was
immense and awkward. Rosa ate her steak like a meditation—bite,
chew, chew, chew—nibbling at everything else, and she refused to
look at Dolores, her mother.

"You know, your father was a shocker to my family too, being
English and German. The one time they met, your grandmother
wouldn't even talk to him. I don't think she believed we were really
married."

Rosa was stunned, but she guarded it closely. "He was English
and German? I didn't know that. I mean, my maiden name was
English, so I assumed he was English."

Dolores took note of Rosa's sudden interest. "His father was
English, his mother was German. I went back to the farm for about
six months and nearly went out of my mind. The women there
worked as hard as the horses, and when they saw me they thought
they had a darkie." Dolores winced at the memory.

"Why didn't you tell me all this before?" Rosa asked, knowing
she wouldn't get an answer.

"I just didn't think this kind of dead-and-buried stuff would
interest you," Dolores said, beginning to be defensive.

Rosa breathed for a while and let the silence grow between them again, to Dolores' discomfort.

Trying to keep her voice as even as possible, Rosa said, "I've never asked you why you left me with grandma. It was probably the best thing in the end—but some time, you know, some time, I'd like to know why you had to. Also, anything you'd like to tell me about my father, and that time, I'd like to know."

Tears filled Dolores' eyes, but she stopped them. "Well, what I'll do is, whenever I think of something you might want to know I'll write it down." She put both hands in her lap like a little girl being reprimanded. But that was only for an instant. "Do you want some more wine? I have another bottle stashed in my room."

"Maybe one more glass," Rosa said.

Dolores came back with it. "It's a good one. What do you think?"

"It looks pretty good. I'd like you to do that. To write things down that I might want to know."

Dolores stood there holding the wine opener, her auburn wig perfectly styled, her flowery blouse billowed over her slightly overweight, but strong—one sensed—body, and Rosa noticed her mother's hands were aging.

Louie came in the door. "What, 're yu two at it agin? Call me a drunk! I only drink but twice a month, but yu two'r at it ever day!" Louie laughed and went to the kitchen.

"Oh, shut up, Louie," Dolores said. "Yak, yak, yak—that's all you do, old man."

"I see yr feelin better. It's the wine. Gives ya false curge. Now, mine's natral." He laughed again.

Rosa would finish this glass of wine and leave. German, she thought, rolling it around in her mind. Of course.

"Rob, it's Rosa."

"Where are you?"

"It looks like I'm going to be a little late. I'm at my mother's. Do you have reservations?"

"For seven." Rob sounded a little disappointed.

"Do you think you could change it to eight? I'll be there by six-thirty. I'm sorry to be late, Rob."

"I'll give them a call. See you when you get here."

"I'll be there by six-thirty at the latest, never fear."

Rob laughed. "No problem, lady."

Rosa hung up and picked up her purse, slinging it on her shoulder. Then she walked to the door, and holding the handle she yelled, "Bye, Louie! Thanks for the chow!"

He came to the kitchen door and said, "Don get friendly with no bears! Take care yrself!" Louie gave a wave and disappeared before she could see his eyes.

Dolores walked into the hallway. There was a pained look on her face that she was trying to hide.

"Bye, Dolores. Don't forget to write anything down that you think I might want to know," Rosa said without smiling. She didn't trust herself to smile. Whenever she'd shown any personal warmth towards Dolores, it'd exploded right in her face. So Rosa just faced Dolores as she would an opponent.

"I guess I always hate to see you go," Dolores said softly.

"Why?" Rosa asked in spite of herself, and it took Dolores by surprise.

"I guess it feels like I'll never see you again."

"That's how I always felt about you, Dolores," Rosa said, opening the door. "Take care of yourself. I'll let you know when I get there."

"Okay," Dolores said gathering herself, "don't forget." And then she added, "I'll write you, too."

Rosa started the car and looked back. Dolores was standing on the stairs, smiling and waving. Rosa waved and drove off. Maybe it's this way with all parents and grown children, but in our case there are no memories—no day to day memories to soften the separation—no love to remember, Rosa thought as some tears finally came. Poor Dolores, poor Dolores, the words came suddenly to Rosa—she had no memories either. Of anyone.

Rosa stopped at a park and sat in a sunny, grassy spot to think and collect herself. She gave herself twenty minutes. A young couple with a baby sat on a bright blanket next to her. The baby was learning to walk, and it fell regularly. Rosa thought of Sean at that age, his dark, curly hair, his huge baby smile, and then like a film his ages unrolled—delight and despair. Yes, I have love to remember. I do.

The sun was wonderful. It filled her as she lay back and closed her eyes. But, then, a shadow crossed her, like winter, a terrible coldness, a thief that could make you forget the warmth of the sun.

Rosa rang Rob's bell and he instantly opened the door. He was dressed in a tweed sports coat, dark slacks, and a deep burgundy shirt.

She gave him a thin, purse-lipped wolf whistle, and laughed. "It's the best I can do. You look great, like you're going out or something."

Rob blushed, "I am."

"Look, I'll change into something else. I brought a dress in honor of the expensive restaurant," she laughed. "Be out in a minute."

Soft, Brazilian jazz was playing, and it soothed her. His stereo system was excellent, with its four immense speakers throughout the house. In the bathroom Rob had stacked wooden crates to hold towels and magazines, and his shower curtain was falling apart. By the window there was a small, flowering cactus sending up a pale, pink flower from the center of its heart.

Rosa glanced at the tattoo; it was entirely scabbed now and very sore. She took out a small bottle of oil and smoothed some on. She'd chosen the purple, fuzzy knit dress, the one she'd gotten half-off because of a rip in the seam. She'd sewn it. And some sandals. She clipped a silver-chained belt to her waist, and brushed her hair.

Rob smiled when she came out. "Very nice. How's your tattoo?"

"It's an ugly scab, but healing, Dr. Simon. You know, it hurts more now than when he actually did the tattoo itself."

Rob laughed. "That's what you get for being wild, Ms. Luján. This place is across town, so we probably should get going."

"Shall we take my car?" Rosa suggested.

"I'm so sure of my masculinity, I'll even let you drive," Rob said with a serious face.

"Hold still so I can barf on you!" Rosa yelled.

"How crude, Ms. Luján. I'm very shocked," Rob said, smiling; his eyebrows arched in that curious fashion of detached delight.

Rob was always nervous in traffic, and he actually asked her to slow down a little. "Too many emergency cleanups as an intern," he said.

"Then why do you persist in driving around on that motorcycle?"

"Why did you get a tattoo?"

Rosa looked at him and slyly smiled. "So, you're taking me to a real French restaurant, huh? I purposely nibbled today for this event."

"How was your mother's? You rarely go, right?"

"Today I remembered why, again. But, you know, Rob, today was actually different. Something happened. Something changed. For one thing, I found out I'm German. How's that? She slipped and told me. Supposedly, she assumed I knew."

"How bizarre." Rob looked at her with genuine sympathy. "Do you mean she never told you what your origins are?"

"Well, like I told you, my grandmother brought me up, and a

gringo was a gringo as far as she was concerned. As for my mother, you'd have to meet her to believe her."

"Anywhere you can find a parking place from now on," Rob said.

Their table was waiting for them, a candle lit, and a red rose to the side in a thin, crystal vase. The walls were exposed wood, bunches of dried flowers were placed at the door in a huge basket, and dried, braided rushes threaded with old, red ribbon hung on the walls making it seem like a country inn rather than an expensive French restaurant in the middle of the city.

"Well, I like it, of course," Rosa smiled.

"I thought you would. Order anything you want, choose the wine, go for it. I'm going to miss you."

"Are you on call tonight?"

"Kind of. Just for consultation. If there's an emergency, someone else'll cover. You know, when you were talking about your mother I started thinking about my own family."

The waiter came at that moment and began to list and explain the specialties of the house. It was a little awkward because the waiter looked so unhappy.

"Well, I know what I want. The beef dish sounds great. I can't say it. The second one you mentioned," Rosa said.

Rob ordered the salmon specialty, baked in wine. Then they chose their salad dressings, starch and vegetable. The waiter seemed to relax when he realized they weren't going to grill him for an hour, and he brought a Sonoma Petite Sirah, opened it, poured the taster, waited for the verdict—it was dry and delicious—and left.

"Poor guy," Rob said. "Maybe he's pre-med."

"Really. I think he was relieved when I couldn't say the beef dish. Do you suppose people practice the menu before they come?"

Rob laughed and took a sip of the wine. "Do you know that I hate my family?"

"What did you say?"

"I said I hate my family. My older brothers kicked my ass the whole time I was growing up." Rob looked bitter.

"What do you mean by kicking your ass? A lot of older brothers beat up their little brothers, isn't that right?"

Rob's face froze into anger.

"I'm not trying to minimize what you're saying. I'm sorry. But what do you mean, Rob?" Rosa asked gently.

"I mean they nearly broke every bone in my goddamned body by the time I was thirteen." Rob's body began to tremble, but he controlled himself.

"Where were your parents?"

"We were well-to-do. My father's a dentist. They just didn't care. Simple as that. When I tried, in the beginning, to tell my mother they'd drag me out, right in front of her, and as I cried she told me not to be such a cry baby. She'd take me in for broken bones and she'd lie and say I'd fallen. They didn't want me, at all. I was totally unexpected." His voice was matter-of-fact, and, therefore, more painful because it was the truth. In a minute Rob's face assumed the expression she recognized as his: irony.

"How horrible. She and your father should've protected you. I'm so sorry, Rob." Rosa reached over and touched his hand with her fingertips.

"The last time I saw them, all of them, at a family gathering, I could barely keep it together. My brothers tried to joke about me being the cry baby, and I told them they were a bunch of sick sadists, and I left. Yes. I hate them." Rob looked at Rosa, closely, to see if she understood.

"I can see why, but it must be hard for you. It is, isn't it?"

The salads arrived, warm bread, and a tureen of soup. They'd requested the soup with the salads. They ate quietly for a while.

"You know, Rosa, I think we come here—to Earth, I mean—to see if we can love in spite of everything. And I mean, in spite of everything. So, I had to put my love somewhere else, the best way I could."

"In spite of nuclear threat, ongoing wars, and the fact that the sun will burn out eventually. Is that it?" Rosa said, trying to smile.

Rob looked up at her. His eyes were fierce. "I don't believe that scientific shit! I don't believe the sun will ever go out! Don't even say it!" he said, almost yelling.

"Rob, are you kidding? The sun is a star, and all stars live and die."

"Not the sun!" he said firmly, lowering his voice, aware of the tables next to them.

"You really believe that?" Rosa was astounded. She'd never seen him so emphatic, so angry.

"Yes, I do."

"Well, since I, personally, won't be around to witness the outcome, I hope you're right." Rosa felt unnerved. On the one hand, she'd just heard Rob tell her a horrible childhood story—and she'd been ready to accept that—but when he told her he refused to believe the sun would burn out, it upset her sense of order. She had accepted the theory that the sun would burn out, and here was this man, a doctor, passionately refusing to believe the scientific theory of his time. She loved him for it. It didn't make sense. Who the fuck cares, she thought, anyway? If the sun went out, wouldn't there be another sun, and another sun, and another sun—even if it were only the sun we remembered?

Rob looked at Rosa, who was deep in thought, and he asked her, "Do you think I'm crazy?" He looked at her without flinching.

She looked back at him and said, "Maybe you're one of the ones who'll remember the sun for us if it ever does go out. Do you think I'm crazy?"

Rob laughed loudly.

Later, as Rosa fell into sleep, she was amazed at how equally elated and exhausted she felt. Briefly, Rosa wondered why she felt so alone in spite of Rob and the others, as though some unnameable part of her were beyond human comfort. She thought of Sean, Sierra, Rob, Julio, and she failed to understand why she felt compelled to leave and change everything.

Was freedom something everyone had to steal? Perhaps, she thought. But first they had to want it. More than love? Perhaps. Perhaps not.

The wolf was back, and she'd brought the north wind in her fur—the sharp edge of the coming winter. She was silent and impatient as Rosa fell asleep.

Part Two

I leave the coast, the city, flocks of seagulls, and drive into the fertile valleys. Cows graze, black, against the shock of green here, the dry, dead grasses there. Tame horses stand still. Nothing really runs. Nothing seems to be filled with what will not let me rest until I come to it. Until I come to it. And when I come to it, will I know that place? Will it be the place I had to go? Will the urge inside me rest, there? Will I come to it? Will I?

So far away. The mountains appear, finally. Color, mass, color, mass. They are not real to me, yet. How stern the stones are. They do not speak to me, yet. The tunnels I pass through are terrible— will there always be light at the end? Will there? And the drops to the river below begin to look enticing, and the river looks so alive, and I feel so dead.

I concentrate on my arms and hands steering the truck, my eyes that guide me, and beautiful things appear though I do not ask them to. A single lily. Enormous clouds.

Exposed rock the color of dried blood. The mountain bleeds. Does it? If it does, we begin to understand each other.

"Do you want me to drive for a while? Just let me know," Sean reminded Rosa.

"Oh, that's okay. You drove to Marysville, and that's fair enough. It's funny driving such a big truck, my refrigerator behind me." Rosa smiled.

Julio was driving behind them with a patient look on his face. They'd packed and cleaned together, moved him in, and now it was Rosa's turn.

Sean would stay with Julio, he'd finally told Rosa. His chances of a scholarship were much better at an urban junior college. "It must be nice," he'd said, "but what the hell would I do out there?"

So, Rosa began to imagine being without him for the first time in her life since he was born, and it stung—no, it ached—like an open wound. A freshly opened wound. But she kept it to herself, and she didn't let her tears even rise because then they'd fall. Hadn't she said it was his choice?

Sean had come home from Lisa's three days late. A call: "I just can't get back yet. She wants me to stay. I'm staying in the guest room." He gave Rosa the phone number, but he asked her not to call unless she really had to. "You're okay, Sean?" He sounded soft-voiced and depressed. "Yeah, I'm okay." "It takes a lot of courage to do what you're doing." Silence. "It takes more to do what she's doing." "Take care, Sean, and see you when you get here. You're insured now, by the way." He laughed. "Thanks."

Rosa looked at Sean from the corner of her eye. Now he knows sorrow, she thought. Now he knows.

They stopped for drinks a few times, and to let Zack out to do his rounds.

In the last couple of weeks, as the separation became a reality, a mutual restraint, a forced respect, emerged between Rosa and Julio. As they packed each room it felt as though parts of their bodies were being disengaged, piece by piece. Which words did that chair hold? That lamp? The dishes?

They became silent, efficient, kind.

Julio brought her a mineral water, and Zack disappeared into the bushes, excitedly. He handed Sean a beer.

"We could just unpack the essentials today, go out to eat, and finish tomorrow," Julio suggested.

"That sounds good," Rosa answered. "Zack!" she yelled. "Get over here!"

Zack appeared covered with dry leaves and panting with pleasure. Rosa opened the car door and he reluctantly jumped in.

"There'll be more, old Zack," she laughed.

As Rosa pulled herself up to the cab of the truck she caught a sulky look of disdain, briefly, on Julio's face. He'd assumed he'd drive the truck, and now Rosa was driving it through the narrow mountain pass. It'd taken her about thirty miles to really get used to it, but now the dimensions of the truck felt familiar.

Julio waved to her as he got into the car to dispel the display of negativity. Okay, mountain woman, let's see how you take to the woods, he thought, silently, sulkily. You can't talk winter out of coming. You've got some things to learn, Rosa.

Now, he couldn't believe he would leave her here. Her carefully wrapped and padded canvases, her clothing, her things. His wife. Julio gripped the steering wheel like he'd strangle it, took a sip of beer, and listened to his breathing. Something—some farfetched presence caught his attention to the left, and when he looked he saw ridge after ridge of forest, and a brief image of a mountain lion came to mind. He laughed deep in his throat. It wouldn't surprise me, he thought, in the least. And the presence, whatever it was, bolstered him. Paws. Paw prints. His mind raced ahead.

"Are you tired yet?" Sean asked.

"Not really. But thanks," Rosa answered.

"I can probably cut at least two cords this week."

"That sounds okay. I'll just have to buy the rest. Don't worry about it." Every time Rosa looked at Sean a strange, cold feeling of distance appeared and disappeared. It disoriented and alarmed her by turns. This is how you say goodbye to your own child, she realized, and it nearly nauseated her with a peculiar despair. She hadn't exactly felt like herself, but then who would under the circumstances?

"Sean, have you thought about the draft?"

He shot her an acutely worried look. "The instant I turned eighteen. I'm supposed to sign up now, you know."

"What're you going to do about it? You ought to have a plan, I think," Rosa said, trying to sound logical rather than distraught. Distraught at the idea of her son being shipped to Central America if the government's support went beyond money, machinery. It was her money—a deep anger exploded inside of her—buying the automatic weapons and helicopters, the military advice that wiped out entire villages and disemboweled pregnant women. No, she would not, unconsciously, give her son to patriotism. She would not *give* him to any war, the military.

"All I know is, there's a jail term and a fine if you don't register now. Anyway, there're no wars right now. Not really." He glanced at her and looked away.

"Sean, you know there're wars. They're unannounced, but if you lived in El Salvador you'd know it was happening. In fact, you'd be a prime target at your age. You'd probably either be forced to join the military, to slaughter your own people, or be picked up, tortured and killed if you dissented. This country supports that, and that's why I worry about the draft. Have you thought about a C.O.?"

"What's that?"

Rosa looked at Sean mockingly. "You've heard about that more than once in casual conversation in our house. Remember Carl and

Tim? They were both conscientious objectors. They did community work instead of going into the military. But it's something you have to think about, carefully, for yourself. What you'd be saying, in essence, is that you're against the taking of human life for the purpose of war."

"A friend of mine was saying they even want you to say you wouldn't even fight to protect yourself. I think that's pretty stupid and unrealistic." Sean took a sip of his beer and opened his window wide. "You've definitely got some mountains here, Mom. There must be good fishing here."

"I think it's unrealistic and stupid, too, Sean, to not defend yourself if someone means you harm. But the military creates the situation for you. If you're placed in a dangerous situation like Vietnam. . . . Sean, are you listening? Because if you're not, I'm going to save my breath," Rosa said, edgily.

Sean shut the window halfway and looked at his mother with guarded irritation.

"I'm saying this because I care what happens to your ass, in short—and it burns me up that so many young men just go. Especially the brown and black ones, the poor, white ones. Cannon fodder, as they say. A purple heart and back to the ghetto, if they're lucky." Rosa stopped and caught herself—to the point, she reminded herself—afraid to lose Sean's attention.

"If you're sent to a place like Vietnam you'd be conditioned to believe certain people are your enemies, and when they start firing on you, you fire back. You kill because you're forced to, and then it all blurs like it did for some soldiers who started killing everyone— women, children, babies." Rosa paused to see if Sean was shutting her out, but she knew she had to say this to him. She just had to.

"It's the situation, the insane situation, that creates men that kill just to kill. And I'm not saying every soldier did, or does it, but do you want to even be a part of something so dedicated to death? Better to state your stand for global life—do you know what I mean, Sean?"

"Yeah, I think so. Like once you're in the military they have you by the balls and you might do anything." He looked at Rosa, gauging her response.

She gave him a direct glance and put her eyes back on the narrow, curving mountain road. She noticed a grove of aspen by the river beginning to lose their leaves in the late afternoon sun. They were yellow and green, full of light, filtering a steady wind, delicately. Fitfully. Now, the river was no longer far below. Road and river ran together, only the river flowed to the sea, and Rosa was moving away from the sea. Now, she felt the effort, the great effort, it took to swim against the current.

"For the individual, the soldier, that's exactly how it is. Exactly. What I mean by taking a stand for global life, is to refuse to kill someone, a total stranger, for impersonal ideology. Someone else's idea of how the world should be at the moment. Their power struggles. Their politics. You know, these questions will make you come of age. Like, what is your conscience, your consciousness? What would you do if you were ordered to shoot a group of terrified people, women holding children, because they're considered subversive?"

"I get your point," Sean said, quietly. "This is stuff I'll have to think about. Okay, but if someone were to come up and try to hit you, would you fight back?"

"I'd protect myself in any way I could. Maybe I'd be able to talk to them, but if that was out, and they were bigger, I'd probably try to surprise them and then get away. And, honestly, if I had to knock someone out and get away, fine. In other words, Sean, if I have to clobber someone I want it to be personal. Very personal." Rosa thought of her Buck Knife and how she slept with it, and now she wondered if she'd really use it. If she could really plunge it into a human body. She couldn't imagine that part; her mind turned away at that point. But the idea of sleeping without her knife was an impossible one. She wouldn't be hurt or raped. She wouldn't be hurt again. She wouldn't allow it.

Sean was looking at the map. "You really aren't that far from San Francisco, but it does seem like a long time getting here. It feels far away." He looked out the window. "Do you think you're going to be okay living out in this cabin by yourself, speaking of self-defense? Why're you doing this, anyway?" His voice sounded almost angry.

Rosa felt his resentment and then a wave of guilt struck her or snuck out of her own being—she couldn't tell which. She forced her eyes to see the trees, individually. Distinctly. She struggled for words. "I have no idea what it'll be like to live by myself here. All I know is that I have to. Maybe this is my stand for global life, or something like that. Sometimes it just feels so much bigger than me," Rosa said in a contained voice. "But most often, like right now, it feels like I'm taking a stand for my own life. Like if I don't do it I'll die," and then she said to herself, and if I do do it, I'll die.

They were on the outskirts of the county seat, the town of Quincy. All the clubs and churches began to announce themselves. A baseball field to the left, green and grassy—a small airport, a bar, a few motels. Yet everything was muted and dwarfed by the presence of the mountains, and the endless, seemingly endless, forest.

The air had changed. Everything seemed strangely alive, and without knowing it Rosa fought against it. It aroused her and disturbed her, almost equally.

"Are you scared?" Sean asked, finally.

They were passing through the town now, a quiet town. One movie theatre, an ice cream shop, other little shops, a Sears sign, catalog it said.

Rosa was in third gear, going slowly. A few heads turned to look at the moving van. Lupine Meadows was about sixteen miles out of town. It seemed forever to Rosa, and this was town. She couldn't even imagine the cabin now, and she was so close to it. She couldn't imagine the wolf, her wolf. She tried, but she couldn't. The howl, the longing inside her was silent, and Sean's question still remained unanswered.

Rosa looked back at Julio. His eyes seemed intent on the back of her head. Zack was standing up in the rear seat, his nose out the window.

"Yes," she said, and her wolf leaped forward, over a small creek, the uneven stones. Something called her back to the cabin.

The rain had packed the dirt road so that the summer dust clouds didn't greet her this time, but the mud was beginning to form and the huge tires spun a few times, then gripped. A few more rains, a snowfall, and she wouldn't have made it in in time.

How long the dirt road was. Narrow. Rocks showed through, and on the side of the road boulders of every size made way, grudgingly, she felt. She couldn't remember the turn to her cabin, so they followed a dead-end road. A house was being built in the middle of some immense pines. A man was on the roof and he waved, smiling. Then he turned back to his work.

Rosa had to back all the way down the road again—she felt like a fool being lost. I bet Julio's smiling, she thought.

"Tell me how I'm doing on your side, Sean. This thing's too big to turn around. It must be further up. Don't forget, I've only been here once."

"Well, it would help if there were street signs. That place with all the houses and buildings—that's the ranch, right?"

"That's it."

"Looks pretty nice. Maybe I'll check it out for some action," Sean laughed.

"Okay, watch the road for cars. Jesus, that ditch!" Rosa backed up onto the main road again, and she was sweating from the effort, afraid to blow it and have an accident so close to arriving.

"Do you want me to take it, Mom?"

"Thanks, I've got it."

Rosa drove up to the next road and stopped. There was a lot number on a tree, but it wasn't familiar. The motor idled smoothly as she coaxed her tired attention to concentrate.

"Is this it?" Sean asked.

"Wait," Rosa said. She looked back at Julio, and he looked pleased with the situation. "Wait, there's the meadow! There it is! This is it!"

There it was. An empty cabin. Her house. It was nearly entirely hidden by cedar and pine, the oak trees in front. There are no street lights here, she fully realized, and no other houses on this road.

Rosa positioned the truck into the small driveway, backing up four times with Sean giving hand signals. She'd almost said, "Here, Sean, you do it. I'll guide you in," she was so nervous. But she clutched herself, internally, and said, No.

There was a steep incline till it leveled out to the driveway, and Sean was giving her the come-on signal. Rosa eased up on the clutch and looked back one more time over her left shoulder, and a dark shape on the porch startled her. She'd actually seen it, briefly—her wolf. Poised, alert, standing. She looked again. Gone.

Rosa turned off the motor. Silence. She'd caught sight of it from the corner of her eye. It unnerved her, but it also made absolute sense, somehow. She'd made it. She'd driven the damned truck to her doorstep. Rosa felt like crying and laughing, but the vision of the wolf sobered her.

Rosa's stomach growled. She suddenly felt like gnawing bones, the last sweet shreds of meat, and she smiled to herself because at the same time she felt the need, in the same proportion, to crawl into a sleeping bag and collapse into darkness.

She fished the cabin keys out of her purse and jumped to the damp ground. The sharp smells of earth, trees, autumn revived her somewhat. A great ravenous hunger returned.

Sean was looking in the windows. "Kind of dark in there," he said. He looked up at Rosa and saw the exhaustion she couldn't hide. "But it is pretty in a rough way. It looks like you bought a boulder farm," he added with a laugh.

"Just what I need—cheerful words."

Rosa opened the door and, for a moment, the emptiness felt like a permanent condition, a threat to her existence. Can I fill this up? she asked herself.

"Kind of small, isn't it?" Julio's voice sounded loud in the empty silence.

"It's big enough for me, Julio," she said, without turning to look at him. "There're two bedrooms. I guess I've got a studio area with this second bedroom."

Sean was in the bathroom. "Hey, you've got a heat lamp in here," he said, flipping it off and on.

"Well, you've definitely got a view—of trees, that is," Julio said, cuttingly. What in the hell made her do this? he asked himself as his mind fought with accumulated rage. "Is there anything we should get unpacked from the van for the night?" he asked as evenly as he could.

Rosa looked at him expecting to do battle, but instead what she saw in his eyes stopped her. They looked shiny, burning, patient. Inhuman, she thought, and dismissed it.

"How about the sleeping bags and cooking stuff from the back of the car. The truck can wait for morning."

"I'm starving!" Sean yelled. "Absolutely starving!" He began to make coyote calls.

"Coyotes, right?" Rosa asked.

"Yeah, heard them all summer. Bet you've got packs of them here. Bet the wolves are all gone, though."

"Maybe," Rosa said. "They spotted the largest mountain lion seen in this area, right here on this spot, I was told."

"Of course," Julio mumbled.

"What did you say?" Rosa asked.

"I said, of course," Julio repeated, patiently.

They slept in the front room around the fireplace. The instant the sun set every trace of warmth vanished with it. Rosa turned all the lights off, resisting the temptation to leave the bathroom light on. In a new house, she told herself, it's hard to find the bathroom at night. The only light was the fire, and what would die.

Each one fell asleep so deeply it was as though the darkness swallowed them, and at the bottom was silence, if they went that far.

The silence is almost suffocating, Rosa thought as she took one last look at the fire. Julio and Sean were asleep, and Zack was in a corner of the room curled into a ball. Then the darkness swallowed her, too. She didn't dream that night. No one dreamt. The darkness was complete.

Julio and Sean were sitting at the kitchen table drinking coffee when Rosa woke up. It felt like she had amnesia for just a moment. Then the dark smell of the cabin and the dead fire reminded her where she was. Finally, she thought. She closed her eyes and the night's darkness returned, frightening her with its vividness. She opened her eyes and listened. The only thing she could hear was Julio and Sean speaking in low voices, and even that sound seemed to disappear as though the silence itself were hungry. Even the farm hadn't been this silent. There'd been neighbors, a much-used road in front, the almost constant presence of children. No, she'd never heard this before. Not this.

"Where'd the furniture come from?" Rosa asked.

"We snuck it in. You were out like a light," Sean answered her.

"Do you want some coffee?" Julio asked. "I'll take you some if you want." He felt tender toward her, watching her sleep. She looked so small in the sleeping bag. Why do I always forget she's so small, really, he asked himself.

"If you don't mind, I'd love some. I'll cook breakfast. Hungry, Sean?"

"Starved. This place is too quiet for my blood, Mom. You might start talking to yourself, you know?" Sean laughed, loudly.

Rosa sipped her coffee and stared out the window. Pine needles moved in a gentle wind, and the sun was thin and new. She got up and walked to the back bedroom window. It was one huge sliding glass window that took up nearly the entire wall. Small pine and cedar trees crowded her view, and behind them two immense trees— one pine, one cedar—stood looking over ridge after ridge of forest. She decided to take this as her bedroom—it got the first sun.

Rosa changed into her clothes and went into the kitchen. "Where's Sean?" she asked Julio.

"He went out to run around with Zack for a while." He got up and made another cup of coffee. "There's some mail I forgot to give you in all the confusion. I'll get it in a minute. It's in the car."

"Anything special?"

"Something from Sierra as I remember."

Rosa's heart leapt. "Why didn't you give it to me? How long have you had it?"

"During the packing I kept putting all the mail into a folder. I'm sorry, Rosa. Do you want it now?"

A rush of anger threatened to explode. Why couldn't he give me my damned mail, she thought. "Are the eggs in the car? Do you mind bringing in the whole cooler? Just give me my mail after breakfast." She felt numb, though the anger had almost reached her. Rosa looked at the loaded truck and a heaviness, a strange tiredness, hit her. No, she said to herself, and made another cup of coffee. Strong.

"Here's the stuff. Do you want it on the floor?" Julio asked in a careful voice.

"That's fine. Thanks," she said, saying the *thanks* in a clipped tone. They'd been polite, in a forced way, for days, and now that Julio would be leaving, and she staying, the tension began to be unbearable again. The unsaid.

She began frying bacon. She opened the back door and stood in the sun. It was warm and direct, though its light still filtered through the tallest trees.

"Are you sure this is what you want, Rosa?" Julio asked in a low, quiet tone. It was so quiet it seemed to become a part of the sun, the silent sun, flooding the exposed kitchen.

Rosa turned and looked at him. His arms were down to his sides in a helpless manner—in a way she'd never seen. His face looked strangely vulnerable, and she walked into his arms.

"Rosa," Julio murmured, pulling her to him, stroking her hair and her face gently in a slow, painfully gentle way. She just held him around the waist firmly, smelling his body, his familiar body, filling herself with his odor.

"The bacon," she said, remembering it. She turned it. "Just in time."

Julio stood behind her, his arms around her belly. Rosa held onto his arms and leaned back into him.

Sean came in to view, in front. "Come on, boy!" he yelled at Zack. "Come on!" Zack jumped up to Sean's chest, holding his paws steady, licking him in the face.

"I'd better finish cooking." Rosa looked at Julio and he kissed her lightly on the mouth, lips open. A shudder ran through her, through him. The current between them was on, again. Again, they read each other's eyes: desire and dread. Again.

"I'll unpack the dishes," Julio said, turning away. Rosa was glad. She didn't want to involve Sean, anymore than he already was, in the see-saw they couldn't escape from. They could only push off into the air, taking turns, up and down, back to earth.

"I'll take a pound of bacon and six fried eggs. You're going to have to feed me to unpack that thing."

"You've got it," Rosa answered. "How was your walk?"

"Didn't see anyone but a deer, and Zack scared her away. I saw some dead wood. It looks good for firewood to me. We could get a chainsaw tomorrow and I'll start cutting."

"Fine. Did you see any other houses?"

"Yeah, but they look empty. No, wait a minute, one of them had a car in front. You ought to find out who's here all winter."

"I will, for sure. Here's your chow, sir. As much as you want while you bring in the wood," Rosa laughed. "Yours is coming up, Julio."

"No hurry. I'll steal some bacon, though."

"Help yourself." Rosa looked at him and saw warmth. A little guarded, but warmth. Should we keep sleeping together? she asked herself. Will it only be harder when he goes? If he stayed it'd be harder, she reminded herself. "Don't forget to get the mail."

"Right," Julio answered.

After breakfast Rosa took her mail in front, on the porch. The entire cabin was built of rough cedar and the porch was roomy— room enough to pile the split wood to come, she noted. The sun was beginning to warm the front of the house, so she sat on the steps.

Through the trees she could see a horizon of trees, an endless valley of trees, stretching out through a clearing, and it, instantly, had the effect of clearing her mind. The numbness lifted, entirely, and Rosa began to tremble.

The earth was damp and steam rose in the morning air. The air seemed so clear, so very clear, as though bubbles, clear bubbles, floated by instead of simply air.

Dear Rosa, I tried to call . . . are you in the mountains? The baby leaps like a porpoise, no rest standing, sitting or lying. Will you try to be here for the birth? Bob wants you to be here too—chalk up the last one to Macho Stupidity— life goes on . . . I think of you . . . HOW ARE YOU? WHERE ARE YOU? LET ME KNOW! Enclosed one poem to make you laugh, the other for straight faces . . . I approach the Full Moon Belly. FUCK! (Isn't that why I'm in this state?) Look, please beam me a return message soon. Hasta la vista . . . con amor,

Sierra y Panza

   The first poem, Sierra pointed out, was from a series of poems,
THE WITCH POEMS she'd written by hand, entitled "Canto de Mujer:
Song of Woman." The poem itself she called "Of/To Man." There'd
be six poems in the series, she said. Let me know what you think . . .
she'd written at the bottom of her letter. The dried honeysuckle
she'd enclosed left dark scarlet smudges on her words, and their
sweet fragrance still lingered.

> *Of/To Man*
>
> You, man, are the snake in
> my garden—
> yeah,
> a snake in the grass.
> Everyone since Eve & Adam's
> been blame ME
> for The First Fuck—and it was
> ME who got knocked up! Well,
> hell, I'm not sorry.
> I can come over & over (spiritual orgasms count, too)
>   and
> you're limited to one
> at a time: Is that the
> main bitch?
> Well, man, my man—
> let's set herstory
> straight. I come IN my cunt,
> IN my clit, you might say
> my whole body is IN the
> act: Maybe you feel gypped and
> someone dubbed me a
> mystery.
>
> Some snakes are dark and fluid
> and compelling—and for the life of me
> I just can't resist them.
>
> Now, there's a mystery.
> Then,
> On Recognizing The Labor of Clarity
>
> 1.
> It is not the clarity
> of the sun

I seek; I seek
its warmth
perhaps
I seek
its tongue on my
face on my
belly (reddening, reddening)
but watch
the sun
it burns and blinds
you (blistering, blistering)
O moon:
grandmother planet,
midwife to earth,
old scarred face;
men count your craters
now
as they once
counted sons.

Cycle after cycle (bleeding, bleeding)

2.
I have heard there are men
that watch the moon
and follow her cycle
as regularly as women
that watch the womb
moon to moon:

empty/full
empty/full

There is a woman
with a nine month
belly,
she stares
at the full moon;
she has
swallowed the moon and
she glows like an x-ray.

She will open her legs
at the appointed hour;

> she will give birth
> to the new moon.
>
> She is a woman of clarity.
> This birth will be no easy
> task.

She's writing in a different vein, Rosa recognized, and then she remembered, with a fresh clarity, how it always seemed that they were working on the same themes in their own mediums. She looked out again at the clearing—"She is a woman of clarity. This birth will be no easy task."

Of course, I'll go to Sierra's birth. Of course. What are we really birthing, Sierra? She thought of her paintings packed tightly in the van. The wheels had sunk a little into the mud overnight, she noticed. Rosa began to imagine the second bedroom with her unfinished paintings side by side—Lilac Sky, Rainbow Sky.

What are we really birthing, Sierra?

A small, white butterfly—a little tattered and tired looking—landed on the dark, wet ground. It opened and closed its wings in the sun in a kind of lingering pleasure. It rested.

Rosa noticed that her breasts were tender to the touch, but she felt no cramping, the beginnings of the signal that her blood would come. She'd been late before and panicked for nothing, she reminded herself. She counted carefully. Yes, she was nearly two months late. Look at everything I've been doing—the pressure, the turmoil, the general insanity. Who wouldn't be late? Rosa stared at the butterfly, but lightly. She'd learned that a too intense gaze always drove flying things away.

"No, I can't be pregnant," she spoke to the butterfly. Not now, she thought. Rosa put the rest of the mail down for later and closed her eyes, putting her face up to the sun. It was such a comfort, the sun, she thought and felt—such a pleasure. And she forgot about the winter.

What are we really birthing, Sierra?

"We finished cleaning up, Mom. Better get started. Where's Zack?" Sean looked at her a little worried. "You okay, Mom?"

Rosa smiled. "I'm fine. Isn't Zack with you? I thought he was inside." She stood up and noticed the butterfly was gone.

"He must've slipped out the back door, sneaky bastard," Sean laughed.

"It's okay. Let him run and sniff to his fill for a change. He's only on a million or so acres of national forest. Why not?" Rosa laughed and looked out at the clearing almost to make sure it was still there, really there.

Everything was finally unpacked, the truck swept out and returned. The refrigerator plugged in and humming, the soft, velvet couch she'd bought second hand for fifty dollars in front of the fireplace, the rubber tree plant as old as Sean in the front room window, some other survivors scattered throughout the house. Julio had kept the bed, so their sleeping bags lay in the middle of the room. She wanted something simple here, just a platform bed. And the studio held the promise of her work—a little shyly, a little stiffly, but the room waited for her now.

Sean brought in an armload of wood. "Downed wood. Dried and perfect for a fire. Tomorrow I cut with a chainsaw, right?"

"We'll go in in the morning to see about renting one and keep it for a week. How much longer till the chicken's done, Julio?"

"Half an hour or so. Why?"

"Do you want to take a walk?"

He came out of the kitchen. "Sure."

"Do you want to go, Sean?" Rosa asked.

"Nah. I'll stay and make a fire and relax. Vegetate for a while."

Zack was on the front porch and followed them down the road. Then he ran ahead.

"He must think he died and went to heaven," Julio laughed, shortly.

"He was gone all day and he's still running like a big puppy. There must be a million scents here and he's tracking them all down. From a back yard to this must be quite a switch in doggie consciousness. Even on the farm, when he was a puppy, we tried to keep him on the property because of all the neighboring livestock. Why don't we go through here instead?" Rosa indicated a small path running into woods. They turned to follow it and then it disappeared, leaving them free to choose any direction.

"You have to watch where you're going around here or you'll break your neck tripping on these rocks," Julio said.

"That's for sure. Do you hear that?" They stood still, listening. "Water. Let's go that way."

They walked straight ahead, toward the water sound, tripping on stones and regaining their balance. They came to a small meadow. Tall, yellow flowers on giant stalks, some almost as tall as Rosa, grew everywhere.

Rosa touched a leaf. "Feel this. It feels like a kitten, so soft."

Julio touched it. "I should've brought my camera. Next time I come I'll bring it for sure. This place has a raw, wild beauty I've never seen. I can see why you've come." Julio faced her and looked directly into her eyes.

"Can you?" Rosa looked back at him.

He reached out for her hand and held it. "Yes, I can." He smiled at her. "I don't think Zack's the only one who can sense things. I've got doggie consciousness, too, I think." Julio laughed, and then he growled. "Maybe I've even got mountain lion consciousness. They're here all right," Julio said, looking at the peak to the left of them.

Rosa thought of her wolf, but she couldn't bring herself to speak of it. She'd seen her—just a quick, dark glimpse.

The sun was beginning to set, sending long shafts of gold through the trees. The chill began to overtake the warmth of the day. They walked toward the water sound and it got louder and louder, and there it was. A small, fast-running creek in the shade of a grove of aspen. Its leaves were yellow-gold. Most of them covered the ground already, soft and wet—but at least half their leaves still clung stubbornly to the stark, outstretched branches that reached up to the darkening sky.

"Do you plan to come back with your camera?" Rosa asked in a whisper.

"Let's not make this anything permanent, Rosa. Maybe we need to do this for a while. I'm willing to see it that way." He paused and then he asked, "Do you still love me?"

She stood up with a cold, wet rock in her hand. The water was freezing and her hands were red from dangling them in it. She handed him the stone, and he took it.

After dinner they all sat in front of the fire, exhausted.

"I'm going to put the wall heater on 'low' tonight. It was pretty cold this morning," Rosa said. "Why don't you add another log, Sean?"

"Got it. I think I'll sleep right here tonight next to the fire. Where're you sleeping, Julio?"

"In the bedroom."

He looked at Rosa and said, "Whatever."

"Good night, Sean," Rosa said, walking toward the bedroom. After she brushed her teeth and put oil on her face she got into her sleeping bag, and it was deliciously chilly for a moment, warming quickly to her body heat.

The sky outside the window was absolutely clear, and the stars looked sharp and pointy. Each and every star was brilliant with light. Tomorrow she'd try to explain to Sean what seemed to be going on with her and Julio, though she really didn't know herself.

She fell asleep instantly, with the same feeling of the night before of being swallowed up by the darkness. It was unpleasant, but somehow tinged with an excitement which made it bearable.

When she woke up it seemed half-dream, half-waking, as though she couldn't decide, entirely, which she preferred. Julio was stroking her thighs and gently sucking her nipples. Shudders of passion ran through her as though he'd been doing it for quite a while. And then his hands found her and she moaned. When he started to enter her she thought, briefly, of her diaphragm. "My diaphragm, Julio." Rosa held onto his hot, sweaty neck, and then spread her hands to the length of his shoulders, and down again to his soft, round nakedness.

"Forget it. Just forget it." He opened his mouth wide, filling her with his tongue and his penis simultaneously, and she had to keep herself from screaming out loud.

Julio began to moan in time to the rhythm of his orgasm, as everything escaped him. As everything escaped him, he held onto Rosa, smelling her, their mingled odors. If it were possible at this moment, he would've gladly eaten her. He put his tongue out and licked her shoulder lightly, softly. She was already asleep.

Julio looked up at the sky and two quick, consecutive shooting stars streaked into the void. Instinctively, he held Rosa close to him as though to protect her from what they didn't know. She felt like a child in his arms, and he refused to let her go.

Vietnam seemed so far away, war seemed so far away—the world seemed so far away, as though they were on the very top of the world where only silence could reach them. The mortars, the helicopters, the screams of dying men seemed so far away that it might never have happened. What proof did he have? What proof did anyone have? The silence answered him: Nothing.

Rosa watches the tattoo on her belly enlarge until she becomes terrified that it's going to burst. Then, gently, a small, white butterfly emerges from the rose. Slowly, the delicate, white butterfly stretches its wings open, opening them wide, then pulling them shut to touch its own softness—wing to wing. They open again, becoming a glowing source of light. "You know," a deep silence tells her.

Rosa's eyes flew open. The whiteness of the butterfly sharply contrasted the darkness she now faced, and the sweat pouring from her body contrasted with the terrible chill in the room. She picked up the flashlight beside her and aimed it at the wall. She crawled over and put the wall heater on medium, and the sweat on her body vanished as though a million tongues licked her clean. The cold was almost shocking and it was only late September.

"Rosa!" Julio reached for her. "Don't go." He looked at her with startled, little boy's eyes. Instinctively, she reached for him and held his head to her, touching his cheek. His cheeks were soft, soft like a baby. Rosa turned off the flashlight and, for a moment, the darkness, as dark as dreams, made the white butterfly appear in mid-air before her eyes. Soft as a small, white butterfly.

What are we really birthing, Sierra? The silence answered her: You know.

Rosa decided to stay at the cabin to put away and clean up, so Julio went with Sean to rent the chainsaw.

"Take your time. I'm going to wander around here in a daze for a while. Don't forget to pick up the food on the list, Julio."

"Are you kidding? It's over thirty miles round trip, and you're always the one who forgets one thing, remember?" he said, laughing.

"Don't remind me. Maybe I'll have to work on developing my doggie consciousness," she said, looking at him with the warmth of her body's memory exposed to him in her eyes. A wave of pleasure surprised her, making her weak, wonderfully weak, in her legs. I must be going up, up into the air now. Let me down gently, Julio, she asked without words.

Sean was in the car. He was going to drive, so he started the motor.

"Is there anything else you want?" Julio asked. "Anything at all?" He smiled slowly. He kissed her lightly, the edge of his tongue grazing her lips, and he ran both of his hands down the sides of her hips. Then he kissed, softly, each of her nipples through her sweater.

Rosa felt unusually sensitive to his touch. She trembled and turned away. "You better get going. Poor Sean. He must be kind of confused. First we can't get away from each other fast enough. Now this." She laughed softly to dispel the pain that never seemed to leave them.

"Don't worry. It'll be okay. I'll see you in a few hours." Julio smiled at her intimately, the way she loved him to.

Rosa waved him away. "Get out of here, and don't forget the list. Or the wine, for God's sake." She corrected herself, "For the Goddess' sake."

"How could I? he answered. "For the Goddess' sake." Julio laughed and shut the door behind him.

They drove off and the silence descended all around her, tangibly. Rosa looked out the kitchen window, at the light. It was so sharp and clear here, she thought, even the shadows are interesting. She walked room to room looking out every window, the eyes of her house.

She went into the studio bedroom and arranged her work table, unpacking the boxes. As Rosa unwrapped the lilac sky painting, she looked up at the sky through the wide window-eye. Large, white clouds slowly moved across the chill, blue air. She looked down at the painting again and back to the clouds. The clouds are closer here, she thought. I can actually see them better. Their edges are more vivid. Or something.

Then the silence moved in on her, making itself strangely present, disturbing her. What's it going to be like when they're gone? she wondered. She thought of putting on the radio—her tapes were still packed—and decided against it, making herself unpack the other paintings and placing them in a semicircle against the wall. Rosa stared at the rainbow painting, and for an instant it seemed the Earth was twirling. It was a brief moment—a trick of the eyes, she thought—but it was a moment of intense peace. She wondered what nasty headlines she'd missed in these last few days. Julio would probably bring a paper, then she'd know.

Sean and the draft, Sierra and her baby, the world and the end of this century, the next century and the unborn. Rosa looked at the Earth on the flat canvas. It was absolutely still, and now she saw only the unfinished work she had to do.

The dream. The dream last night, she remembeed, and her heart froze with anxiety. I'll have to take myself to a doctor and see what's going on. Could I actually be pregnant? Now? The image of her rose tattoo expanding on her belly made her hold her breath.

Rosa stood up and listened to her body. No cramps. Tender breasts. But no nausea. No morning nausea like Sean, she thought. The incredible nausea I had with Sean. But these dreams, damn it. "Not now," she said out loud, but the silence answered her with the words of her dream: You know.

She refused to listen, and she rushed to unpack some more boxes, fast and efficiently. Then she swept, leaving the back door open. Sunlight poured in, and its warmth.

Rosa made a peanut butter sandwich and drank a glass of milk. I did a lot, she thought, looking around the house. Now for a walk, before they get back.

She took off in the direction of the creek again and followed it down a half mile, circling back, she guessed, toward the cabin. Light and trees and stone. Always stone—and the sound of water. The tall peaks, the ones behind her cabin, were visually exhilarating. The light was in constant flux, bringing them to life in a kind of sustained creation.

"Zack!" Rosa yelled. Zack came running toward her with dark, fresh dirt on his nose.

When Rosa came to a road she realized it was the road before hers. She decided to walk through the woods rather than taking the trouble to walk to the main road. It was thick here and she thought of rattlesnakes. She peeled her eyes to the ground and walked carefully.

There was a sound of a saw up ahead, and then she saw the house that was being built. The one she saw the other day with the man on the roof. There he was with a chainsaw in his hand. He had goggles on, and a wild mass of red hair stood up on his head. He also had a beard, and that was red as well.

Rosa stopped, a little embarrassed, because she was probably on his property. She was about to turn back when he yelled, "Hi!" He turned off the chainsaw and pulled off his goggles, walking up to her in a slow, confident pace, smiling.

"Hi," Rosa answered.

"What, did you just move into that cabin over there?" he asked, pointing in her cabin's direction. "You bought that place, huh?"

"That's me," Rosa smiled. Zack edged up to Rosa panting in a relaxed way, but slightly wary. She patted him, letting him know he was doing the right thing.

"Nice looking dog. A malamute-wolf mix, isn't he?" he asked, reaching his hand out to Zack, but Zack stayed next to Rosa.

"He's a malamute as far as I know, but I wouldn't doubt a wolf strain somewhere. I'd let him get to know you first. He's a good dog, but that's how he is." She looked at him evenly.

"Yeah, nice mask, boy," he said, looking at Zack. "What's his name?" Then he looked back at Rosa and said, "I'm Forrest," putting out his hand to her.

"I'm Rosa. Rosa Luján. Is that your real name?" She laughed and shook his hand.

"Forrest McBride, ma'am," he said with an exaggerated politeness. "Is Rosa your real name?" He looked at her, piercingly.

"Damned straight," the words shot right out of her.

He laughed. "Don't get excited. You asked me first, remember? Are you planning to be here through the winter? If you are, you better get a four-wheel-drive and plenty of wood. Don't forget a snow shovel, either." His words came out slow and smooth, one after the other, and he never took his eyes off her.

"Yes, I am. And you?"

"This place isn't ready yet and my wife's pregnant, so we're staying in town. We'll probably move in next summer, for sure. Are you going to be living there by yourself?" He saw her eyes become guarded. "That is if you don't mind my asking. Don't mind me, I'm just nosy by nature."

"You don't look old enough to be married," Rosa said, almost without meaning to, but then she saw he wasn't offended but flattered. "Anyway, it looks like I am. Do you know of a good place to get wood?"

"I can get you some. How much do you need?"

"How much do you charge?"

"Fifty per cord. Pine, cedar mix, a little oak thrown in, split and delivered."

"How much is the oak?"

"Seventy per cord. Where you from?"

"I grew up in San Francisco."

"I'm from a little place in Montana, so I'm used to the mountains, you might say. Been here since I was twenty, four years now. How much wood do you want? I can get it to you by next week." He sat down on a log facing her and looked off towards his half-built house.

"Okay. How about two cords mixed and one cord oak? What day will you deliver it?"

"How's next Saturday? Also, you might go on down to the ranch and get in good with them. They're the ones to plow you out all winter, you know." He smiled at her.

"Isn't this county maintained?" Rosa asked in disbelief.

"Only up to the paved road. The ranch takes care of all the cabins up here."

"But doesn't it close all winter?"

"For guests. The top guys live here all winter and there's a deal that they plow out these roads. But you might remind them you're up on that side road."

"Well, thanks for the information. I'll see you Saturday, Forrest. It looks like I'd better trade in my Volvo as soon as possible."

"I would if I were you. That Blazer's mine over there. It churns through three foot drifts." He stood up and smiled, surveying her with a candid expression. "It's been a pleasure, ma'am." The exaggerated politenesss again.

Rosa winced inwardly. "The pleasure was all mine, Mr. McBride."

As soon as her back was turned he started up the chainsaw, making her jump. She hoped he hadn't noticed. "Stupid bastard," Rosa muttered. Then she remembered the rattlesnakes again and watched out for them. Were his eyes green or gold? She couldn't remember.

The trees were dense through here, and the pine and cedar trees mulched the earth with a thick, silent cover. Manzanita, huge bushes of them, with their reddish thorn-like branches, grew in clusters making her weave around them. Besides, rattlers were known to like their shelter—but didn't they hibernate in winter? Yes, they were probably all bunched up together, she imagined—huge, coiled, round one another, preparing to hatch their young for the spring. Spring. Rosa couldn't imagine spring; she was trying to imagine winter. Snow. Three foot drifts of snow. Up to my waist, she realized. Four feet, five feet—"Five foot drifts," she muttered. And the county's not responsible to plow me out. The ranch. Well, I'm glad someone told me. And I've got to see about a car. Spring? I can't imagine it, but I must, I must begin to imagine winter.

Rosa came to a meadow. A small meadow, but open to the sky. Little grassy spots showed through, and the sun, the autumn light, made it look like a clear yellow bowl filled with its last sweet warmth.

She walked to the center of the meadow and saw the roof of a cabin. She walked further on and realized it was her own cabin, with a jolt of surprise. This was the meadow next to her place. Her car was parked in the driveway. They were back.

She sat down facing the meadow. The sun lulled her. Rosa walked over to a grassy area close to a stand of oak. Oak, pine and cedar droppings mingled in the dense, scratchy grass, but it felt good, and it was dry. She turned on her stomach and the smells were so rich it startled her. She looked around for Zack, but he wasn't to be seen. Must've run up ahead. Sean's probably petting him right now, she thought.

Then Rosa did something she'd never done before. She stuck her nose into the leaves and took quick, deep sniffs, getting a little dirt up her nose. She sneezed and did it again, more carefully, and she thought of a deer. No, deers. She laughed out loud. Suddenly, Rosa felt like crawling around and sniffing, but she decided that was going too far, so she moved around a little, sniffing some more, and she thought of coyotes. Her wolf? No, she couldn't see her wolf. She sat up and looked, quickly, over her shoulder the way she'd glimpsed the dark wolf-shape on the porch. Nothing. Not even Zack.

Rosa lay back down, belly up, feeling the sun press against her gently, subtly.

She woke up with something panting in her face. Zack. "Bad breath, boy," Rosa gasped, sitting up, petting his thick fur. But there were patches, she noted, where he'd scratched himself bare from fleas. "Poor old dog—bad breath and fleas. I'll put some oil on you tonight. How's that, Zack?" He leaned against her affectionately, and she stood up. "How long have I been here? Huh, Zack?"

His tail was curled to attention, and she pounded his sides the way he loved it. "You're a solid old dog. You know that?" Rosa brushed herself off and began walking to the house. "Come on, wolfie," she called to him. He ran ahead and was on the porch with Sean when she got there.

"Where've you been? We've been back over an hour."

"I just took a walk. I actually fell asleep over in that meadow." Rosa pointed to it. "Bad Breath, here, just woke me up. Doesn't the sun feel good? I feel like I should soak it up before it gets away. Did you get the chainsaw?"

At the mention of the chainsaw Sean's look of displeasure turned to interest, somewhat. "Yeah, a good one, too. I rented it for the week till Saturday. So, I'll start cutting tomorrow. I cut a little wood for tonight. There's some dead stuff behind the cabin. Perfect firewood. In fact, I think I'll start right back there. There's quite a bit back there."

"Okay, but show me first. Don't cut anything living, right?"

"I know that, Mom. Come on!" Sean looked at her irritably.

Julio stepped out on the porch. "Been on a walk?" he asked, keeping his voice pitched to a pleasant tone, but his eyes were dark and guarded.

Jesus, Rosa thought, what is this, the fucking inquisition? Maybe

I look too relaxed for their taste. And then her guard went back up. "Yeah, I went on a trek and met an elf who said he'd sell me some wood." She kept her face straight though the thought of Forrest's wild, red hair sticking up made her feel like laughing. He had rather looked like an elf.

"What?" Sean asked. "A what?"

"You know that man we saw on his roof the other day? Well, I just met him circling back here. Anyway, we made a deal for some wood. Three cords, and he's bringing it Saturday."

"Some elf," Julio said, caustically. "How much is he charging for the wood? Free?"

"Hardly, Julio. Fifty for mixed pine and cedar, seventy for oak—split and delivered."

"That's not bad," Sean said. "Not at all. Well, that takes a load off me. I'll cut as much as I can, though. And split it. That's a lot of work. The guy's charging you more than a fair price."

"You mother's a good looking woman, Sean, don't forget," Julio continued in the caustic tone.

"Julio, I believe that's a fair price here in the Plumas National Forest." Rosa shot him a killing look. Damn you, goddamn you, here we go again, she thought. Her back crawled with fury up to her shoulders, making her neck rigid. She imagined her shoulders were made of steel, and then she looked out at the clearing, the horizon of trees stretching out into the distance, and she stopped herself. No, my shoulders are softening, softening to flesh. My flesh, she told herself.

Rosa looked at Sean. "Look, I'll stack everything. You cut, split, and I'll stack. I think I'll start some dinner. You hungry?"

"I sure am," Sean answered, not looking at her, aware of Julio's presence right behind her. He didn't want to get in the middle, at all.

Julio was silent, but his presence wasn't.

Rosa walked by him without a word, ignoring his eyes on her. She went to the bathroom and as she washed her hands she looked into the mirror, muttering, "Fuck him." She put on fresh lipstick, and that helped. It always did.

As she began chopping onions and mushrooms for the spaghetti, Julio came into the kitchen. "You're got leaves all over your back, Rosa." He reached over and took some off, holding them in his hand. "Were you laying down for a while?" His voice was ominous and he glared at her.

Rosa spun around and faced him. "What are you insinuating, Julio?" She kept her voice low; Sean was still on the porch with Zack. "And keep your voice down."

"Well, you were gone for so long, and then you come back with news of this guy bringing you wood Saturday. You should see your back, it's a mess."

"I don't believe this. I really don't believe this." Rosa's mind teetered for an instant with rage and disbelief, and then she forced herself to focus on his face. To see him—two eyes, a nose, a mouth. A human face. In fact, one she knew, very well.

"You'd better back up, Julio. You'd better back way, way up. You expect us to still have some kind of relationship and say—even think—things like this? Not me, man! Sure as hell not me! This is one of the reasons why I came here—to get away from this crazy shit," Rosa said, keeping her voice down. She looked out the front room window and Sean was gone. He must've heard us anyway, she realized, and her anger mounted.

"Okay, okay," Julio said, retreating an inch or two from his confrontation. "Buy why is your back full of leaves, and why were you so late?"

Rosa put the butcher knife down, slowly, with a conscious effort. She looked at the chopped onions and the half-chopped mushrooms, and her stomach reminded her she was hungry. Then a hint of nausea announced itself. She groaned inwardly. No, it just can't be.

Julio was waiting for an answer, and his face was impassive, relentlessly impassive.

"Would it make you feel better if I told you that I sold my body for three cords of wood? I can't believe we're even discussing this! It's so fucking stupid!"

Julio crushed the leaves in his hand. "Do you want me to get the rest off your back?"

"I fell asleep in the sun, you idiot!" Rosa yelled.

Julio's face seemed to come back to life as though Rosa's anger jolted him out of a trance. He tried to take her in his arms, saying, "I'm sorry, Rosa. Come on, I'm really sorry. Please, just let me hold you."

"No, don't touch me. Just leave alone. I want to cook this damned dinner. I'm hungry. I mean it, Julio. Don't touch me." She moved away from him to the refrigerator and got some cheese and some bread. I'm probably getting nauseated because I'm starved, she told herself.

"Rosa, I'm going back tomorrow. Can't we forget this?" He tried to move toward her.

"Do not come near me. Go make a fire, take a walk, something, but just leave me alone right now."

"This doesn't change anything, does it?"

"I don't know. Please just leave me alone right now, Julio." Rosa waited for him to leave the room and then she took a bite of the bread and cheese. Better. She opened the bottle of zinfandel and poured herself a glass. She could hear Julio balling up papers for the fire. She looked for Sean but he was still gone.

Rosa turned on the burner and put some margarine to melt for the onions and mushrooms. As the onions began to fry the odor hit her with an unaccustomed intensity, and the taste of the wine seemed exceptionally strong. How dare he? she thought, and tears came to her eyes, but she stopped them and took a sip of wine. She could hear the first twigs crackling and the grate being gently moved.

Julio fed the fire its first large pieces. His anger had cooled and now his back felt chilly. She probably won't let me sleep with her tonight now, he thought. Damn it, he sulked. He heard Rosa go out the back door, and he got up to take a look. She was brushing off her back, angrily.

Julio went back to the fire and reached for his sweater. There's more of those guys here than she'll know what to do with, with that ranch down there, he thought, and his anger surged up again. The fire shifted and fell. One of the logs rolled out of the fireplace, and he grabbed it with his hands and threw it back in, burning himself slightly. Julio readjusted the fire again and made himself sit down on the couch rather than go try to speak to Rosa again. And he had to go back tomorrow.

Will she even let me come back? the thought came to him. He resisted another urge to go try to speak to her, as he added a long-burning log at the very top of the pile.

Sean came in and saw Julio on the couch. He could tell by the set of his shoulders they were arguing. "Hey, I put some more wood on the porch. May as well bring some in." He went back out and brought in an armload of wood, dumping it on the side of the fireplace.

"Hi, Sean! Put the wood in those boxes I put there," Rosa yelled.

"I did, Mom. How long for dinner?"

"Thirty minutes."

Sean came into the kitchen and took some mushrooms from the pan, eating them. "Do you think you're going to miss having a TV? I sure would."

"I know you would, but I didn't really watch it that much to begin with."

"So, anyway, this guy's delivering the wood Saturday?"

Rosa indicated Julio with her eyes. "That's what he said."

"Do I have time to take a shower?" Suddenly, Sean almost dreaded going in the front room with Julio.

"Go ahead, there's time." Rosa heard the shower running and Julio turning the pages of a newspaper. The nausea was subsiding. It must've been hunger, she told herself.

Rosa managed to avoid Julio until bedtime. She'd refused to let the silence at the dinner table bother her, and finally Sean plugged in the stereo and found a rock station, which helped. Her anger just wouldn't dissipate—she didn't want it to. It felt strangely good to be angry again. Maybe it'll be easier this way, she thought, as she got into her sleeping bag.

Julio knocked on the bedroom door. "Rosa, I just want to talk to you, just for a minute."

"Okay, come in," she said, flatly.

He came in and sat down with his back to the wall facing her. There was something in his hand. "I want to give this to you, if you want it. I thought you might feel better with it here." He unwrapped a gun from one of his old flannel shirts. Julio held it in the palm of his hand. It was dark and covered his hand, entirely. "Do you want it?"

"Where in the hell did it come from?"

"My father brought it back from World War Two, from a German soldier. I've shot it a few times. It works pretty good. I've kept it in good condition."

Rosa was stunned, but she managed to straighten her thoughts and ask, "Do you mean you had that gun all the time?"

Julio flinched, then he raised his voice an octave. "Yeah, but it was put away. I kept it in my darkroom. Anyway, I thought you might feel better with it out here." He placed the gun on the rug between them.

"How did you get it, Julio?" Rosa stared at the gun. A German gun, she thought. She almost felt sick to her stomach again, and this time her full stomach made it worse. She looked up at Julio.

"I didn't tell you this, but I met my father once when I got back from Vietnam, after my grandmother's funeral. I mean, he visited us maybe three times when I was little, but they were brief, and when I tried to hug him once he pushed me away. I guess he was embarrassed. Anyway, after the funeral we went back to his motel room and we drank and talked about our wars, like men." Julio looked away, and the words "like men" echoed, cynically, wall to wall and back to the gun again. "At the height of our stupidity he pulled out this gun and told me, 'I'm giving you this gun because now you're a man. You and I, we seen The Elephant.' That's what he said, 'We seen The Elephant.' And he shoved it into my stomach. So, I've taken care of the damned thing. Do you want it?" Julio looked at her with agonized eyes.

Rosa wondered if he'd cry if she touched him, just touched him on the cheek. She wanted to but she just couldn't do it. "Let me think about it. I'll tell you in the morning." It lay there between them with its violence intact. That's what she felt most of all—its violence. Dark and ugly—hideous. Was it taken from the soldier the year I was born? Rosa thought. She stared at it.

Julio picked it up. "Look, it's easy to use. Just flip this safety, after you load the bullets. I have a box of them." Julio turned the barrel, cocked it and pressed the trigger. It was a small, terrible sound in the room, and a part of Rosa cringed and a part of her wouldn't turn away.

"Here, hold it," Julio said, handing it to her.

She took it in both hands. It was heavy, and, for an instant, her shoulders ached.

"Hold it in your right hand and get a feel for it. You never know, Rosa, you may need it here by yourself."

Rosa held it in her right hand and the pain shot right up her arm, vividly this time, to her shoulder. Horror and sorrow, she thought, and the image of dead men came to her mind—and then the image of the little girl in her dream, surrounded by the other children, preparing to die, surfaced, and Rosa held the gun tighter feeling its awful weight in her hand. "I'll keep it," she said. "Throw me the shirt." She wrapped it and took it to the closet, putting it away as far as she could reach.

Rosa slid into her sleeping bag. Her heart was pounding in her ears, and the room looked altered as though its emptiness and lack of furniture had catapulted them into some other time. Instinctively, she held her belly, and then she thought of her nausea, her missed menstruals. The white butterfly.

"Can I sleep with you tonight?" Julio asked in a small, quiet voice.

"I'm not going to make love to you, Julio," she answered him.

"I just want to sleep next to you. That's all."

"It's up to you. Why don't you turn off the light? I'm exhausted." Her voice was neutral, without expression. She felt cut away from the familiar, detached, as though anything were possible, and it didn't terrify her as it usually did. She continued to hold her belly. But if I am pregnant, I just can't have it. I'll have to get an abortion, she told herself, taking her hands away from her belly, leaving it exposed. Don't start that, don't you dare start that. A baby is out of the question.

Julio got into his sleeping bag. "Good night, Rosa. I'm glad you took the gun. I won't worry about you as much."

Rosa lay in the darkness, keeping her silence, staring out at the night. The stars are fierce here, she thought—fierce with light. She felt Julio's hand touch her leg, resting itself against her, and she let him. She could almost feel its warmth through the sleeping bag. He has such warm hands, such warm hands—and then she wanted to put his hands on her belly and tell him, "I think I'm pregnant." She wanted to cry and be held and tell him about her dream of the little girl in the concentration camp, that she knew she was German, the gun, the small, white butterfly. But she couldn't. The fierce, white stars wouldn't let her.

Then the darkness swallowed them, and the room was flung without pity into space. Julio's hand was the last thing Rosa remembered. Then dreams beyond remembering.

Toward dawn Rosa woke with the certainty that Julio was gone. She reached for him and he was still there. He opened his eyes, feeling her touch, and took her into his arms. He tried to kiss her but she turned away. They fell asleep again, in each other's warmth, as a thick frost formed on the window.

"I'll be back up again weekend after next, if you want," Julio said. They were sitting in the car waiting for the Greyhound driver to begin loading up. Steam rose from their cups of coffee and the chocolate doughnuts took the edge off their hunger.

"Maybe you can get breakfast in Sacramento," Rosa said, staring straight ahead. She'd poured cool water on the windshield for the morning frost. Now the steam from the coffee and the warmth of their breath began to block their view. She opened the side window to see if the driver was back.

"I said, do you want me to come up weekend after next?" Julio repeated.

Rosa looked at him. "Okay, but no bullshit. I really can't stand it, Julio. Do you understand, at all?" There was a sense of anger and desperation in her voice. She was slightly nauseated again.

"I promise. If any bullshit attacks threaten to occur, I promise to leave without a protest. I'll bring you a surprise." He looked at her and smiled.

She couldn't return his smile. She wanted him to leave; she didn't want him to leave. We're about to say goodbye for the first time, she thought. We're about to let each other go. Rosa looked at Julio and saw that his smile was forced, hollow. There was a sorrow in his eyes like an old wound.

"Okay, but I have to repeat this—the incident yesterday was pretty off the wall. Why do you think we're separating, Julio?" Rosa said softly. "I mean, there are other reasons, too—my own reasons. But why are we separating? What I'm saying is I'm not going to be here and keep fighting with you. I'm just not. Believe it or not, I'm trying to work some things out on a level I don't really understand yet, and I can't stand to keep tripping all over the same damned thing whenever I try to love you. I just can't stand it." Tears rolled down her face without her consent. She wiped them away, quickly.

"That won't happen again. I promise. Things are going to be different whether we want them to be or not, the way I see it. You're staying here and I'm leaving. It won't happen again, Rosa." He stared at her intently, but she wouldn't turn to meet his gaze.

She kept looking out the window, staring at the shadows of things—the bus, the trees, the man walking. Short, dark, intense shadows. They gave her a sense of relief as though the absolute reality of things, the density of things, were lightened by their dark twins. What's real? Rosa thought—me, Julio, my nausea, the gun in my closet? This gave her relief, otherwise it was stark reality: pain.

"Don't tell Sean that I have a gun. I'd rather keep it to myself. I don't know why, I just do."

"Sure. I'll show you how to use it next time. We'll take it out somewhere and really shoot it."

"There's the bus driver. You'd better get going." Rosa turned to look at him.

"Give me a kiss," Julio said, leaning forward. His eyes held no pretense now, only the old wound tinged with a kind of anger.

They kissed and they memorized lips, taste, smell. But it wasn't enough, so they clung for a moment longer, and that wasn't enough. There was only pain, and it was time to let go. Separate.

"Call me when you get the phone. I'll see you Thursday night week after next." He shut the car door. Passengers were beginning to board. Julio came around to Rosa's window. "I love you, Rosa. Do you hear me? I love you."

"I'll see you Thursday. Take care of yourself."

Julio hesitated as he waited to hear her say it, that she loved him, but she didn't. He turned and walked toward the bus.

"Te quiero, cabrón!" Rosa yelled. He turned as she closed the window. She started the motor and drove away. She began to cry, and then she made herself stop. Sean will have to face my swollen eyes again, she told herself. Poor kid.

Rosa turned back toward the center of town and decided to have breakfast by herself. She sat in the car until the pain in her throat subsided and her head cleared to a state of relative calm. The nausea was worse—there was no denying it.

She closed her eyes and concentrated on her womb trying to feel the beginnings of cramps instead of her increasing nausea. She felt like crying again, like crawling in the back seat under a blanket and crying until every tear was gone, gone out of her. Her eyes felt heavy with their accumulated weight, as though she were holding back the tide.

Rosa looked around. Not here, she told herself. Besides, I'm hungry. I want some damned coffee. Now. And she got out of the car and walked into the restaurant.

There was an empty table by the window, so she headed straight toward it. Rosa sat facing the window. She didn't care to be looked at or smile or be smiled at. It was warm inside, a nice place cozy with plants, and watercolors hung on the wall. She looked behind her and there were more. Very interesting watercolors of natural scenery as far as she could see. The one over her table was of a waterfall tumbling into a pool, and boulders on all sides. It was done entirely in blues, pinks and purples. Pastels. Nothing vivid. Extremely simple. Rosa looked at the name, a woman. An austere, feminine heart, Rosa thought, and she was glad she chose this table. After she ate, she'd take a tour of the others. Yes, they were truly lovely.

A sudden wind stirred the grape arbor on the trellis in front of her. Most of its leaves were gone, and the ones that remained were brown and brittle. Rosa was still nauseated, but becoming calm as the light shifted through the trellis.

As Rosa turned to see if she could find some service, she saw the source of the warmth—a Franklin stove in the center of the room. No wonder I smell wood, she realized. She'd been in such a hurry to sit down she hadn't seen it. The waitress smiled at her, giving her the one-minute signal with her finger in the air. Coffee, Rosa mouthed, and the waitress nodded.

The customers here were the young, hip crowd. The decor was

rustic San Francisco. She liked it. Rosa could almost hear the early morning metaphysical conversations. With a name like Lightning Strikes. She had to laugh. And there was flute music. Rosa imagined Julio relaxed into his seat. Or was someone talking his ear off? The thought of him brought its weight back to her eyes. She looked back to the trellis. Its shifting light and shadows.

Rosa began to be impatient, and as she turned to see the waitress coming she heard, "Morning, Ms. Luján!" in a loud, scratchy voice with a hoarse laugh in it. It was Forrest, smiling and waving. A pretty, young, blonde woman was with him. His wife, of course. Rosa waved hello, and then turned her attention to the waitress who was pouring the coffee.

"Could I have some toast now? Whole wheat."

"Sure. Sorry I took so long. I'm the only one this morning," she said, smiling. She was maybe twenty-five with long blonde hair, with grey in it, Rosa noticed. And she was very slender and graceful. Almost an old-fashioned gracefulness. She was pretty in a serious way. "Do you know Forrest?"

"I just met him the other day. I bought a cabin close to where he's building." Rosa couldn't bring herself to smile, but the young woman didn't seem to expect it.

"So, you're new here. That's what I thought. You'll need to get winter boots pretty soon," she said, looking at Rosa's clogs.

"I suppose you're right. Forrest's also delivering some wood. So maybe I'll survive after all." A smile crept into Rosa's voice.

"Do you want to order? I could take it right now, if you want." Her face was very thin, almost matronly when she became serious.

"Huevos rancheros, please," Rosa said without hesitation. "Do tortillas come with it?"

"Two corn tortillas."

"Great, skip the toast. Thanks."

She poured her some more coffee and left with an unhurried grace, pouring coffee table to table to table. Rosa hoped her food wouldn't be too long. The coffee was good, but it increased her hunger, and her nausea.

There was the voice again. "Having a bite to eat, I see."

Rosa looked up to Forrest's broad grin. His red hair still stood up, even indoors. His wife was next to him.

"I want you to meet my wifey, Cheryl. Cheryl, this is Rosa, the lady who's going to keep us in groceries for a few weeks." He burst out laughing and Cheryl flushed.

"Glad to meet you, Rosa. He's always this way. Try not to pay any attention," Cheryl said, rolling her eyes.

Rosa looked from one to the other and couldn't help laughing out loud.

"That's it. Keep your sense of humor," Cheryl said. "It's your only defense."

"Come on! You make me sound like a monster. Don't I deliver?" Forrest smirked. "Good wood, that is."

"Oh, Jesus," Cheryl muttered. She looked at Rosa. "And I'm pregnant."

Rosa stopped herself from laughing. "When are you due? You certainly don't look it. That's the secret, keep your weight down," she said, trying to cheer her up. They were obviously arguing.

"I'm five months along. It's my first. Well, it looks like we'll be neighbors. That is, if the house gets done." Cheryl shot Forrest a decidedly dirty look. "Excuse me, I've got to go to the john," and she was gone.

"Do you mind if I sit down?" Forrest said.

"Help yourself, Mr. McBride."

Rosa's breakfast arrived, steaming and delicious smelling. "If you want some more tortillas, let me know," the waitress said.

Before Rosa could respond, Forrest said, "Thank you so much, Iris."

"You're not welcome," she laughed and walked to another table.

"Their huevos rancheros are my favorite. Of course, they'd be yours, with a Hispanic surname, as they say."

Rosa took a bite, swallowed, and said, cuttingly, "Now, that's very perceptive of you."

"Strike two," he said. "Forgive me, I left my brain at home this morning, but my mouth doesn't know it yet." He looked up without smiling.

"Whose watercolors are those? I really like them," Rosa said, changing the subject. She didn't feel like getting involved in another quarrel. Especially this morning.

"Deft of tongue, are you?" Forrest shot her a look of irritated recognition. "Iris is the artist. The woman who just brought you your huevos rancheros."

Iris. Of course, Rosa thought. The tiny iris drawn next to I. Lily Swan. "I like her work very much. Very delicate and very strong. Are you an artist of any kind?"

"Besides being a lazy bum and building my house," Forrest said

as he saw Cheryl coming back, "I do a little charcoal drawing now
and then, and I play the piano." His eyes brightened up a little, the
energy flowing back into them.

The elf-look, Rosa thought.

"You ought to hear Iris play the piano. She's a trained pianist.
Hey, Iris! Can I come by and pound a few on your Steinway?" he
yelled.

Iris turned and looked at him. "Come on by," she said. She
couldn't keep the amusement out of her voice.

"Jesus, do you have to yell clear across the room, Forrest? We
should be going. I promised I'd be there a half-hour ago."

"Okay, let's go. See you Saturday with the promised quality
wood. Maybe I'll even help you stack it."

"It was nice meeting you, Rosa," Cheryl said. "I have to drag him
out of here every time, or we end up staying for dinner."

"See you soon, and good luck on your creative process."

Cheryl smiled and headed for the door.

"Hey, Iris! How's tomorrow night around seven? I'll bring the
wifey, too," Forrest yelled. A few laughs went around the room, but
most everyone seemed to be used to the sound of his voice and didn't
even bother to look up.

"I'll check your technique for improvement," Iris managed to say
without yelling.

"This lady likes your pictures. Her name's Rosa. Tomorrow
night then," he bellowed, and then he continued to say goodbye to
various people in the room. Cheryl was out the door and gone.
Forrest went over to Iris and got the coffee pot from her hands,
bringing it to Rosa's table.

"Would madam like some more coffee?"

Rosa burst out laughing. "Are you trying to get a tip out of me?"

He looked at her, shrewdly, and said, "I'll take anything I can
get," in a low voice. "Madam, is the coffee satisfactory?"

Rosa felt herself blushing, but she managed to say, "Yes, thank
you, James."

"Give me the coffee pot," Iris said, standing behind him.

Forrest put it down on the table, gave Rosa another look, and he
was out the door. There was something familiar about his eyes, but
she couldn't remember what it was. She also couldn't remember the
color of his eyes—gold or green? Cheryl's had been a clear, childlike
blue, and Iris, who was standing in front of her, had deep, green eyes.
Wise eyes, Rosa thought, for such a young woman. But, again, she
couldn't place Forrest's eye color.

"He's always like that. A very brilliant nut. But I guess Cheryl wants him to be a regular husband now that she's having the baby. Not that I blame her." Iris's voice trailed off.

"Well, Iris, as Forrest said, I'm Rosa, and I do like your water-colors, very much. I love your use of color, the space you suggest by not cluttering. Do you paint with oils, too?"

"I used to, but I'm not as comfortable with oils, so I came back to watercolors. They make me happy," she said, a little defensively. "Do you paint?"

"Yes, I do. Mainly in oils. Anyway, I think your pieces are pretty reasonably priced. Do you sell many?"

"If I keep them up long enough, I'll probably sell at least half. I've already sold a few. What're you planning to do out here?" Iris asked, keeping an eye out for customers.

"I'd like to teach, but I could end up doing anything," Rosa answered.

"That's how it is around here," Iris laughed. "My husband's the cook, and I wait tables. I like it up here in the mountains, don't get me wrong. No complaints." She spotted some anxious eyes. "We'll have to get together. Give me your number."

"I don't have one yet."

"Here, I'll give you mine." She wrote it on a slip of paper, drawing a hasty iris next to it.

"Tell your husband the huevos rancheros were great," Rosa called after Iris.

"Thank you!" a voice yelled from the kitchen, and Rosa saw a young man with long, blonde, curly hair smiling at her. He lifted his spatula in a salute and went back to his cooking.

Rosa finished the last tortilla with butter. Her stomach felt set-tled, and then she thought of Sean. Well, he can cook breakfast and get along, she reminded herself.

"Would you like another cup?" Iris asked.

"I'd better not or I'll fly back," Rosa laughed.

"Well, call me," Iris said as she turned to go.

"I'd love to hear you play the piano, so you know I will."

"Do you play the piano, too?"

"I'm sorry to say I don't, because I really love it."

Iris's face lit up with a smile. "Do you like Chopin?"

"Yes, Rosa smiled.

"All right!" And she went to pick up a steaming plate waiting for her under the heat lamps.

Rosa remembered the other watercolors she wanted to see, so she took a quick look, table to table. There were also a few portraits, well done and probably extremely accurate, Rosa thought. There were people eating at each table, so she felt a little awkward lingering to stare for too long.

As Rosa got into the car she thought, Why do I love the piano so much? The memory of Dolores playing the piano, at her aunt's wedding, came to her. She'd played elegantly, flamboyantly. Beautifully. And then later when Rosa had gone back down to the church basement, her mother had been quietly playing a classical piece on the beat-up piano, her head bent over the keys, by herself, as though she were all alone in the world and she didn't mind. When she'd seen Rosa standing at the door, small and silent, she'd stiffened and closed the keyboard with a slam.

Outside the car window the mountain's beauty flew by. Changing trees, the autumn, and fast-running creeks full of quick lights laced the road. Rosa wondered if she'd ever take it for granted. She turned into her driveway and saw that the chainsaw was gone from the porch. When she turned off the motor she heard it. Sean was close by cutting.

This week, she told herself, I must see about a four-wheel-drive, and get an appointment with a doctor. Tomorrow the phone will be in. That is, if they can find my cabin.

Sean stomped his boots on the porch and came in. "There's a lot of wood out there. Maybe two cords. I'm just going to get a snack and go back out. You okay?"

Rosa smiled. "I'm fine. Just a littled tired. Did you have breakfast? I assume you did." Sean nodded. "I'll start dinner around five. How's that?"

"Sounds good to me."

After Sean went back to work Rosa thought about Forrest and the way he irritated her, but she had to laugh. It's like fencing, a playful fencing, she thought. But, then, he's not my husband.

She began to unpack the larger boxes, occasionally stopping to look out the windows. What am I doing here? she asked herself.

While Sean showered Rosa set the table, placing two candles in the center. It was dark and she'd closed the curtains. Music played on the stereo—a piano tape. It was on low, and it was exceptionally beautiful in the silence. Silence. Not a sound. Not a car, a plane overhead, or another human voice—just the soft sound of the shower running and the audible, absolute silence.

Rosa opened the back door and stepped out. She stood there for a full minute, but the darkness terrified her beyond reason. She looked up, quickly, at the stars and went back indoors. Rosa shuddered and wondered what had terrified her so much. Certainly, it's vast, not my little back yard or a camping trip with someone else. Why is this different? she asked herself. Is it because this part of the forest is mine? . . . the darkness is mine, connecting to that immensity out there. That immense, dark forest surrounding me. Entirely.

"This darkness is mine," Rosa said out loud, shuddering again. She lit the candles. Silence and sound, darkness and light were not safe, intellectual symbols here. No, she could see they were real, and alive. Did closing the curtains and doors keep the immensity out? the thought skittered across her mind. The depth of her sleep, the feeling of being swallowed whole answered her: no.

"Well, I was starved. I'm going to have one more slice of that ham," Sean said, wiping his mouth.

"Help yourself. I got that ham to eat off of for a few days, and there's plenty. How about going out to dinner tomorrow night?"

"Sounds okay to me. I'm going to cut for two more days and then start splitting." Sean sat back down and then got back up to get some more broccoli. "I might turn into Paul Bunyan if I stayed here on a permanent basis," he laughed.

"You'd have to start hunting for your keep."

"I can't, remember? I'm a C.O.," Sean teased her.

"Killing to kill and killing for food are two different things in my book, dear dodo," Rosa replied. Her stomach still had an edge of nausea and it made her feel slightly off-center. "And as we discussed before, if there's no other, absolutely no other recourse, and you must kill to protect yourself or those you love, that's life."

"All right, all right. I don't want to get you started, Mom. I was trying to make a joke. Ha-ha, get it?" Sean saw Rosa's face register impatience and he said, "Anyway, I'd hunt here, for sure. Maybe I could try my bow out, but probably, if you're serious about eating, a rifle would do it."

"You kill it, you eat it. Over and out. I love deer meat. We've had it before, remember? Those steaks and ground meat David brought us on the farm?"

"Yeah, it was pretty good," Sean said, finishing his plate. "Do you mind if I borrow the car to go down to the ranch? I want to check out some cowboys. Maybe there's a shindig going on or something," Sean laughed.

"Go ahead. Just drive carefully around here. There're no street lights, and there are some giant gullies on the side of the road. Also, park my one and only in a safe place. You know, I'm going to have to see about a four-wheel-drive this week. When are you leaving, anyway?"

"Sunday, I guess. I'll go with you to see about the car if you want. Are you going to be okay here in the middle of nowhere, Mom?" Sean asked, irritably.

"It's not the middle of nowhere, Sean. It's the middle of somewhere. Don't smile like that. I mean it."

"Are you still scared?"

"What's that got to do with it? There are some things you have to do in spite of your so-called better judgment, and it's always unpredictable, it seems to me. You know that now, don't you?"

"Don't bring that up again, Mom. Okay?"

"Oh, I see. We can only talk about my stuff, but not your stuff. Is that right?"

"Okay, Mom, you made your point. I don't even want to think about Lisa. There's no use in it. I'd like to forget about it. She may as well have said she didn't want to see me again. Well, I feel the same now."

"I'm talking about the baby, Sean. About being responsible for that choice as well," Rosa said, thinking of her persistent nausea. Mild, but always present now. Yes, I'll be responsible—damn it, she thought—and get an abortion as soon as possible.

Sean stood up to clear his plate, angrily. He shoved his chair back and stomped over to the sink. "I'll wash these pots, okay?"

"I'm not saying your choice, really Lisa's choice, was wrong. What I'm saying is that you shouldn't forget. That's a part of it. Or you become inhuman, Sean." Tears came to her eyes and she turned away.

"What about your moving here by yourself? Isn't that kind of inhuman? I mean, I don't know why you're doing it, to tell you the truth," he sneered, openly.

Rosa stood up. "Okay, that's enough. I think we've both said enough for tonight. Here're the car keys. Drive carefully, please. I'm going to bed."

"Can't take your own medicine?"

"I said, that's enough, Sean. You have a lot more growing up to do before you can even begin to question my life," Rosa said in an angry voice. "Just don't get too hard, Sean. It doesn't suit you." She turned and left the room.

Sean was furious. He banged the pots as he washed them. He

snatched the keys from the kitchen table and slammed the door behind him.

Rosa heard the car disappear into the night, and her heart slowed down. She went back into the kitchen to straighten up and turn off the lights, leaving the front porch light on. She took the candles into the bedroom and lit them again. Now she was alone in the cabin for the first time. The silence descended. Rosa looked up at the uncovered bedroom window and realized if anyone were out there they could certainly see her, especially with the candles on. She'd have to make curtains. Suddenly she felt defiant, grabbed a book to read, and faced the window, but she was sleepier than she thought. Her body felt unfamiliar, as thought her usual pace were beyond her. The words, I'm pregnant, flashed across her mind, and stayed there this time.

Rosa blew out the candles and she instantly wished she'd left the kitchen light on. It was so dark she couldn't see in front of her to the closet. She felt for her Buck Knife. It was there. And then she thought of the gun in the closet, the box of bullets right next to it. No, no, I'll leave it there. It stays there.

Zack came into the room, lying at the foot of her bag. Rosa could hear his breathing, so loud, in the silence. Zack never barked for nothing. She trusted that. Yes, I trust that, she thought. It feels like there's no one really left to me. I'm alone. Alone with my choices. Rosa couldn't stop the darkness from finding her.

In the morning Rosa took her coffee back to bed, climbing into the warm sleeping bag. She couldn't remember sleeping, much less dreaming. The only thing she remembered was the car waking her up, Sean coming in, then the first grey light of dawn. Like amnesia, she thought. But I feel pretty good. Rested. No, recovered. The nausea. Rosa got up the make toast.

The smell of the frying bacon didn't stir her appetite as it usually did, but she knew she had to eat it. She opened the back door for air. There were enormous, dark clouds gathering and shifting with the morning light. She heard Sean get up and go to the bathroom.

Rosa came back in and turned the bacon. She wondered if she'd be able to paint today, just a little. It'll settle me down, she thought. Next week, for sure.

"Guess who I saw down at the ranch?" Sean asked.

Rosa thought about it. "Julie, right?"

"She's turned into quite a cowgirl. She said to say she'll be coming by. There was a dance last night. Poker game, pool table. There's a little swimming pool even, but it's closed for the winter. It's not a bad place."

"How's Julie?" Rosa asked.

"You'll have to see her to believe her. I'll let it all be a surprise." Sean was smiling in a calculated manner, and he knew she didn't like it.

"Anyway, I ought to go down there and talk to someone about plowing this road during the winter. I'm told the ranch does it."

"You'd better. I heard they get up to eight feet here," he said, clearly enjoying himself.

"Do you want a couple of eggs while I'm at it?" Rosa asked in a clipped tone.

"Yeah, I'd better get out there quick. I guess I can work in a little rain, but I'm sure not looking forward to it," he said, looking out the window. "There're some real cowboy types down there. Some real sleaze-balls. A couple of nice guys, though. Most just work there for the season, and I was told most of the summer guys are gone."

"You smell like a booze bucket. Did you drink?"

"A little beer. They have a pretty loose bar down there. They asked me if I was twenty-one and that was it." Sean felt pleased with himself.

After breakfast Rosa went down to check the mail and make an appointment with a local doctor. Now or never, she told herself. She chose a name and called, making an apointment for the next day. She'd also stop at the used car lot while she was in town. May as well do it all at once, she thought with a sigh. Rosa thought of her studio room, her work, and she felt bleak. Who cares if I paint? No one but me, she answered herself.

To her surprise there was some mail, all forwarded. A letter from Rolf! Inside was a xerox of a photograph of him waving, with one hand, and holding a child's wind-turner with the other. Underneath it he'd written "Self-portrait, or couldn't get anyone else to take my photo at the time." Colored glitter fell out of its folds, cheering her up as though he'd actually arrived by mail.

My friend Rosa,
I'm back home and up to my old tricks. Your memory is still fresh. I'm not a good letter writer, so please excuse my pathetic attempt. I began work on a new piece and classes have started. How goes your work? I think often of our

conversations, our meeting. It was admittedly a brief meeting, but meaningful, no? Isn't that what counts? Write me when you can, tell me how you are. It's gloomy here in winter, time to sip brandy and make fires. Much happiness to you!   amor, El Gringo

Rolf xxoo

Rosa looked at the German stamps on the envelope and touched them. The glitter sparkled in the light. How wonderful the unexpected is sometimes. Yes, she thought with a smile.

Was she seeing things or was there actually a horse tied to a tree in the front of her cabin? It was definitely a horse—a very large, brown one. As Rosa got out of the car an ear-piercing whistle, that sounded like in the movies when they're rounding up cattle, brought her to a halt. Then, "Long time no see!" and Julie was striding up to her with a cowboy hat, chaps, and a pair of silver spurs attached to real cowboy boots. Not the kind that are bought for fashion. These had mud all over them.

"Julie! How are you? Jesus, let me take it all in!" Rosa laughed, moving toward her to hug her.

Julie stopped her with a hand shake, but she was smiling without pause. "Well, was I surprised to hear you moved up here! What the hell brings you here?" Her horse began to paw the ground and dance around nervously. Julie reached over and grabbed the halter, calming him down.

"I thought you came up here to teach elementary school! I didn't know you were working as a wrangler! What happened?" Rosa couldn't take her eyes off the sharp little spurs on Julie's boots. "Do you actually use those?"

"Only when I have to. Look, I brought some wine. Why don't I open it. By the way, Sean's grown into a hunk. I wouldn't mind breaking him in for you, Rosa." Julie winked at her.

Rosa stiffened a little, but Julie was probably just stretching a point, she told herself. "I think he's already been broken in, to tell you the truth. Sorry," she said with a trace of annoyance.

"Well, I could finish the job," she laughed gustily. "I could barely keep my hands off him last night. I'm sorry but the man's sexy. It's not my doing." Julie looked at Rosa and laughed again.

"Frankly, it's up to him." Rosa was clearly annoyed now. "How about that wine?"

"I put it in your refrigerator," Julie said, bounding ahead of her. "So, where's your old man? What the hell are you doing here?" Julie poured the wine. "We have to finish the entire bottle before I go." She laughed loudly.

"To make a long story short, we've separated," Rosa said, looking at Julie, trying to find a point of contact.

"He always was a jealous son-of-a-bitch, wasn't he?" Julie's eyes glittered with a hint of maliciousness.

"Well, that's really making the long story short." Rosa had to laugh. "To be honest, your letters, and the mention of Lupine Meadows, sparked my imagination. I began to imagine this place. In fact, I dreamt it."

Julie scowled. "What does that have to do with it? You know, I don't live here in Lupine Meadows. I live in town. Kind of on the edge of town. A little ranch. With the head wrangler." Julie waited for Rosa's reaction.

"I certainly didn't follow you here, Julie. As I said, I dreamt this place, this cabin I've bought, and we're sitting in it. We used to talk about things like this. Dreams. I gather you don't subscribe anymore."

"Oh, sometimes I do, but it sure hasn't helped me out. I'll tell you what's helped me out—knowing the head wrangler. I couldn't get a job for shit. Small town politics and all that."

"Have you thought of going back to the bay area?"

"Nah. Wrangling's hard work but I kind of like it. I must've gone through half the wranglers the first year, and some of the guests are another matter." Julie licked her lips, playfully. "I guess I'm tired of doing A, B, C, D, E, F, G and all that. Here I can work with a horse between my legs." She laughed. "I'm just so turned on. Hot pants. Can't explain it. I think it happens to women our age."

"How does your boyfriend feel about your hot pants?" Rosa was becoming intrigued.

"As long as there's enough left on the stove for him he doesn't mind. He's older. Kind of a father-daughter thing. We each do what we want, just don't bring anyone home."

"Are you happy?"

"For now. Why not? Anyway, I want you to come down and meet some people. We take off for Reno and party once in a while." Julie looked at Rosa. "You'll be competition, but what the hell," she said, laughing.

Rosa hardly recognized the woman she'd liked so much for her warmth and exuberance. Exuberance, yes. That had been her trademark. Well, now she was exuberant about other things. Julie's reddish-blonde hair was short and curly. Little golden horse shoes hung from her ears, shimmering as she moved her head, which was often. Rosa looked at the freckles, the hazel eyes, the pretty, determined face that was Julie's. But her eyes which had once paused for understanding now looked harsh and hungry. Is this what happens to women our age? Rosa thought of Rolf, even Forrest, with a sigh.

"First what I have to do is set up my work area. The second bedroom's going to be my studio. And then see about work. I'm applying to the junior college for teaching, and in the meantime anything else."

"Anything?" Julie asked, cynically.

"Well, I have my limits, shall we say. For example, I don't think I'd do wrangling because I'm not that hot on a horse. No pun intended. As far as prostitution, I suppose I'd have to be desperate and the price about right." Rosa's cheeks were flushed from anger. "Look, actually, I moved here to be by myself for a while, so I'm really not into being anyone's competition or partying at Reno. Maybe we can just get together once in a while. You know, to talk?"

"A recluse. Well, in the winter you'll get your wish out here. There's no one back this far in the winter. The ranch'll plow you out. I'd remind them if I were you." Julie was beginning to look bored.

"The guy that's building his place across the meadow told me the same thing." Rosa poured herself a half glass of wine.

"Oh, Forrest. He's cute but a snob. A real hard-to-get number. He works at the ranch in the summer, wrangling a little, clean-up. I wouldn't mind getting into his drawers."

"He's married, you know. I mean, a little discretion goes a long way, right?"

"So what? This is a real Peyton Place, you'll find out," Julie laughed. "How about going riding Saturday to the cookout?"

"I can barely stay on a horse." The ranch was becoming less of a source of curiosity by the second.

"I'll save you a safe one. Guaranteed. Come on—it's almost free to the homeowners up here. Just five bucks to cover your grub. Steak and plenty of beer and wine."

A horse and its rider rushed into Rosa's front yard sending dust in all directions. If there's a clump of grass left after this it'll be a miracle, Rosa thought to herself.

"Shit, it's Jake! Now, what does he want?" Julie looked at Rosa. "It's daddy," she said, sarcastically.

"Julie!" he was yelling at the top of his lungs. "Julie!" Julie's horse was dancing nervously again, and trying to pull free from the tree. Jake was in his sixties, strong looking, with a sweat-stained cowboy hat that seemed permanently attached to his head.

Julie walked out on the porch. "What's so damned important, Jake?"

"What's so damned important? We're workin the horses, that's what's so damned important! Git yr raggedy ass down to the corral, on the double! Do ya hear me?"

Rosa walked out on the porch. Julie yelled, "Jake, this is Rosa!" Jake looked disgusted and rode off without a word.

"Charming, isn't he?" Rosa said, angrily. "The only place I've seen a scene like that is in the movies. B movies."

Julie unwrapped the halter from the tree's branch and calmed her horse. "Oh, he was just being an outrageous asshole for your benefit. I guess he wants you to know who's boss."

"Then why are you going? Do you have to leave?"

Julie looked at Rosa with the first hint of vulnerability she'd allowed herself in a long time and she was instantly sorry. "He is the boss." Julie got on her horse and kept her anger to herself; she'd revealed enough as it was. "Look, come to the cookout. He's too busy showing off to be an asshole in public."

"I'll think about it, Julie. Come by again when you get a chance." Suddenly Rosa felt sorry for her. Maybe that's what she's had to do to get by with someone like that. Julie had changed, almost beyond recognition.

"Be at the ranch by one o'clock. Bring the hunk with you! Don't forget my offer!" she laughed loudly. Julie spotted Sean. "Hi, Sean! I'm inviting you and your mother on a horseback-riding cookout this Saturday. All the steak and beer you want. In fact, anything *you* want." She laughed again. "See you both Saturday." She glanced once at Rosa, and rode away smiling to herself.

"That was a regular John Wayne scene. Who the hell was that guy on the horse?" Sean asked.

"You saw that? I didn't know you were watching. That was Jake, her boyfriend, certified he-man, and head wrangler," Rosa said with heavy sarcasm. "He was too much of a man to say 'Glad to meet you' or anything—even 'Hi' would've done it. Did you see that trip?"

"Yeah, I saw it." Sean had vaguely enjoyed it, though he did think it was an asshole thing to do. "Isn't he kind of old for her? He's in good shape and all, but he could be her father. He was playing cards last night, and, come to think of it, she was kind of avoiding the area."

"Probably because she was trying to latch onto you. Was she coming onto you or what?" Rosa could see Sean was enjoying her anger, so she took deep breaths.

Sean smiled. "You might say so. She wanted to dance with me, but I felt a little funny about it. I started talking to some guys there and she left me alone. One of them told me to run for my life."

"I think we'll skip the cookout scene. Jesus."

"Oh, come on, Mom. Aren't you curious? She said there'd be steak and beer. I could go for that. It'd be fun to ride a horse."

"I'm not that curious. I sure don't like what's going on with Julie. Are you through cutting?"

"Almost. She doesn't bother me. She's harmless. I can take care of myself," Sean said, defensively.

"I'm not going, Sean."

"Then maybe I'll go," he said, walking back to the downed wood.

"Did the phone people come?" Rosa yelled.

"Yeah, it's in the bedroom. It even works. What's for dinner?" Sean yelled back.

"We're going out, remember?"

"Great! I'm starved!"

Rosa stood looking at the pawed-up earth. I'll have to get a good shovel and rake—too bad I left mine on the farm. And a snow shovel, she reminded herself. Tomorrow the doctor and a four-wheel-drive. My Volvo should be a good trade-in.

She took Rolf's letter out and read it again. The sparkling glitter made Jake's face disappear. Making love to him would be work. Real work, Rosa thought. Like a thousand an hour. She laughed out loud. She folded the letter up and placed it back in the envelope, and went to her bedroom closet. She brought down the gun and unwrapped it, holding the cold, dark metal. "Germany," Rosa muttered. She wrapped it up again and placed it back on the farthest shelf, and then she placed Rolf's letter on top of it.

Rosa picked up the phone. The dial tone was loud and clear, and it was dark brown like the rough cedar on every wall. It was beautiful, the stark design of the wood repeating itself, over and over. But at the same time, as she lay there looking up, the walls and ceiling gave the impression of a coffin. Walled in, she thought.

Her bedroom boxes were half unpacked and she could see a bright fuchsia shawl, its fringe hanging over the side. Rosa took it out and spread it across the wall over where she planned to put her bed. That's better, she thought. Color. And more color. She thought of calling Julio, but decided to wait until the next night.

Tomorrow the doctor. A urine test, no doubt. A pelvic. But I'm nauseated again, she thought, and she was. I'm pregnant, but I have to make sure. Where do I get an abortion around here? The dream of the child came to her again, almost like a punch to her stomach. And it was a daughter, she thought, remembering the sweet, little genitals she'd glimpsed in the dream. A girl. Then what in the hell am I doing here? By myself? No, she almost yelled out loud. I just can't do it. It'd be crazy.

Rosa went to the kitchen for a snack to ease her nausea and fixed herself a cup of tea. She took her tea into the studio and sat on the floor looking at her paintings. Four of these will go in the front room, three in the bedroom. Maybe one will sell in San Francisco this month. Maybe I can get an exhibition up here. Of course, I can. The voice inside her regained its confidence by a notch or two. Rosa looked at the unfinished globe, Earth, and she imagined the rainbow again. Next week I start, no matter what.

The realtor had pointed out a restaurant and hotel sign on the house tour, telling Rosa that they served some of the best meals in the county. Sean and Rosa were given a table for two in a small dining room. Sean ordered the roast beef special and Rosa ordered stuffed clams in a thick, white sauce covered in mushrooms. Sean had milk; she white wine. Two things spoiled her dinner, but it was delicious nonetheless—the nagging nausea and the realization that the waitress was being nasty because she assumed Sean was her lover. It seems, Rosa thought, like a week ago that I was taking him for some new tennis shoes, ones that could make him fly, and here we are being given bad service because the waitress wants him.

"Don't take it so seriously, Mom. That's her problem," he smiled. "Besides, she's a dog," he said, making barking noises.

"Okay, Sean, cool it." When did this start? she wondered. Of course, I've noticed he's attractive, but I thought that was a private observation, not a public declaration. Then Rosa got angry and gave a dose of bad manners to the waitress, which worked. Rosa was always amazed at what worked, though Sean looked a little embarrassed.

The nausea remained. As they got in the car the paradox of her situation revealed itself to her—people thought her son was her young lover and, in fact, she was pregnant, at her age, and separated from her husband. The rich clams made her feel instantly sick to her stomach as the car heater began to work.

"Mom, do you feel all right?" Sean looked at her face.

"I'm okay. I think the clams were a little too rich, that's all. But it was good, wasn't it?"

"It sure was. Thanks. I felt like saying MOM real loud there for a while, but, you know, it's really not her business. Arf-arf." He laughed.

"Well, Julie's after you too, Sean. She wants to break you in, as she put it." Rosa looked at him without smiling.

"She actually said that?"

"I told her you were already broken in. Too late for that, anyway, thank Goddess."

"Thank Goddess, huh?"

"Yeah, thank Goddess." Rosa opened her window, hoping the air would relieve the nausea.

"I told some guys I'd come down and play a little pool tonight. I'll take the car, okay?"

"Go ahead, but watch out for the tigers."

Sean laughed. "No problem. I'm not a kid. Remember?"

"Watch out for the ruts, hunk, and see you in the morning."

"Do you think I'm a hunk, really?" he teased.

"Oh, Jesus, Sean! Julie does, take it from her. No, don't take it from her," Rosa laughed in spite of herself.

Sean grabbed the keys, throwing them into the air and was gone.

Rosa opened a 7-Up and took it to the bedroom. The heater was on and that would have to do tonight. She was too tired to make a fire. She looked at the phone and thought of calling Julio. No, not tonight, she decided. Maybe he's not even home. She tried to imagine him out at a bar, the serious set of his shoulders, the line of his cheek in the light, his full lips set into silence. She imagined him alone, but maybe he wasn't. If I'm pregnant, will I even tell him?

The light in the kitchen was still on and it eased the absolute darkness. Zack was at the foot of the sleeping bag, and though the darkness still opened its mouth to swallow her, she didn't dread it as much. Her stomach was settling as she lay still on her back. The silence is beautiful, she thought. Unbroken. Not a car. Perfect.

Rosa waited for the presence of her wolf, but it was as though she, the wolf, were everywhere at once, running, running, sniffing, unable to lay at rest. Or, Rosa thought, as though I've set her free. As though she set me free?

A group of riders—large, muscled horses beneath them—slowly ride ahead.

The riders look unhappy, serious. Rosa realizes she must hold on to the back of her horse no matter what. Sean is up ahead, talking and laughing, unaware of the seriousness. The horses are beautiful, and Rosa feels that they long to throw the riders off their backs. She sees Julie and wants to warn her, but a voice tells her not to. It will make no difference. She won't listen. But Sean. I must warn Sean.

Julio got home after midnight after meeting some friends at a bar in North Beach. A couple of photographers, a poet, a painter—all of them brown and black. When he'd graduated from the university he'd personally congratualated himself; this brown, Indian-looking kid getting this white boy's piece of paper. He'd gotten so drunk it felt like he had to get to know himself all over when he came to.

The apartment looked inhospitable, unapproachable, and the bedroom even worse. Where would his flesh fit in here? he felt, slumping to the floor. The sauna had sounded so good—now it just seemed like a sweat box in the basement.

He'd seen them, the sweat boxes where they kept prisoners. Horrible. He thought of his initial rage of abandonment—as though love itself had abandoned him to war. Didn't my mother start it all by leaving me at birth—then my first wife, my grandmother, now Rosa? The old rage returned, and he remembered.

At first he volunteered for night patrol, painting his exposed flesh, his entire face, black. Black, dark, invisible, he'd lived through a couple of weeks of night patrol, never coming face to face with the enemy out there, but he'd heard the screams, he'd seen the body bags, and a couple of his friends never came back.

One night they stopped an old Vietnamese man who was obviously late getting home. Julio had seen sheer terror in his eyes as he looked at each grotesque face, and he saw himself through the old man's eyes. The old man was released in the morning, or at least that's what he'd been told. You never really knew the truth unless you actually saw it in Vietnam.

Julio sat up on his elbow and looked around the room. A shimmer of ocean shone in the distance. Rosa was up on a mountain in some cabin trying to paint a lilac sky or something. He laughed out loud. Maybe you can't believe it even when you see it.

I love you, Rosa, Julio thought the words, and their opposite, I hate you, Rosa, were also in his heart, in equal measure, unsaid.

The landscape is split in two. On the right is jungle—men in uniform, mortar fire, the smell of death, violent death. Yes, he smells it. On the left is the desert, silent. Gonzales is crouched down and hidden. The smell of water is in the air. The hunt. On the right it is dark. On the left it is day, morning. The water hole is sweet, and death is fair. They will eat. Julio enters the left side, the desert, and Gonzales puts his fingers to his mouth. Silence.

Sean was still sleeping when she got up to go to the early morning doctor's appointment. While she drank some coffee and ate a piece of toast—the nausea was now an unmistakable condition—she wrote Sierra.

> Dear Sierra, Well, I'm finally here. Got your poems, think they're fine, especially the woman of clarity. Of course, I'll try to be there for your birth. As far as I can see, that is. Bob and I were once friends, but I can no longer be friends with a man like that. I know he's your husband, but look, I don't even live with Julio. If this situation makes you uncomfortable with my presence, especially at your birth, I'd rather be told now. Because that's how I feel. We each have our own lives, that's clear to me now. That's very clear. I think of you with love. (Sean won't be living here after all—will buy a snow shovel today—SNOW!)   Rosita

Rosita. What her grandmother had called her, and what Sierra had called her when they were girls. No, I won't change a word. It goes in the mailbox this morning.

The car dealer thought her Volvo and the Landcruiser were an even exchange, but Rosa argued that the Landcruiser was nearly five years older. The manager had come and agreed with her, offering to throw in an eight-hundred dollar check. She'd pick it up next week.

The lab results would be ready Monday. "You're either pregnant or very late. You are swelling. It's been eighteen years since your last pregnancy?" "Yes." "This must come as quite a surprise," he'd said, smiling. "Yes, it is," she'd said.

Rosa put the red snow shovel with the wooden handle by the front door. Well, it looks official, she thought. Now it can snow. She was exhausted. She dozed off for a quick nap, and when she woke up it was almost midnight. She'd slept through, though she could hardly believe it. Something deep inside of her needed to sleep and sleep and sleep. To rest.

Sean had written a note: "Down at the ranch. Where else? I didn't want to bother you. See you in the morning."

Rosa fixed a cheese sandwich and some tea. She put the heater up to medium; Sean's fire was down to ashes. She ate the sandwich quickly and fixed another cup of tea, taking it to her room. She forced herself to brush her teeth, and then fell back into the sleeping bag. The night was cloudy, but the persistent stars poked through.

Suddenly, she remembered Julio. She'd forgotten to call. She picked up the receiver and the numbers glowed. He answered in a sleepy voice.

"It's me, Rosa. Sorry to wake you up. I could call back in the morning."

"No, I've been waiting for you to call, you know. How are you?"

"Alive. Actually, I slept through the afternoon till now. I guess I was more tired than I knew. Anyway, how're you doing?"

"I'm okay. Is anything wrong?"

"No, I'm just tired, finally. That's all. I think I got a car. A Landcruiser."

"I miss you, Rosa. Do you miss me, at all?"

"I must admit I do, sometimes. I guess that's why I'm calling. Here's my phone number."

"Okay, great. Are you sure you're okay?"

"Yes, I'm fine."

"I don't like this. In fact, I hate it. I don't think you're safe up there by yourself. Don't women usually live with men in those places?"

"Don't start that. I can take care of myself. I'd better because I'm here. I bought a snow shovel today."

"Have you tried firing that gun?"

"No, Julio. I called you just in case you were up, but I'm still sleepy. Look, I'm sorry if I woke you up. I'm falling asleep with the phone digging into my ear."

"I'll call you back tomorrow. We'll take it out for some shooting while I'm up there. I miss you. Good night."

"Good night, Julio," Rosa said, hanging up the phone.

Julio called back. "Aren't you going to say good night? You almost took my ear off, you hung up so fast," he said, angrily.

"I did say good night. Didn't you hear me?"

"Sounded more like goodbye. Forever."

"Julio, are we going to start fighting long distance, too? I said good night. *I* called *you*, remember? I'm really sleepy."

"Okay, good night, Rosa. I'll see you next Thursday."

"Good night, Julio. Do you hear me?"

"I miss you, Rosa."

"Take care of yourself," she said and hung up, pushing the button down with her finger. Tears jammed her throat again. Rosa turned off the lamp and stared into the darkness listening to Zack breathe.

The sound of the chainsaw woke her up. She glanced at the clock: eight-twenty. The heaviness of the day before was gone, and a distinct feeling of renewal ran through Rosa's body. She sat up and the nausea was more pronounced, as though it'd finally gotten permission to assert itself. Otherwise, she felt an incredible sense of health as though she were a very young girl, twelve, or thirteen. Rosa thought of her inexhaustible energy at that age and it made her feel good. It was as though she'd plugged into a human energy outlet—a mysterious source of energy. Yes, she felt plugged in.

Rosa's sleep had been so deep it was as though her dreams couldn't reveal themselves in form, anything recognizable. But instead, walls of color had floated through her mind. The darker the color, the more dense the wall, and the lighter colors had been transparent, lovely with joy. The walls had appeared and disappeared, sometimes the dark walls overpowered the light pastels like a battle between sorrow and joy. The battle within herself. And then it seemed the walls blended, merged, and what was left flashed for a frustrating, ecstatic instant. She hadn't seen it, but she'd felt it. Yes, she'd felt it.

"Have you eaten breakfast, Sean?" Rosa yelled from the back steps.

"Not really!" Sean yelled back.

"What're you doing out so early for a change?"

"I'm going tomorrow, remember?"

She'd actually forgotten, so she gathered herself, quickly. "Do you want pancakes and bacon?"

"Love some! Be there in ten minutes!"

Rosa shut the back door and the chainsaw receded. She put on a flute tape and started the batter, nibbling on toast and sipping coffee. She ran to the bathroom and threw up, and she instantly felt better. Fuck, she thought, this is exactly how it was with Sean. "Damn it, damn it to hell!" she said out loud.

The chainsaw stopped. Rosa went back to the kitchen, poured some more coffee, and started the pancakes and bacon. The bacon smelled too strong. Of course.

"I thought I'd get started as early as possible to try and finish it up. Isn't that guy with the wood supposed to come today?"

"These are almost ready," Rosa said, keeping any visible trace of her nausea hidden. "He said he'd deliver today."

"I hope he's here in time so we can go on the cookout. You must've been out of it. You slept about seventeen hours." Sean poured himself some coffee. "You look pretty good, so you must've needed it."

"Are you still planning on going to that damned cookout? I really don't think it's such a hot idea. Anyway, look, the temperature's dropped and it's clouding up," she said, irritably.

"Yeah, they said this is the last week for cookouts. Julie said to tell you she's saving the gentlest horse down there. She was going to come by last night, but I told her you were knocked out," Sean said, remembering Julie's reply: "You ought to be in bed yourself. Want me to tuck you in?" she'd asked, running her eyes over him, head to foot. She wasn't a dog or anything; she was just too obvious. It would feel like I was doing her some kind of favor, he thought. What a weird trip.

"Yeah, I bet Jake'll put a nice, friendly burr in my saddle, or whatever they do around here." Rosa looked at Sean and he looked entirely pleased with himself. Attention will do it every time, she thought with irritation.

"Come on, Mom. It's only five bucks."

A truck drove up and parked at the top of the driveway. It was Forrest. Rosa opened the door.

"Your car's in the way. I have to back up to unload. How're you doing? Great day, isn't it? All nice and gloomy!" Forrest laughed. He was wearing what looked like a child's ski hat.

"Do you want some pancakes? I'm cooking some right now. So, gloomy weather's your natural element, I take it." The bright, red ski hat with white snowflakes on it, with a red tassel on top, made her want to laugh. He had it pulled down over his ears.

"It makes the firewood trade brisk. Maybe I'll take some after I unload. If you give me your keys I'll move the car," he said with a hint of command.

Sean came out on the front porch.

"Sean, this is Forrest. Forrest, this is my son, Sean," she said, watching a slight shock register on his face.

"Big for a twelve-year-old, aren't you?" Forrest laughed.

Sean reddened, but before he could say anything Rosa answered, "He's eighteen and bigger than you, it appears."

Forrest stepped forward to shake Sean's hand. "No offense intended. That just makes your mother a little older than she looks. You are pretty tall there, Sean," Forrest laughed again. "I'm half-inch from six feet, but that's all you need." He looked at Rosa. "I'll be polite and not ask your age. After thirty it's always twenty-nine, right?"

"Very cute, McBride. I'm thirty-four and three-fourths." Rosa went into the cabin to get the car keys. She heard Sean and Forrest talking and laughing.

"I'd help you unload but I'm trying to get as much wood in as I can. Do you sell much wood around here?" Sean asked.

"It's a pretty good side line, that's for sure. I work at the ranch in the summer months and part of the spring. I'm not full-time because I don't kiss the head wrangler's ass."

"You mean Jake, don't you? Do you know Julie?"

"Don't remind me," Forrest said and they both burst out laughing.

"She's a friend of mine, Sean." Rosa shot him a dirty look. She handed Forrest the keys to her car and went back in to eat her breakfast.

She heard Sean start up the chainsaw, and thought of tomorrow morning when he was scheduled to leave. I won't see him every day, she told herself—a glimpse in the morning, dinners once in a while. He'll be there, I'll be here. Rosa looked around the cabin in the gloomy light—alone. Sean's morning fire was beginning to die, so she built it up again until it began to send out a bright, steady heat.

Forrest knocked on the door and opened it. "Do you want to tell me where to stack the wood? You also might want to take a look at this quality wood here." He looked proud and boyish. "You may as well see what you bought, Ms. Luján." His eyes challenged her.

Rosa followed him out and looked at the wood he'd tossed by the carport. She picked up the oak pieces and they were dense and heavy. The pine and cedar were solid, dry.

"Very good, McBride. This isn't all of it, I assume."

"Very observant of you, no. I'll bring the other load in the afternoon. So, where do you want these gems?"

What you need is a bell at the top of your hat." Rosa looked at his snowflake ski hat. "Then you could be Santa's helper." She began to laugh.

Forrest became serious, obviously slighted.

It felt good to laugh, but she stopped herself and tried not to look at the tassel at the top of his hat. "How about half the oak on the porch, and the rest of it, just leave it laying right here. I can stack it later. Thanks, anyway."

"Suit yourself. Would you have a cup of coffee?" he stared the request right into her eyes—a command more than a request.

"It's on the stove. Help yourself." Rosa looked out toward the clearing. The ridges of trees, sprawling in an endlessness that seemed ringed with light. An Earth light. Not a light from the sky, she thought, but a light coming up from the Earth itself.

Forrest was beside her with his coffee. "I see you can tune out quarrelsome entities—men," he said, laughing to himself.

Rosa looked at him. "Not entirely, but I keep trying. So, you work at the ranch. Do you like it?"

"It pays okay and it's work I don't mind. However, the hierarchy down there can get fairly oppressive," Forrest said in a confidential tone.

"You mean Jake, head macho wrangler, alias John Wayne? See all this pawed-up earth? His horsie did it the other day. Quite a show."

"Yeah, the man's quite a show, that's for sure. What're you doing here, anyway? And you know Julie?"

"I've known Julie for a few years. She used to teach elementary school in the bay area when I knew her. Anyway, I'm here probably for the same reasons you are—a little solitude and silence. I'm a painter, and, usually, I teach."

"I see," Forrest said, staring at her. "Is your son going to stay?"

"Rosa looked away. "He's leaving tomorrow," she said, guardedly.

"Some people can't handle the solitude, you know. Well, I'd better get to work. I'll deliver the rest of your wood this afternoon. A painter, huh?" His eyes held a mocking tone.

"How much do I owe you?" she asked, sharply.

"It comes to one hundred and seventy dollars." He stared down the steps, putting the coffee cup in her hands. "Thanks for the coffee, Ms. van Gogh."

"Fuck you."

Startled, Forrest turned. "What did you say?"

Rosa looked at him. "I said, fuck you."

He stalked to the truck and began throwing wood non-stop.

His eyes are more gold than green, Rosa noted with silent satisfaction. She wrote him a check and placed it in an envelope. "Here's your check!" she yelled, putting it in between two pieces of oak.

He looked up but didn't answer, continuing to throw the wood. When he was finally done he started the motor, then winding each gear to its absolute limit, he drove away.

"Overgrown teenager," Rosa muttered.

Sean came in. "Are you going to the cookout or what? We have to be there by one and it's almost twelve now."

Rosa looked at him and thought of her ominous dream of the horses. "I guess I'll give it a try. Look, I had a dream about this outing. A kind of warning dream, so pay attention to any strange occurrences."

Sean looked impatient. "It'll be okay, Mom. I'm going to haul in the last of the wood so we can get going." He turned and left.

Already he seems to be someone else, Rosa thought. And his dismissal of her dream hurt and angered her. Will he dismiss his own dreams as well? Little boys, men, growing away from their mothers, and in this culture any shred of the mother in the son is considered failure. Did I fail? she asked herself. I was strong, loving. Strong. Maybe that's it, she thought. Too damned strong. An indescribable sadness held her in a grip that was soft and harsh at once.

Julie had saved her the gentlest horse, but the gentlest horse was hardly docile. The horse sensed Rosa's anxiety and began to nip at her legs, baring her teeth.

"Just punch her right between the eyes!" Jake yelled. "Show her who's boss or she's goin ta take ya for a ride." He came up to the horse and punched her squarely on the forehead above the eyes. The horse shuddered and then stared straight ahead.

Rosa felt the punch sharply between her legs, then it echoed throughout her body. She refused to meet Jake's gaze and he rode away. She touched the horse's neck and held her hand there. Look, she thought to the horse, if you don't nip at me, I won't hit you. The horse's neck twitched where her hand was, and Rosa patted her like she patted Zack.

"That's not a dog there, Rosa," Julie said, caustically.

"I don't think punching them in the head like that's absolutely necessary. Anyway, I feel like patting her."

Julie jerked her horse and rode to the head of the line. Sean was up ahead on a grey gelding. The horses started moving and Rosa's horse followed. Julie said something to Sean and he turned around, and both of them laughed.

Rosa flushed with anger, but tried to concentrate on being flexible or the rolling motions of the horse jarred her. Plus her nausea was having a field day. Well, isn't this fun? she thought, holding onto the saddle horn. She looked back at the other riders and most of them looked deadly serious, as though they couldn't wait to get to where they were going. Like the dream.

They came to a stream and the horse hesitated. Rosa tightened her knees gently and moved her body forward, and the horse crossed it, carefully placing her hooves into the water. "Good girl," Rosa said out loud.

"Talking to the horse now?" Julie said, riding by to the back of the line. She spurred her horse bringing it to a gallop. An unnecessary gallop, throwing dust and making the other horses nervous. Rosa put her hand on the horse's neck, and it seemed to calm her.

Julie rode back to the front of the line again, falling into place beside Sean. There was an unmistakable flaunting attitude to the way she sat in the saddle. Rosa realized that the best she could do was to stay glued to her horse. Period. Like in the dream.

Jake, who was at the front, looked back at Julie and Sean. "How bout bringin up the rear an doin yr job?"

Julie jerked her horse around angrily and dug her spurs sharply into the horse's soft sides. When she got to the back of the line her horse reared up, pawing the air. Julie screamed one loud scream and was thrown against a pile of stones.

Rosa held onto her horse with both hands, legs tight against the large animal.

Jake was kneeling next to her, yelling, "Damn it! Can't you handle yr horse, Julie?"

"A goddamned snake spooked him. Ran right under his legs." Tears were running down her face and she clutched her arm.

"Hey, Jake, she's hurt pretty bad. Why don't you let up on her," an old man said.

"I don't see where it's any yr busines," he said, looking up at the man and back to Julie.

"Messed yr arm up, it looks ta me. Okay, let's git ya to the emergency."

Julie held onto her arm unable to stop crying. The pain was almost unbearable.

"You on the rag or what?" Jake asked loudly.

The older man looked disgusted and turned his horse back to the ranch. A group of people followed him.

Rosa got off her horse, leading her to where Julie was. "Are you okay, Julie? Can I do anything?"

"There ain't nothin you can do. Gonna give that horse a whippin though. Yr too soft on yr horses, that's all," he said, glaring at Julie.

"How're you going to get her back?" Rosa asked.

"Put her on my horse. You go on with the others."

Rosa ignored him. "Are you okay, Julie?"

Julie steeled herself. She was so ashamed to be sitting there crying, holding her arm. "I'm all right. Go on back like Jake says," she said, angrily.

Jake looked at Sean and said, "Maybe if yr mind had been on the job this mess wouldn't a happened."

"Jake, will you shut up?" Julie yelled.

Rosa got on her horse and left, following the trail back, slowly.

"Jesus, what an asshole!" Sean said, hotly.

"That, Sean, is the understatement of the century. I just hope she's okay."

"It looks to me like she's not your friend anymore."

Rosa smoothed the horse's mane, patting her neck. "I think you're right."

"She must've shattered her arm. She was lucky she didn't land on her head."

"That's for sure. She said a snake spooked her horse."

"Is that what she said? I didn't hear that."

"That's what she said. Do you mind cooking something? I'll get the dishes."

By the time they got home a drizzle had started and the air was getting colder. Rosa put on some tea water and went to the bathroom. She could hear Sean getting the food ready.

"How about fried chicken?" he yelled.

"Sounds good. Put some cream of chicken soup over it after you fry it for a while, and let it simmer around fifteen minutes."

"Do you want rice?"

"I leave it up to you, Sean."

Rosa went to the bedroom and lay down on her sleeping bag. She opened the note Forrest had tacked to the door. "Here's my phone number. . . . Call if you need any more wood. F. McBride" He'd stacked half the wood, she'd noted. She dozed off and the next thing she knew Sean was in the room saying, "It's ready, Mom. It's really raining now. It looks like I got that wood in right on time."

"Okay, here I come, believe it or not. Boy, I'm tired. I feel like my brain's not connected to my feet."

"You sure are tired lately, aren't you?"

"I have to catch up with myself is probably what's the matter," she said, getting up. Rosa poured a glass of milk, sipping it slowly, and that settled her empty stomach somewhat. They were both hungry and ate without talking until seconds.

"This is great, Sean."

"My farewell dinner." He smiled wryly. "I guess Julie got to the doctor's by now. You know, not all the guys down there are like Jake-the-jack-off. I didn't know guys like that still existed."

"Me either. But do you notice that Julie's buying it? By the way, what were you and she cackling about today? You know, when you looked back at me while on the great grey gelding."

Sean looked embarrassed. "Oh, she made some stupid remark about how pretty soon the horse would start talking back and all. So, did you really dream what happened today?"

"Pretty much. That's why I came, to tell you the truth. Only I didn't dream Julie falling off the horse. What I dreamt, basically, was a sense of danger."

Sean smirked. "But did you actually dream the horses and all that?"

"Yes, I did." Rosa looked at him and asked herself, Where's my son?

Rosa started soaking the dishes and then she made some hot chocolate with brandy. They sat by the fire sipping their drinks. There was an unaccustomed stiffness between them. A feeling of mutual distrust and animosity. The soft sound of the fire, with occasional explosions and flying sparks, drew their attention like a living presence. The fire's warmth, in the deepening cold, sealed that impression.

"Why do you suppose Dad never answered my letters? I mean, he never answered one." Sean stared at the fire.

Rosa saw the hurt in his face and decided, for once, just to say it. She'd always sheltered him as a child by telling him his father drank too much, he was a very unhappy man, his own father never gave him any affection; and all of that was true. And more. "Because he's a coward, Sean. He's a goddamn coward."

Sean riveted his eyes on his mother. "What do you mean?" he asked almost angrily.

"Because he feels sorrier for himself than for you, and, therefore, he cannot love you. He'd rather blame life than try to change it. He's a coward because he's chosen not to love you. He makes me sick. Self-pitying bastard."

"Do you hate him?" Sean asked with a kind of relief and sense of shock.

"No, I don't think so. I just can't stand him. I guess I always kept these feelings to myself because I didn't want you to get mixed up in my anger. But that's the truth. I can't stand him."

"You know, I was glad when he left. I was scared of him. I remember that. Like his good mood would change and you never knew what was going to happen." Sean's face tightened with pain. "I hated him when he was drunk. And that time I saw him hit you, I wanted to kill him. I really did. But I knew I was too little, and I was so damned scared."

"Do you hate him now, Sean?"

Sean was silent. He leaned forward and added a small piece of oak to the fire. When he finally spoke his words had a gentle quality. "No, not now. In a way, it feels like there's no one left to hate."

"He missed out, Sean. He's the loser. You're going to be a fine man. Don't make that face. I mean it. There, I said it. You *are* going to be a fine man." Rosa laughed.

"Is Zack back?" Sean got up and opened the front door. "Mom, it's snowing!"

Rosa ran to the door. "Don't let Zack in. He's soaking wet. Get your jacket!" She put on her coat and grabbed a Japanese paper parasol. "Come on, Sean!"

"You're going to have to get something sturdier than that!" he said, laughing.

"It'll do!" Rosa lowered her parasol and snowflakes were stuck to the bright-red, oiled paper. She looked up to the sky and the night was aiming a steady stream of stars at her. Soft, cold stars. As soon as she caught one in her hand it melted. "Look, they're shaped like stars!"

Sean put out his hands and then stuck out his tongue to catch them. They ran around the meadow laughing and screaming. Zack ran and circled them in a state of ecstacy. Finally, they sat under a huge cedar, a circle of soft, dryness beneath it, and they watched the snow fall—soft, soft, silent.

"It's so damned quiet, it's hard to believe," Sean said. There was wonder on his face.

Rosa smiled. "I've never—I mean never—seen anything like this."

They sat there in the dark for a while longer as the world became white and beautiful and silent. This is my son, Rosa thought. We've found another sheltered place—different, changing. But it's always love, isn't it? And she asked herself, like a wish, to remember because she knew she would forget. There would come a time, as there always did, when she just wouldn't be able to see it. *Do not forget*, a voice told her that seemed to come from the depths of herself and the night at once.

Sean was gone. He'd been so excited to go and get back to his car, school, track, his new freedom, that Rosa had felt embarrassed to display any parting sorrows. So, they joked a little and sat quietly in the early morning frost. The streets were powdered with snow, little drifts frozen by the curbs.

"I'll be coming back up for Thanksgiving. You aren't coming down, right?" Sean asked.

"No, I'll be here. I'll make a feast. There's the driver, Sean." Rosa's heart almost stopped. He'd leave now.

"Stay warm. You've got a lot of wood to stack." Sean glanced at her, and he saw a self-sufficient woman. Not a mother who was letting go of her child.

"Eat breakfast at the change-over. Do your homework, Sean, put oil in your car and change your underwear."

They started laughing.

Sean shut the door and walked quickly to Rosa's window. "Anything else, Mommy?"

"You might give me a kiss," she said, offering her cheek.

Quickly, he pecked her cheek. "Take it easy, Mom," Sean said, turning to go.

"You'd better not take it easy! See ya later, alligator!"

He laughed and waved.

Rosa put up her window and drove away. She drove straight back to the cabin wanting to keep her silence intact. Her first day alone. The elevation in Lupine Meadows was higher than town, so the drive back was a climb, and the snow became deeper and branches were heavy with the fresh snow. Her nausea was becoming a constant companion and hunger made it worse. Tomorrow I'll call the doctor and see the results. Officially. I know I'm pregnant. I just know it, she thought.

As she passed the ranch she looked out on the immense meadow where they kept the horses, and they looked dark and stunning against the whiteness of the snow. Everywhere, there was snow. Each fence post had a neat, white dollop perched so perfectly that it seemed someone with an absolute eye for beauty had created the scene before her.

When Rosa stepped out of the warmth of the car, the air assaulted her like a dose of consciousness, and it seemed even her nausea had its place in the chaos of her life. The car had just made it up the dirt road. She'd have to see about getting the Landcruiser tomorrow. And I must see about an abortion as soon as possible.

Rosa looked at the perfect beauty—yes, it was perfect—surrounding her, and she knew everything had its place. She was exactly where she had to be, as chaotic as it might seem to someone else. Downed wood, growing trees, and grown trees—dead things and living things—made up this composition of beauty. Wasn't this chaos and absolute order: beauty?

Her stomach complained loudly and a wave of nausea threatened to overwhelm her. As Rosa opened the front door Zack hurtled past her and she let him go. He disappeared at once. The fire was down to small, orange embers, but she started some sausage first, turned on the tea water and made two pieces of toast. Then, nibbling the toast, she built the fire up to three blazing logs, and brought her breakfast back to the couch in front of the fire. She ate in silence and comfort next to the naked fire.

After two cups of tea her nausea subsided, and the sausage and eggs hit the spot. Yes, she missed Sean already, his persistent presence, the child-shadow presence that had comforted her since his birth. But this was wonderful too, she thought—to know that the sausage and eggs had hit the spot. Rosa smiled to herself.

She poured a third cup of tea and got out her stationery.

> Dear Rolf, What's it like on the other side of the world? I'm sitting here trying to imagine it. You in Germany. Is there snow? What color is the sky? Are you sitting by your fire with that brandy? Are you working in your studio? Yes, that's what I imagine you're doing at this moment, working in your studio (actually, you're sleeping with snow falling through a dark, German sky, or you're teaching a class, eyeing your prettiest student, am I right?) Well, this is the kind of letter writer I seem to be. I loved your photo, thanks. I'm here by myself in the mountains, a small village called Lupine Meadows. My son left this morning after cutting much wood for winter fires. Snow fell here last night, Sean and I ran through the woods like idiots. IT WAS EXQUISITE. It still is, all white this morning, you know, *perfectly* composed. The silence here is astounding, so is the dark. There are no street lights, or any houses within eye-distance, therefore the forest calls all the shots (more forest than people). So, here I am, no La Casa, flamenco guitar or

dancing, or Sangre de Toro (well, maybe I can get some
Sangre de Toro). It seems alien and familiar at once, kind
of how I felt when I first met you . . . and guess what, I
recently was told that my father was also German. It's a
long story, but believe me it makes sense. When I see you
again I'll tell you all about it (it'll probably sound to you
like some far-fetched fairy tale, but I bet everyone's life is if
you take the time to look at it.) Well, drop me a line. How
do you feel about the American missiles being placed in
Europe? Anyway, next time you write please tell me the
color of the sky in Germany at *that particular moment*. I'm
working on a sky painting, and maybe it'll help, I haven't
been able to hit the right color yet. Good luck on your new
work and take care.   Con amor, the half-breed,
                                                          Rosa

Rosa walked into the small bedroom studio. Anyway, the light's
not bad, she thought. I mean, it's not good, but it's not bad. She
looked at the globe she was painting, the Earth. She imagined Germany and she got out the atlas she was working from, and saw it
much more clearly. Then, she imagined Lupine Meadows and it
seemed like an inconsequential dot. Who would think a dot could be
so beautiful? But it was. And the Earth itself? Incomprehensible.
The atrocities occurring side by side with the ever-present beauty of
the Earth.

Rosa set up her work area in preparation for next week so it
might welcome her, just a little. Yes, she'd begin the rainbow, but
first she had to complete the Earth. Rosa looked at the shawl in the
lilac sky, at its very beginnings. The two black spiral roses. Who
knows, the sky may never look right to me, she thought. But I must
complete the shawl. Quetzalpetlatl's shawl that comforts the Earth.

After she straightened the area to her satisfaction she decided to
go for a walk. I'm going to be alone today, tonight and tomorrow,
and the day after that, she told herself. She circled the creek, this
time keeping away from Forrest's property. In the middle of the walk
she sat down on a huge tree root by the running creek. Beauty is also
desolate, she thought. Huge ice prisms dangled like transparent,
gnarled water roots, exposing the movement of water beneath them.
The cold began to penetrate her clothing, so she got up to continue
the walk, thinking, and beauty will not tolerate any form of inertia,
but between those moments are eternal stillnesses, so still that the
world seems permanent. Permanent, she laughed. Her laughter

seemed frail in this place. What a harsh beauty this is. It's as though it wants to kill me.

As she walked her body heat regulated itself, and she was warm again. Zack was on the porch when she got back. Rosa had kept the front room wall heater on low, but the cabin was still almost as cold as the refrigerator when she opened it to think about dinner. The silence was tangible, settling itself all around her. It was so alien she wanted to escape into town for a cup of coffee or something, but at the same time it welcomed her like an echo of an old longing. Like a constant sorrow she couldn't pinpoint. A familiar sorrow that rose only in solitude, but now, in the silence, it threatened to speak with a voice of its own.

She walked to the studio and leaned in the doorway. This is where she'd always resolved her sorrow's presence, twisting it into a strange blend of joy—personal and universal, universal and personal, she crashed and pushed and tore through its layers, imagining herself and the Earth, the people, all of them, sharing the Earth in some kind of balance. A balance she couldn't explain or rationally understand—but a balance that always made it possible to begin the work. To create, she thought, what has never been before. No, not quite from scratch, but a kind of remembering. A remembering into being.

Rosa built up the fire and put the heater on medium. Look at that snow—a miracle, she thought. And I'm all alone in it. Her nausea reminded her otherwise; not quite. She brought her snack into the studio. It'd be getting dark in a few hours.

"Spider," she asked out loud, "are you still there?"

The spider emerged between the black, spiral roses, and Rosa felt herself merge with the consciousness of the weaver. Finish this shawl, the words came to her, and you'll finish the painting. Next week the globe, and then the rainbow. But today the shawl.

Rosa worked meticulously for an hour and a half, engulfed only in the design of the thin, black spirals connecting to the next and to the next. Webs and webs of lace sprouted into a blossomed, black rose. Her attention wandered for an instant, for relief, and she looked at the lilac sky. Too light, too damned light. Then she looked out at the grey, darkening sky.

Wind moved through the trees as pine needles flew swiftly to the ground. Rosa put two more logs on the still pulsing fire and returned to her canvas. She looked up to the grey sky and back to the lilac sky, and she wondered, again, what she was really trying to imagine. Sunset and sunrise? Maybe. Haven't I seen this color, this particular color, at those times? she asked herself. Then why am I so dissatisfied? Why can't I accept this damned shade of lilac? Too light, too dark. What color do I see and why do I want to see it?

Then, she thought of the sky in her dream—the dream of the child dying. That sky was blue, a clear summer blue. Warmth and harvest in the land while the children died, shivering, with empty stomachs. Tears came to Rosa's eyes, but she stopped them. The child had *seen* the sky through the walls, Rosa thought fiercely. *Through the walls.*

Paint, don't think, she told herself—it's getting dark. Rosa turned on two more high intensity lamps and worked for another hour.

Snow was falling again. Zack was curled by the window, twitching as he ran in his dreams. His paws made funny running motions and he whined as he caught his prey.

"Did you catch a rabbit, old Zack?" Rosa laughed, rubbing his ears. He woke up and licked her hand. "Are there rabbits around here? Huh, Zack?" He panted excitedly, rising to his feet. "False alarm, Zack. Go on back to sleep."

Zack went to the door and whined softly.

"Oh, okay. Go for it," Rosa said, letting him out. She watched him run through the snow, kicking it up, smoothly, as though it were the ocean. Then he was gone.

She put on some left-over chicken to warm and made a small salad. Rosa noticed that the rubber tree plant dominated the front room window, taking in all the available light, and she hoped it would make it. She'd had it since Sean was a baby. And then she noticed the small plant, Julio's philodendron, inside the planter. She remembered Julio putting his plant inside her rubber tree saying, "My little plant is lonely." The philodendron had done better under the older tree's branches that went in every direction now.

It won't get any light there, she thought. She picked it up to put it in her bedroom window and it seemed stuck to the planter. Its roots had grown and twined around the rubber tree. Rosa got the scissors and began to gently cut the roots. She began to cry. The tears she'd denied came, suddenly, with the taste of salt. "I didn't know this would happen," she said to the plant. Deep sobs, ripples of grief, ran through her body, and her tears refused to stop.

When every root was separated Rosa took the plant to her bedroom and placed it by the window. It looked small and naked by itself. One entire side had even stopped sprouting leaves where it had rested on the rubber tree's trunk. Yes, our roots are entwined, more than we knew. Which side of me is naked, Julio, without leaves, growth?

I can cry now if I want, as much as I want. I can sleep in and get up and speak to no one. I can work until midnight without explanations, if I want. Which side of me is naked? Julio, what have I done?

Rosa got into the sleeping bag just to get warm, and then the phone was ringing.

"Rosa? It's me," Julio said. His voice sounded very far away. "Rosa, are you there?"

"Yes." Her voice came out thickly. All that crying, then sleep.

"Were you sleeping?"

"Yes, but it's okay. Is Sean there yet?"

"I picked him up around five. He's down in the weight room."

Rosa looked at her clock radio, fifteen to nine. "Well, I passed out. It's so quiet here, Julio. It's snowing. You won't believe it." Her eyes began to focus, and then she saw the plant by the window.

"Are you okay and all?"

"I'm fine. I discovered today that the philodendron you put in my rubber tree planter had rooted itself in a pretty permanent fashion. I had to cut its roots free. Anyway, that got to me. Do you know what I'm saying?" Her voice broke. No, I don't want to cry again, she told herself.

"Does that mean you miss me?" Julio asked softly.

"I suppose so. I mean, I had to snip the roots so that I could put it in its own light, or else it'll die." Rosa's tears started again, and she gave up trying to stop them.

"I love you. Do you hear me? I love you."

"We have so much to work out, it's frightening."

"What do you mean?" Julio's voice stiffened.

"I mean everything. Like the plant, the light. Growth. Fuck, and the rest of it. What . . . I don't know what I mean. I feel like someone just snipped my roots and put me in my own light. It hurts Julio. It just hurts."

"Yes, I know. You can change your mind, Rosa. You don't have to stay there."

"Julio, I bought this place." Suddenly, Rosa remembered that Zack was outside and the door might not be locked. It was pitch black outside her window, and anxiety gripped her. "Hold the line for a second, okay?"

"Is something wrong?"

"No, just hold on for a second."

Rosa let Zack in and locked the door. It had been open. She

quickly shut the curtains. They were ugly. She'd have to make her own.

"I let Zack in. I forgot about him."

"You could rent the place till it sells and come back down," Julio said again.

For an instant Rosa was tempted to tell him about her nausea, but, no, she decided not to.

"It's not that easy, Julio."

"Look, we'll talk when I get there Thursday. Is there anything you want?"

"Pan dulce, of course. How about some Sangre de Toro?"

"It's yours."

"Okay, see you then. Tell Sean to give me a call. Is he okay?"

"He's fine. He's excited about school. Also, the car," Julio laughed.

"Okay, see you Thursday. Drive carefully and have a good week."

"Don't forget to water my plant."

Rosa looked at it. "No, I won't. I'm thinking of getting him some friends."

"It won't be the same."

"Nothing's ever the same. Good night, Julio."

"See you Thursday, for sure. Good night, Rosita."

She felt terrible. She'd forgotten to eat her dinner. The fire was out and the cabin was freezing. Rosa brought the food back to the sleeping bag and ate the chicken cold with milk. One more chore. Her teeth. She got back into the sleeping bag, with an extra blanket on top, and fell asleep instantly.

She is in a field with two horses. They are immense and muscled and untamed. One is white and one is black. Rosa realizes they are connected to her wrists by slender ropes, and that they obey her by the subtlest turn of each wrist. This knowledge fills her with an inexplicable, wild joy.

The dawn was so cold she could hardly believe it. Snow weighed down the branches outside her window. Snow. But the day was clear, and the sky looked smooth as stone. She made herself get up and began to roll paper for the fire, adding small twigs for the kindling, and then the larger pieces began to burn. Her nausea was already loud and clear.

After breakfast Rosa called the doctor's office and the nurse confirmed it; she was pregnant. There were no more tears this morning, just the words being said: "Your test was positive. Congratulations." She was pregnant. On a mountain, up a dirt road, by herself, pregnant. Congratulations.

She sat down by the fire and stared at its center. Pregnant. Eighteen years ago I was pregnant. Pregnant? Pregnant. The baby in my dreams. A daughter. No, I can't think of that. It's impossible. I just can't do it. I left Julio. I'm here now. This is where I am. Congratulations.

Rosa looked around the room and got up to look at her paintings. Pregnant. The black roses she'd completed look vivid. The shawl had begun to shape itself, magically, in the lilac sky. Pregnant. The lilac sky still didn't satisfy her. Pregnant. What in the hell is it trying to tell me? Pregnant. She tried to imagine the circle of orchids, but she couldn't. Pregnant. The Earth was incomplete on the flat canvas. Pregnant. She hadn't even begun the rainbow. Pregnant. Are we going to survive this fucking century? Pregnant. How much life will die today because of our stupidity . . . atomic testing in the Pacific, the relocation of its people, their jellyfish babies that die within hours of birth, the villagers slaughtered in El Salvador, the children clubbed to death to save bullets, the bullets this, my, government supplies with my money, Guatemala, Nicaragua, South Africa, missiles, missiles, anti, anti-missiles cover the globe. Pregnant. Where is the fucking rainbow pointing? Pregnant. I'll need to get a job. Pregnant. She thought of the miniature child in its dark, red world listening to her thoughts. I just can't do it. She thought of her grandmother, Luz. This would be her great-great granddaughter. Pregnant. I just can't, I cannot do it. I can't be pregnant. Not now. Congratulations. "Confuckinggratulations," Rosa muttered.

The car dealer was still interested. They made a contract, gave her a check for eight hundred dollars, and she drove away with a dark green Landcruiser. She felt like she was driving a tractor. Just as long as it gets me in and out of there, she thought, as she looked at the metal dashboard. I'd better stop and talk to someone at the ranch about plowing me out. Today, she thought.

Rosa felt a little conspicuous driving what looked like a tank to her. All metal. But she was definitely more confident knowing she could put it into four-wheel drive if she had to. The salesman had shown her how to change the hubs and work the extra gear shift. "Change your oil regularly and check the air filter. Living up that dirt road's going to give it a work-out."

She'd deposited the eight hundred. There's enough put away for a while, she told herself. That'll help. Now, where can I get an abortion?

Rosa pulled up to the building where she'd paid for the cookout. There were some kids throwing snowballs out by the pond, and some horses were saddled for rides. Otherwise, it was quiet, smoke curling up from the various log cabin buildings.

There was a fire in the lounge as she walked into the main room, and a coffee pot and cups on a table. A young woman in a cowboy hat stood behind the desk.

"I was wondering if the manager's around?" Rosa asked.

"Can I help you with something?" she answered in an impatient tone.

"I just moved in up the road and I'd like to remind whoever's in charge of plowing not to forget my side road."

"I see," she said. There was a distinct feeling of unfriendliness in her manner. "Well, you don't want to talk to the manager, you want to talk to Dale. He's in charge of plowing out the roads. He's probably in the chuckhouse," she said in an uninterested, flat voice.

"Where's the chuckhouse?" Rosa asked, loudly.

"First building to your left. Can't miss it." She immediately shifted her attention to some papers as though they were extremely important.

Rosa turned, without a word, and walked to the chuckhouse. It was a huge dining area with an immense, open fireplace with, what looked like, tree trunks burning in it. There was a group of men, all in cowboy hats, sitting at a long table, drinking coffee and talking in low voices. They looked up as Rosa walked in. She felt herself flush. Were they all like Jake? Dread ran through her. They watched her approach with vaguely curious, unsmiling faces. The local mask, Rosa thought. Shit.

"Excuse me," she said. "Is one of you Dale?"

"I'm Dale, ma'am," a tanned face answered her.

"I'm Rosa Luján. I just moved in up the way. I was wondering if I could talk to you for a minute?" They were all staring holes into her.

Dale stood up. "Why, sure." He was very tall and moved with a measured slowness. The others went back to talking among themselves. Loud laughter punctured the air, and they glanced over at Rosa, then back to their coffee.

Rosa gave them a dark look, and then turned to face Dale. "I just wanted to remind you that I'll be up on that side road this winter, so you don't forget to plow me out."

His face looked slightly amused but straight forward. He looked her right back in the eye. "Aren't you the woman who just bought that place on Wild Cat Road? Julie's friend, I hear."

"My road doesn't have a street sign, but it's supposed to be Wild Cat Road."

"I know the place. No problem. I'll be plowing you out as soon as we get a good snowfall. This place closes next month, you know. I didn't catch your name?"

"It's Rosa. Rosa Luján. Do you happen to know how Julie's doing?"

"She's in a cast as far's I know. Busted her arm up pretty good, I hear. You going to be up there by yourself this winter?"

The other men stopped talking.

"That's what it looks like."

"Well, give me a holler if you need a hand. Here's my card. I sell a little real estate on the side. Helps keep body and soul together," he laughed softly.

"Well, thank you," Rosa said, taking the card. She liked his eyes, his face. He implied a certain respect and distance. A vague warmth. But she couldn't be sure. Now they all know I'm going to be up there by myself, she groaned inwardly. "Don't women usually live with men in places like that?" Julio's voice echoed against her mind.

"No problem. What kind of car do you have, Rosa?"

"I just got a Landcruiser. Today, in fact."

"Sounds like you're set."

"Got your wood in yet?" one of the men yelled.

Rosa looked at him. "Most of it."

"That's Tony, the manager." Tony smiled, an undisguised, greedy look on his face. "Well, it's been a pleasure, Rosa," Dale said, tipping his hat to her.

Rosa put out her hand, and Dale, quickly and firmly, shook it. His blue eyes held no reservations about shaking her hand, but he never really smiled.

As Rosa shut the door behind her there were hoots of laughter. "Charming bunch of bastards," Rosa muttered. She wondered if Dale was laughing with them. She imagined him sitting down quietly, pouring himself another cup of coffee. She hoped, anyway.

Strong, patient eyes, about forty-five. Maybe he thought it was funny, too. The little Mexican Rose up the way shovelling her way out of the snow. Rosa drew in deep breaths. I hope not, she thought. I could use a friend or two around here.

She started up the car and drove home feeling strangely abandoned. Alone. What did you expect, a welcoming committee? she asked herself. The snow was starting to melt and the mud showed through, but the Landcruiser gripped the road all the way.

After a good dinner in front of the fire her stomach felt settled, and the encounter with the men at the ranch receded. Tonight Zack stays in, she thought. He never barks in the house unless something's wrong. "You're going to earn your keep, boy," Rosa said, petting his muzzle. Zack lay at her feet for a while, but he really preferred his own corner, so he moved, circling his spot, and settled with a sharp exhalation of breath.

"You're getting old and grouchy, Zack boy," Rosa laughed.

The sun had set. The doors and windows were locked, the curtains shut. A delicate, crescent moon hung in the horizon and it would set soon. The light from the moon had a peculiar clarity, like the sun during the day seemed to almost hum in the sky. The elevation. Awareness. The air itself, she guessed. The awareness that I'm pregnant.

There was a small advertisement in the local paper, toward the back, for a women's clinic in a town seventy miles away. "Abortion counseling," it said. And "Sliding scale." If I'm going to do it, I've got to do it right away. Next week. Next week at the latest. I'll call tomorrow. Tomorrow.

A piano piece played on the stereo, beautiful and flowing. She felt torn in half. Julio will be back in a couple of days, she realized. Maybe I just won't tell him. Just do it. I'm the one that left; it's my responsibility. It's my choice, isn't it?

Rosa read a little by the fire and dozed off. The dying fire woke her up. She placed a couple of pine logs on and got ready for bed. The dream, the dream of a daughter. Can I do it? I've got to. I can't be pregnant here by myself. The conflict had exhausted her, and she let go of consciousness with gratitude.

Zack was at the bottom of her sleeping bag, not touching her, but aware of her fear. Of her listening for sounds. But there was only the silence and it covered them both like raw, wild honey. Rosa fell to the bottom of the jar. It wasn't terrible. Dark, liquid honey.

The moon had set hours ago, and if there was a light, a clarity, she'd have to find it in her dreams. Luz, she thought. Mamacita. Los estoy juntando. (I am gathering.) Estoy juntando la luz. Una estrella. No más una.

Her face was puffy the next morning. A violent nausea gripped her. The invasion had begun in earnest. The first time I was seventeen, she thought as she doubled over. Now I'm almost thirty-five. She made herself eat, and she stared at the clinic phone number.

Rosa finally called. They were the closest women's clinic, with abortion counseling, to Plumas County. Yes, there was a sliding scale for fees. Yes, the woman at the other end understood. She was thirty-five years old and just separated from her husband. Yes, she had a choice. Rosa's heart felt like it would come out of her chest. She made an appointment for the following week. She'd stay at a motel overnight. She was pregnant, but she had a choice.

It was her choice.

Rosa worked on the globe until the afternoon. The silence was continuous, punctuated by one car the entire morning and a dog barking in the distance from time to time. It was entirely silent now. It was as though time unrolled, smoothly, from pure, white sheets of paper. Enough paper to wrap the day, entirely. And the night was of the blackest shade imaginable, with snow falling from it or stars poking through bold with light.

She took her drawing pad and began to sketch in an abstracted, unconscious manner, the way she did when fresh ideas, a particular vision, came to her. It was a small, serious face. A lovely face. A little girl. Tears rushed to Rosa's eyes. My daughter. That's who you are, aren't you? Rosa looked at the half-finished drawing and she knew if she completed it she would have the child. She remembered the dream of giving birth, and the others. She remembered the little girl beginning to walk. Toward Julio.

Rosa put the drawing down. The child had thick, dark hair and large eyes. Wise. Aren't all children's eyes wise? Rosa thought. Haven't I seen these eyes before, the expression? Stop it, she told herself. But she picked up the drawing again and shadowed the curve of the cheek. How soft it looked. How lovely. A little girl.

She closed the drawing pad and put it back on her work table to the side. I drew her face. My child's face. Tears came again. She let them. She let them fall like the sky releases the countless, starry snowflakes. The little stars that melted in the warmth of her hand.

The globe, the Earth, began to come to life. The oceans seemed to move, and the air to sparkle, if she stared at it long enough. Maybe no one else will see it, but I will, she thought. But, of course, I want everyone to see it, so there's more work to do. I'll *make* it spin.

When she finally cleaned up it was late afternoon. Rosa hadn't spoken to or seen another human being all day. She felt strangely vacant and wonderfully full at the same time. A curious balance. She looked at the drawing pad and left it lying where it was.

While her meal cooked she wrote her mother, Dolores.

> Dear Dolores, Just to let you know I'm here on a street, dirt road I should say, called Wild Cat Road (only there's no street sign). It's starting to snow, tell Louie I bought a Landcruiser to keep me a step ahead of the bears. If you don't have one of these I understand you don't get in or out during the winter around here. Well, I'm freezing my ass off. It gets cold fast when the fire (in the fireplace) goes out, but the wall heaters keep the place from freezing up. I guess I'm not used to it yet. Write when you find the time. Say HI to Louie for me. It's so quiet here, I assume the bears (and everything else) are in hibernation. Well, take care,
> Rosa   The snow is BEAUTIFUL.

After dinner she walked outside in front and sat on the porch steps. It was overcast again; not a star to be seen. Perhaps it would snow tonight. She thought of the child's face on the drawing pad; her appointment next week. Next Wednesday, ten in the morning. A shiver of fear and cold ran through her.

"Come on, Zack. Come on inside."

The feeling of solitude, chosen solitude, she'd felt earlier was gone. Now she only felt alone. Alone and scared. Alone and pregnant with a bunch of cowboys down the way. But wouldn't they be gone in a few weeks? The manager, Tony—he'd probably stay. The creep, she thought. And in the spring, will there be bears and rattlesnakes all over the place? Wouldn't I be a sight pregnant?

Rosa remembered Forrest's words, "Some people can't handle the solitude . . ." Can I handle the solitude? she asked herself. What in the hell am I doing here?

As she passed the studio the urge to take one more look at the drawing held her, but she didn't. Next Wednesday at ten in the morning, she answered herself.

The sleeping bag warmed quickly to her body. Again, Rosa lay absolutely still, till even her breathing was silent, and she listened for any sound. The two doors, the windows—everything was ground floor, close to the earth. She looked out her bedroom window, the only window without curtains, wide open to the sky. And eyes. Anyone over five feet could look in. Does this make sense? she thought. She tried to imagine closing the curtains at night. Because of fear, she said to herself. No, these windows will not have curtains. If anyone looks in or bothers me at all, I'll shoot. Well, they can take a peek if they're desperate, but they'd better not try to come in. The thought of the gun in the closet comforted her, and for an instant she almost got up to get it—but no. A German gun taken from a dead German soldier next to me all night, Rosa thought. No. But it's there. Which is worse, the cowboys or the damned gun?

She touched her knife. It was beside her. She felt like calling Julio. No. Rosa stared out at the dark sky. Then she fell, she fell, she fell to the bottom of herself.

The air is warm. Summer. Rosa is alone. The stars are so close. One begins to move toward her, becoming larger, until the expanding, brilliant light becomes a dove. A white dove. Gentle, graceful, lovely. And then it turns in mid-air, exposing an incredible strength. Its muscles flex with movement, and it faces Rosa with an eagle's face. Frightening, yet, strangely, full of love. Love. A great feeling of love flows from its fierceness. The eagle. "The child's name is Luzìa," it says. Rosa forces herself to not turn away from her stare.

Rosa woke instantly, and, with a sense of shock, astonishment, remembered the dream. "Luzia," she murmured. Luz, Mamacita, the eyes. Of course. A spark of my grandmother will live in her great-granddaughter's eyes. Her soul. Am I saying it? she asked herself as panic gripped her. The nausea overwhelmed her as she rushed to the bathroom, but nothing was in her stomach. Just a bile like bitterness.

After Rosa made herself eat some toast and tea—no coffee, it only made the nausea linger—and then an egg, she took the drawing pad to the couch in front of the morning fire. She opened the pad to the child's face. The eyes, Rosa thought. Luzia, is this you?

As she began to finish the sketch, a feeling of peace, an unexpected peace, filled her. She would have her daughter, yes. She would have her because she wanted to. No man, no laws would force her to. It was rational. It was irrational. It was her decision, and yet the dreams were absolutely clear. The birth, the stages of development, and now the voice saying, "The child's name is Luzia." And then Julio's face came to her, his eyes large in his face, staring at her. Angrily, patiently. It's our child. Mine and Julio's. Her tears fell. A child of our union, my love for him, she realized and at once recognized its truth. I'm here, he's there, but it's true that I love him.

Rosa finished the sketch, the blending of their faces. "An Indian child," she murmured. Both of us Yaqui. Then perhaps those genes

will dominate. But you will also be Spanish, English and German.
"German," Rosa said out loud. "You will be a child of the Earth, a
Native Person of the Earth," she said in a loud voice, and her words
rang in the silence of the cabin, cushioned by the new snow, with a
force that surprised her. "Will we survive this century, Luzia?" she
whispered.

She imagined the child within her duplicating the ancient miracle of creation. The brain, Rosa thought. Have you completed your
brain? At six weeks, she remembered, the brain is complete. And the
heart, the miniature organs? And if I'd chosen, in spite of everything,
abortion? the question came to her. The Earth is earthquake, flood
and fire as well, she thought, and not all of us, or life, survives each
time. I've chosen life this time. Yes. Birth and death. The endless
harmony filled her as though she'd begun to paint.

Luzia. Luzia. I think I begin to understand.

Snow fell during the night, and flurries continued all morning. By
afternoon a steady snowfall had begun. Rosa started the rainbow
encircling the Earth, and the colors commanded all of her attention.
She'd stopped for a snack to quiet her nausea, and a part of her still
couldn't believe she'd made that choice. The part of her, the human
part of her, that knew she'd grow huge and vulnerable. The human
being that wished to survive at any cost.

Rosa looked out at the snow. How would I walk through that in
my last months? I haven't even told Julio. Well, he comes tomorrow.

Luzia's face was propped on the window sill. The white light
flooding in from the snow gave it a sense of intensity and focus as
though the face had come to life. Color, Rosa thought. That's what it
needs. A little color. Will you really look like this, Luzia? she wondered. The child's face gazed back at her. A two-year-old's face.

The sound of a tractor in the distance seemed to be approaching.
Rosa went to the front room window to watch. Zack was on the porch
sitting up and alert. A snowdrift began to form at the bottom of the
steps. Then the tractor was closer. Very close. And then it came into
view. The tractor was plowing her road.

Rosa watched from the window, and someone inside waved.
Probably Dale, she thought. She waved back, but she doubted that
he could see with all the snow on the side windows.

Dale did see her wave, but just her arm, the movement of her
arm, going back and forth. What the hell is she doing there? he asked
himself. By herself. He shook his head involuntarily. One of those

feminist gals, no doubt. And with a name like Rosa. Looks Mexican and something else. Wish I'd sold her the house. The thing is, with that kind of woman, you never know whether to sleep with your boots on or not. Dale turned the tractor around.

Rosa watched the tractor disappear as it left a clearing in its path. Tomorrow I'll go into town for supplies. Tomorrow I'll call the Women's Clinic and cancel my appointment. Tomorrow I'll see Julio. Tomorrow.

She ate dinner with one candle, facing the last light of the day that turned the fresh snow into scenes of another planet. Only six hours from here people walked on cement, clocks ticking everywhere—on their wrists, buildings, walls of supermarkets, shopping malls, banks. But here the clock on the stove and the clock on the radio were less important than the last light holding the pale snow, still, in her astounded vision. Less important than the fire she fed piece after piece of wood. Less important than the absolute silence that held her in its grip. Rosa held her breath without knowing it. She'd never witnessed beauty, a sheer beauty, of this magnitude.

Then it was dark and the candle reflected its single flame in the window, and her own face looked back at her through the darkness. I am alone with the darkness, she thought.

Rosa closed the curtains and carried the candle into the bedroom, bringing her drawing pad with her. She added color to the face and hair, but she kept the eyes black, unfinished.

The phone rang. "Yes," Rosa answered.

"Mom, it's Sean."

"Sean! Your voice sounds so close. How's it going?"

"Pretty good. I'm taking a full sixteen units, running track and working part-time. But some of the grants came through so I'm cutting back two work days, and that'll really help. How's the wood holding out?"

"I'm warm enough with two sweaters and a turtleneck underneath," Rosa laughed. "It's been snowing. I've even been plowed out. I got the Landcruiser, by the way."

"Great. Have you driven it in four-wheel-drive yet?"

"No, but tomorrow I probably will. Tomorrow's go-to-town-day."

"I just got a registration warning, damn it," Sean almost whispered.

"You've got to do a C.O., Sean."

"It says here if I don't register there's a fine and a jail sentence. It looks like I have to register to keep them off my goddamned back."

"What about a C.O.? Have you looked into it?"

"I'll do it, but I think I've got to register, Mom."

"You don't want to be drafted, do you?" Rosa's throat felt so tense she wanted to scream.

"Are you kidding? I'm definitely not into being dumped in the middle of someone else's war."

"Okay, Sean, then pay attention and see what your alternatives are. Talk to a draft counselor, okay?"

"Yeah, I will. Guess I'll get back to my homework. Julio wants to talk to you."

"Look, take care and see you soon, and talk to a draft counselor. Find out what's going on, Sean. No one can do it for you. With Central America simmering, it's no joke."

"I said I would. Here's Julio. Bye," he said with irritation.

"I'm coming up tomorow, remember?" Julio said in a low, intimate voice.

"I remember."

"How're you doing?"

Rosa thought of everything she had to tell him and said, "I'm fine. I've been painting and feeding the fire. Next week I'm going to see about a part-time job of some kind. As far as I can see my expenses here are pretty low. Plus the money that's left helps. You know, song and dance. I bought a Landcruiser and got eight hundred as part of the trade."

"Well, okay. Everything's okay then?" he asked as though he didn't believe her.

"I'm fine. How're you doing?"

"I miss my darkroom, but I made a deal with Curt to use his, so it's working out. My classes are going good. I miss you, Rosa."

"I'll see you tomorrow for dinner. Something good. A surprise," and to herself she added, A real surprise.

"Good night, Rosa. Te quiero."

"Te quiero también, sometimes," she laughed softly. "Good night."

Rosa turned off the light, but decided to let the candle burn. She stared at it until her eyes seemed to absorb the flames, until her eyes burned. She blew out the candle. She could hear Zack breathing. She touched her knife. Her hands covered her belly, protectively, and she thought of Sean who she could no longer protect. Her son.

Morning. Grey and patches of sky clearing, fitfully, with the freezing wind. The sun about to rise. Rosa ran the shower hot till steam filled the air, turned the heat lamp on, and sipped some milk to quiet her nausea. She would go into town for breakfast.

She scraped snow off the windshield and the back windows. The snow was heavier than she'd expected. The hubs were frozen, so she had to turn them with pliers. The tires gripped as all four wheels dug into the snow and churned together up the slight incline of the driveway onto the road.

How fresh everything was. Even her bones felt alive. Alive. Alive. This is winter, she told herself, and this beautiful snow could kill me. Look how the branches hold their white weight. Magical. It all looks magical. Yet this beauty would kill me if I didn't take care.

Her stomach growled and she wondered if she could make it to town. She felt suddenly empty, as though she'd never eaten in her life, and the child within her clamored for sustenance. Waves of nausea overtook her. Take care, little one. Luzia. "Luzia," she said out loud, and her breath was a puff of warm air in the face of winter.

Shafts of sunlight made the snow unbearable with light. Crystals, crystals—an ocean of crystals everywhere she turned.

"Iris, do you mind bringing me some tea right away?"

"Sure. Do you know what you want?" she asked, noting Rosa's pale color.

"I'll take hot cakes and sausage. Thanks."

"Coming up," Iris turned away.

Rosa had called the women's clinic and cancelled the appointment, thanking them for their support. The woman had asked her, "Are you sure, Ms. Luján?" "Yes, I am. And part of being sure was knowing your clinic was there. I'll be sending you a little donation. Not much, but everything must help."

Rosa sat in the same chair as the last time, facing the grape arbor, but this time the trellis had ice crystals lacing it, which the sun filled with shimmering rainbows. Blinding rainbows of light. She looked away and began to read the paper. Three nuns raped and killed in El Salvador. A shudder of horror ran through her. She thought of Sierra and herself on the camping trip during the summer. The terrible photographs she'd never see of nameless women dumped under the open sky; their dead unborn still swelling within them. Or as Sierra said, slashed and ripped from their bellies. Congratulations, Rosa thought. Yes, men and war can do this—in fact, blow us all to hell within minutes—but a woman, a woman, cannot choose to birth or destroy what will live within her own body without an endless struggle to keep the right to choose. There are no qualms about war, only abortion, she thought bitterly. Now will they take my son and make him a soldier? Congratulations.

For an instant Rosa could see the nuns struggling on a stark, grey landscape to the sounds of laughter and jeers. Their own cries for each other. Then silence.

Her tea was in front of her and Iris was walking away. The warmth of the cup filled her hands and the wood stove crackled behind her. Rosa sipped her tea, slowly, and thought of Sean in a soldier's uniform. Rage filled her. Then sorrow. The wars continue to sweep the Earth, as women continue to bear their young, she thought. A son, now a daughter. A child of the next century. Will we make it, Luzia?

"Here's hot cakes and sausage. More tea?" Iris asked, looking at Rosa closely.

"Yes, please." Rosa smiled at her.

"Coming up," she said and left.

The food was delicious, but she ate slowly, afraid to upset what was becoming a precarious balance between nausea and normalcy.

"Would you like anything else?"

"No, I think that does it. Thanks, Iris."

"Look, I'm going to give a small recital at my place this weekend. Do you want to come? Here's a map to get to my place. It starts around seven. We're about eight miles out of town. Butterfly Valley." Iris looked at Rosa without smiling, almost defensively.

"Here's my phone number, Iris. I didn't call because I've been trying to settle in, whatever that is. But I'll definitely be there. Should I bring something?"

Iris gave a hint of a smile. "Some wine or a finger food would be nice. Got to go." She walked over to another table with the same sense of grace Rosa had noticed before, as though there were nothing else she'd rather be doing. Only her face betrayed her, just a little. As she wrote the order her hands were pressing chords, perfectly.

By the time Rosa got everything on the list it was close to two o'clock. Julio would be coming in a couple of hours. How will I tell him? Maybe I should keep it a secret for a while, the thought crossed her mind. She considered this and it made her feel calmer.

As Rosa got to the ranch a line of riders were coming back, so she stopped to let the horses pass. Jake was in the lead. As he passed he stared at her without a hint of recognition. Most of the other riders

gave her a friendly wave as they rode by. "Screw you, John Wayne," she muttered to herself.

Dale was by the tractor and he turned to wave. Rosa stopped. "Thanks for plowing me out."

"All in the line of duty," he said, looking at her from under his cowboy hat. "How's the Landcruiser taking the snow?"

"So far so good. It started right up this morning. I had to change the hubs with pliers though."

Dale laughed. "Yeah, sometimes you've got to do that. I notice you don't have snow tires on it, though. You'll probably do best to get some when you can."

More money, Rosa groaned inwardly. "Won't these do? They look like new."

"I'd save those for the dry months. If there's a heavy snowfall you can't get out on the highway in those. Without chains, that is. Got mud and snow on that." He pointed to a truck.

"I appreciate the advice. Thanks. What does everyone do here in the winter, anyway, besides make fires? I'm a painter, by the way. I also teach, though I doubt I'll be teaching up here. I am painting though."

"I see," Dale said, taking a good look at her. "Well, I'll tell you, we're a boring bunch. Mostly cards and television around here. You play poker?"

"I can play, but I'm a lousy gambler. Well, I won't keep you. Drop in for some coffee next time you plow the road."

"Oh, I wouldn't want to be going in your place with these muddy things on," Dale said, indicating his boots with his eyes.

"You could take them off," Rosa said, smiling.

"Never thought of that." His eyes flashed warily as he turned away, with a wave of his hand.

Just a friendly cup of coffee, Dale, she thought. I'm not trying to get in your pants, believe me. Rosa couldn't resist laughing at the entrenched cowboy syndrome so apparent at the ranch. It isn't like that at Lightning Strikes, or that crowd. But here I am up the road from the ranch, she told herself.

A grey BMW was parked in front of the house. Who could that be? Rosa wondered. Julie got out of the car. Rosa rolled down her window.

"I was just about to leave," Julie said, without smiling. In fact, she looked angry. Her arm was in a cast, cradled by a sling.

"How bad is it?" Rosa asked.

"Bad enough to keep me in this for a while. Fractured the whole damn thing."

"You're lucky you didn't land on your head." Rosa looked away from Julie because her face was registering anger again. "Look, I'll park the car."

Julie walked over to Rosa's car. "I can't stay. I waited for around twenty minutes. Are you by yourself?"

"Sean went back, if that's what you mean. Here's my number, Julie. Give me a call and come by in the evening. I'll make dinner."

"Maybe I'll take you up on that. We're planning on a trip to Reno in a couple of weeks, if you're interested. It almost always gets interesting, if you know what I mean." Julie laughed.

"What about your arm?"

"I'm not about to let a fracture get in the way of my fun." Julie's face became bored. "Well, I'll give you a call."

"Don't bring Jake."

Julie spun around. "What do you mean by that?"

"I think he's a pain in the ass," Rosa said, reaching for her groceries.

"You'd better watch that attitude. You won't be too popular around here, Rosa." Julie's gold horseshoe earrings twinkled in the afternoon light, but otherwise she almost looked like a man except for the swell of her hips.

"Being popular was never my goal. Not even in high school. Take care of yourself, Julie." Rosa walked into the house with the first bags of groceries, stepping carefully through the snow.

Suddenly, Rosa was nauseated again, and hunger rumbled around in her stomach. "Shit," she said out loud. Pregnant and unpopular, she thought, that's me.

Julie drove away with a stony look on her face. I wonder if being a cowperson is contagious? she asked herself, and then ran to the refrigerator to quell her nausea.

After the enchiladas were made, finally, she sat by the fire. The cheese sandwich had calmed her stomach, and now she sipped a glass of dry cabernet. She sipped it slowly and cautiously, and hoped wine wouldn't have to be given up like coffee. A glass or two of wine at night was a special friend of hers. Rosa loved good wine.

Well, here I am pregnant with enchiladas in the oven—a real prime target for the Mexican Man. First I'll gauge Julio's face, and then, maybe, I'll tell him.

Rosa picked up the drawing pad and closed it, leaving it by the

couch. The fire was so warm, her stomach was settled, and the wine was rich and full. Her two paintings waited for her in the bedroom studio. Another painting had begun to form itself in her mind. A painting of Dolores playing the piano, the way she remembered her as a child—before she looked up and saw Rosa standing there. Dolores had looked like she was dreaming.

She woke up to loud knocking at the door and Julio's voice, "Rosa! Rosa! Open up!" Then she remembered the enchiladas. "Oh, shit," Rosa muttered. "Just a second, Julio!" she yelled, running to the oven. Relief flooded her. They were cooked a little dark, but they weren't burnt.

She put them on top of the stove and ran for the door. "Sorry to keep you waiting. I thought I burned the dinner. Fell asleep by the fire."

Julio's overnight bag was on his shoulder and various packages were on the porch. Zack ran past him into the house. "If you hadn't opened up pretty soon I think I'd of frozen to death. Even Zack wanted to come in. You really picked a spot, didn't you?" he said irritably. He looked at Rosa's face which was regarding him cooly. Very cooly, he thought.

"Long drive." Julio reached over and kissed her with his mouth open, and smiled. "Here, let me get the goods."

His smell and touch affected her, almost against her will. I love his lips, his full lips, Rosa thought—and he smells like my brother. My lover, my brother, my lover. "Did you get the pan dulce?"

"Dare I even knock on your door without it?" he laughed. "Also, various bottles of wine for madam. Champagne, Sangre de Toro, chardonnay."

"Great. I'll open the Sangre de Toro. Guess what I made for dinner?"

"I can smell it. Enchiladas."

"Are you hungry?"

"Are you kidding? When you said something special, I knew it was enchiladas." He pulled her close to him. "You know I love your enchiladas, Rosita."

They kissed again, gently, and then Rosa pulled away. "Okay, look, they almost burned. Now they're getting cold. Let's eat. Why don't you put all this stuff away and I'll serve. I'm starved." The nausea was creeping up on her. Not like the morning nausea which was almost violent, but subtly like a threat.

"You look good. Rested," Julio said, looking at her. "The solitude agrees with you?" He couldn't keep the hurt out of his voice.

"I don't really know yet, I suppose. But it seems to. I guess I've always wanted to know if I could do it. Be completely alone. Anyway, I've started painting. How're the enchiladas?"

"I want fourths tonight. That's why the Romans threw up, to eat it all over again. Sorry about the symbolism," Julio said, noticing Rosa's wince, "but they're that good."

Rosa took a sip of her wine and dispelled the thought. "It is good, isn't it? Do you want more salad? Help yourself." Rosa caught herself treating Julio as a guest. Well, he is visiting me, isn't he . . . the realization made him seem clearer somehow, as though a heaviness had been shed. An unnecessary skin. Rosa thought of her dream by the river. The beautiful, rainbow, snake skin. Now she knew she would tell him.

They quickly cleared the dishes and went to sit by the fire. Rosa emptied her glass of cabernet. Julio's had been empty for a while. They stared at the fire for a moment. The dinner had been delicious and Rosa's stomach, the child, was quiet. She leaned into his outstretched arm.

"Do you miss me?" Julio asked.

"I have something to show you," Rosa answered him softly.

"I asked you a question, Rosa." Julio looked at her face and she looked like she was waiting for something. Maybe she wants some more wine, he thought. "Do you want to open another bottle of wine? Which one do you want? You choose."

Rosa could see he was trying to please her. To please her. Yes. She reached for the drawing pad beside her and opened it to the child's face. Luzia's face. She handed it to him.

"What's this? A new drawing? Do you want that wine?" Then the words caught him, 'I'm pregnant.'"

Julio looked at her in disbelief. In utter disbelief. "What is this, Rosa? 'I'm pregnant?' What's going on?"

Rosa looked back at him, straight into his eyes. "That's our child. That's a drawing of our child. I'm pregnant."

Julio was stunned, but he kept staring at the drawing. "Why didn't you tell me? When did it happen? Are you sure? Are you absolutely sure?"

"Yes, I'm absolutely sure. I think I'm close to two months along. I want this child, Julio. Do you?" Rosa stared at him with all her soul. Her soul was exposed, utterly, in her face.

"Rosa, Rosa," Julio murmured, "she's beautiful. Almost as beautiful as you. Are you sure she's a girl?" Julio laughed.

"That's what I dreamt, more than once. I never wanted to tell you. I didn't want to be pregnant, especially not now." Rosa began to laugh, tears streaming down her face.

Julio took her into his arms, stroking her hair and back. Tears stung his eyes and joy grabbed at his throat. "Don't you think this calls for champagne, mi Rosa?"

Julio's lovemaking bordered on violence, and it aroused her in an unexpected way—as though his kisses had to be met, his tongue had to be met, his teeth had to be met. Rosa matched him until he collapsed across her in an attitude of surrender. Whose surrender? It was difficult to tell. They lay silently as though an answer would arrive, the way their orgasms had arrived, the way the child would arrive. From the mystery itself.

Finally, Julio spoke, splintering the silence. "You aren't staying now, are you? You can't stay here now. Pregnant, I mean."

Rosa was silent.

"Rosa, do you mean to tell me that you're pregnant and that you're still going to stay here? That's crazy, Rosa."

"I don't know. Don't ask me now." She paused to look at Julio. His face was tense and angry. "But I've got to be honest, I think I'm staying. I think I've got to stay."

Julio exploded. "How in the hell are you going to pull this one off? Pregnant, here, by yourself? Now you'll really need a man. Me, remember?"

Rosa stiffened at his words and sat up. "Between a part-time job and the money that's left I think I'm fine for a while. Maybe even my grant will come through, but I won't know till December. Anyway, my expenses here are low. I can't, I honestly can't imagine going back right now. I feel like I've got to finish whatever it is I came here to do."

"And what might that be? Tell me! I want to know!" he shouted.

"Julio," Rosa stared straight ahead, "I'm not going to go back because I have to. If I do go back, it'll be because I want to. Do you understand me, once and for all?"

"Then, once and for all, what about this pregnancy? What about that little item?" he said, trying to control himself.

"I wasn't even sure if I was going to tell you," Rosa said evenly.

"And why not?" He raised his voice again.

"Because of the reaction you're having now. Look, I set up an appointment to have an abortion. I'm not saying this to hurt you, I just want you to know. I've decided that I want this baby. It wasn't easy, but I decided with everything in mind."

"Do you love me?" Julio sat facing her, staring at her lips for an answer.

"This is our child. She looks like a relative, doesn't she?"

"Do you love me?"

"Yes, I do."

Julio sighed. "Come and lay in my arms and finish this champagne."

The fierce stars were out, and they hunted without a sound. It would freeze tonight, and they were aware of their bodies stretched out, warm, against the other. The champagne was gone, so Rosa turned to face the sky through the curtainless window.

Julio cupped her belly in his hands. His hand wandered down to her pubic hair and he stroked her gently. "You think it's a girl?" he asked.

"That's what I've dreamt," she answered him sleepily.

"Did you dream that face?"

"No. I just started to sketch it. That's what I think she'll look like." Her voice trailed off.

"Shouldn't you put curtains on these windows?"

"Then I wouldn't be able to see the stars. Good night, Julio."

"Have you considered the view goes both ways?"

"I don't care."

Julio held his breath for a moment. "Good night, Rosa."

Rosa woke to a dazzling sun, and the brief dream came, clearly, to her. They'd slept in. Julio was on his side, breathing softly, covered up to his eyes. She'd go make a fire, immediately.

The dream, she thought. The dream. She'd decided to leave— this had been very clear—she'd decided to go back. And then the tattoo began to melt. To disappear. A great sorrow engulfed her, as though she, herself, would disappear. No, I can't do it, she told herself. I can't leave. I'm staying.

Rosa shut the bedroom door and started some tea water, then the fire. The cabin was freezing. She felt it on the exposed areas of her face. She opened the back door and the sheer whiteness, the cold, assaulted her. How would I shovel myself out nine months along? She shut the door and started breakfast.

"I smelled the coffee," Julio said, coming into the kitchen. "Are you planning to cook something for breakfast? I'll do the dishes." He smiled at her.

"I was thinking of a German pancake stuffed with apples and cinnamon. How's that?"

"I'll do the dishes for that any day. You aren't having coffee?" he asked, noticing the tea bag in her cup.

"It nauseates me."

Julio began to laugh as he drew Rosa into his arms. "I forgot to give you something." He took something small out of his shirt pocket, a small metal heart with a purple ribbon tied through a hole at the top of it. A safety pin was clipped onto the ribbon. "A milagro, for you."

Rosa took it and felt its small strength. She fingered the smooth, purple ribbon. "A miracle. Of course. Could this be your heart, Mr. López?" Rosa smiled at him.

Julio took the heart and pinned it over hers. "Now I don't know whether to pin it over your heart or your womb." His eyes were shining.

"That'll do, Mr. López, for now. Here, the coffee's ready. Let me get breakfast." She kissed him lightly on the lips.

"I'll be sending you two hundred a month to make ends meet until you decide to come back. I want you to come back. Do you hear me, Rosa?"

Rosa fingered the milagro. "I hear you, loud and clear. If I don't eat pretty soon I'm going to be sick."

"This is delicious," Julio said, looking at Rosa. "Do you feel all right? You look a little pale."

"It's always like this until the food properly settles." Rosa poured herself some more tea. "I can't believe that the smell of coffee almost turns my stomach." She looked at Julio and said, "I seem to be turning into someone else. That's what it feels like."

"You know, your telling me you're pregnant makes me feel a bit altered; but to actually be pregnant must be like changing into someone else." Julio paused. "Were you really not going to tell me?"

"I was contemplating it."

"Why?"

"Have I ever told you about the Mexican Man?"

Julio laughed. "No, I don't think so. Someone I know?"

"He's the man I never wanted to marry. He's the man I've seen women make the endless piles of tortillas for, as he grows fat and stupid while his brain shrinks to fit his narrow mind that dictates boys are better than girls, boys become men, girls become wives, men have moments of freedom, release, women count the tortillas and the children. Men have affairs, women become whores. Puta. La Puta. You know, that word used to send shivers down my spine. 'Puta.'" Rosa said it deep in her throat, like the sound of coughing up something disgusting she was about to spit out and get rid of. Something so worthless it deserved to lie on the ground, the Earth, and be forgotten. "That's the way they said it. It was like the woman

deserved to die. Fuck!" Rosa looked at Julio with a strange desperation on her face.

"Rosa, I may be a little overweight, but my brain's not shrinking.
Okay, I guess I've had trouble with your freedom. I was brought up
by the women who served me the endless tortillas. But why the
Mexican Man? Do you see me as the Mexican Man?"

"Sometimes. It just creeps up on you. I don't think it's something
you consciously know that you're doing. But didn't you just say it?
You were raised by the women who served you the endless tortillas.
Dolores just told me my father was also German. Maybe that makes
me la hija de La Gran Puta."

"Rosa, what're you saying? Take it easy. I am not the Mexican
Man, for Christ's sake."

"What I'm saying is that in our culture, the culture we were
raised in, the puta was the woman who fucked who she wanted to
and didn't fuck who she didn't want to, because she liked to fuck.
Maybe she loved her body. Maybe she loved being a woman. The
Mexican Man was in opposition to all this."

"Do you still have an interest in other men, even now?" Julio
asked, suspiciously.

"Watch it, Julio. He's creeping up on you again. I may be pregnant, but I'm not dead. In fact, I feel especially alive."

"Don't women feel motherly when they're pregnant? I mean,
isn't that what's happening?"

"I was a mother before. Was I only motherly before? All I know
is, my body feels like it's reaching out for the stars and the center of
the Earth, simultaneously. I feel like fucking you right now like La
Gran Puta." Rosa laughed, reaching for his penis, rubbing it, slightly
swollen and soft, under his jeans.

"The Mexican Man surrenders to La Gran Puta, gladly." Julio
shivered with excitement, and let her rub him to a full erection. As
she took his penis, carefully, out of his pants he threw his head back
and moaned loudly as the warmth of her mouth surrounded him. He
drew her up and they collapsed on the couch.

"You'd better throw a log on the fire," Rosa mumbled.

"Forget the fire. Take your clothes off."

"Take your clothes off. And throw on a log."

Julio put the log on the fire, and then another one. It would last
for a while now. He stripped off his clothing in a few movements. His
penis stood out in front of him, proudly. It had no eyes, but it knew
where it wanted to go—inside of Rosa. Will I remember this in my
old age? The thought flickered and disappeared.

He faced her thrusting out his penis, with his hands, for her scrutiny. For her admiration. And then he saw it. The tattoo on her belly. "Rosa, what's on your belly?" Julio stood there staring at her, holding his penis with one hand.

"What does it look like?"

He sat down on the couch and touched it. "A rose tattoo. Is it real? Not a glue-on?"

"It's the real thing. Do you like it?"

"When did you get it?" He was flabbergasted.

"A couple of months ago. Do you like it?"

"Do I have a choice? Why did you get it?"

Rosa thought of her dream of the melting tattoo and said, "Because I had to."

"Why?" Julio insisted.

"I don't know." Rosa's voice sounded far away and she turned her face toward the fire.

Slowly, Julio bent over her. He kissed her tattoo, and then he licked it, encircling the softness of her ass with his arms. "You taste so good, Rosa."

"Puta," she reminded him.

"Puta," he echoed. His tongue found her again.

"Do you realize I can hear myself think here?" Julio laughed. "And do you know that I love that you're pregnant? The tattoo I'll have to get used to."

"Are you surprised?" Rosa was lying on the crook of his arm staring at the fire.

"I'm still in shock, I think. But I love it. Would you have had the abortion without telling me?" Julio stroked her neck softly.

"I think it's enough that I told you. It's been hard for me. Don't ask."

"Okay. Fair enough. Do you want to take the gun out for a few rounds?"

"Take a look outside. Do you want to shoot a gun in that?"

"I think you should practice with it. What if you have to use it?" Julio's body stiffened.

"Come on, Julio. Let's go for a walk. We could follow the creek. We'll take some brandy."

"On one condition. We make love again." Julio kissed her.

"Save that for tonight, M.M. Let's go."

"Have it your way, La Gran Puta."

They threw pillows at each other for a while and eventually they got dressed.

"Are you really pregnant, Rosita?" Julio held her in his arms and stared, directly, into her eyes.

"It looks like it, M.M.," Rosa laughed.

"Okay, come on. Let's take this walk out in the tundra. I guess I'm ready." Julio looked out from under a ski hat folded down over his ears.

"You look like a pissed-off grizzly," Rosa laughed loudly.

"Listen, I'm from the desert, woman. I am pissed-off. I ain't supposed to be in no snow. Sheeit!" Julio growled at her.

"Do you have your camera, Mr. Bear?"

He growled and nodded yes. Zack was waiting for them on the porch.

"Mush, mush, Zack! Tally ho!" Julio shouted and jumped off the steps.

"You'd better watch it! You're going to fall on your ass!"

Zack ran ahead toward the creek. He was beginning to know which way Rosa would go. This time she decided to walk the opposite way—to cross the creek and follow another trail. The snow was deeper here. The trail led to a meadow covered by the sloping smoothness of fresh snow. Not a single footprint, human or animal, was on it. Then the trail forked and a smaller one followed the creek through the trees again.

"Well, it's beautiful. Look at those peaks in the distance. Nothing but white. And the shadows are incredible, aren't they?" Julio asked, aiming his camera, full of concentration. He hardly heard her answer. He was seeing more than hearing.

"Yes. It's absolutely beautiful here."

They sat on cold, grey stones facing each other. The creek flowed in front of them.

"There's a composition everywhere you look, isn't there?" Julio bent over the water to capture the ice prisms dangling in weird shapes.

"The ice is so still and the water never stops."

"What did you say?" he asked.

"I said, the ice is so still and the water never stops. I like that. They look like water roots. Winter roots."

"I've never seen anything like it. I guess if it gets deeper out here you'll need snowshoes to walk through."

Rosa poured the brandy. "I guess. I'm going to have to equip Zack with a brandy barrel and put it around his neck." Zack ran over at the sound of his name. "How about it, Zack? Do you want to carry the brandy?" Rosa smoothed his ears, and then he was gone, running along the creek.

"He sure likes it here. Doggy's paradise. No fences. I'm glad we stopped here. My feet were beginning to freeze," Julio said.

They sipped the brandy slowly, listening to the swollen creek.

"Do you ever think about making it into the next century? If we're going to survive into the next century? I mean, the whole planet." Rosa stared at the ice prisms as they caught the available light.

Julio looked at her. "Not constantly, but from time to time. You can't help but wonder which missile's pointed on your head. I know in the bay area there're quite a few pointed on it, that's for sure."

"This child of ours is headed for the next century, you know."

"That's right. I hadn't thought of that. Pour me another, would you?"

Rosa poured them both another.

To the Earth and our baby," Julio said, softly, putting his glass out to Rosa's.

"And to transformation." The brandy burned a little, filling her mouth up with its fire.

That night as Julio put his arms around her belly, he asked her, "Have you thought of a name for this tattooed baby? If it's a girl, that is."

"I call her a Native Person. She's a mestizo, a mixed-blood. That's what a Mexican really is—a mestizo. We're all mestizos."

Julio laughed. "How's that?"

"She'll be a Native Person of the Earth, that's what. If we're going to survive into the next century, we're all going to have to be Native People. You know?" Rosa stretched against Julio and it was hard to remember tension at that moment.

"But have you thought of a name for this Native Person?"

"I'm going to keep it a secret until I see her. Why don't you think of one, too."

"Are you really going to get big, Rosita?" Julio's voice was thick and sleepy. He waited for an answer and when she remained silent he asked, "You aren't going to stay here by yourself, are you?"

"Yes, I am." Her voice sounded small in the darkness. It was as though they were in a narrow tunnel.

He grabbed hold of her. "I won't let you. You've got to come back with me now. You know that."

"Not now, Julio. Go to sleep. I'm so damned tired."

Rosa fell asleep almost immediately, and Julio struggled, alone, in the dark tunnel until he passed into the brightness of his dreams.

He is following tracks, lion tracks, and then they disappear. They simply disappear. He begins to laugh with joy. He sees that the desert's in bloom. Flowers among cactus needles, fertility within the sand. Spring. Julio cups a handful of sand, and when he opens his hand, the sand is gone.

When Rosa woke, Julio was already up. She could hear him in the kitchen, and the sound of the morning fire. Her dreams, there'd been many small ones, seemed like one continuous thread. Deep, dark and unbroken. Maybe these are the ones that guide me best, the thought came to her, blindly. She smelled bacon and coffee, and the familiar nausea returned with an unusual force.

"Are you up?" Julio asked, looking in.

"Not quite. I feel absolutely lousy." Rosa turned on her side and looked out the window. "Do you mind bringing me some tea and toast? I would sure appreciate it."

"Coming right up. Do you want bacon and eggs?"

"I'll tell you after the tea. Thanks."

They ate breakfast by the fire. Bach played on the stereo. Peace.

"I let Zack out. I fed him, too," Julio said.

"Look at the sun. What a day. Do you want to go for a ride later? We could do some exploring up by Buck's Lake."

"Sounds good to me."

"Also, tonight I was invited to a piano recital—a woman I met at a local restaurant. Her name's Iris. She's also a painter, and a good one. Do you want to go?"

"We don't have much time together. Do you have to go?"

"I want to go."

Julio's face darkened. "Well, then, I guess I'll go with you."

"Okay, the map says the highway goes out to a deserted Mobil station, and the next left by a school bus shelter. It seems longer than eight miles, doesn't it?"

"Seems like eighty," Julio answered.

"Here it is," Rosa said, turning the car onto a narrow dirt road. "There isn't as much snow down here, at all. Just a powder. I enjoyed our snow fight today."

Julio lit up a joint and smiled. "Me, too. Got you good, didn't I?" he laughed. "Do you want some?"

"Maybe later. I got you good back, though, didn't I?" Rosa

teased. "The house is set back, but a banner with a crescent moon will be hung by the fence, it says here."

"Hippieland," Julio muttered.

"What do you mean, hippieland? You're an artist, aren't you?"

"These are white people, right? I mean, it's okay, of course. I have some white friends, but they're just a lot harder to get to know. I mean, I hope we don't have to sit around chanting OM or something."

Rosa laughed. "You can sit around chanting *mierda* for all I care. Anyway, her name's Iris. She's a waitress in town and I like her."

"There it is. Must be that place with the lights on and all the cars." Julio pointed to it.

Forrest opened the door. "Well, it's Ms. Luján! How's the quality wood? Come on in. I'm supposed to welcome everyone. Right, Iris?"

Iris smiled and waved. She was sitting at the piano. A group of people sat on chairs and pillows in a semi-circle, facing her.

"Has she started?" Rosa asked.

"She just started up. Grab a pillow."

"Forrest, this is Julio." Rosa glanced at Julio and he didn't look overjoyed.

They shook hands. "Welcome to the show, Julio. Talk to you in the intermission. I see you brought food and libations. Excellent, I'm starved," Forrest laughed. He went back to his pillow next to Cheryl.

Julio was frowning. "Who in the fuck was that? Golden Boy? I plan to eat some of this myself."

"He's the guy I bought the wood from. Actually, he's going to be my neighbor. Sort of. That's his wife next to him," Rosa added.

Iris looked over at them, briefly, and began to play on a piano as beautiful as Rob's. But, obviously, she was a much better pianist. Her hands took control of the keys, immediately, and the notes rolled fluidly into the small room like a gift. The notes quickly filled the room; every corner seemed filled with its richness. She erased the notes with a silence, and then she began again.

"Go on and sit down." Rosa motioned Julio toward some pillows. "I'll bring some wine. Isn't she good?" Rosa whispered.

"Very. Very good," Julio answered, making his way to the pillows. His largeness dwarfed what seemed to be a roomful of fine-boned people—but he was agile. Agile as a cat.

Rosa handed the wine to Julio and sat down on the floor. A wood stove with a glass door, a square of red warmth, heated the room. On the walls were some watercolors and a large oil. They all had her trademark of delicacy and strength, like the ones in the restaurant.

The oil was bold, though. Striking. A pair of dark horses, very realistic and solid, stood facing each other in a dreamlike plain of light corals. Rosa gazed at this painting while Iris played, glancing occasionally at her face which followed the music that she heard in her head.

"Iris, that was wonderful." Rosa reached over and touched her hand.

"Thank you, Rosa. And thanks for coming." She looked at Julio.

"Iris, this is Julio."

"Very beautiful, Iris," Julio said, smiling.

"I'm glad you enjoyed it. I really am. Have you had some of the food? Help yourself. That is, if you can beat Forrest to it," Iris laughed.

Julio looked at Rosa. "She isn't kidding. Are you hungry?"

"Just a little. These look good. I wonder what they are?" Rosa picked up a cabbage leaf filled with something.

A dark-haired woman answered her. "They're a kind of dolmas filled with brown rice, raisins, chopped vegetables and walnuts." The woman's dark eyes were wide-open and intense. She had high cheek bones and full, sensual lips without lipstick.

"Are these yours?" Rosa asked.

"Yes, they are." She smiled, slowly.

Rosa took a bite. "These are delicious." She put the rest of it in her mouth. "My dish is the tacos." Rosa looked over at her plate and laughed. "Or rather, my dish was the tacos. I'm Rosa," she said looking at the younger woman.

"My dream name is A——. My waking name is Diana." She said this in a low voice, looking at Rosa, closely, to see her true response.

"Are you Indian? A—— sounds like an Indian name. I think your dream name is lovely." Rosa looked back at her and the air between them was charged with a restless energy.

Diana's long beaded earrings caught the light and then melted into her thick, dark hair. "My mother's Cree with some Mexican thrown in. Did you just move here? I haven't seen you before, so you must've. Is that your old man?" She indicated Julio.

"Well, first of all, my grandmother was Yaqui Indian, but after my grandfather a good dose of Mexican was thrown in, and my father was English and German. Thought we'd get that straight."

They both laughed.

"And, yes, that's my husband, but I moved here by myself." Now it was Rosa's turn to scrutinize her response. "Do you mind if I call you A——? I love it. What does it mean?"

In a soft, low voice she said, "One who seeks." And then she changed back into her speaking voice which was rather loud. "Well, it appears we have some things to talk about, Rosa. There aren't many Mexican or Indian people up here. Well, there is what's left of the Maidu, the Native People of this area—but they make it a point to keep to themselves. I don't blame them." Diana paused, then asked, "What do you do?"

"I'm a painter and a teacher. I've been painting oils for about ten years. I don't know what I'm going to do here. The college is locked up tight, it seems. Anyway, what do you do up here?"

"For one, I'm a midwife, and I also run the county nutrition and prenatal program on a part-time basis." A little boy around three years old ran up to her and held onto her long, full skirt. "This is Joel. Do you have any of these?" she laughed.

"Mine's eighteen and on his own now. Why don't I give you my number. I live in Lupine Meadows."

"Do you like it out there? I've heard it's Machoville with the ranch there and all. But the lots are pretty nice, and there's only so many of them. Are you renting something back there?"

"Actually, I bought it. Why don't you come by for dinner sometime? Do you live out here?"

"Most of my friends live in Butterfly Valley or Spanish Peak. I live about six miles out toward Spanish Peak. I'll give you my number if you'll lend me your pen."

"Do you live by yourself—with your son, that is?"

"Yeah, but there's a group of us in a small cluster of cabins, so it's kind of supportive. It'll be a little tricky living out in Lupine Meadows all alone, I imagine." Diana kept her eyes on Rosa's face.

Loud voices made Rosa turn around. It was Julio and Forrest.

"Did I ask your opinion, or what?" Julio was enraged.

"Well, I didn't mean anything by it. Take it easy!" Forrest said angrily, but it was clear that he was intimidated.

"You ate all the damn tacos! What's your trip?" He wanted to shout Golden Boy.

Rosa took Julio by the arm. "What's going on? Come on, Julio."

Then Forrest got brave. "It looks like he can't handle his tacos."

Julio rushed toward him and Forrest backed into the food table spilling things. Iris came over and grabbed onto Forrest saying, "You'd better shut up, Forrest."

"All I said was that the tacos were some of the best I'd ever eaten."

"Yeah, well you ate nearly all of them, asshole!" Julio yelled.

"Come on, Julio. It's not worth it. Come on!" Rosa dragged him out the door. "Jesus, calm down!"

"You calm down! I don't have to put up with that shit! First the tacos are good, then you're good, or whatever that asshole said."

Rosa started up the motor and let it warm. Iris came out to the car. She had a shawl around her shoulders, and a concerned look was on her face. "Rosa, Julio, you don't have to go. You really don't. I'm planning to do another set in about ten minutes."

Rosa glanced at Julio and his face was still angry. "Thanks, Iris, but I don't think we should. But thanks for coming out like this." She didn't know what else to say. It was embarrassing.

"Look, Iris, I'm sorry," Julio said, leaning forward toward the window. "I didn't mean to cause so much trouble back there." His voice sounded strained with effort.

"Don't worry about it. It happens," Iris said, looking at Julio with a trace of impatience. "I'll see you soon, Rosa. Bye, now." She turned and ran toward the house.

They were quiet all the way to town, though it took every effort at silence for Rosa to hold her tongue, and Julio could feel it like a hollowness in his ears, loudly.

"Twenty degrees. It's a bitch tonight. Did you leave the heater on?" he asked in a subdued voice.

"Why did you get in that fight with Forrest?" She asked in a tempered tone because she remembered that Forrest had also pushed her button.

"The tacos are great, and Rosa's not so bad either," Julio mimicked Forrest's voice.

"It seems that the guy can be a pain, but do you think that explosion was worth that measly comment?"

"Yeah, I do! I sure as hell do!"

"Julio, maybe a short, but lethal, comment would've done the trick. I think you overdid it."

"That's your opinion," Julio said in a harsh voice.

"That's right! That was damned embarrassing. I have a feeling if we'd been around people you know, you'd have been a fucking diplomat. If you really didn't want to come, why didn't you stay at the cabin for a few hours?"

"Oh, right. Now that would've been tons of fun." Julio laughed angrily.

"All I know is, there've been plenty of times when I could've really used your back-up, but you left me on my own." Rosa began to cry. "It seems like your possessions were in jeopardy back there, that's all."

"Oh, Christ, not that again. Does it always have to come back to that, Rosa?"

"Apparently, it does. Okay, look, just forget it for now. But why did you apologize to Iris back there?" Rosa shot him an angry look.

Julio started to speak and then he fell silent. Finally, he said, "I guess I thought I owed her an apology. Do you know that I'm leaving tomorrow?"

"Yes, I know."

Julio reached over and touched her hand. "Can't we be friends?"

"That's what I keep trying to do, Julio." She started crying again and pulled her hand away from his.

"Okay, I apologize to you for the scene, but I'm not sorry I did it."

"Great. Then that means, in essence, that you'd do it again."

"I said I apologize, Rosa," Julio said with an edge of anger.

When they got into their sleeping bags Julio reached for her, but she shrugged him off.

"I don't believe this. I'm leaving tomorrow. Will you at least let me hold you in my arms?"

Rosa turned and put her head on his shoulder. Then he tried to kiss her. She turned away.

"I'll lay in your arms, but I just don't feel like making love, at all."

"Great. That's just great." Julio stared out the window. The night was clear and the stars were brilliant with light. An unusual amount of light, he thought. But they were no comfort to him. No comfort at all. He was in the middle of his life with nothing to show for it but a couple of failed marriages, a few bittersweet affairs. The child, he thought. There is the child. And Rosa will probably come back when she starts to get big. At least there's the child . . .

"Good night, Rosa," he murmured, snuggling up close to her, smelling the back of her neck. But she was asleep, as the child was asleep inside of her. Inside of her, he thought with yearning. God, this place is quiet—too damned quiet. She'll come back soon enough. I'll give her two months in this place.

He continued to stare at the stars, and he thought angrily, She ought to put some damned curtains up. Suddenly, he was fourteen camping out for the first time in the desert, and though the night had frightened him, the stars had kept him up with excitement. They'd looked so close. He hadn't killed yet. The next day he would kill his first rabbit. Everything was gone now. The rabbit's flesh, its soft fur, Gonzales, the boy in the night, wrapped by the night; silence instead of screams, a slow burning fire instead of flares, light instead of loneliness.

Now, he opened his hand, and it was true—even the sand was gone. Entirely. No one owns the desert, the words came to him, not even the sand.

Julio left the next day, and the joy they'd felt when he first arrived, that first night, was equal to the sense of sorrow they felt as he left. Rosa felt drained of any real emotion, and Julio had only one left. Anger. So they parted again, both of them vaguely feeling what would become familiar to them both. Despair.

"I'll send you the two hundred dollars next month. Take care of yourself," Julio said. "Look, I'll take the baby right after it's born. I mean it."

"Oh, sure. I'm just going to give my baby away. Right, Julio."

"It'll be my child, too, you know."

"Goodbye. Have a safe trip." Rosa was anxious for him to go, though she knew an immense wave of loneliness waited for her. She knew it was there waiting for her, as though it were a gate to her solitude.

"I want to come back week after next." He tried to kiss her, but she turned her cheek to him, pulling away from his hold.

"Call me during the week. Bye, Julio." Rosa closed the door as he walked to his car. Pregnant and alone, the walls whispered.

The drawing of the child hung over the fireplace. "Luzia," she said out loud. She could no longer hear Julio's car. Then Rosa walked into the studio, and her sense of despair included the unfinished paintings. Maybe I am losing my mind, she began. Maybe I am, finally, just seeing things. Who else cares about the fucking lilac sky but me? As Julie said, with my attitude I'm not going to be too popular around here. And then last night. A hermit. And a pregnant hermit at that.

Then she started to laugh, and every time she'd start to calm down, the image of a serious-faced, pregnant hermit made her gasp with laughter all over again. I must be nuts, she thought, laughing by myself.

Rosa took a look out of the front room window. I wonder what old Dale would think of this? Probably call in a posse. This made her laugh even harder. I'm a lost cause, that's what. "A lost cause," she said out loud.

Suddenly she was hungry. Very hungry. She waited for the nausea, but it didn't come. Rosa heated up the leftovers, putting candles on instead of lights. The night's swallowing the forest, she told herself. Let it. Just let it. She felt like laughing again, but, this time, because the food was delicious. Let it.

Rosa woke to the phone ringing. She brought it to her ear. "Yes?"

"Rosa, are you really there?"

"I think so."

"It's me. Sierra. Did I wake you up, you lazy bitch!" she laughed.

"That's me." Rosa looked at the clock. "I slept in, I guess. What're you up to?"

"I'm just calling to say that Bob and I want you to be at the birth. Are you still coming?" Sierra asked in an anxious voice.

Rosa gathered herself. "Only if my being there's not going to get in the way. What I mean is, if you'd rather just have Bob there, I understand." I wouldn't have before, but I do now, she thought silently.

The icyness in her voice betrayed her because Sierra said, "You're still pissed-off, aren't you? I mean, do you really mean that about not liking Bob?"

"Yes, I'm sorry, but I do."

Sierra's voice stiffened. "Okay, well, he was an asshole that day, but things are better now. A lot better."

"It doesn't mean I have to like him."

They were both silent for a few moments.

"I want you to be here, okay?" Sierra began to cry.

"When's your due date?" Tears jumped to her own eyes.

"November fourteenth. I'm so big now, it feels like tomorrow."

"I'll come if you want me to," Rosa said, softly, "but it'll take me about six hours to get there. So, you're going to have to call me at the first sign so I can make it. Guess what?"

"What?"

"I'm pregnant."

"You're what? You're kidding!"

"You heard it right. I'm pregnant."

"What the hell are you going to do? You don't like Julio either, right?"

Rosa laughed. "I'm going to have the baby. That's what."

"Well, you can't stay there now, right? Jesus S.! Aren't you pretty secluded out there? What does Julio think?"

"I'm staying. I've got a gun, you know," Rosa laughed. Then, in a serious voice she said, "Julio wants the baby, too. I just can't live with him. Not now."

"How bizarre. For you, I mean," Sierra said with a note of embarrassment.

"Everything's bizarre, Sierra."

"Jesus S., girl, can't you do anything right?" Sierra said, laughing. "I suppose you've thought of an abortion?"

"I even made the appointment. I want this baby. That's what I realized."

"I can't believe it! But I'm glad for you if that's what you want."

"Well, I certainly wouldn't have chosen this time, but, now, that's what I want." Rosa's nausea arrived. "Sierra, I'm starting to get nauseated. You know, morning sickness, so I've got to go. Anyway, I'll be there. Just call me right away."

"Are you okay?" Sierra asked, concerned. "And where'd you get a gun?"

"Yes, I'm okay. I got it from Julio. Look, I'll call you back this weekend."

"Don't you think you should consider going back to Julio, at least for a while, for some support? We all need it."

"This is where I'm staying. Anyway, see you next month or so. Thanks for calling. . . ."

After breakfast Rosa decided to work on the rainbow painting, and tomorrow she'd get a paper to see what kind of work was available locally. Well, living here I won't go out much, and the house payment's low. I have plenty of clothes. All I need are some long johns and a pair of pregnancy pants. Maybe, she told herself. Or I'll just tie rubber bands at the waist like I did with Sean. Anxiety gripped her, but she forced herself into the studio and began work on the rainbow.

The painting of her mother, the one she wanted to do, flashed through her mind. She thought of Iris the other night, sitting at her piano, bent to the music—transfixed. I'll probably never hear Dolores play again, the thought came to her, and with it a strange despair.

She put on a tape of piano music and then, slowly, as she began to work the rainbow became the most important thing in the world.

Rosa glanced at the shawl and decided to do at least one rose. Yes, at least one, she thought. It hung there, in the lilac sky, incomplete.

The walk had been beautiful, cold and curiously lonely after Julio's visit. The Mexican Man and La Gran Puta have blown it again, Rosa thought, wryly. The walk following the creek was like being on the moon—white, still and silent. She thought of Sierra's situation—Would I rather be there? No. Would I rather be with Julio right now? I could just leave. I could just go back and sell this place. No. No. No. You're supposed to be on the moon, La Gran Puta, Rosa answered herself.

The phone rang in the silence, jarring her. It was twilight and she hadn't lit a single candle yet. Zack was still out, running somewhere. The open fire had calmed her, and she was tempted not to answer it at all. But she did.

"Is that you, Rosa? This is Diana. Remember?" she asked in a confident but cautious voice. She certainly had a loud voice.

"Of course, I remember. I was just thinking how being up here in the snow's like being on the moon. I just got back from a walk."

"Exactly," Diana laughed. "That's exactly what it's like. Do you still have that invitation open? I'd like to come out, if it's all right."

"Of course, it's all right. If you're talking about Julio, he's gone back to the bay area."

Diana laughed. "Yeah, I could tell you wanted Scotty to beam you aboard the other night. Anyway, Forrest is the kind of guy you don't take too seriously. He's a nice guy. In fact, he shows every sign of being brilliant, but his energy and his mouth run away with him sometimes. But, I'll tell you, he's a really good friend when you need one. He's done some pretty nice things for me. So, when do you want me to come?" she asked, changing the subject.

Rosa laughed. "How's tomorrow night? Or how about afternoon, around four. I'll fix an early dinner."

"I'll bring a salad, okay? Four sounds fine. Do you need anything from town?"

"No, but thanks for asking. See you tomorrow, A——."

"Hasta la vista!" she almost yelled.

Well, maybe I won't be a hermit, entirely, after all, Rosa thought. And tomorrow morning I'll have breakfast out. Then Rosa remembered Iris. She got her number out and called, but there was no answer. "Oh, well, I'll see her tomorrow," she said out loud.

Zack was at the door. Rosa grabbed a towel from the porch and

dried him off. "Hey, boy, your fur's getting thick, and no more fleas."
Zack was ecstatic, or he appeared to be so. He seemed to be panting
and smiling, his tail in a stiff curl. Again, she realized how much she
loved his malamute mask.

"Hey, wolfie, where you been?" She and Sean had picked him out
from a litter. Sean had been twelve, his face wild with expectation.
They'd never owned their own dog. Sean had knelt down to see the
puppies better, when the largest one there leaped on him, licking his
face.

"I think your dog's found you," the man had said.

"Looks like it," Rosa'd said, watching Sean let the dog lick every
inch of his face.

"Do you miss Sean, Zack boy? Bet you do." At the sound of
Sean's name, Zack's eyes held a sharpened awareness.

Rosa picked up the phone and dialed Sean's number. He answered.

"Oh good, you're home. It's me, your mother."

"Yeah, I'm going to be home all night. Studying."

"How're your classes?"

"They're not that hard, but I want to get a high grade point
average. Helps with the scholarships. Universities love that stuff. Is
it still snowing?"

"No, it's clear, but there's snow on the ground. And it is freezing.
Sean, I want to tell you something. Nothing bad, okay? But startling
news. Are you ready?"

"I guess so," Sean answered warily.

"It looks like I'm going to have a baby."

"You've got to be kidding! Aren't you a little old for that? I mean,
you're up there by yourself, for chrissake," Sean said, angrily.

"Hey, hold it, Sean. I'm not too old, and I'm telling you something that's already been decided."

"Well, if you ask me, this is crazy. So, what does the father think?
No wonder he's been in a lousy mood."

"Do you mean Julio?"

"Who else? Jesus!" Sean sounded exasperated.

"It's okay, I suppose. We just talked about it, and we both want
to have it. The baby." Rosa struggled to keep her voice low.

"Okay, but you're coming back now, right? What're you going to
do about that cabin now, Mom?"

"Live in it. I'm not coming back, Sean. I'm staying here," she
said, raising her voice.

"Mom, you've lost your mind. Do you know that?"

Rosa was getting angry. "Sean, if you say that one more time I'm going to hang up on you. Do you hear me?"

"Go ahead and hang up on me, cause that's what I think."

"Is that all you have to say?"

"What do you want me to say, congratulations or what?"

"I'll talk to you later, Sean." Rosa said, slamming the phone down.

She took the phone off the hook and cooked dinner. Rosa poured a glass of wine and sipped it, thinking, We'll see who's too old or who's lost their mind. Her face felt hot with anger. Sheer rage flowed through her, warming her blood like fire. Crazy at seventeen and crazy at thirty-four, that's me. Yeah, that's me, Sean, you little bastard. No, actually you're a big bastard.

Rosa let out a loud yell of fury. If only my arm could reach, she thought, I'd slap him. She'd slapped him only once in his life when he'd called her a bitch at fourteen. This would've been the second time, if she could've reached him. Rosa imagined Sean trying to call her, and it gave her some satisfaction.

As she got into her sleeping bag she thought, This is going to get old real quick. I need a bed, goddamnit. She felt for her Buck Knife, and rolled onto her stomach. She listened for sounds, alert, alert like a wolf. No, the wolf wasn't running. Its paws had changed into feet and hands. The last thing she heard was Zack shifting his position.

Rosa is in a warehouse full of huge machinery. She knows she's not supposed to be there, so she hides. Two little men, short but muscular, carry a bucket of fire into view. Rosa feels she shouldn't be watching, but she has to. One dwarf turns his back to the other, hunching over with his ass in the air, and slides the fire between his legs, slowly, toward the other dwarf. Then, they sense her and one of them yells, "Who's there?" Rosa's terrified, but she says, "I'm sorry, sir. I seem to be lost." One holds the bucket of fire and one points to an exit. I saw it! Rosa thinks like a shout. I saw their sacred fire!

The dream was curious to her at first; it had been so strange. The muscular dwarfs and their fire. As she drank some tea and ate a piece of toast, it simply settled in. Sacred, masculine fire, she told herself. Rosa stared at the snow, and the tea was hot in her hands.

Rob came to mind and she looked at the clock, quarter to eight. So, she decided to call since she hadn't written him yet.

He picked up the phone on the second ring. "Who's calling at this ungodly hour?"

"Guess who?"

"Rosa?" Rob laughed.

"Why're you so uptight, Robert?"

"Not enough sleep, long hours, bad pay, and I was almost killed yesterday." He made it sound like a shopping list.

"What happened?" Rosa was used to his low-key approach to the horrible, so his words made her jump. "What happened, Rob?"

"A drug addict walked into my office with a gun in his hand and demanded that I give him some dope. I walked right past him and told the desk clerk to call the cops. Goddamnit, that pissed me off! He had no right to come marching into my office, sticking a gun in my face! I've worked too damned hard to be treated like that!"

"I've never heard you so angry." Rosa thought of the night he'd told her about his family, but even then he'd quickly subdued it. "That was certainly an asshole thing for that idiot to do, but, Rob, promise me something. Don't you ever do that again. Give them the fucking dope. Don't ever do that one again. It's not worth it, Rob."

He was silent.

"Rob, do you hear me?" She thought of the miles between them, the mountains, the snow, the highways—Maybe he can't hear me, Rosa thought.

Finally, he said, "I couldn't let him get away with it. I'd do it again." Rob lowered his voice to a familiar pitch, but a tremble of anger remained. "No one's going to get away with that, goddamnit."

"He could've killed you! Do you want to die for some dope? Some replaceable dope?" Rosa was angry. She couldn't help it. The thought of him flaunting his life made her furious. "Do you want to die or what?" she asked, raising her voice.

"Have you thought of going into counseling, Dr. Luján? Look, thanks for your concern, but I guess it's like the sun—I can't help it. It's how I feel. Do you understand?"

"I think I do. But unlike the sun issue, I disagree. I'd like you to promise me you won't do that again. Do not walk past a man with a loaded gun," Rosa said with angry frustration.

"I can't promise you that, Rosa. Let's change the subject, okay? How're you doing up there? Any visits from Big Foot yet?"

"It's beautiful, with elements of the old West such as macho cowboys, not to forget the cowgirls." Rosa paused. "And I'm pregnant."

Rob was silent.

"Did you hear me, Rob?"

"Well, that's better news than near-murder, but is it good news? Do you want to be pregnant?"

"I don't know if I *want* to be pregnant, but it appears that I am, and I've come to the conclusion it's okay. I'm going to have this baby."

"Well, you see, Rosa, you're as bad as me." His voice was full of amusement. "You have no business asking me to promise you anything. We're both going to do what we want anyway."

"Wouldn't you say the circumstances are a bit different?"

"Not really. Think about it. Are you all right up there?"

"I'm okay. I even got a Landcruiser, so the road should be no problem. Also, plenty of wood. It's been snowing here. You ski, don't you?"

"I was thinking of that. How would sometime in December be? Probably the second week. I'll bring my cross-country skis up."

Rosa thought of Julio and winced. He just won't be able to come that week. Do I want him to come back, at all? she asked herself. "That sounds fine. I'm sure there's somewhere in town I can rent some skis. You know, I've never skied before. So, you're going to have to show me how. Do you mind?"

"I'd love to be the teacher this time," he laughed. "I'm not as nice as you though. I warn you. Now, seriously, do you feel okay? You know, with a pregnancy in your thirties you ought to have close contact with a doctor from here on out. You're in great shape, so I'm not trying to worry you. Just some free advice, okay? See someone right away."

"I'll take your advice, if you'll take my advice and be careful when someone's pointing a gun at you."

"You never give up, do you?"

"No."

Rosa found a seat and looked for Iris. Another waitress was working. When she came to take her order, she asked if Iris were off today.

"Iris and Danny are gone to Baja for a few months. Wish I were there. Didn't I see you at Iris's the other night?"

"Yes, that was me. My name's Rosa."

"I'm Jade. You're new here, right?"

Rosa felt disappointed, and sure enough, when she looked into the kitchen, a dark-haired woman was cooking. She looked at the want ads and it was worse than she thought it'd be. The only real jobs seemed to be out of the county, as though the hint was, leave the county if you want a job. There were a couple of part-time ones. One at a stationery store, the other at a newspaper.

"You aren't going to find anything here in the winter, and you'll be lucky to find something in the spring." It was Forrest. "May I join you for a cup of coffee? Or tea, I see." He was standing there, smiling.

"Where's Cheryl?" He certainly can smile when he wants to, Rosa noted.

Forrest sat down across from her. "At the doctor's. Thought I'd wait for her here." He leaned forward as though he were going to tell her a secret. "Sorry if I caused you any trouble the other night. You can tell that to—what was his name?"

"Julio."

"Yes, please tell Julio I meant no offense. Just enjoying myself, as usual. Battle at Fort Taco, I guess. But it was all my fault," he laughed. "Well, are you going to speak to me or what?"

Rosa started laughing. "Do I have a choice, McBride?"

His face got serious. "I suppose you do. You're not a hostage or anything."

His youth and his red hair was enough to make her laugh for some inexplicable reason. "What else do you do besides build houses? I hear you're brilliant."

"Who told you that?" A smile played around his eyes.

"So, what're your secret talents?"

There was something about Rosa that made him want to say the worst thing that came to his mind. She challenges me. That's it, he thought. She just looks at me. Forrest controlled himself and said, "Well, I'm not bad on the piano, but much better on the guitar."

"What do you play? By any chance, do you play flamenco?"

"Sure. And rock and ballads."

"Do you sing?"

"Not too hot. Can't do everything," Forrest answered with a trace of annoyance.

"Well, I love flamenco. I mean, I love it. Do you play around here?"

"Once in a while I play Friday evenings here. Also, at Peak's, a couple of blocks from here. But I've never played flamenco in public. I usually play rock, country or the ballads."

"When are you playing next?"

"Peak's, Saturday night. If you come, leave me a tip. I make it on tips," Forrest smiled at her.

"You'll have to play flamenco to get a tip out of me."

"Hard to please, are you?" He sipped his coffee.

"Where did you learn flamenco guitar?"

"A Spaniard, actually. An intense guy that claimed he knew Manitas de Plata. Worked as a bartender and taught students on the side. He was good, too. He could really play." Forrest seemed to be calming down. His voice was almost gentle. "Actually, I play flamenco mostly when I'm alone. You know, music of the gypsies and the soul."

Jade appeared with a coffee pot. "Do you want some more, Forrest?" She eyed Rosa, curiously.

"No, I'm about done."

"No, thank you," Rosa said, wishing she were Iris. "Iris is gone to Baja, I hear."

"Yeah, till February or so. I'd give my left testicle—excuse me," he laughed, "to go. But it's hard on Cheryl now. Anyway, I should go do a couple of things before the wife returns," Forrest said, getting up.

"I'll try to be there Saturday. I'll even tip you. Maybe. If you play flamenco."

A flicker of hurt went over his face, but then he laughed, and was out the door.

The job at the stationery store was already taken, so Rosa opened the door to the newspaper office. It was in an old house, and the office was part of the front room. Very comfortable, with a wood stove and a couch.

"I'm inquiring about the part-time job," she told the receptionist.

She gave Rosa the once-over and said, "I'll get Ted," and left the room.

A tall, dark man, with serious eyes, came out to greet her. "I'm Ted Mahoney, the editor here. You're here about the part-time job?"

"Yes. I'm Rosa Luján." They shook hands.

"Well, basically, you'd be covering for Inez who'll be gone for three weeks. Three days a week, with some paste-up. Have you ever done paste-up? It's not hard. I could show you. It's five bucks an hour. You interested?"

"For three weeks?"

"Inez is going on vacation. We might be able to use you off and on during deadlines, but that's not a promise."

"When does it start?"

"First of November."

"Sure. I'm interested."

"You're hired. Just fill this out. Basic questionnaire. I assume you type."

"About fifty-five words a minute. Do you hire everyone first and then look at their application?" Rosa laughed.

"Yeah. It usually works every time. There's some coffee in the kitchen. I'll be in my office," he said pointing to a room, "when you're done."

Rosa poured herself some coffee and put lots of milk in to offset the nausea it gave her. It was only one page, so she quickly finished it and took it to the editor.

"A little over-qualified, aren't you, Rosa?" he said, smiling. "Well, that's how it is up here. Oh, by the way, bring your own mug. You paint, I see. Maybe you can give us some advice with layout. Do you sell your work?"

"From time to time. I have a couple of paintings in the Oakland Museum and the San Francisco Museum of Modern Art, and other places. I guess that's what I'll really be doing up here. Painting." The coffee started to nauseate her and she remembered the baby. It was funny, she hadn't been pregnant in so long she had to remind herself she was pregnant.

"Well, I'm sorry I can't offer you anything more permanent. So, how's the first at nine A.M.? You get a paid lunch hour."

"Sounds fine. You don't want me to take a typing test or anything?"

"Nah, I'll take your word for it." His phone rang.

Rosa waved and was gone.

As Rosa drove home she realized that the town barely had a ground cover, but as she got nearer to Lupine Meadows the snow was still a solid foot. Must be the difference of five hundred feet in elevation, she realized. When she got out at the post office to get her mail she was aware of the silence the snow created, like an insulation.

She wondered who lived in the row of cabins next to the post office. The post office was in an old building that had once housed a store, with two Mohawk gas pumps next to it. This must've been a road stop at one time, but now the highway takes all the traffic, she thought. Lupine Meadows Trading Post was on the front windows of the store, with a fish painted in. It was in a jumping pose and the words "Ray Harris' Hand Made Flys" were next to it. The windows were papered so she couldn't look inside. There was a wooden bench on the sloping porch, and a pay phone, that looked too modern, next to it.

There were some letters. One from Erica, and one from Dolores, an opening for a sculptor she knew, and a notice saying to ring for a package. Rosa pressed the buzzer twice and was almost ready to leave when an angry face appeared at the grill of the post office window. Inside, it looked like an old fashioned bank, and the scales and equipment were old and dusty. Everything seemed to have layers of dust, as though time, current time, was secondary, and a spider's web given preference. She liked it.

"What can I do for you?" an older man with a red face asked with a bark.

Rosa handed him the notice. "This is it."

He took it and walked away, and he came back with a package in his hands. He lifted the grill and shoved it toward her.

"Thanks," Rosa said. "By the way, my name's Rosa."

He closed the grill, loudly. "It's part of the job. The name's Ray." He scowled at her.

"You make the flies?" Rosa persisted.

"That's me. This place may look like a dump ta ya now, but I used ta be busy tryin ta keep up with my customers. Thinkin of openin the store agin. Maybe even the pumps. Save everyone a trip ta town, the way I see it. What's yr name?"

"Rosa. I live up past the ranch."

"Good thing it don't snow like it used ta. Ya'd never get outta there. Twelve foot snows in the forties back there. Got ta git goin."

"The store sounds good, by the way," Rosa said, smiling.

"It all depends on money, like everythin else," he said and walked away, slamming the door behind him. Then he yelled, "Those books there's the town lendin librarer, Roza." That's how he said it: Roza.

She looked at the worn paperbacks and magazines. Some of the magazines were new. The sign said, "Trade or return." Rosa took a magazine. She didn't care for Louis L'Amour or mysteries. But wait, there was The Snow Leopard. She took that too.

As she passed the ranch Tony, the manager, waved as he fastened his glinting little eyes on her. Fuck, she said inwardly, but she waved back, and then kept her eyes to the road.

By the time Rosa got home she felt exhausted and nauseated. She made a quick sandwich and drank a glass of milk. She reminded herself to stay away from coffee. Well, anyway, the job will help a little, she told herself. I'm hardly spending any money at all here. It'll work out.

Diana was due in a couple of hours, so Rosa started the quiche. A midwife, Rosa thought. I could certainly use a midwife. She's pretty young, but she probably knows what she's doing. Rosa put the quiche in the oven and then lay down on the couch in front of the fire.

Rosa picked up the Newsweek she just got from the post office. There was an article inside about anti-nuclear demonstrations in Berlin. And then a color photograph of some young German people dressed up like Indians. "Back To Nature Movement" it said. She looked for Rolf in the group, but he wasn't there. It looks a little silly, but they were trying, weren't they? she thought. They were trying to be Native People. Native People of the Earth.

She remembered her letters and her package. They were still in the car. She threw on her coat and tennis shoes. Zack was on the porch. "So, you're back. Wait a minute, you're soaked, Zack."

Rosa wiped Zack down with the towel and let him in. She opened the package first. It was two pair of long johns with roses on them. Then she opened Dolores' letter.

> Dear Rosa,
> I thought you'd need these. Had them sent directly from Macy's. Things are the same here. Louie grouching like a housewife. Thought of this. Your father's mother wanted to keep you when I left. Told him, Lionel, not in a million years. It was in Louisiana you know. You would've been a farm hand. Probably never sent you to school, or as little as possible. And you had dark hair. They were all blondes, except for a couple and they were red-headed. I think the best part of my childhood was playing the piano. Well, that's all over now. My parents tried, but I don't think either of them ever liked this country. Hope these keep your ass warm. ha ha ha And the rest. Got to get up early to get to the office and get away from Louie. Enjoy the mountains. It all seems to slip away, Love,
>   Your Mother

Rosa folded the letter up, quickly. She fingered the long johns and smelled them. They smelled like something new. I love the smell of new things, she thought. Newborns. I've forgotten what newborns smell like. I'll be three months in a couple of weeks. Most daughters, I suppose, would want to tell their mothers they're pregnant. I have no desire to tell Dolores. Why does it all seem to slip away? she asked the folded letter. In order for the new to come, a voice deep inside of her, and part of the silence that surrounded her, answered.

Erica's letter began:

Rosa,

Just to say I have a downtown gallery interested in a group show of women painters. Four of us, I figure. If you're interested send slides immediately. It's the kind of gallery where things move, so I'm excited. They also have a sister gallery in New York, so we'll see what happens. Write and let me know how things go. I don't see getting up there till maybe summer. If show comes together, we could get together here for the opening. Spend the night here. I miss our talks.

Take care and love,   Erica

A car pulled up and Rosa was amazed to see Diana sitting in a Volkswagen Bug. How in the hell did she get up in that? Rosa thought. Diana got out of the car with Joel by the hand, balancing a couple of bags and a bowl.

"How did your Bug make it up here?" Rosa laughed and took the bowl from her hands.

"I got up enough speed so I could fly. These things can churn pretty good, though." Diana's dark eyes flashed with obvious pleasure.

"Hi, Joel. Are you hungry?" Rosa smiled at him.

Joel ignored her and walked into Rosa's studio.

"He's always hungry. So, these are your paintings. Very accomplished, I see."

"Thank you. These are some of them. The ones in the front room are from the days I lived on a farm in Sonoma County. Another era. I'm sorry, but Joel won't be able to stay in here."

"I understand." Diana laughed loudly. "I brought plenty of toys and crayons for him. Do you have some extra paper I can give him?"

"Sure." Rosa walked into the studio and got some scratch paper and shut the door behind her.

"This painting of the continents in the shape of a woman's body is exquisite. And the baby! You certainly got the feeling down!" Diana's voice seemed to get louder the longer she spoke, and then she'd lower it to start all over again. "What's cooking?"

"Quiche. It'll be ready pretty soon. You mentioned you're a midwife. How do you go about it? Do you come to the house?"

"You're not pregnant, are you?" Her wide, intense eyes fastened on Rosa.

"Yes, I am, and I'd like to give birth at home this time. With Sean, eighteen years ago, it was an automatic saddle-block, forceps, hospital rules, the whole bit. This time I want to do it by myself. Here." Rosa took the quiche out of the oven. "I was pretty young, so they got away with everything."

"I can hear that. I had Joel with a couple of friends and his father in a tepee, so no one messed with me. I can imagine what a bitch it was for you." Her eyes filled with compassion, and then the moment passed. " Well, I'd better make the salad. All the stuff's in the bowl, I just have to chop it up. I must admit, I'm taken by surprise, being that you're by yourself. You are by yourself, right?"

"Julio and I are separated. I didn't know I was pregnant until I moved here. Then, I had a dream—actually, a few of them about this child. So, I'm going to have her."

"Her?"

"I dreamt a girl. I seem to do that. I dream it. I live it. Like I dreamt this place and then I found it."

"Of course. I haven't gotten that far with it yet, but that's what it's all about. Okay, you know you're high risk because of your age. You're in your thirties, I assume."

"I'll be thirty-five in a couple of months."

"That's the only thing that worries me. And you haven't had a child in eighteen years. Obviously, you were really young when you had your first. I think you should definitely have a backup doctor, but I'd love to be your midwife." Diana smiled widely. Then she proceeded to ask her questions about her diet, her nausea, and began giving her advice on food, vitamins and exercise.

Rosa served the quiche and Diana served the salad.

"Do you want some wine?" Rosa asked.

"Sure. But as your midwife, I'd advise you to limit yourself to one glass a day. Two wine glasses at the very most."

Rosa took offense, involuntarily.

"You asked me to be your midwife," Diana smiled at her. Then in a serious tone, she said, "I'll write down a couple of the doctors I like up here, and I think you should go see them. Check them both out, if you want, as soon as possible. Don't be surprised if they freak out at the mention of the word *midwife*—but they usually agree to meet at the hospital. So far, they respect me because of the work I do in the community, and I've never—knock on wood—" Diana reached over and knocked on the pine wall in the kitchen, half-humorously—"had a problem with a client. So, I haven't had to use a backup system. They resent me a little, but they keep agreeing to the hospital backup."

Rosa could see that if she didn't break in now Diana was going to continue. "I'll do it next week, for sure. Where did you grow up?"

"In northern Washington on a semi-official reservation. My grandmother brought me up. My mother drank herself to death." Diana paused. The memory still stung her. "So, I found out I can't live in cities. I tried it for a while. Went to school. You know, when I first came here I was living with a bunch of women way out in the woods, and a rattler came into the front yard. It was like something made me pick up a shovel, and I marched out there and beat it to death. And, you know, the snake is my dream animal."

Rosa was stunned, but she reached out her hand and placed it on Diana's shoulder. A few tears rolled down Diana's face as she stared out the window. It was nearly night, and the candles began to reflect their fire against the window.

"Do you dream the snake regularly? Rosa asked.

"The last dream I had, I walked into my bedroom and it was full of snakes. Snakes of every color and size. There was a large white one, a pure white one, coiled on my pillow, but I was too frightened to go toward the bed. I had the feeling I was supposed to touch it."

Rosa thought of her wolf, but that had been more of a waking experience. Still, it'd led her here. She also felt a vague sympathy for Diana. Snakes had always repelled her.

"I think that's it. The white snake sounds so healing, waiting there for you on your pillow, where you dream. But you have to get past a roomful of snakes. You have my sympathy," Rosa laughed.

Diana laughed with her. "I think I'll have another glass of wine. No more wine for you, though, mother." She took a sip of her wine. "What's your dream animal?"

"The eagle, I think. It's pointed things out to me in dreams, so clearly. When I felt like chickening out about moving here, I dreamt an eagle hovering right over the cabin." Then Rosa remembered Quetzalpetlatl, Feathered Serpent Woman. The highest, the lowest. The eagle, the snake. Rosa shuddered. She preferred to have nothing to do with snakes, personally.

"Yes, a clear dreamer would need an eagle. You know, the eagle and snake are on the Mexican flag. In a sense, they're natural companions. One for clarity, one for depth. Joel's been quiet. I'm going to take a look."

Rosa looked at her reflection between the candles. Hadn't Julie said her horse was spooked by a snake? Wasn't she denying the depths of her being?

Diana returned. "Joel fell asleep on your sleeping bag. I put him inside. Do you mind?"

"Of course not. I'm going to have to get a bed pretty soon. A good piece of foam would be great. Have you ever heard of the Mexican Goddess, Quetzalpetlatl?"

"Isn't that Feathered Serpent? You see what I mean? But isn't that a male God?"

"This is his older sister. She's hardly ever mentioned. Feathered Serpent Woman."

They were sitting, side by side, facing the window. The table was right up against the wall under the wide window. Their faces reflected, between the candles, onto the darkness outside.

"I see," A—— said, softly. "How interesting."

After Diana had gone, Rosa thought of her for a long while. She brought her sleeping bag to the couch and added a piece of oak to the fire. And she poured herself a half-glass of wine, a little guiltily. The fire lulled her. Her Buck Knife was under the couch, its handle within her reach.

Diana was twenty-five. She'd been separated from Joel's father for over a year. Her grandmother died when she was sixteen, so she left for Seattle after high school. College for two years. Sierra and I were so close when we were twenty-five, Rosa remembered. Am I trying to establish a similar friendship? I don't think so. It's just not the same. I'm different, and Diana is not Sierra.

It was as though there were no transition into sleep—as though the dream were real.

An immense snake, in an upright position, rushes toward Rosa. It merges with her in one horrible moment.

Rosa woke trying to scream, and found herself moaning deep in her throat. She thought of Diana and, inexplicably, a great anger welled up within her. That snake was monstrous, she thought. Monstrous. She was dripping sweat and the wine was sour in her mouth. Rosa got up and brushed her teeth, and the chill air cooled her, immediately. She brought a glass of water to the couch and got back into the sleeping bag.

What did it mean? Rosa asked herself, but only vaguely. She really didn't want to know yet. She still struggled against it.

The next few days Rosa worked on the rainbow painting. She wanted to complete it by the end of November. She saw and spoke to no one for three days, not even going to the post office to get her mail. It could wait.

The weather was clear and warmer during the day, so the snow was melting. But at night she huddled down into her sleeping bag. It dipped below freezing.

By Friday she realized she might be done with the rainbow painting by mid-November. Rosa stepped back and the Earth spun for a moment. The living quality of light was becoming effective. The vivid rainbow circling the Earth seemed to pulse in the afternoon sun, as it tapered to a spot in southern Mexico. After this painting, the second painting in the series, she'd begin the third. The final one. The close-up of what the rainbow seemed to be pointing to. She also wanted to begin the painting of Dolores playing the piano. At the same time Rosa wanted to work on the shawl.

By the time she completed an entire black rose—"Intricate, it's so damned intricate," she muttered—it was getting dark, and her stomach was growling with an edge of nausea. The fireplace was throwing out a steady heat, but the beginning of night made her shiver with its abrupt drop of temperature. Rosa put on another log and went out to the front porch, shutting the door behind her, quickly, to keep in the accumulated heat.

The sunset was a series of purple slashes across the sky, and the clearing through the trees into the valley was unearthly in its beauty. The clearing, the length that the naked eye could envelope, depended so much on the sky, Rosa realized, that it was as though every time she gazed out at it, she was witnessing the ancient marriage of Earth and Sky. Yet it was earthly, and, in a sense, she was always trying to approximate it in her work. How would I attempt to paint this clearing? she asked her eyes.

She framed it, the expanse of trees, with a beautiful light, but a morning light holding it whole. Then she saw an eagle in the distance—not actually, but in the painting she'd framed. Its wings would be large and dark and edged with the glow of the rising sun. Its underbelly would be on fire. Yes, she thought, I'll put it in the foregound, with eternity behind it. The eagle with its view of eternity. The snake with its existence grounded in eternity. The eagle with the snake dangling from its talons, and she thought of the Mexican flag. Rosa took the snake out of the frame, and a sense of relief flooded her. I'm not about to paint a flag, anyone's, in a painting of mine, she reasoned.

The first star appeared in the west, bright in the delicacy of the new dusk. Then she asked herself, What would Feathered Serpent Woman look like? She tried, but she couldn't imagine. She couldn't imagine a face, at all.

The phone was ringing. It hadn't rung in three days. In fact, she'd picked it up to see if it still had a dial tone.

"It's me, the Mexican Man. How are you? Shall I address you as La Gran Puta or simply Rosa?" Julio asked in a serious voice.

"Rosa will do, Julio. I'm okay."

"How's the morning nausea?"

"I just have to watch what I eat, that's all."

"Are you still angry?"

"I guess I dread the next round."

"Okay, Rosa, but you are pregnant, and I want to see you. If you have something planned while I'm there, I'll just take some time to myself. I was thinking of coming up weekend after this one. In other words, I'd come Thursday again."

"How would you feel about making me a platform bed while you're here?"

"Sure, why not?"

"Also, if you'd bring a piece of three-inch foam, queen-size, from one of the discount places, I'll be set. I'd appreciate it."

"Will do. Then, I'll see you next Thursday." Julio sounded pleased with himself.

"How's Sean?" Rosa tried to sound matter-of-fact.

"Hasn't he called you?"

"No."

"He's gone a lot, so I've hardly seen him."

"I was just wondering, Julio. Okay, then. I'll see you Thursday."

"He did say you hung up on him because he told you what he thought of the situation," Julio said, sensing she was about to say goodbye.

"Well, he was more than a little rude, and I don't need it."

"I guess he has a hard time understanding the situation."

"So do I, actually. But I don't need an eighteen-year-old judging my life. Anyway, he's okay?"

"I think he wants you to come back. Like me, I guess. He's doing everything—going to school, training and working. And I think he's seeing someone." Julio seemed amused.

"Why's that?"

"He left a package of rubbers in the bathroom cabinet. Ribbed." Julio laughed.

"He's obviously alive and well, then. And learned from experience. That's something. Don't tell him I'm asking about him, but let me know if anything comes up. I guess this is called living your own life."

"I guess," Julio echoed. "Do you miss me?"

His words threw her back to her pain.

"I suppose I do, sometimes. I suppose I'm trying to adjust to this place, just being here, and being pregnant all at once. Last week didn't make me miss you."

"Okay, sorry I asked. I'll bring the foam and do the bed while I'm there. If you need anything, give me a call."

"Goodbye, Julio."

"Take care of yourself. Do you hear me?"

"Take care of yourself," Rosa said, hanging up.

Zack was on the steps, so Rosa let him in. Suddenly, the night seemed as dark and lonely as the first night she'd arrived. I wonder if this will happen regularly? she thought. And then dread settled itself firmly in her chest. It was as though her pregnancy wouldn't allow it to settle in the pit of her stomach, but the heart had nothing better to do.

In the morning a series of dreams haunted her. Brief, intense dreams of losing and finding Sean at different ages, and each time the loss seemed greater. That's the way it is, she told herself. Isn't it? That's the way it is.

Rosa made herself get up and start the morning fire. The light will be beautiful today, she thought, looking out the studio window. She decided to begin work without a morning walk.

The rainbow painting would be done sooner than she'd expected. Maybe just the light, more light like the clearing, she thought. That light. Does the rainbow circling the Earth make it spin? she asked herself. I'm losing perspective, somehow. I just don't know anymore. I can only keep going until I know I'm done. Then, she thought, The continents look exactly like continents, and I'm satisfied with that. And the oceans do seem to move if I stand still long enough . . .

On her afternoon walk Rosa was sorry to see that all the water roots were melted. All that remained of the snow was a deep, slippery mud. The sky was so clear it seemed like a vast mirror reflecting itself, without pause, against the Earth. Rosa felt strangely exposed with such a sky so close to the top of her head.

Tonight, she told herself, I'll go to Peak's and see if Forrest can really play the guitar. Plus, I'll be able to see and hear other people. Deciding this, she felt like a hat had been placed on her head.

Ray was on the post office porch reading the paper, but he didn't lift an eye as Rosa walked by saying, "Hi, there."

There was junk mail, a letter forwarded by a student, and a letter from Rolf. He'd cut out and glued a post card to the outside of the envelope. People were strolling through a beer garden. The colors were gaudy, and it made her laugh.

As she walked back to the car, Ray said in a low voice, "My son died over there in Europe. That was my only son."

It caught Rosa by surprise, entirely. "Do you have any daughters?"

"Just the boy. Couldn't a kept him from goin. The war an all."

"How old was he? If you don't mind my asking? I have a son myself," Rosa said, gently.

"Too young. All of em too damn young. How old's yer boy?" Ray stood up, glaring at her.

"Eighteen."

"So was mine," Ray said, starting to walk toward the cabin next door. It had a wooden sign on it with raised white letters: The Old Fisherman. "It'll be snowin by the end a the week." He stopped. It seemed a great effort to walk. He seemed to be, at least, in his eighties.

He looked up at the sky and tugged on his baseball cap. "This is a good day fer thinkin, Roza, if ya can hang onto yer thoughts."

"I'm sorry about your son, Ray," she said, waiting for him to respond, but he kept his back to her. "I'll see you later. Bye."

Rosa got in the car and drove away. She looked through her rear view mirror as Ray began to walk again. How alone he was, and angry. He reminded her a little of Louie. Only Louie's humor was a cushion that made her comfortable. Ray seemed to look out at the world for information, facts, and his eyes glaring out at her made her want to run away. Maybe he hasn't thought of his son in years until the post card today, Rosa thought. Eighteen years old. Like Sean.

She sat in front, in the last of the sun, and read Rolf's letter. Zack rolled in the exposed, wet grass the color of dried hay.

A piece of colored paper fell from the letter. It was a light turquoise piece of tissue. The letter began:

> This, Rosa, is the color of today's sky at about one in the afternoon. I think of you there in the Sierra Madres—you aren't too lonely I hope. You see, I can't imagine living anywhere in the world but Berlin. I love this city. It is ugly and beautiful. What more could I want, no? You must send

mé a sketch of what you look at from one of your windows,
so that I can imagine it more clearly. No, I don't like the
missiles in Europe, but if war were waged even you up
there on your mountain wouldn't be safe. I plan to go on a
protest march, my friends and I. Are you proud of me? I
came across these words by a Japanese poet—"When you
look into a mirror, you do not see your reflection, your
reflection sees you." Rather like looking at another human
being. You see, I don't see myself reflected in nature (the
way you do, though I continue to look)—well, then, does
nature look at us? Does it care? Does our reflection care?
You must excuse me. I've been alone all morning. But do
you see what I mean? We were not taught this kind of
"crazy thinking" and I like it very much. I like it, also, that
you're German. Does that make you a Gringo, as well?

con abrazos, Rolfxxoo

Rosa tacked the tissue paper over her studio window. She ate a
half sandwich and drank a glass of milk to settle her stomach. Then
she went to the bathroom mirror and looked at her reflection, but
this time she felt herself looking back at herself, like an old friend, a
patient friend, who asked no questions but answered all of hers. She
saw her friend shed a tear, wordlessly. I accept you as you are, her
eyes seemed to say. Thirty-five years old, pregnant, unemployed,
separated from your husband, your son thinks you're nuts, and your
closest friend wonders what you're doing. It's only right that you're
plagued by Quetzalpetlatl's face, the rainbow around the Earth, the
lilac sky. What else is there, really, to think about? Then Rosa saw
herself full-term, and she wondered what the locals would think,
pregnant and without a man.

Her reflection looked back at her, and Rosa began to laugh.

A waitress sat her at the community table, as she called it. A long,
wooden table with candles lit and two bunches of dried flowers in the
center. Rosa ordered the chicken dinner with a half-litre of white
house wine. She nibbled on the French bread. The smells from the
kitchen made her realize how hungry she was. She also realized she
was the only woman by herself, and everyone else seemed to know
each other. So, she was also unfamiliar.

The table was filling up, so it was hard to tell she was alone now.
The food arrived and it was perfect. Chicken smothered in onions

and mushrooms, in a wine sauce, wild rice, broccoli, and a green salad. She forgot about the cowboy types behind her, at the bar, who'd been staring holes in her back.

A guitar was being tuned, softly. Forrest had walked into the room unnoticed, the way he liked to when he was going to perform. He'd spotted Rosa eating with total concentration, and it made him smile, inwardly.

"You goin ta fool around all night up there, Forrest, or you goin ta play? Get a move on!" a man yelled from the bar.

A round of laughter went up around the room.

"Give the man a chance! He's a goddamned artist! You always was simple-minded, Charlie!" another man yelled back.

The laughter in the room increased.

Not a brown or black face in the room, Rosa realized, looking around as if for the first time. What am I doing, she asked herself, in the middle of cowboy country? Plumas County. Plumas. Feathers, she reminded herself. The Spaniards, before that the Maidu, and still the eagle.

We all belong here, here and now, I suppose, she thought as she sipped the dry white wine. Rosa turned around and looked at Charlie sitting at the bar. He winked at her, smiling. Maybe, she silently added—but the playful look on his face made her want to smile.

Forrest adjusted the microphone and sat on a stool. "This is for all you uneducated cowboys. Especially you, John," Forrest looked at the second man who'd yelled and laughed, more to himself.

"Better make it good!" John yelled back.

Forrest began to play a ballad straight through in a richly patterned composition, so rich and woven Rosa wondered what it was until Forrest began to sing in a low voice, "Mama, don't let your babies grow up to be cowboys . . ." People whistled and stamped their feet. When he finished singing it through, he played it again. Then he played "Don't Fence Me In," and he made it echo in a haunting way. He could really play.

People spoke quietly as Forrest began what sounded like a Scottish ballad, and as he began to sing his voice took on a soft-slurred accent, "My love is fairer than any maiden . . ." The women in the room loved it. A love song. The atmosphere changed.

Rosa looked around for Cheryl, but she wasn't there. Just as she was beginning to wonder if Forrest knew she'd come, he met her eyes, briefly. Then he began another song. His audience was with him.

"Going to take a fifteen-minute break. Be right back, folks."
Forrest picked up his drink and stopped to talk to a group of people.

Rosa was done eating and, feeling a little tired, she was thinking
of going home. She'd parked her car less than a half block down the
way under a street lamp in front of some friendly looking houses.
Street-smarts do not die easily, she thought. Well, why should they? I
don't know if I'm safer here than on a city street. What if these guys
knew I lived by myself back there? And then she remembered Forrest
knew.

He was walking toward her and, grabbing an extra chair from a
nearby table, sat down next to her. "Do I get the tip?"

"No flamenco, no tip."

"You drive a hard bargain, Ms. van Gogh."

Rosa glared at him.

"I know what you're going to say. Don't tell me," Forrest said,
laughing.

"I'll tell you what, McBride. You can call me Ms. van Gogh, if I
can call you Johnny Appleseed," Rosa said, without taking her eyes
off him.

"If you promise not to tell me the F word again, it's a deal."
Forrest smiled wickedly.

"How does your wife stand you, anyway?"

"She likes my apples, I guess, Ms. van Gogh."

Before Rosa could answer he got up, flashing his eyes into hers,
and then she saw it. The fire. Where have I seen that look before? she
asked herself, trying to remember. But she couldn't.

As Forrest tuned his guitar, Rosa thought of Diana's words,
"Forrest is the kind of guy you don't take too seriously . . ." I guess
not, she thought. His apples. I mean, his apples. Rosa took a sip of
wine and noticed how the one spotlight made his wild, red hair catch
fire. Again, she tried to remember what it was, but she just couldn't.

He even looks neat tonight, she noted, with a good shirt tucked
into well-washed jeans, and those tucked into worn cowboy boots. I
bet his apples aren't bad, she couldn't help thinking. And then she
stopped herself with the irony of her pregnancy and Cheryl's pregnancy, and at what an opposite end Julio was to Forrest. What a
great mess that would be all around. A little reality, Rosa, she told
herself, firmly. Plus, that's all I need—he's almost Sean's age.

Just as she was about to stand up and leave, Forrest said, "This is
for you, Ms. van Gogh," and without looking at Rosa, he began to
play flamenco. A thunderous flamenco that gathered in intensity

until he began to sweat from the exertion; and then, finally, he let his fingers fall like liquid over the chords as he surrendered to a gentleness, to a kind of giving, that surprised her, that took her completely off guard.

Forrest's head was bowed over his guitar like a private worship as though he were speaking to the music that barely left his hands, and his neck looked so vulnerable, so young, it hurt her, inexplicably. It hurt her to see him so exposed.

As Forrest paused shouts of olé, whistling, and foot stomping punctured the air, the opening he'd created. Then he lifted his head and, somehow, took it further. He took the music further into a wild sense of joy, like explosions of joy that flowed, one after the other, into the room.

No one spoke. Everyone's eyes were riveted to his hands and glimpses of his face. He was on fire.

When the music came to an end, Forrest just sat there for a while as though he were stunned, while the crowd enjoyed shouting olé and whistling again. Then he said into the microphone, "How bout a beer?"

"Where da ya want it?" someone from the bar shouted.

A woman yelled, "Oh, shut up, and give him a beer!"

There didn't seem to be any of the Lightning Strikes crowd here or, for that matter, any of the people she'd seen at Iris'. Different crowd, that's for sure, Rosa thought. I guess he moves between them. Yes, he's an artist, and he works at the ranch, she reminded herself.

"Play s'more that olé shit, there, boy!" Charlie yelled from the bar.

Forrest laughed. "That's enough for the night." He drank his beer in a few gulps.

"Oh, come on! One more, Forrest!" a woman shouted.

Rosa recognized the piece he began to play. It was Villa-Lobos. A slow, delicate piece that she loved. The crowd was obviously disappointed. What they'd wanted was another explosion.

As soon as the piece was done Forrest launched into a song. She took some money from her purse and walked over to where the basket was, next to him on a piano. As Rosa leaned over to put the money in, she said quietly, "Olé, Señor Appleseed."

"Don't go," he mumbled.

"I've got to. I'm pooped. I loved it. You're excellent," she said, waving goodbye.

As Rosa paid her bill and walked toward the door, Charlie said,

"Been a pleasure knowin ya. Drive careful now." He touched the brim of his hat as she passed and she felt herself flushing.

Rosa glanced back at Forrest. His hair was still on fire.

There was no one on the street. The smell of wood smoke was in the air. She looked back a couple of times to see if anyone was following her, but the street was absolutely silent and empty, and it was cold. It looks like the weather takes care of street crime around here, she thought. I liked those people, their spirit. I guess Julie's so-called boyfriend isn't the norm. I bet Forrest has a hard time with Jake and vice versa. The car finally warmed up and she pulled onto the highway. "Johnny Appleseed," she murmured, and laughed out loud.

The moon was nearly full, so the night was lit up with it. Pools of pale light and shadow made the ride home strangely exquisite. The forest was so beautiful in the moonlight, she was grateful to be seeing it this way. It felt as though some wonderful secret, a secret world, was being revealed to her. Rosa's eyes felt hungry for this sight she'd never seen before.

Could I paint the moonlight, like this? she wondered. A creature would have to be in it, she thought—a beautiful, terrible creature.

As she got into her sleeping bag, Forrest's music echoed in her head, filling her with a longing she couldn't name. Moonlight flooded her room, and, for a moment, the beautiful, terrible creature revealed itself to her. Then sleep took the memory away.

By the day Julio was to arrive Rosa had seen the backup doctor, and she liked him much more than the one she'd gone to for the pregnancy test. Dr. Walker made it clear that he preferred her to give birth at the hospital, but that he'd meet her there in case of an emergency. He also wanted to see her throughout the pregnancy. She agreed to that, gladly.

But she wanted to have the baby at home, and he seemed to understand, though he'd said, "I don't like doing these backup deals, especially with a woman in her thirties. You look in good health, so we'll give it a go. Just realize how much responsibility you're taking."

"I know," she'd answered, and that was it.

The rainbow painting was nearly done. Now she'd begin the third and final one in the series, and the portrait of Dolores. There was an urgency now, in her work, to get done. The baby, of course. The baby would come, small and lovely, and capture her time.

Next week the part-time job at the newspaper would start, but it was only three days a week for the three weeks. Then back to her own work and the solitude she was becoming accustomed to. And maybe, just maybe, the artist's grant she'd applied for would come through. The notice would arrive by late December.

During the days, as she worked, she played her flamenco records, but none of them touched what Forrest had done the other night. The sheer energy still echoed in her memory, vividly, as though he were still playing in the same room. Must be the silence of this place, she thought. By the third day she'd gone back to flute and piano music.

Now it was Wednesday and Sierra hadn't called, Sean hadn't called, and storm clouds were beginning to gather. She'd written Erica and sent her the slides.

Erica,
What good news about a show—enclosed are the slides (some of these are in storage in Daly City). Well, I have news, so I'll tell you straight out—I'm pregnant and I've decided to have the child in question (I dreamt a girl). Well, do you think I'm crazy—just tell me. The other night when I told Sean he told me I was too old *and* crazy—how's that? At this point I figure I'm so far out on a limb the only thing I have to do is die. Only you will probably understand this—when I was considering having an abortion I began to sketch a face and it turned out to be *the child* at around two years of age. I knew if I finished the drawing I'd have her. That night I had a dream telling me her name (I can't say what it is till she's born). The next day I finished the drawing. She's going to be lovely, Erica—isn't this how it all starts? I love Julio but I can't stand him—I just left him but I'm pregnant—and I'm eyeing young men—do you believe it? Keep all this to yourself—burn this letter. No, really, only harmless looking (smile). Meanwhile, the world goes its merry way, killing people left and right—I've asked Sean to not register with the military, but at this point it's up to him. So, I'm going to vote for the human race, I suppose, with this mid-life baby—my own very personal vote of confidence (which I don't have yet) for the next century—but I have a feeling when I see this daughter I'll find it. Enough. Let me know how you are,

what you're working on—send me a recent slide, and if everything works out about the opening and all, I'll try to make it. It'd be great if some paintings sold. I always wondered if I'd go crazy in solitude—you know, the final test—I suppose it's too early to tell (I can hear you laughing), but though it *is* scary, I'm in the right place. You wouldn't believe how dark and silent it gets here at night. Well, I think the Goddess approves of my with-child-hermitage. Also, I have a midwife, a wonderful young woman (part Cree, Indian face) who's becoming a good friend. So, come up anytime, of course.

Con amor,
Rosa

Tomorrow Julio would come, Monday she'd start the job, Wednesday she'd go to Diana's for dinner; her due date was mid-April. Dr. Walker had said it with such certainty: mid-April.

Will the air be soft and fragile? Early spring . . . will there be wildflowers by the creek? Will the rattlers wake up, and will my wolf return? Will there be eagles here in the warmer months? Will you be taking milk from breasts that have only been breasts for so many years in mid-April, Luzia? Rosa imagined the small human being within her listening to her blood and her heart.

I am a pregnant woman, Rosa told herself. She felt the slight swelling of her belly, and a great tenderness invaded her and held her in its sweet, fierce arms. Wings. Immense, soft wings.

"I am making life," Rosa murmured.

Snow fell during the night. Its peculiar silence told her before she stood up to look out the window. Even her dreams were muffled, though, once, during the night, toward dawn, she'd distinctly heard voices saying, "She's waking up." She'd had the feeling that her bedroom was crowded with presence, beings. Instead of frightening her it had given her the safest feeling she'd ever had. Protected. For the first time in her life, alone in a cabin surrounded by forest, she felt utterly protected.

Rosa woke up, rested. She gave her nausea no time to creep up on her. After breakfast she drove down for the mail. Two letters. One from Sierra, one from Sean. The post office was empty, though smoke curled from the chimney next door where Ray lived. The sign, The Old Fisherman, made her smile. She was tempted to knock, but decided against it.

Rosa added more wood to the fireplace and settled into the couch. A steady snowfall continued. She opened the first letter.

Dear Mom,
I don't mean that *you* are crazy. I mean that what you're doing is crazy. It really is. And lets face it you're 40, right, or almost. When you told me you were moving there I thought it was pretty insane, but this is ridiculous. How're you going to have a baby by yourself up there? It's bad enough isn't it? Twenty miles to town and all. What about Julio? I know he wants you to come back and I think you should too. He wants to help and I think you'll need it. Of course, it's your life so I'll shut up now. It looks like I might have to register for the military if I want to get scholarships and grants. I'm doing okay. I eat as many of my meals as I can get away with at the restaurant. The cooks like me so I eat regularly. I don't think I'll be able to get up there for Thanksgiving, but I'll try to get up for Xmas. Watch out for Big Foot.   Sean

Dear Rosa,
I guess I'd rather write this than say it . . . do you think it's fair to Julio for you to be pregnant up there, and him down here? Also, aren't you making it kind of hard on yourself unnecessarily? No one would think you'd "failed" if you moved back down. In fact, I'm surprised you moved there at all. Perhaps "spiritual journeys" aren't for women with children, especially pregnant women. Anyway, I'm worried about you. I spoke to Julio on the phone last week, and, of course, he's worried about you, too.
       Marlin's gone to live with her father for a while, at least for the semester. It's peaceful again, and I can give Tomás more of my time. I think I was wrong about Bob. In fact, I know I was. Things are much better, and he's so much better with Tomás now.
       I'm feeling immense, so I'm going to save the "Goddess Poems" for later, after the birth. Have you thought of that . . . getting *big,* your time scattered all over the place. It'll pass, but it'll pass a lot easier with Julio to help you, so you can get back to your work, at least when he's around. By

the way, Julio *did not* encourage me to say any of this. Just
wanted you to know. I'll call you as soon as I feel a thing.
Bob and I both want you here.

Mucho Amor,
Sierra

The letters infuriated her. "Patronizing bunch of assholes!" Rosa
yelled out loud. She knew she couldn't work, so she grabbed her
jacket, hat and gloves and slammed the door behind her.

It was snowing steadily and fast now. Huge, weightless snowflakes filled the air. Rosa marched toward the creek trail, as Zack ran
ahead of her. She felt bleak with solitude, and tears flowed from her
eyes without any restraint. The cold felt good, bitterly good.

How dare they! she thought—how dare they insinuate I can't
take care of myself, pregnant or otherwise. Who the fuck asked them?
Rosa's thoughts screamed. I wouldn't be with that bastard Bob for
anything on Earth, and I wouldn't be eighteen for anything, and I
wouldn't go back to Julio for anything. She continued. I don't have
to do any-fucking-thing but die, and I'll even do that in my own
fucking way. Damned straight! Screw them, one and all!

Rosa ran up a slope and collapsed at the top, lying there, letting
the snow just land on her. If she stared at the snow, straight up at it,
the snowflakes aimed right for her eyes.

She opened her mouth to the wind. It tasted harsh like a mouth-
ful of sea when it yanks your legs from under you and you forget
which way the shore is, or for that matter which way is up or which
way is down. But you grab hold, and though the sea could certainly
kill you—your throat burns from its salt—you grab hold of nothing.
Something as slim as the wind, but it's yours.

Zack circled her, playfully, and put his nose into the snow, snort-
ing it out forcefully, his snout bent low between his paws.

Rosa shouted, "FUCK EVERYONE!" into the soft, falling stars that
nearly covered her, and, laughing, got up.

Julio's car was in front. His tires had chains on, and he'd parked
it facing down toward the main road. She dried Zack off and let him
in.

"So, there you are," Julio said smiling.

"Welcome. Make yourself at home. I'm going to take a bath. I'm
freezing my ass off. There's a casserole in the fridge with foil on it.
Would you stick it in the oven at 350?" Rosa said, heading straight for
the bathroom.

Julio knocked on the door. "Do you want me to make a salad?"

"Fine!"

"Are you okay, Rosa?"

"I'm just fine, Julio." She took a look at her tattoo and slipped into the steaming water.

After dinner Rosa made it clear she wasn't going to make love to him, and though it made him angry and frustrated, he decided to settle for sleeping next to her. Patience, Julio thought. Sip by sip, or the desert will claim me again. He looked out at the snow and laughed to himself.

In the morning he brought her tea and toast and made breakfast.

"Do you still want me to make the bed? Are you sure you're staying, Rosa?" He looked at her, steadily.

"Yes, I still want the bed."

"Okay, we'd better take your truck for the wood. It's clearing up again. You're really staying, then?" Julio held his breath.

"Yes, I am." Rosa looked out at the dark, naked branches holding their harsh gift of whiteness.

After they bought the wood and got back from town, Julio decided to make the dinnner.

"You could do the dishes. Fair enough?"

"Sounds fair to me. Do you want some wine?"

"You've been evading me all day. May I kiss you?"

"I don't want to fight anymore, Julio."

"I'm not asking for a fight, either," he said, drawing her close to him.

They kissed, briefly, and then Rosa pulled away. "I found a midwife. I want to have the baby at home."

"You're kidding. The hospital's almost twenty or more miles away from here, isn't it? Don't you think that's kind of risky?"

"I have a backup doctor who'll meet me at the hospital in case of an emergency."

"So what's this midwife going to do, boil water? I don't believe it! Don't you think it's bad enough your being here alone—now you're going to have the baby, here? Here in this cabin?"

"I'll call you immediately when my labor starts, so you can be here. Or maybe toward my last weeks you can take a leave of absence, if you want, and wait it out. But all I know is I'm going to try and have this baby at home. I hated Sean's birth, the way they drugged me. I'm not going to argue about it, Julio."

"You've got a doctor backup?"

"Someone in town. A Dr. Walker."

"I'll take some of that wine."

After dinner they sat by the fire, quietly. Buying the wood for the bed had finally made Julio realize she was staying, and it depressed him.

"The foam's in my car. We could sleep on it instead of the floor. I brought you some vitamins, too, with lots of calcium." He looked at Rosa like he would cry.

Rosa took Julio into her arms. "If I went back now, I'd hate myself. I've got to stay. Do you understand, at all?"

"I'm trying. But I want you to come back. If not now, then after the baby's born." He kissed the back of her neck, softly. "It'll be different. I promise."

"Did you notice my painting? It's just about done."

"It's very beautiful. It really is. I'll take another look in the morning."

"I can turn on the lamps."

Julio stared at the painting, and then he looked at her. "You made the Earth spin, didn't you?"

"Do you see that?" Rosa asked, excitedly.

"It's hard to miss that rainbow. I think it's very fine. I developed the contact sheets from last time. Do you want to see them? Tell me which ones you like."

They made love that night, slowly, gently. Julio completed the platform bed the next day, and they made love again that night. Her orgasms squeezed her womb, and the intensity made her wonder if the child floated within her in a kind of ecstacy. But it didn't last. They argued the morning he was leaving. About the midwife.

"Since it's my insurance that's covering you, I insist you go to a hospital, Rosa."

"You don't have to pay for the midwife, just the doctor. I don't want to talk about it anymore."

"It's not the money."

"No, as usual, it's control. And that's why I'm here. It's the same old shit, Julio."

"Enjoy your bed!" he shouted, leaving. Then he came back, trying to apologize. "Look, I'm sorry. Try the midwife, but be careful."

It didn't work, and they both knew it. Rosa shut the door and listened to him drive away, and she knew it was true that she loved him, but that she also couldn't stand him. Maybe I just don't love him enough, she told herself, but something deep inside her—perhaps the becoming child—told her otherwise.

And if he loves me, why does he continue to insist that I relent and relent and relent. As though that would be proof that I love him. This is why people kill each other, she thought dismally. This is why nations war. And does the secret flower preparing itself to bloom in our mother, the Earth, tell us otherwise? The simple wildflowers that cover the Earth. The image comforted her, and eased the sense of loneliness Julio left behind.

The fire was warm, so she brought pen and paper to the couch and began:

> Dear Sierra, I forgot to tell you that I have a tattoo, and like the tattoo, my decision to stay is irreversible. When you asked me to not interfere anymore with you and Bob (really your life), it hurt me, but I think I begin to understand. In the same way, you must make the same effort. I won't tell you to leave Bob, please don't tell me to leave here. It took all my courage to get here, now I'm staying. Again, if my being there for your birth interferes with anything, I'll understand—and it is a long way. I might not even make it, but if you want me to come, I'll try to be there.
>
> Con cuidado,
>
> Rosa

By evening she'd completed the second rainbow painting, working until nearly ten o'clock. Then Rosa began a sketch of Dolores playing the piano. She also planned to start the final rainbow painting next month. The lilac sky would have to wait, as it seemed to want it that way, anyway. Rosa continued to struggle with it on a level she was unaware of—and it stared at her whenever she worked on the other paintings. The little spider waited for her touch, and she, the spider, had an eternity to spare. Rosa longed to complete the shawl, especially when her eyes followed the spiralling curves of the black roses, but the lilac sky wouldn't let her. No, it whispered, not yet.

When Sierra called after dinner Rosa almost didn't recognize her voice. They hadn't spoken in nearly a month, and Sierra's voice was careful and strained.

"Rosa, it's me, Sierra. I'm calling to tell you my water's burst, and I'm starting labor, it looks like. Are you coming?"

"Are you sure you want me to? Why didn't you answer my letter?"

"Maybe we could talk about it while you're here. I'd like you to be here, Rosa. Can you come?"

"Are you in hard labor yet?"

"No, just starting. I always take a while," Sierra laughed softly.

"Okay, I'll be there. See you in six hours or so. Bye."

By the time Rosa was halfway down the mountain she remembered the job at the newspaper Friday. It's my last week, anyway, she thought. I'll call Ted tomorrow.

Working for Ted had been an undemanding task, and they'd gone out to lunch a couple of times. He wasn't sure if the newspaper was going to survive in the small town where the main newspaper, extremely conservative and right wing, held sway. Ted's paper explored environmental issues, the hidden political issues of the community like the trucking of nuclear weapons through the narrow mountain passes to an army depot in a small mountain town on the California/Nevada border.

There'd been talk about the *Gazette*'s anti-American article, and so-called negative reflection on the community. Rosa had gotten a few callers saying things like, "Junk like that shouldn't be printed in this community," or "Why don't you people go back where you come from?" Then they'd hang up. Most of the irate callers asked to talk directly to Ted. She could tell he dreaded it, but he always answered, "Yes, may I help you?"

The paper also poked fun at the rather sombre community with "The Sheriff's Log," like the time they reported "Sick chipmunks on Green Valley Road sighted by local resident. Resident was sober." So, in a sense, Ted got his revenge, Rosa thought, laughing to herself.

Reading the *Blue Mountain Gazette* definitely made Rosa feel at home, and working there, even briefly, had given her a true sense of the community and how it worked. There was still a kind of hangover of the white settler mentality, and the irony was that most of them had migrated from the cities. It was a clash of values, and Ted poked them, over and over, to remind them they'd left nothing behind—that their conservative views would be challenged, even in the mountains.

If Ted's paper folded, there'd be the one newspaper again with its predictable views. And the cover of the *Gazette* was always in full color and artistically beautiful. She'd miss that, too.

Rosa liked Ted. He reminded her, just a little, of Rob. But she knew there was no time for a friendship, and he seemed to know it as well.

She thought of Julio. His last visit. They'd had one wonderful day together. Taking a walk, talking, Julio taking photographs. Intense lovemaking, again. Then the inevitable fight. The showdown. The angry goodbye.

Zack was getting restless in back, so she stopped by the side of the road to let him out. It was seven-thirty, so she'd probably get to Sierra's by one in the morning. A cup of tea, that's what I need, Rosa thought. I'll stop at the next drive-in.

The front porch light was on, but the house was dark. Rosa stretched her legs and was amazed at how much warmer it was in Sebastopol. It was cold, but not freezing. The night was clear and there'd be frost in the morning. Even the stars look gentler here, she thought. Not so fierce and close.

"Go on, Zack. Take a quick run," she said, letting him out.

"Rosa, is that you?" Bob called from the back porch, turning a light on.

"Hi, Bob. Is Sierra okay?"

"Yeah. She fell asleep. Her labor's probably going to be slow, so there's plenty of time. Do you want a hand?"

"That's okay. I've got it."

"The extra bedroom's made up, or should I say Sierra's office? See you in the morning," he said with an edge of sarcasm. He was referring to Sierra's attempts to make it, strictly, her own writing room.

Rosa groaned inwardly, thinking, Here we go again. She called Zack and brought him in with her. She was too exhausted to consider Bob any further, and, anyway, hadn't she come because of Sierra? Remember that, she told herself, and turned off the light.

Sierra is swimming without effort through warm water. She realizes it's the exact temperature of her body. Small tropical, rainbow fish flash by her in quick, sharp movements. She, the largest thing in the water—she feels immense—must give birth. Sierra looks for the others. The immense ones like herself.

"Rosa, do you want some coffee?" Sierra opened the door a notch and looked in.

"What time is it?"

"Almost nine."

"How're you doing? Are you in labor?"

"Off and on, but it's definitely getting stronger. I almost pissed the bed last night," Sierra laughed. "I haven't done that in years. I dreamt I was a pregnant whale. At least that's what I think I was, and the water was perfect. I guess I got too relaxed there for a minute."

"What a good birth dream. You look pretty relaxed. Do you have any tea? I'll be right up."

"Tea?"

"I'm pregnant, too. Remember?"

"But, of course, sister whale, I almost forgot. Are you nauseated?" Sierra couldn't help smiling.

"Only if I don't get the tea and toast right away. Are you okay running around like this?" Sierra was huge, but she carried the child in a confident balance.

"This is great to be able to get up and walk around in my own house. I just sit down when the contractions start up. I'll get some tea and toast," Sierra said, closing the door.

"Be right there." Zack was anxious to get outside, so she dressed quickly.

"I'm just going to let him out. That's no problem around here, is it? Would any of your neighbors call the pound?"

"There're some sheep in the next field, but Zack doesn't bother sheep as I remember. Here they come, Rosa." Sierra sat down and started to breathe deeply, her face absolutely calm with concentration.

Rosa let Zack out and came back to the kitchen. She stirred her tea and sat down opposite Sierra in silence, not wanting to break her concentration.

Sierra exhaled out and relaxed her concentration. "Well, those were good and strong. They're definitely getting stronger. Off and on. That's how they've been."

"You certainly look ready for them. You look pretty strong there, girl," Rosa laughed. "Have you eaten yet?"

"I was waiting for you. Do you want some huevos rancheros?"

"Sure. But I can cook. Come on, sit down."

"No, really. I'd rather be up and cooking."

"Okay, I'll get the dishes. Where's Bob?" Rosa asked, trying to keep any dislike out of her voice.

"He went to town with Tomás and a list. He said you got in pretty late. Well, I'm glad you're here." Sierra paused and looked at Rosa. "Have you notified your midwife?"

"She's on the alert. Also, the doctor and the hospital, just in case."

"I found a midwife I like a lot. So I'm going to go for a home birth as well. The doctor backup is much more paranoid up there, though. That's for sure. Very conservative, White Person's Paradise kind of trip. I have mixed feelings about the place, believe me. Not about the cabin or the forest, any of that. I mean, not that way. It's a kind of wild west—you know, The White Settler number that some, not all, the white folks are trying, very hard, to keep alive up there. It'd be funny if it weren't so damned offensive sometimes."

"Sounds pretty crazy. Though, as you know, there's some of that red-neck shit here. Remember? Remember Slave Day? I loved the look on that principal's face when we stormed his office." Sierra laughed.

"I remember well. We got them to stop the grand old tradition in both schools. I couldn't believe it when Sean came home with that story—selling slaves for 'fund-raising,' as the principal called it. It boggles the brain," Rosa said wearily. "Anyway, when's your midwife coming by?"

"Karen said she'd be by around noon to see how I'm doing. I wish these contractions would speed up. So, you've got a midwife up there in the wilds?"

"It feels like an old-new meeting in many ways with Diana, my midwife. An almost instant familiarity. One of those." Rosa smiled. "There's a few people up there I'd like to know better, and I'm sure I will." Forrest came to mind, but she made him go away.

"Anyway, I found a doctor who I can relate to humanly, and though he tried to discourage me, he's promised to meet me at the hospital in case of emergency."

"How far's the hospital?"

"Around twenty-five miles."

"Isn't that kind of far away? I mean, my hospital's just four blocks from here. What if the weather's bad? You know, I really do think you'd be better off coming back while you're pregnant."

Rosa's face darkened with anger, and in a precise, clipped tone she said, "Sierra, I promise to stay out of your most personal choices, but you've got to do the same for me. I'm staying up there, and that's all there is to it."

Hurt and anger flashed across Sierra's face, but she kept her back to Rosa as she cracked some eggs into a pan. Finally, Sierra said, "Do you really have a tattoo?" She began serving the food.

"On my belly," Rosa answered, edgily.

"Well, aren't you going to show me? I know you ain't shy, girl." Sierra started to laugh, but she sat down again with contractions. She stared out the window, breathing deeply and evenly until they were gone.

"Do you think you should have huevos rancheros just before your baby's about to pop out? Are you okay?" Sierra looked a little tired after that one.

"Those were stronger but didn't last as long. I'm just going to have a little, but I'm going to have some. I can eat anything I want as long as I don't overdo it. Well, are you going to show me this tattoo or what?"

Rosa stood up. "Are you ready? Cause I don't want any more shit! By the way, it'll cost you a buck!" She lowered her jeans and exposed her belly.

"Bitch, you've gone and lost your mind!" Sierra howled with laughter. "No, I like it. I really do. Did it hurt?"

"I thought I'd die," Rosa said in a serious tone. Then she laughed loudly seeing Sierra's expression. "This little tattoo is a pinch compared to what you're about to do—and what I'm going to do in a few months."

As they finished eating Sierra's contractions started again, and they both looked out the window at the sun shining thinly through the few leaves left on the skinny branches. The wind had spared a few, for now.

After Karen left, Sierra wanted to take a walk.

"We could just take the loop. It's less than a half mile. Like Karen said, it'll probably really get my labor going."

"You can rest when it hits. We'll sit on people's doorsteps," Rosa said, laughing. "It appears this one's going to be stubborn from the start."

"Jesus, that's all I need. Come on, let's get going. I want gravity to have a talk with this kid."

As they walked up to the road Bob's car appeared. He rolled

down his window. "Where do you think you're going?" he said, looking at Sierra in disbelief.

"For a walk. Nothing's really happening right now, so some jostling might get things going. Karen came by. She'll be coming back tonight." Sierra looked at Bob almost apologetically.

"I just don't think it's a good idea to take a walk right now. What if you go into hard labor or something?"

"I'll deliver her under a tree," Rosa said impatiently. "Hi, Tomás! Are you ready to see your new baby?"

"I sure am. Sure is taking a long time. I think I'm getting tired of waiting. Are you getting tired, Mommy?" he asked Sierra.

"Just a little, honey. But I think the walk's going to help him hurry up."

"Hi, Zack!" Tomás yelled, rolling down his window to pet him. Zack jumped up and licked his fingers. "Can I go, Mommy?"

"Not this time, Tomás. I'll be back in a little bit. Look, Bob, I'm okay." She reached up and touched the window, but Bob seemed frozen. Distant. In a low voice Sierra said, "If I don't start some strong contractions by tomorrow morning, I might have to go to the hospital, Bob."

He looked at her as though it were her fault. "Go ahead if it helps. I'll be inside the house in case you have to call. If this doesn't work, maybe you could try jumping rope." His voice was caustic.

Sierra pulled back her hand as though it'd been burned. "I'll see you when I get back. Why don't you smoke a joint or something?"

Bob looked from Sierra to Rosa and, without a word, pulled into the driveway.

There was a persistent wind picking up the dry, fallen leaves and whirling them in small, intense circles. Sierra was silent, but Rosa saw the tears on her face. Then her face tightened up. "Here it comes again."

"Sit on the grass, Sierra. Look, what did I tell you—there's our tree," Rosa laughed, indicating an immense, gnarled oak.

Sierra sat down on the soft, damp grass, stretching her legs out in front of her. "Are your teeth sharp enough?" she asked between breaths.

"For what?"

"To cut the cord." Her breathing was normal again. "Well, not as strong as the ones in the morning."

"I wouldn't worry about it. In fact, you ought to relax. After this walk, how about a glass of wine?"

"I've been drinking enough birth tea to float a fleet. A glass of wine sounds good. There's some champagne, by the way, in the fridge. For the big moment." Sierra gazed at the huge oak. The wind had stripped every leaf from its branches.

They got up and started walking again.

"How're you doing?" Rosa asked.

"You know, it's like Bob's been better because he's guilty. Oh, I don't know, maybe I'm just being paranoid. He's been home on time and everything for a while now. But I just keep feeling things, you know?" Sierra stared straight ahead. Zack had disappeared around a barn.

"I don't think you should be concerned about what Bob's doing, or not doing, right now. You've got enough to do, don't you think?" Rosa made herself stop and not say anymore.

Sierra looked at her. "I can't believe you're pregnant. Yet," she laughed. "How're things with you and Julio?"

"It depends on the weather, I think. Something like that. I believe I'm having a girl. I sketched a little girl when I was undecided."

"Do you have it with you?"

"No. I rushed out like a maniac last night. Anyway, I think Julio's starting to understand I'm not going back just because I'm pregnant."

"Here they come. I'm going to stand up this time. Here, let me lean on you, if you don't mind," Sierra said, drawing in a large breath of air.

It sounded like dogs fighting in the distance, and Rosa looked for Zack, but she couldn't see him. Sierra's body leaned into hers and she imagined the urge that filled Sierra's body. The impossible urge to empty one's body of an excruciating, living fullness. To surrender to a pain older than death, and the longing to hold what's never been before and make it one's own. For a while, Rosa thought. Just a little while, really.

"Those were longer, but not that strong. I can feel him. He's just right there, locked into the birth position," Sierra said, smoothing her huge belly. "Aren't you, little one. Little stranger."

"Is that your dog?" a man yelled, breaking the moment. Zack ran toward Rosa with his ears and tail down.

"Yes," Rosa answered. "Is something wrong?"

"There sure as hell is. Your dog just about killed a dog back here. I don't know who this one belongs to, but you'd better take a look."

Rosa grabbed Zack by the collar and jerked him toward her,

hard. "Zack! You're a bad dog! Bad dog, Zack!" She followed the man, holding Zack tightly.

"Well, the dog was here. It was bleeding pretty bad. Look," he said, pointing to some dark blood on the ground. "You'd better chain your dog. If I hadn't hit him with this board he would've ripped that dog's throat out."

"He's never done this before. I'm sorry this happened. I'm staying down the street at 788. The white house with red trim. If you find the dog, I'd appreciate it if you'd let me know." Rosa thought of Sierra waiting on the street. "I've got to go."

"I'd chain that dog if I were you."

"I will as soon as I get back to the house."

"What was all that about?" Sierra asked, holding her belly as she leaned on a fence.

"It looks like he almost did in another dog. Damn him! I'm going to have to chain him up." Rosa jerked Zack's collar. "You're a bad dog! Bad dog!" She noticed he was bleeding on his face. "Serves you right, Zack! Damn it!"

"I guess we'd better head back. I'm getting a little tired, anyway. Hold it. Here comes another one."

"Here, sit down this time," Rosa said, indicating a stretch of brick lining a garden.

After the contractions passed they sat there for a while longer. Sierra said as much to the air as to Rosa, "It's really a beautiful day. The wind keeps me from sweating and the sun is just warm enough. You know, I could just lay down under a tree and do it."

Bob was in the kitchen cutting up vegetables by the sink. "I thought I'd start the stew. The meat's on. You were going to cook stew?"

Sierra smiled widely. "Yes. And it smells so good, too." She kissed Bob on the lips, leaning over to make room for the child wedged tightly in her womb. "Where's Tomás?"

"I put him down for a nap. He really needed it." Bob continued to cut the vegetables, quickly and efficiently, as though he were being paid by the hour.

Rosa came in with Zack by the collar. "Do you have a long chain I could use? I've got to chain Zack. He just had a fight with another dog."

"I think there's a long one in the garage, Sierra. Do you know the one I mean? It's hanging up by the tools. Is he okay? He looks pretty cut up himself."

"It's just on his face. Supposedly, the other dog almost got his throat torn open." Rosa had only seen him do that once, when he was about two, really a puppy. Come to think of it, twice. Once when he'd killed one of their ducks and they'd tied it to Zack's neck and penned him, and the other time in a dog fight when she'd had to pull him away from another dog. He'd been slashing at the dog's throat. Rosa'd beaten Zack for that, and, as far as she knew, he'd never done it again. Or killed again. She made sure he was well-fed.

"Look, I'll get the chain. Be right back." Bob started out the back door.

Sierra started her contractions again, so they waited in silence, punctuated by Zack's panting.

"They aren't as strong as this morning's. Oh, well, maybe they'll start up again tonight and get going. Babies like to get born when it's convenient. For them."

"Just sit there. I'll pour us both a glass of wine," Rosa said.

"Here's the chain," Bob said, handing it to Rosa. "Do you want some towels for his face?"

"Some paper towels and hydrogen peroxide would be great." Rosa looked at Sierra. She looked tired. "Look, we'll do everything. Go lay down and drink that wine," she told her.

"I'll take you up on that this time."

After dinner Bob and Rosa cleaned the kitchen, and as they worked together the stiffness between them eased up.

"Your stew wasn't bad, Roberto."

"Old family recipe," he laughed. "If you want, I'll come up and make some for your labor. So, you're pregnant?"

"That's what it looks like," Rosa answered, guardedly.

"And you're staying up there, anyway? Don't you have that Landcruiser just to be able to get in and out of your place?"

"That's why I got it. You know, it's quite beautiful up there, and silent. I also have a feeling Zack's getting a little wild with so much new territory. He really does have the run of the forest. The summer people are gone and, I guess, their dogs."

Bob was rinsing out the sink. "How does Julio feel about your staying up there, pregnant?" he asked, fastening his eyes on her.

Rosa met his eyes. "That's just the way it is, Bob. I'd better go let Zack off the chain for a while," she said, turning to go.

"I'm glad you're here, La Rosa."

Rosa turned around.

"I really am. We used to be good friends, remember?" Bob said, leaning against the sink. He looked like he wanted to tell her something.

"I remember, Bob."

Tomás ran into the room. "Mommy's having tractions again."

"It's okay, Tomás. That's how babies get born. That's how you were born," Rosa told him. His eyes were wide open. "You okay, Sierra?" she yelled.

"Yeah!" she yelled back. "Got any ice water?"

"I'll get it. She probably could use a back rub, too," Bob sighed. "Come on, Tomás, you can take Mommy the ice water."

As Rosa let Zack off the chain the midwife pulled up and went into the house.

There was a crescent moon, turning a deep gold, about to set. Its prongs were sharp and pointed against the sky, as though it might refuse to leave the night sky, and hold itself there forever.

"Come on, baby," Rosa whispered. "Come on out." Three Mile Island, nuclear testing, the endless wars—is that why you'd rather stay in the darkness? she thought, as she watched the moon begin to set, slowly, reluctantly, filling her eyes with gold, gold, glowing gold. Then, gone.

She could see Zack in the back field, so she followed him out there and sat for a while in the night, watching him roll in the short, new hay beginning to grow again.

"Get over here, Zack!" Rosa called.

Zack ran over and, without a trace of guilt, stood in front of her, panting.

"You were a bad dog, Zack! That's why you're chained up. You just can't do that. Do you hear me, Zack? You're a bad dog! Bad!" she said, severely.

Zack hunched down as though he understood her. Usually she'd pet him in this position, but, instead, she said it again, "You're a bad dog, Zack! Bad dog!" He started to get up and Rosa grabbed his collar, making him lie down, firmly. Then, she let him go again.

The constellations commanded the night sky, and it was pleasant, even though it was cold, without the usual buzzing of mosquitos. Rosa fixed her gaze on the brightest star, Sirius. Sirius, the dog star, she remembered. She looked at Zack just in time. He was about to dig under the barbed wire.

"Get over here, Zack!" she yelled.

Sierra was in bed stretched out, comfortably, sipping tea. "Where've you been?"

"Out in back keeping an eye on Zack while he took a run. What did the midwife say? What's her name, again?"

"Karen. Well, I'm coming along, but slowly. She said the doctor wants me to come to the hospital tomorrow if things don't start happening." Tears filled Sierra's eyes. "I don't want to do that, damn it!"

"How about a glass of wine instead of that tea? I bet your friend gets sick of being cramped up by morning. The moonset, by the way, was beautiful. A crescent."

"I'll take a half-glass. This tea is starting to taste like piss. I can feel him, right there. But he's so still, Rosa," Sierra said with a worried look.

"The little sucker's gathering his energy for the sunrise, I bet. Watch out for dawn, is my guess," Rosa laughed softly.

"Of course," Sierra smiled a little. "The birth of the sun/son."

"Here's your wine. The poet speaks. Keep on going." Rosa sat down next to the bed with her glass of wine.

"First, I'll light a candle. May as well do this right. Would you hand me those matches? There. That helps." Sierra focused her eyes on the flame.

"The birth of the sun/son, I call on you, my Mother." Sierra paused and held the sides of her great belly. "Isis, Mother of all—the flower, the egg, the sun/son, the moon's daughters—be with me as I birth. As I birth the sun/son." Sierra's face reflected the light of the candle as she spoke.

They were both silent for a while. The sounds of Tomás taking a bath drifted into the room, and Bob's voice telling him to put his head back, the sound of water pouring, a slight struggle.

"Here they come," Sierra said. "Here they come."

Both women watched the flame, which was between them, as it made little leaps as the currents of air in the room touched it.

"Those were longer, but about the same strength." She took a sip of wine.

"Are you tired? I'll leave you alone if you want to go to sleep."

"I'm tired, but I'm restless. Stay a little longer. Have you met any interesting people? What are the men like up there?"

"So far, to be honest, the only interesting men are the younger ones. Mind you, this is just speculation and coincidence, I guess," Rosa said with a laugh. "Anyway, there's this young guy named Forrest who's building his place across the meadow from me. He has red hair and plays flamenco guitar like you wouldn't believe. First of all, he's married, his wife's pregnant, I'm pregnant. So like I said, it's purely speculation. I have never been attracted to anyone with red hair, and he looks like an elf." She laughed again at the thought of his crazy, red hair sticking up in the air.

"Rolf was blonde, right? As I understand it, Isis liked, or rather likes," Sierra smiled, "young men herself. Her own son becomes her lover, but I think this is symbolic. In our time, anyway."

"I knew there had to be an explanation for these lustful impulses. I like Isis more and more. Do you want me to rub your legs? I'd be glad to."

"You read my mind. I'll do the same for you. When're you due, girl?"

"Mid-April or so."

"What's your midwife's name?"

"Diana. She's quite beautiful. Half Cree Indian and grew up on a reservation in northern Washington. Anyway, you would not believe Julie. You met Julie a couple of times, didn't you?"

The candle continued to burn. A small, brown, intricately patterned, moth found it and began its dance of death. Once, it made the candle sputter as it flew into the wick.

"Should we blow it out?" Sierra looked at Rosa.

"She'll only find another candle. Maybe it's the best part. Who knows?" Rosa watched the moth approach again.

"It's terrible, isn't it?" Sierra said, sadly.

"To us. If you want to blow it out, go ahead."

The moth circled the flame, then entered it.

"I think I will. I'm getting sleepy, finally."

"Okay. If anything happens, just wake me up. Good night, Sierra."

They kissed each other.

"See you in the morning, or sooner, Isis willing," Sierra said with a laugh.

Bob had fallen asleep on Tomás's bed with the light on, a book still in his hands. Rosa turned the light off and went into the spare room. There was a budding violet plant on the low table next to the day bed, and a candle. She took the throw pillows off the bed and turned off the lamp. The candle. She had to light it. For Isis, Rosa thought. For Sierra's sun/son. And for the moth. "The moth," Rosa muttered.

She found some matches and lit the candle. Her shadow was huge against the wall. Perhaps we can't bear to watch anything so naked. Especially death, Rosa thought. Tomorrow birth. Tomorrow naked birth.

She felt herself flying to the candle, but she couldn't feel the flame. It's the brightness, like the sun, the thought flickered across Rosa's mind, that draws me in.

Three women stand together holding candles. Rosa stands in the middle. The two women on either side of her are very tall and stately. Their candles burn without effort. They are goddesses. Rosa's candle is small, held in a silver dish. A great wind threatens to extinguish hers, and she must shield it with her body. Now, Rosa knows how much she loves the fire.

"Rosa." Bob was kneeling beside her. "Sierra's in hard labor."

Her eyes flew open. "Is the midwife here? How long's she been in hard labor?"

"The last couple of hours. I've got some coffee on, if you want some. Karen's coming pretty soon. She only lives a couple of miles from here."

"I'll be right there." It was still dark, with the slightest hint of dawn. The candle still burned, barely, in its pool of wax. The dream, she reminded herself—the intense feeling of love for that small flame. Love, she thought, and tears came to her eyes. My own faltering love.

Rosa automatically bent over to blow the candle out, but she stopped herself and left the room.

Sierra was laying on her side, resting.

"Morning. I hear you're in hard labor." Rosa sat down on the bed and put her hand on Sierra's feet.

"They're coming all right, about every ten minutes or so. This must be it. I'm getting worn out. It'd better be." Sierra looked up at Rosa with an exhausted look.

"Why don't we open the curtains so we can watch the dawn. It's coming, you know." Sierra nodded.

They had sliding glass doors that revealed a small patio, a grape arbor and a wide stretch of sky. To the far left, the back fields could be seen in the daytime, but not yet.

Sierra began panting as she stretched herself out, positioning herself with pillows. She held onto Rosa's hand. When they subsided, she asked, "Where's Bob?"

Then they heard the shower running.

"I guess he's going to take a quick one. Look, Sierra, the sky's beginning to lighten."

She turned onto her right side and looked out the window. "Isn't that the Morning Star? It must be. Look how bright the damn thing is. Remember the legend of Quetzalcoatl, or however you say it—Feathered Serpent. Anyway, he turned into the Morning star," Sierra said, surprising herself with the memory. It'd been tucked somewhere in the back of her mind.

"Did you know that Quetzalcoatl had an older sister named Quetzalpetlatl? I don't know if I'm saying them right—tongue twister names. In the painting I'm doing, the one that I told you about, the lilac sky one—I'm painting her shawl, a black, lace shawl. I imagine it as the color of the night, holding the stars. Really, holding everything."

"How beautiful. I didn't know about this older sister. Where'd you read about it?"

"I'll lend you the book if you want. By the way, she's also her younger brother's lover. These goddesses don't want to leave anything alone, do they?" Rosa laughed.

"Look where it gets you," Sierra laughed softly. "Damn, the sky's so fucking beautiful at this time. I wish Marlin were here. Damn it!" Sierra began panting again, holding onto Rosa's hand.

"Those were good and strong, weren't they?" Rosa asked.

"They sure the hell were. I think Karen better get here," Sierra said with an anxious look.

"I think you're right." Rosa knocked on the bathroom door. "Bob, I think you'd better call and tell Karen to get here, right now."

He opened the door. "Are they getting worse?"

"They sure are. She's getting ready. Is Tomás going to watch?"

"That's what we planned. Okay. I'll get hold of Karen."

Rosa sat back down on the bed. "Keep it going. You're right on schedule. Look, it's almost dawn."

Sierra rested on a pile of pillows and stared out the window. "Marlin didn't want to be here for the birth, she said. But she said she'd come up after the baby's born. What if I hadn't wanted to have been at her fucking birth?" Anger stiffened her body and then tears dissolved it away.

"I think that's a teenager. You know, Sean thinks I'm nuts. A bona fide crazy," Rosa said with a smile. "I'm here. I hope that helps. Well, the sun's going to be popping up pretty soon."

"If I squeeze too hard, tell me," Sierra said. "I am glad you're here."

Bob came into the room. "She's on the way, Sierra."

"Come here, Bob. Hold my hand. Rosa, do you want to get Tomás? He said he wanted to watch his brother come out." Sierra smiled at Bob.

"Why're the curtains open?" he asked.

"To watch the sun be born. You know, s-u-n, s-o-n."

"Of course," he said, looking at her. "How about a back rub?"

"When you really get the urge, bear down, Sierra," Karen said, slowly. "Just bear down, but don't strain. Take your time. You don't want to tear."

The first shafts of light filtered through the grape arbor and the sun was beginning to rise. It was a deep-red dawn with a pulsing orange halo, but the sky was quickly changing to the color of rinsed blood.

Rosa held Tomás in her lap, and Bob was at Sierra's side holding her hand. Sierra's body was glowing with a gentle sweat as she panted and bore down.

"Look, Tomás, the sun's coming up," Rosa whispered. The sun had cleared the tallest trees and the shafts of light were thick and golden as they reached across the room in an instant, like a miracle, warming everything in its path.

"Okay, don't strain," Karen repeated. "You're doing real good. I can see the head."

Rosa held Tomás tightly and kissed him on his smooth, soft cheek. "Isn't that great, Tomás? The baby's head's just about to come out. That's called crowning, like a queen. Your mommy's going to be a queen, Tomás."

Sierra readjusted herself onto the pillows until she was almost in a sitting position, with her legs bent and wide apart. Soft moans escaped her lips as she panted and bore down, panted and bore down.

"Rosa," Bob said, suddenly. "Trade me places." He repeated the request with his eyes. He looked terrified.

"Are you sure?" Rosa asked. "Are you sure you want to do this?" She looked at him in disbelief.

"Go ahead, Rosa. Trade places. Just do it," Sierra said, impatiently.

Bob took Tomás and Rosa sat next to Sierra on the bed. Sierra reached for her hands. Both of them.

"If I squeeze too hard, just yell," Sierra said in a husky voice. Her eyes gripped Rosa's eyes with the ancient message of feminine terror: Do I have to?

Rosa looked back—You can do it. "Squeeze as hard as you want."

Sierra bore down, squeezing Rosa's hands, which lay across her breasts. Her moans were soft and constant. Rhythmic.

"Hold it, Sierra. Just hold it for a minute," Karen said.

Sierra's legs trembled. Then she bore down again in a powerful urge, so powerful it consumed her, entirely.

"Hold it, Sierra. Just hold it for a minute. You don't want to tear," Karen repeated.

Sierra's legs began to tremble violently from the sheer effort not to surrender to her urge.

Rosa found herself shouting, "Push, Sierra! Push! Go for it, goddamnit!"

A low, growling sound came from Sierra's throat as she was consumed, and surrendered to her birth, completely. The head, the shoulders, the entire body emerged from her sex. A boy. A glistening, red son. The thick, spiralling umbilical cord pulsed with life. Life. The room held the gathering warmth of the risen sun.

Sierra reached her arms out, "Let me see him."

Karen handed the baby to her, the cord still connected to his belly, pulsing its womb message to him while his lungs drew air. He never cried. His eyes were wide open, and his look was one of recognition instead of pain.

"Felipe," Sierra said softly, and he suckled at her breast for a moment.

"She could've torn, you know." Karen looked at Rosa, angrily.

"But she didn't, did she?" Rosa turned and asked Sierra, "How about that champagne? Are you ready?"

"I'd love some," Sierra said, glancing at Rosa. Then she handed the baby to Bob.

"What's his name, Mommy?" Tomás asked.

"Felipe. Now you're going to have to teach him how to be a big boy, just like you."

"He looked at me!" Tomás exclaimed with delight.

"Here comes the placenta," Karen said, catching the multi-colored organ in a bowl. "I'm going to sever the cord. Do you want to be the one to hold him?"

Bob glanced at Sierra and nodded his head affirmatively. His heart pounded as Karen clamped the cord, cutting it, then cutting it closer to Felipe's belly. He was astounded at the calmness on his son's face, as his own confidence returned.

Rosa brought the champagne in on a tray and handed a glass to Sierra. Sierra looked at Rosa with tears on her face. "Well, we're separated. He's born."

"Do you want to keep the placenta? It's certainly healthy," Karen asked.

"We'll plant it with a tree. A tree for you, Felipe," Bob said, looking at the baby.

Rosa handed the glasses to everyone, including a small one for Tomás. "Shall we toast?"

Karen looked at Rosa with a shrewd expression and said, "You may as well do the honors."

"Gladly." Rosa lifted her glass, touching Sierra's, and since no one else made the gesture to touch glasses, she continued, "Happy birth day, Felipe. Sierra."

"Happy birth day," everyone repeated, and Tomás began to sing, "Happy birth day to you, happy birth day to you. . . ." in a high-pitched, happy voice.

It was early March and Rosa sat drinking her morning pot of tea facing the kitchen window. The constant fire in the fireplace offset the grey rain. It'd been raining for nearly four days straight. The temperature refused to drop to freezing, so it rained and rained. The trees were a violent green against the wet, dark mud of the earth.

The tattoo had expanded as her dream had predicted months before, and the child moved forcefully and, it seemed, constantly as though she resented the cramped quarters of Rosa's small body. The child was unusually quiet this morning as Rosa thought things over as she gazed at the inexhaustible rain. She looked at the outside thermometer: thirty-eight degrees.

She felt strangely responsible, as though some part of herself refused to harden into ice and snow, but preferred the soft, yielding rain. Rosa listened to the rain as though it were telling her secret things. Necessary things.

Sierra had been distant since her birth. Rosa remembered saying goodbye the morning she left. It was nothing Sierra said, but her eyes had reproached her. Yes, there'd been a hard reproach in Sierra's eyes. Since then, cautious letters, cautious phone calls.

Rosa could hear Bob, "She had no business telling you to push." Maybe. Maybe that's what he's saying, Rosa thought. Didn't he ask me to trade places? Didn't Sierra hold onto me? I don't understand, Rosa repeated, inwardly, as though to an old wound. And Sierra, was she saying, "She had no right to take over like that." Maybe. Maybe, Rosa thought sadly.

Rob lingered in Rosa's mind like a small, warm pleasure. She turned it, slowly, and it eased her wound. His five-day visit had been an almost constant exchange of friendship, going up and down, down and up, to the many levels each one was capable of. He taught her to cross-country ski, and she'd finally learned with a clumsy persistence. The bottle of brandy Rob had tied, in a scarf, around Zack's neck, so they'd had to wait for Zack to join them in order to get a drink.

Rob had said, "If you'd marry me, we could be old socks together. You're good old sock material, you know that?"

"I'm already married," Rosa had laughed until she thought she couldn't stand it.

Then Sean had arrived on Rob's last day and Sean's judgment had been severe. "Don't you think it's kind of weird to have a man visiting you like you weren't married? Or pregnant, for Christ's sake!"

"No," Rosa had said angrily. "And, anyway, who the hell made you sheriff of the world?"

"When're you moving back to civilization, anyway?" he'd persisted.

"And just what, dear boy, is civilization? And to whom?"

"You don't give a damn what anyone thinks, do you?" Sean had yelled.

"No!" Rosa had lied, because she did, but there was something of more importance than even what she thought of herself. And she couldn't begin to explain it.

Sean hadn't called in over a month, so Rosa knew how he was by talking to Julio. Julio had come in February. A sad, strained visit. A moment or two of tenderness, and then the immense anger that flew out of both of them, always a little too late to call it back, safely.

"Sean told me Rob stayed here, Rosa. You just don't know where to stop, do you?"

"He's my friend, not my lover, Julio."

"Tell that to someone with half a brain. Not me. Okay?" He'd shouted.

"It's because you've got half a brain that I can't even speak to you! Don't come back. I don't want you to come back while I'm pregnant. Do you hear me? Do not come back here!"

"I'm sorry. I'm sorry, Rosa."

"No, you're not. You won't let me love you, and you don't want me to love anyone else . . ."

Rosa's thoughts trailed back to Rob and his visit. It had a feeling of completion, as though the sustained intensity of the visit would have to last them a long time. He'd sent her a card, after he left, with the words, "Rosa, Thank you. Rob." The card had been a painting of a mythically beautiful woman standing in a world of snow, surrounded by stars. She held something bloody in her cupped hands, and it dripped, red, onto the white snow.

Rosa remembered him saying, "You know, I always thought that being a doctor would solve the problem of loneliness. Almost as though I could make people love me." He'd laughed.

"Maybe we all do that in one way or the other. Maybe we can't imagine someone loving us for what we are," she'd said.

"Sometimes I feel like quitting the doctor business, especially when funds get cut again. Maybe I'll become a shrink and pretend to know what's wrong with myself because I know what's wrong with everyone else." He'd laughed loudly, flinging his arms and legs onto the couch, in front of the fire, in a ridiculous pose. "You know, I have saved some lives with these," he'd said, waving his hands in the air.

Rosa got up to stretch her body, and the child wedged under her ribs. She went into her studio. The third, and final, rainbow painting was nearly complete. On an enlarged map of Mexico an Indian woman kneeled. Her skin was brown and her body was strong; a little heavy, but not fat. Yet not slender or frail. Her face was still blank. Rosa kept putting it off and sketching it, waiting for the one that felt right.

The woman was naked and her deep brown, almost black, nipples commanded the viewer's attention. They were lovely, as though they'd suckled many children.

She wore a back-strap loom, and she was weaving the rainbow that encircled the Earth. The woman kneeled in a desert landscape, ringed by mountains. Light, purple mountains. It was at the southern tip of Oaxaca. Rosa smiled to herself. The Sierra Madre del Sur. Am I not in the Sierra Madres, Mountain Mothers, to the north?

The urgency to complete the woman's face seemed especially strong today, so Rosa decided to sketch all day if necessary. Dolores' painting was coming along, and in this one she'd completed the face almost immediately. A young woman's face, surrounded by heavy, black hair, was bent over the piano keys, dreaming. Her dark purple dress seemed to age her and pull her firmly to the piano seat. Rosa realized, looking at the painting, that it was a wish, as though the purple dress could've kept Dolores rooted to the young woman, instead of looking up in anger at the sight of her daughter's longing.

She'd decided to not tell Dolores about her pregnancy, and she wondered if she'd ever show Dolores this painting. What would Dolores see? Rosa asked herself.

The shawl had grown bit by bit, and the single, black fold, as it hung in midair, began to look as though it belonged that way, permanently. Its design revealed itself, beautifully, against the pale lilac sky. Yet the sky continued to haunt Rosa, disturbing her with a persistent sense of imperfection. A flaw, she thought. The sky is somehow flawed.

She went back to the kitchen and sat down, again, facing the steady rain. As she poured the last of the tea she thought of her Aunt Maria and she was tempted to let her know she was pregnant. But she just might tell Dolores, out of loyalty or competition, she reasoned. Besides, Rosa thought, my aunt's always influenced by her husband, and that I don't need.

The Mexican Man loomed up at the thought of her uncle—the uncle of her childhood. The few times Rosa had stayed with them had given her a good glimpse of him, and though her aunt had complained to Rosa, the moment he came through the door, it was serve, serve, serve.

Then, Rosa thought of her grandmother, Luz, and the story of her wedding night. She'd been terrified by the largeness of her husband, and she'd locked herself in the closet. Later, because he'd been patient, her grandmother'd told her, she'd come out to find her husband sleeping. Her mother-in-law had hung the bloody sheet from the window the next morning. "I was so ashamed," she'd said, giggling like a girl, as she arranged a long, grey braid with a rubber band.

The sound of rushing water made Rosa focus her eyes in front of her. A wall of water was rushing toward her, as it came over the barricade of rock and soil.

"The creek," Rosa whispered. "It's the fucking creek!"

Instantly, it began to rush around the cabin. Dale, she thought— I'll get Dale. She dialed his number, but no one answered. Throwing on a parka, Rosa ran out to the car and headed for the ranch. Will the damn place still be there when I get back? she thought as the car churned mud up to all the windows. The rain, quickly, cleansed them.

Rosa found Dale by the corrals, and now he was behind her with the tractor. Dale went around to get to where the original wooden dam should've been. She parked the car on the road and hurried toward the sound of the tractor. The cabin looked like a houseboat in the middle of a rushing stream, but it was still there.

The tractor was scooping earth and stone to create a new dam, and the water began to change direction. Rosa followed the stream up as Dale worked the tractor. She bent to scoop a drink from the clear, cold water, and she followed it with her eyes as it disappeared up the slope of the mountain.

When Rosa got back to the cabin, the creek was flowing in a trench toward a newly created pond beside it. The pond was less than twenty feet from the cabin, and the sound of the creek was loud, like voices singing at perfect pitch, together. Rosa was drenched, but she stood and listened for a while, amazed at the appearance of the creek. And then she thought, The voices sound like praise.

"Do you want a cup of coffee or some brandy? I really do appreciate your coming to the rescue, Dale."

"I'll take some brandy, thank you," Dale said, noticing her pregnancy for the first time. "Looks like the trucks broke down the dam. We're going to have to seal off that area or it's going to happen again, that's for sure."

"Well, that's enough excitement for one day," Rosa laughed. "That sounds like a good idea to me. Besides, it's just a shortcut. How long have you lived up here?" She liked his eyes. They were aware, with an element of kindness in them.

He finished his brandy and Rosa offered him another. "I used to deep-sea dive down in South America a few years back." He took a sip of his brandy and let it linger in his mouth like a small fire.

"No kidding! So, you weren't always a cowboy? You know what I mean—living here and all." Rosa hoped she hadn't insulted him.

Dale laughed. "Not hardly, but I like it well enough. Do you want to hear a good shark story?"

Rosa nodded. "Sure. Since we're on the subject of water, right?"

"That creek is pretty loud. Puts me right to sleep." Dale cocked his head and stared out the window. "The coral cliffs at the bottom of the ocean, down there, are something to see. Like mountains, but full of every color. Anyway, one time I was down there and ran into a Great White. A big one. So I held still while it nudged me with its nose. Then it circled me a couple of times and left. Beautiful, but deadly, down there at the bottom."

"So, now, you're at the other end, on top of a mountain."

"Still beautiful and deadly, but at least I'm surrounded by air, the way I see it. Well, I don't want to take anymore of your time."

"Drop by again sometime." Rosa smiled at him.

Dale stood up and walked toward the door. He looked into her studio and paused. "Interesting," he said, with a touch of embarrassment. "You look pretty busy up here," he said, looking at her swelling belly. "Take it slow, now."

Rosa watched him walk away, his shoulders hunched forward against the rain. Then the tractor started up like a dinosaur coming back to life.

After she cleaned up and ate lunch she worked in the studio until dark, but still the face didn't come. In Rolf's last letter he'd enclosed a piece of fabric the color of a deep fuchsia. "Sunset," he'd written on it with a black marker. Rosa touched the cloth and decided to stop for the day. What was it he'd said—a quote from a photographer he admired. She got his letter from the closet shelf, stored on the top of the German gun.

"My aim is increasingly to make photographs look as much like photographs that unless one has *eyes* and *sees*, they won't be seen—and still everyone will never forget them having once looked at them. I wonder if that is clear. Alfred Stieglitz"

Yes, that's it, isn't it? Rosa thought. I still don't have the eyes to see this face yet. Not yet.

The phone rang. It was Carmen. Like her last letter, her voice was very reserved.

"I was just thinking about you, I guess. How are you? You must be getting big by now."

"Oh, I'm fine. Not too much longer to go at this point." Rosa thought of the creek but decided not to mention it. "How're you doing?"

"The same old thing. How's Julio?" Carmen asked.

I can't stand him, she wanted to say, but she stopped herself. The conversation ran down to goodbye, and after Rosa hung up she felt lonely for the first time in weeks. She thought of calling Diana, but decided against it. Maybe in the morning, she thought.

They saw each other three or four times a month, and each time it took on the quality of a celebration. Each time they learned something new about each other, or really about themselves. There seemed to be a tension between them, a kind of chemistry of possibilities that they mirrored, readily, to one another, so that Rosa sensed the balance they maintained between celebration and conflict was a delicate one. Like mothers and daughters, Rosa couldn't help thinking. And, in this case, would my daughter also be my midwife? Rosa smiled at the thought of Diana's long stride and enormous sense of confidence, carrying a bowl of food, a bottle of unfiltered grape juice, her stethoscope as she usually did when she visited.

Suddenly, Rosa felt like cleaning up the studio, thoroughly. After everything was put away, cleaned and orderly, she felt exhausted. There was enough food in the refrigerator for a couple of days, she noted. After some leftover soup she took a warm, oiled bath and listened to the sound of the creek, singing. Singing its watery praise.

Four strong-looking women stand, each one, on a huge, grey boulder—one north, one south, one east, one west. Their legs are far apart as they stand, slightly squatting. Blood pours down between each woman's legs, spilling a stream of red on the stones as they birth.

When Rosa woke up she couldn't believe it—she'd pissed the bed. Did I? Did I piss the bed? She looked at it, and there was so much of it, and it wasn't like piss, at all. My water's broke, she realized. My water's broke! I'm a little over seven months along—it can't be true! She looked at the warm liquid pooled on her bed, and she knew it was true. The baby was very still. Still.

Dr. Walker checked her, gently. "Yes, you've lost your water. This child's on the way, Rosa. We're going to have to put you on medication to stop the labor till we get you down to Chico where they have good preemie facilities. I'm going to fly you down."

They strapped her into a narrow bed, facing two round portholes. The medication dripped, slowly, into her arm from the clear plastic tubing. The plane was small, and as it climbed into the air it felt like she was in the belly of a large bird climbing, then soaring into the clouds.

"Do you mind if I look out?" Rosa asked the nurse sitting next to her.

She smiled. "Well, if you feel like it, go ahead. Just be careful with the drip."

It was incredible. The highest peaks still had snow on them.

Sheer granite tapered down to an endless, living green. And the clouds moved, gently, beneath the plane, the bird. The eagle, Rosa thought. This I can grasp. A jet is always beyond me. Too fast. "We're flying, Luzia," Rosa murmured.

"Isn't it beautiful up here?" The nurse looked out her own windows. "You're my first patient to get up and take a look," she said, laughing.

"I figure I may as well enjoy it. It really is beautiful." It was becoming valley and the mountains began to disappear.

"Is this your first?" the nurse asked.

"No, this is my second. My first one was born eighteen years ago, though."

"I see," she smiled. "You're in good hands here, I should tell you. A good place for preemies."

"Do you have any children?" Rosa asked. The nurse looked to be about her age.

She looked right into Rosa's eyes and said, "I had four pregnancies, full term, and lost all of my babies. You've had one live birth, haven't you? Well, chances are this one will be live, too." There was absolutely no bitterness or sadness in her face—only acceptance.

Rosa remembered, clearly, the dream last night—the four women giving birth. How has she done it? Rosa thought. How has she achieved that acceptance? North, south, east, west—I'll need all of you.

As Rosa was being lowered into the ambulance, the nurse told the attendant, "Take good care of her now. Take good care of her for me." She turned towards Rosa. "Good luck. The best of luck to you."

When Rosa was secured in the ambulance, she watched the young woman who was dressed in a uniform that made her look more like a cop than an ambulance attendant. She became uncomfortable with Rosa's gaze.

"Your IV bothering you?"

"No, I'm okay."

"Slow down!" she yelled. "No one's dying on this ride!" Then she wedged herself between the two men in front, glancing back at Rosa, from time to time, with a look of superiority she made no effort to hide.

The ride was mercifully short. They could've been hauling a side of beef. As they unloaded her, the young woman asked in a bored voice, "Do you know who your doctor is?" as she glanced at her watch.

"Why don't you just take me inside, and I'll figure it out from there. Wouldn't want to keep you," Rosa said, caustically.

"Well, aren't we snippy."

"Just take me in and get the hell out of my life."

Without a word, she wheeled Rosa in, gave some papers to a nurse and left.

Well, there goes my home birth, Rosa thought, angrily.

They put her in a private room, asked a list of questions, secured the drip and left. After a while a nurse came in to readjust the drip.

"When will the doctor be here?" Rosa asked.

"Dr. Miller should be here any minute," the nurse said, irritably, as though the question were impertinent.

"Do I have any messages at the desk?"

"I really don't know." The nurse looked up meeting Rosa's eyes.

"Would you mind checking, please. Now." The old hospital game, Rosa thought wearily. I haven't been in a fucking hospital for eighteen years.

The nurse turned and briskly walked away, leaving her nurse-smell behind. Another cop. "That's all I need," Rosa muttered.

The rain splattered the window with huge, slanting drops. An old pine was right outside the window, and small, brown sparrows fluttered from branch to branch shaking the rain from their wings.

"There is this message," the nurse said, handing Rosa a piece of paper. "Husband on the way. Ruth."

"May I have a glass of juice when you get the chance?"

"You can't have anything while you're on this medication." She looked at Rosa like she'd lost her mind.

"You're kidding."

A hint of a smile pulled at her mouth. "Afraid not. The doctor will explain it all when he gets here."

Rosa hadn't eaten anything when she'd run out the door. She'd put food out for Zack and left him outside. Dale wasn't home, so she left a note asking him to feed Zack once a day, explaining she'd gone into labor. She decided to call Dale later to see if he had gotten the note and the ten-dollar bill inside the envelope.

A wave of hunger hit her, but she told herself to forget it. I can lose some weight, that's for sure. Her stomach felt like an empty bowl, except for Luzia who pushed on it, waiting to be born.

Rosa listened to the steady rain and imagined the stream beside her cabin running over the smooth and jagged stones. Then she saw the four women of her dream, blood between their legs. A dark, dark red. The color of birth.

"Mrs. Luján," a voice called her. "Are we awake yet?" A very white, fleshy face was connected to the voice. A man's face. "There we are. I'm Dr. Miller, dear."

Puke, Rosa thought. She gathered herself. "I beg your pardon?"

The doctor backed away. "I understand you're Dr. Walker's patient, Plumas County. An early starter, is that right?" His voice hovered between condescension and authority.

"That's right." Why him, she thought with an inward groan. If he can't be daddy or doctor, he's bound to be an asshole. "I understand I can't eat while I'm on this medication. How long will that be?"

Unexpectedly, he smiled widely as a teacher to a bright student accustomed to dullards.

FUCK—the word crowded her thinking. She made it budge so that she could hear him.

"I'd like to keep you on this medication for at least three days to give the fetus time to strengthen its lungs. Not only are we stopping your labor, we've added medication for the fetus as well." His voice held no emotion at all, though his face kept smiling. There was an odd discrepancy about it.

Rosa tried to imagine Rob. He'd probably be leaning on the bed, trying to make her understand the situation—and his face would synchronize with his words.

"So, for three days I won't be able to even have a glass of juice? I mean, if that'll help the baby's lungs, fine. But isn't three days a bit long, Dr. Miller?"

"You look like a strong, healthy girl."

Rosa's face reddened with fury.

"You must be a libber. Excuse me. *Woman.*" He said the word *woman* with a strange emphasis as though the creature no longer existed on the face of the Earth.

"How about a glass of water, Dr. *Miller?*" Rosa asked, giving his name the same emphasis.

"Ice is all I can do for you. Only ice for the next three days. We'll see if we can last that long." The smile was glued onto his face.

Do you have a turd in your pocket? she wanted to ask, but her look seemed to be enough. He kept quiet.

"Rosa! There you are! Are you okay?" Julio was smiling.

Inappropriately, she thought. Like we're two long-lost lovers. Slow down there, Julio. Rosa made her face as sombre as possible and said, "So they got hold of you. It looks like I'm going to be here for a few days." She put an emphasis on the word *I*.

"If you'll excuse me, Mr. Luján, I have to examine your wife. You may wait in the hallway. It'll be just a minute." Now his voice was man-to-man.

"My husband's name is Mr. López. And it's fine with me if he stays in the room. I think that's how I got in this predicament."

Dr. Miller laughed nervously. "If it doesn't bother you, it certainly doesn't bother me." He turned to Julio and said, "Just make yourself comfortable, Mr. López."

Julio turned and stared out at the rain. A regular bitch on wheels, he thought to himself. He glanced at Rosa. She never took her eyes off the doctor.

"Well, things look in order," Dr. Miller said hurriedly. "We'll transfer you to a private labor room. You should be comfortable there."

"May I have some ice?" Rosa asked.

He shot Julio a slightly despairing look of complicity, and then said, "I'll have the nurse bring you some."

Rosa sucked on her ice, and Julio sat on the chair next to her. "Well, I must say, getting here was fun. I flew down on a small plane. The mountains were amazing from up there."

Julio smiled at the curiosity, plain, on her face. Now that the doctor was gone she wasn't so bristly. "When did all this start?" he asked.

"My water broke this morning. Also, yesterday the creek that used to run where the cabin is came back. I had to get Dale, down the way, to bring the tractor up and detour it. I mean, it was a mini-tidal wave coming toward the kitchen window."

"Jesus." He looked astonished. Then his eyes narrowed suspiciously. "Who's Dale?"

Rosa's eyes locked onto Julio's. "Julio, he's a person who works at the ranch. I just want you to know, right now, that if there's going to be conflict, I'd rather be alone, goddamnit."

Julio's hand flew forward and rested itself reassuringly over her own. It quieted them both, and without either of them knowing it a truce was declared.

"There's no phone in here. Would you mind going to give Dale a call? I left him a note to feed Zack once a day. I hope Zack's okay out there by himself. There was nothing else I could do."

"Sure, I'll call him. Are you comfortable? You look kind of red in the face."

"My heart's going pretty fast. The medication, I guess. Also, you might call Sierra in case she wants to come. Tell her it's up to her. Do you have to go back, Julio?"

"I'm cancelling everything. I'm staying till you give birth. Okay?" He looked at her as though he wanted to pour all his strength into her, and it pierced her as no anger ever could.

She wept for a while and then said, "So, you're going to stick it out here with me, old friend?"

Julio pushed the hair off her forehead in slow, sweeping movements. "I'm going to charm you with my latest gossip, run errands, get magazines if you wish. Flowers."

Rosa let that great comfort he offered her settle itself into her, but stopped herself from asking him why it was always temporary. Do you hate me, Julio? she wanted to ask. But she couldn't. Not now. He was trying to give her something, and she would take it. Whatever it was.

"Are you going to go give Sierra another call now? While you were gone the doctor came and I asked him if someone else was okay to have at the birth. He winked broadly and told me a birth coach would be okay. So, tell her, if she wants to be here, it's all right. That guy gets on my nerves, like he's doing something illegal, just for me." Rosa's face mirrored her distaste.

"He's not exactly Dr. Kildaire, is he?" Julio said, wryly.

"You'd have liked Dr. Walker. Just person-to-person. He didn't feel they had the proper facilities up there. You know, Julio, when I allow myself to think about it, I am starved."

"I'll bring you burritos—whatever you want—after." He smiled.

"Don't even say the word burrito."

"I went to your opening last month."

"You didn't tell me that."

"We were fighting, remember? Anyway, I was impressed. I think your work was the best stuff there. You sold three paintings, didn't you?"

"Yes, and it sure helps. That and the grant. Really, the grant. Now I make it another year, clearly. Also, the gallery offered to keep two on consignment, and they want to see my new work as well."

"How's the shawl coming, La Gran Puta?"

"I'd hit you but you're too far away, and, for once, I'm grounded." Rosa laughed, softly. "Anyway, M.M., it's definitely beginning to hang there like it should. Then I begin the orchids. I wonder what it's going to be like to work with a baby in the house?"

"I'd like to be able to help you, Rosa."

She looked out the window, and, from the angle she was at, a solid grey sky like steel was all she could see. Rosa looked back at Julio, trying not to betray herself or him. "Why don't we see what happens with everything before we talk about that."

"I just wanted you to know, that's all."

"Does Sean know I'm here?"

"I left him a note. I'll give him a call, too."

There was a knock on the door. Julio opened it and an older woman introduced herself. She'd come to read to them from the Bible during their difficult time. Julio shot Rosa a look, and the woman began to sit down.

"I appreciate your offer," Rosa said, "but perhaps someone else here can use it more than us. Thank you, anyway."

"Oh, I was just planning to stay for a minute, and then move on to the next room. What a nice couple you are. Here, together, by yourselves," she said, with misplaced sincerity.

"You see, we aren't Christians," Julio told her.

"My goodness! I'm sorry! What religion are you, if you don't mind my asking?" she asked in a horrified voice.

"We're Native People. We worship the Earth as a living being," Julio said in a clear voice. He'd never said it out loud, and it surprised him as his words rang true.

The woman was flustered, but she was persistent in her mission. "What tribe are you people?"

"We're Yaqui from Mexico," Julio answered her.

She started for the door, clutching her Bible tightly against herself. "Well, my goodness." She opened the door. "Well, God bless you, anyway." She smiled, quickly, and was gone.

"May the Earth bless you," Julio returned, starting to laugh.

"And the Goddess." Rosa started to laugh but the pressure in her cervix stopped her.

Julio returned, early, the next morning with three white roses. Their perfection calmed Rosa as though an omen had been handed to her.

They'd increased the dosage of medication as the urge to bear down increased by the hour. She felt exhausted from the muted labor, and pent-up with an energy that made her heart want to leap out and leave her lying there.

"Why don't you bring that glass with some water? These are lovely. Gracias, Julio." Rosa devoured their scent like food.

Julio leaned over and kissed her again, and then went into the bathroom to fill the glass with water. "I called Sierra back and she said she'd be here tomorrow morning." Julio could see her disappointment, so he continued as he handed her the glass. "Sean will be here tomorrow, after his meet. He said to tell you to hang in there."

"Where's his meet?"

"Sacramento. So it's really on his way."

"I see," Rosa said in a controlled voice. "Did you get hold of Dale?"

"He said, no problem. Seems like a nice guy."

"He is. One last person to call, if you don't mind. Would you call Diana, my midwife? Just let her know what's going on, and tell her I'll get back to her after the birth."

"I'll go get some coffee downstairs and give her a call. Just lay back, Rosa. Doze a little." Julio was becoming more than worried. He'd never seen her look that way. Almost helpless. It doesn't suit her, he thought.

After Julio shut the door behind him, Rosa turned her face and stared at the white roses until they seemed to grow wings. Shimmering, white wings. Butterflies. She thought of all the women in the world giving birth at that moment. With me, she thought, and I with them. Then she thought of the nuclear testing, and she wondered if men crouched behind their instruments and fortified structures, watching death, like little boys playing with firecrackers, while she, a woman, struggled with life between her legs, lodged there at the tip of her sex.

And then she thought, with no nod to rationality, This medication feels like death. A test to see how long I can last. Then her rational mind answered her, Calm down, it's for the baby, for her lungs. For Luzia's lungs. Control, control, death, her other voice answered in return. This was the voice Rosa trusted, but she'd have to see where the rational would lead.

The doctor was back, fresh as a daisy and smiling his superficially cheerful smile. Rosa felt like a bed of thorns. Sunset had passed without any change of color behind the steel of the sky. Only the rain was soft, escaping as it did, from the locked gate of the sky where the sun was kept. Where the sun was locked away.

Rosa imagined a sunset so intense with color that its warmth flooded her—and the sun pulsing down, orange and red, entered her. She was soaked in sweat and her heart seemed to have a life of its own as it visibly moved under the thin hospital gown. The pressure in her cervix was almost unbearable.

"I have to start pushing," Rosa told Dr. Miller in a voice louder than she'd intended. "The pressure's becoming unbearable."

He kept smiling at her. "That's an urge to move your bowels, my dear. That's your problem right now. You're constipated."

"I'm that too, but I'm talking about the urge to bear down and give birth, Dr. Miller," Rosa said, answering him in an exacting tone.

There was a nurse and a woman doctor in the room, and Julio was sitting next to her watching what was becoming more and more of a drama.

For the first time Dr. Miller stopped smiling and said, "That is an urge to move your bowels, Mrs. Luján. Nothing more. Now, we have another day to go with this medication and I know we can do it. The pressure is in your bowels."

Rosa sat up on her elbows, upsetting the drip and yelled, "I think I know my pussy from my asshole, and I am about to give birth!"

The nurse turned her face as a smile overtook her, but the woman doctor was outraged at Rosa's words.

"Well, I can't deal with this," Dr. Miller said hotly. At that moment another doctor came into the room and looked at Rosa. He'd checked her pulse twice that day, but each time he hardly spoke to her. He seemed almost shy.

Rosa could hear him speaking to Dr. Miller in his Swedish accent, "Don't you think the patient's reaction to the medication is becoming a threat? Look at her response. I don't think her heart can keep up with it."

Dr. Miller mumbled, turning his back to Rosa, "I'll start a lesser dose. She has to wait another day, the way I see it." He stared hard at the other doctor as though to say, Mind your own business. Then he turned to Rosa and said, "I'm going to lower the dosage, but if you begin to feel any contractions, tell the nurse."

Rosa just looked at him. Then he stalked out of the room. The woman doctor said something to the Swedish doctor, her eyes cutting over to Rosa, angrily. Then they left.

The nurse walked over and stood beside Rosa. "How're you doing?" she asked.

"All I know is that when I begin to feel my contractions, I'm not going to tell anyone." Rosa looked at the nurse.

"Don't tell me about it," she said, laughing. "You do what you've got to do." She met Rosa's eyes and touched her hand. "Look, I'll be right back."

"Should you do this?" Julio looked confused and a little desperate.

"I'm going to give birth right now, or I'm going to die. That's what it feels like. I'm going to do it, Julio." Her face was still extremely red, but her heart was beginning to slow down.

Julio got up and brought paper towels dipped in cold water from the bathroom, laying them on her forehead and wiping her face. Rosa took them and wiped her breasts and underarms.

Then the contractions began, almost immediately, and they were wonderful because they were hers. They strengthened quickly, breaking through the medication, opening wide her gates.

"I feel the head. She's coming. Right now."

The nurse came into the room.

"I feel the head," Rosa told the nurse. "I'm going to do it. Right now."

"Okay, hold on." The nurse opened the door and shouted, "Delivery! Right now!" She unhooked Rosa from the tubing, throwing everything to one side, and it was as though the enforced passivity was left dangling with it. Her body felt free, finally.

As they wheeled Rosa into the delivery room an image of a woman flashed across her mind. The woman's torso was like a snake, and great wings spread out across her back. She was crouched down, hands holding the Earth.

The room was all white and steel, with great pools of light poised to reveal any mysteries.

"I'll have your bed ready when you're done in here," the nurse said.

"Would you order me a meal? I'm starved."

"Do you want a dinner?" She smiled with amusement.

"Yes, that'll do it."

"You've got it," she said and left.

The woman doctor was at the foot of the table. "Okay, strap her in," she said indifferently.

"No, I won't do that. I will not be strapped in."

"You don't have too much of a choice here." She glared at Rosa. "Besides, it's for the baby's safety, not yours."

Rosa's mind teetered at the edge of a sheer, black rage, but she knew if she surrendered to it they'd have an excuse to strap her down. "I will not be strapped in. I do not give you permission to strap me in, and that's final." The contractions were steady, one after the other. "Where's my husband?"

"I told him to wait in the hall until we're prepared."

Before Rosa could respond, someone came up behind her and clapped a mask over her face. She grabbed it and threw it against the wall.

"What are you doing?" a woman's voice said, stiff with anger. "It's only oxygen!"

"I don't care what it is! I don't want it on my face! I want my husband in here, now," Rosa said, looking at the doctor.

"Tell her husband to come in," she said to a nurse in a voice cold with anger.

The nurse brought him in and Rosa could see she was pregnant. "I understand she planned for a home birth," she told the doctor.

"This is a hospital," the doctor said, slapping her rubber gloves on.

The head moved down. Luzia was ready. Rosa looked at Julio. He had his camera in his hands. He touched her shoulder and said, "Go for it!"

In one swift movement, the first real movement she'd felt in days, she got to her feet in a crouch.

"My God, just what do you think you're doing?" the doctor yelled. "Make this woman lie down!" But everyone froze.

Rosa cried out, harshly. The head emerged, dark and wet, between her thighs. It dangled there.

"Another push then," the doctor said as her hands held the head.

"A girl!" Julio shouted. He followed the child to a table as they measured and weighed her. Then the pregnant nurse wrapped Luzia in a blanket and ran from the room.

"Luzia, Luzia," Rosa murmured, feeling every cell in her body alive, alive, alive. She was lying down as the placenta slipped out between her legs.

"I'm going to go see where they've taken her," Julio whispered into her ear, kissing her cheek.

"I want to keep the placenta," Rosa told the nurse. She felt a stabbing pain in her belly, and when she looked down the doctor was probing her with an instrument.

"Get that out of me, goddamn you!"

"I have to do this. Now lay back!" the doctor said, preparing to probe again.

"Don't you dare touch me with that!" Rosa raised her foot.

"I'm through with this patient!" she said, furiously, slamming down the instrument.

As Rosa lay in the recovery room, she burned with an intense energy as though her blood, rushing through her, had finally found the sea. She entered the sea, wide awake. Outside the window clouds began to move aside for a bright light. For a moment, Rosa had to find the word in her mind: moon. A nearly full moon. There seemed to be a film, a piece of tissue, over the moon, like blood.

Julio's words hadn't prepared her for the sight of Luzia connected by wires and tubes to the complex machinery surrounding her, as Rosa looked at her through the thick, silent window. She opened the door to the nursery and walked toward the room where Luzia lay.

"Are you a mother?" a voice asked.

"My daughter is the one in there." Rosa gestured toward the room. "I want to see her."

"You'll have to put these on." The nurse handed her a gown and mask. "I'll go in with you."

Luzia's eyes were shut tight against the bright room, which made her look a little like a boxer after a long fight. But her face was sweet and still. The sight of her raw umbilical wound brought stinging tears to Rosa's eyes, but she stopped them. She's as small as my hand, almost, Rosa thought. Luzia's face twitched as though to cry, and her breathing quickened, but instead she became still again.

"May I touch her?" Rosa asked the nurse.

The nurse turned from her task of arranging things on the other side of the room and said, "You have to be extremely careful not to touch any of the wires. Here, let me tell you what they are."

As Rosa put her hands, one at the top of Luzia's head, where an IV was inserted taped down, transparently, and her other hand at the bottom of her feet—she felt her daughter's body become whole to her. She was startled to feel the smallness of the bones in Luzia's feet, and her tiny head was so painfully vulnerable.

"I'm going to step out for a while," the nurse said, gently.

Rosa nodded. It was a little painful to be up so soon, standing. The dinner last night had revived her, and the shower this morning. Her hair was clean, thick and bushy. And my first healthy shit, she thought, is an experience I'd rather forget. When Dr. Miller, that bastard, comes by I'll tell him I owe my recovery to the healthiest shit of my life. A wicked smile spread itself over her face.

"I had to fight for our lives, Luzia, little Luzia," Rosa whispered, beginning to rub her daughter's tiny legs. Her eyes never opened, but Rosa knew her daughter had recognized her.

After a stinging piss Rosa got into bed. Her body felt so good, it was as though all the bones in her body had melted into ecstacy.

A black nurse walked in. "So there you are! I've been looking for you. I understand you went to the nursery. I don't think you should be up so early. I understand you had a particularly hard time—but, of course, it's up to you. Do you want breakfast?"

"I'd love some." Rosa smiled at her.

The nurse walked over. "Washed your hair even, I see. Well, good for you. Okay, here's your menu. If you do it real quick, I'll take it back with me. You can choose everything on there, you know." She laughed.

Julio opened the door and came in.

Rosa handed the menu to the nurse. "Thanks a lot."

The nurse looked at Julio and said, "She's been up already. Thought she'd disappeared on us. Well, you can't keep a good woman down's what I say." She closed the door behind her, laughing to herself.

"What were you doing up?" Julio asked with amazement.

"I just went down the hall to see Luzia. I touched her, Julio. She's so delicate, so tiny." Rosa smiled, remembering her fingers on the thin, tissue-like skin, the small bones beneath like a little bird. A grounded bird. I'll teach her flight by touch, Rosa thought, so that she can fly beyond her pain, and then, finally, leave it far behind her.

"You got to touch her?"

"I think you can go in, too. After all, you're the father. Just go down and talk to one of the nurses. You have to wear a gown and mask. Luzia is plugged into just about everything, isn't she?" Tears came to Rosa's eyes and fear clutched her solar plexus.

"Luzia's going to make it. She's a fighter like her mother. I like 'Luzia' very much, by the way—one of the light." Julio continued to stand next to the bed. "I was thinking of naming her after my grandmother, too. How would Luzia Ramona be?"

"Of course, Julio. It's beautiful." She put her hand out to him and he gathered her in his arms till their breathing synchronized.

There was a knock on the door and it was Sierra. She looked nervous and a little angry. "I took off at the crack of dawn and I'm just getting here. What a drive!" She walked over and hugged Julio. "Thanks for calling me last night." Then she turned to Rosa. "I see you have a phone."

"It must've arrived this morning."

"Look, Rosa, I'm going down to see if I can touch Luzia," Julio said, laying his hand on her shoulder, lightly. He felt the tension thicken in the room.

"Could I come too?" Sierra said, excitedly.

"I think only the parents can go in the room, but you can look in if you want," Rosa answered her.

"I'll be right back, then," Sierra said, going out the door with Julio.

Rosa was stunned. Stunned and hurt. Not a greeting. Not a touch. Something went hard inside of her, like a door slamming shut.

After everyone had gone—Julio, Sierra, Sean—Rosa thought, These are, were, are the closest people in my life. Sean had been distant, anxious to get back for his early morning workout. Only when he looked at Luzia did he crack, "She's so damned tiny, but she's cute. She's real cute, Mom." But when Rosa tried to reach him, he pulled away.

When Sierra left it'd become apparent how strained it was between them, so there was very little pretense of intimacy.

"Well, we all have our little problems now, don't we? I'm thinking of leaving Bob. I mean, it's not easy for me either, you know, Rosa."

"Do you think it was easy for me when I drove down to be with you? Do you imagine that it was easy?"

"I wanted to be at your birth, but you beat me to it. Anyway, Julio came through it seems," Sierra answered, defensively.

For a second, Rosa was going to ask her why she was leaving Bob, but she didn't. I will not ask, Rosa repeated to herself.

The silence became unbearable.

Even Julio's warmth had lessened during the day as though he didn't want to be in a minority. And Rosa had too much pride to demand his warmth.

"I've never felt so alone in my life." Rosa probed Sierra's eyes.

A flicker of victory spread over Sierra's face. "Well, what did you expect moving so far away?"

Rosa locked the door. "Not much, I guess. Do you mind asking the nurse to bring me some tea on the way out, Sierra? I'd appreciate it. Also, would you please turn off the overhead light?"

Sierra turned, slowly and stiffly, towards the door. She fumbled with the handle and looked back at Rosa. "I'll give you a call later." She turned off the light.

Why? Rosa wanted to say, but instead she said nothing.

The stars were out tonight, soft and twinkling. Up on the mountain, up on my mountain, Rosa thought, they're hard and fierce. The moon had risen and it shone on everything, equally, like the sun. She imagined her childhood friend driving home under the full moon, as she lay, stationary, still bleeding her dark birth blood, under the same bright moon.

There's one. Rosa saw it. A hard, fierce star. Are you Sirius? she thought. And then she slept.

Julio had to go back to the city for the week, and the doctor in charge of Luzia's care told them that she wasn't stable yet. That she'd probably be there a few weeks more. After Rosa called Diana she contacted some friends of Diana's who lived in Chico, who Diana said would be glad to let her stay there. They were a couple with a small child. Gentle people. They drove Rosa to the hospital every morning, and she spent the day holding Luzia. Luzia was recovering quickly.

Sierra called and left a message at the desk, but Rosa didn't return the call. When Julio came back up it was disappointing, but it seemed inevitable—the intimacy, the truce had been broken.

He'd brought an immense box, from Erica, full of baby clothes. I don't even have diapers, Rosa realized. Inside every piece of clothing there was a small, delicate seashell or some dried flowers, and a note with the word "ENJOY" at the end of a rainbow. Yes, it was a storm, Rosa thought, but it's not over. This is a respite.

The doctor wanted to keep Luzia at least another week, suggesting that Rosa go home and come back.

"I'm not leaving without my baby. She's stabilized. You told me that the other day. Why can't I take her home?"

"Are you willing to be responsible for your decision to take her from the hospital?" he asked her.

"Yes, I am."

"Then, at this point, I'll leave it up to you. You do realize you must keep her body temperature stable. If her temperature drops rush her to an emergency, and put her under a doctor's care immediately. But, as I've said, you must be responsible for your decision to take her from the hospital." He looked at Rosa, fully expecting her to concede. They almost all did at this point.

Rosa fought with herself for a second, visualizing Luzia's small-ness out in the world. "I accept that. I'll be taking her tomorrow morning then. Thanks for all you've done," Rosa said as the doctor turned to leave. No, the storm's not over. Not quite, Rosa thought.

The drive through the valley had been strewn with the first signs of a violent spring. Everything was deep with green and clumps of purple lupine lined the road. Once when Rosa had gotten out to use the bathroom, she'd noticed a bunch of wild iris growing serenely by the busy gas station.

Julio drove as she held Luzia, her small warmth, in her arms. And when she suckled it was so soft and tentative, Rosa worried that she wasn't getting enough. In the hospital she'd expressed her milk into bottles so they could see how much Luzia was taking. But she ate every twenty minutes or so, so she seemed to be doing well.

Julio was petulant and falsely cheerful by turns, but when Rosa felt herself getting angry her breasts got hard as though her milk would go bad, so she made herself empty. Suddenly, she remembered the feeling of compromise she'd felt with Sean as a small child. When, to protect him, she'd disguised her fury from his father. Empty, empty, empty, she thought. For now.

As they began to climb, the signs of spring began to disappear. By the first tunnel they were gone, entirely, and the first peak dis-played a dazzling cap of light. Snow. Now, in the canyon, each peak seemed to bow like a sentry, terrible in its beauty. Now, it threatened Luzia who must keep all of her heat in order to survive.

Spring was behind them, a world away. The mountains held the winter, and Rosa's fear, in their implacable grip.

It was clouding up again by the time they reached the cabin. The road had been recently plowed, so the chains on the tires struggled but gripped. The Landcruiser was parked at the top of the road, but it would have to be dug out of the snow that sealed the doors shut. Diana and a friend had driven it back for her from the doctor's office.

"The guy at the store told me one of the worst storms of the season just blew in. I guess. Look at all of that snow," Julio said, irritably.

"Look, why don't you hold the baby while I go in and warm up the house. Just keep the heater going."

The cabin was exactly as she'd left it, but it was freezing. A long, thin icicle hung from the kitchen faucet. Zack's dish was full out on the front porch, but there was no sign of him. I'll worry about him later, Rosa thought, as she turned on all the heaters at high. Then she started an enormous fire in the fireplace. She turned on the hot water faucet in the kitchen sink, and, finally, it ran hot. She turned on the bathroom faucets and they began to run hot. The temperature was rising, slowly but surely. Rosa's mouth was dry from anxiety, but the steam rising from the bathtub reassured her.

Someone had shovelled the way to her cabin. Dale, she thought. "Thank you, Dale," she murmured. Rosa put some water on for tea, and went out to get Luzia.

The one thing Rosa had prepared was a small, woven straw bassinet. She'd bought the ribbon to twine through its sides, but she hadn't had time to do it. A small, droplet crystal hung from the hood by a red string. Luzia disappeared inside the small basket, wrapped by a receiving blanket, two thermals, and a beautifully woven one, with pink rosebuds on each end. Erica'd sent it.

The cabin was warming, the fire blazed, and the subtle silence, that descended like a mantle, told her that it'd begun to snow. Bach's Brandenburg Concertos played softly, and Rosa became aware of a healing deep within her mind, as though the opposing sides within herself were becoming acquainted. But it's just begun, she realized, staring at the fire.

Julio brought a load of firewood in. "Guess who I found outside?"

"Zack? He's back?"

"He looks great, but he's soaked. Should I dry him off?"

Zack's fur was as thick as a bear's, and his chest looked larger and stronger. "Have you been hunting, old Zack? Where've you been? Good dog, good dog, Zack." Rosa petted his luxurious fur, and he licked her with excitement.

Luzia began to cry her soft kitten call, and Zack went to the bassinet and sniffed it. He registered a genuine surprise and went, immediately, to a corner.

Rosa fed her again, as she watched her small head stubbornly cling to the largeness of her breast. "You're a healthy one, Luzia," she said to this tiny creature. Her daughter.

Holding Luzia in her hands, Rosa approached Zack and held her out to him. "It's a baby, Zack. It's a baby." Fully alert, Zack sniffed at the blanket, gave it one lick and went back to his corner to clean himself.

"Can we keep her?" Julio asked. He walked over and watched Luzia sleep, dark and still beneath her blankets. Only the fluttering breaths kept him from saying, "She's okay, isn't she?" like a chant. How can Rosa stay here in the snow, now, with her? Julio held his breath, but it didn't help an anger he felt beginning to rise. She should come back with me. We'll do the best we can, that's all, he thought.

He looked at Rosa. "Are you hungry? I'll put together the chicken. How's that?"

"That sounds good, Julio. Save the back for Zack, and anything else, okay?"

He would talk to her tonight, after dinner. She'll go back with me. She has to, he thought. When Julio went to turn the record over he saw that Rosa'd fallen asleep, crouched, by the bassinet. But what if she won't leave? he asked himself, and his anger rose a little higher. I could kill her, the thought came to him with a violence he thought he'd forgotten.

The dishes soaked in the sink and they sat by the fire. Luzia slept, hidden beneath the single crystal that hung overhead, reflecting the fire as it burned.

Julio's body felt like a bomb, tense with repressed violence. They skirted each other like dancers, barely speaking, and what they said was as carefully chosen as ambassadors from foreign countries. Countries on the verge of annihilation.

"Rosa," Julio began in a careful voice, "you can't stay here now." He saw her features stiffen. "If you stay here, she might die. Don't you know that?" He raised his voice. "How are you going to take care of her and get wood and food, and get in and out of here, for that matter? Do you want her to die? Is that it?" He began to shout.

"Don't you dare say that! Do you hear me? Don't you dare say that to me!" Rosa's body began to tremble with rage. "How dare you say that after what I've had to do! You son-of-a-bitch!"

"You can't stay here. That's all there is to it. Even Sean thinks you've lost your mind. Do you know that?"

She could feel her breasts beginning to drip milk as they hardened from her anger. "You aren't going to spare me a thing, are you? I wouldn't go back with you if I had to live in an igloo. Yeah, that's how crazy I am, you mother fucker."

Luzia began to cry and Julio moved to pick her up. Quickly, Rosa moved ahead of him and took Luzia from the bassinet.

"Give her to me," Julio said in a deep, angry voice.

Rosa held her closely. "Don't you dare touch her! Do you hear me?"

Julio's hands made a desperate movement toward the baby and Rosa turned her body and ran for the bedroom, locking it behind her. Rosa's breath came sharply, like an animal fighting for her young. Her lips pulled back, involuntarily, over her teeth.

Luzia began to cry, and, instead of turning on the lamp, she sat in the enveloping darkness, calming herself with the words, We're safe, Luzia, unsaid in the silence.

For an instant, Rosa thought of the gun, the German gun, under Rolf's letters, at the back of her closet. Then she made the steel image of the gun go away with the sound of his laughter.

After Luzia was fed and asleep, Rosa went out to the front room. She had to go to the bathroom, but she didn't want Julio to take advantage of it and go into the bedroom where Luzia was. She was calmer now. She thought.

Julio lay on the couch in the dark smoking a cigarette. He seemed to take delight, a silent one, in her great agitation and fury, lying there stretched out and maddeningly confident.

"Until you apologize to me for what you said, Julio, you may not touch her. Do you understand me?" Rosa repeated, "You may not touch her."

Julio remained stretched out on the couch, and with an unfeeling calm said, "I pay you two hundred a month for my child. You have nothing to complain about."

Sheer rage shot through Rosa, of a kind she'd never felt before. She grabbed the long, black, steel fire poker, its tip like a spear. She held it in both hands and, for a split second, she imagined herself plunging it right into his upturned belly.

"Why don't you do it? Why don't you kill me? Then you could really brag about something to your feminist friends." Julio's voice lost all control. There was anger, hatred, and a strange sorrow all at once.

Rosa could do it. He continued to lay there like a perfect target. Yes, she could certainly do it.

"I'd never forgive myself, Julio." Rosa slowly hung the black poker back up, steel for steel. The matter was finished in her self. She locked the bedroom door and passed out.

Luzia's cries woke her, louder this time, with a sense of anguish. She must've been crying for a while, Rosa realized with despair. Despair for her hunger, her helplessness—her small helplessness. Despair for them all.

All night Luzia fed every twenty minutes. Sometimes it was a half-hour. Rosa watched the clock. She was just too small to get enough at once.

At dawn Julio brought in a cup of tea and toast without a word. There was bacon cooking. Rosa was hesitant to eat it, but she was hungry and very tired.

A foot of snow had fallen during the night, and only the white smoothness of the snow could be seen. And it was silent.

Julio came to the bedroom door. "The nurse gave me the placenta. Do you want it? It's in the car." His eyes were wounded and his voice held thick tears, so that his words were choked with the effort to speak.

"If you'd bring it in, I'd appreciate it," Rosa answered, coldly.

Why can't I say it? Julio asked himself, again and again, as he walked to car and back. He watched Rosa bend over Luzia to make sure she was asleep. Then she met his eyes and they said, Don't you dare touch her. She picked up the white carton and got a shovel from the closet and walked out the back door.

Rosa chose a stand of pine by the running creek. She sat down within their circle and began to dig. Then, she stood, and taking the top off the carton, she offered it to the hazy disc of sun in the sky, and then she turned toward the peaks where the moon always rose. Rosa said some words he couldn't hear. After she covered the placenta entirely, she shovelled fresh snow on top.

Then she began to cry, sobbing in great heaves, with her face to the snow. Julio ran out to her, holding onto her.

"I'm sorry, Rosa. I'm sorry, I'm sorry, I'm sorry."

After Julio was gone, a storm blew in that bent the tallest trees toward the ground like toothpicks, and the sound surrounding the cabin was like full-speed locomotives rushing by, one after the other. When Rosa saw that the cabin could withstand it, she allowed herself to see how beautiful, how terribly beautiful, the storm was—but watchfully.

Everything bent to this storm. Everything. There's a time for a storm like this, Rosa thought, listening to the powerful wind that destroyed the boundaries between Earth and Sky. I must remember this, always, she told herself. The windows were solid with flying snow.

There'd been letters from Dolores, Maria and Rob. Dolores' letter was brief.

> Dear Rosa,
> Full of surprises, aren't you? This check's from Louie. I'll be sending you a good sweater when I get to Macy's. Well, now you have a daughter.
>   Dolores

Her aunt's letter was longer, and she was obviously slighted at not being told of Rosa's pregnancy, her silence in general, and when was she coming to visit, and how wonderful she'd named her Luzia, "after mi Mamá," and Julio, where was he, and Sean, and Julio . . .

As the storm lessened in its intensity she picked up Rob's letter again.

> To The Wild Rose,
> Enclosed please find a check. I can already hear you, "I can't take this" but I say I want you to. I have so much money saved it's ridiculous (I buy steel garbage can for the kitchen to last a lifetime) But if you still feel guilty you owe me a painting, how's that? Or just a loan. I'll borrow that lilac sky one for six months. Now don't you feel better? I laugh every time I think of you telling that pompous bastard that you knew your pussy from your asshole. You are the stuff of legends in that hospital now, believe me. Who knows, maybe you changed his outlook (joke) though I doubt it. I've had fantasies of punching that kind of guys lights out. When I was in med school an older woman doctor took me to one side once when she saw the unmistakable rage on my face and she simply told me "You're not crazy." So now I say to you Rosa— *You're not crazy.* I want to come up in June, probably the third week. Let me know if this is kosher. I will come bearing gifts for the new one you've named Luzia. Maybe even something for you. Who knows? Take good care, rest as much as possible. I know all will be well, and we will never die like our sun.
>   Mucho Loveo,
>   Rob

Luzia was hungry again, and as she picked her up Rosa realized she was smaller than a roasting chicken and she laughed out loud.

Rosa licked her cheek once, and said to the blind groping that was her daughter, "But you're tasty, Luzia." Luzia began to suck a little more forcefully. "That's it, Luzia. Take what's yours."

Dawn found Rosa in the same spot, in front of the fire, feeding Luzia. It was grey and still. Utterly still. Utterly silent. The storm had passed. Then the strengthening sun revealed a brilliance of light, surrounding the cabin, that was painful to look at. It was like being inside of a diamond.

A diamond. The image followed Rosa all day. She was too tired to concentrate for any real work, but she took the plastic off the unfinished canvases and worked sporadically on the shawl. I want to complete the shawl by June to show Rob, she thought. Maybe even the orchids. Luzia should start sleeping three-hour stretches by May, at least. She looked at the blank face on the woman in the painting and it tugged at her, but she knew she didn't have the concentration to deal with that. So, she let it go.

The sun was setting because it was getting dark. There was no sense of sunrise or sunset, but only of the diamond's brilliance; the light lying on the Earth that would glare and glitter through the night with or without the sun.

As Rosa finished cooking her meal, with the light on over the stove, Luzia slept. Maybe she'll sleep long enough so I can eat if I hurry, Rosa thought. She brought the kerosene lamp to the table and lit it. There was no phone yet, but she was glad the electricity was on. That meant the heaters for Luzia. Dale said her phone might be out for a week, but the electricity was almost always reconnected in twenty-four hours. Luxury and necessity, Rosa realized.

Rosa had spoken to Dr. Walker before the phone had gone dead, and he'd said if Luzia's temperature was stabilized and she was eating, she was fine. That's what Rob had said.

Tonight, maybe every night, she thought, I'll use only the kerosene lamps. It's so beautiful. So gentle. Rosa was tired but hungry, and, as if in a dream, she turned to the stove to serve herself and brought her food to the table facing the wide kitchen window. The expanse of the diamond's light.

Then she saw it. She saw the face. Huge and sculpted. Perfect. It revealed itself to her. How many times did I look out of this window today? Rosa asked herself. The face was at least ten feet high and made of snow, rock and tree limbs. It was a woman's face. Mayan. Infinitely powerful and, at once, equally, serene. Her eyes stared downward to a world only she could see. She possessed infinite beauty. She was perfect. She was complete.

Rosa's face felt like it was on fire. "Quetzalpetlatl," she murmured softly like a prayer. "She knows," Rosa stared at the Goddess and the word came to her, "everything." And then her face felt like ice.

Slowly, the darkness took Quetzalpetlatl as Rosa wept with joy. Luzia stirred and began to cry. She'd blown out the lamp, so she lit it again. Then she fed her daughter and herself at the same time.

Sean was gone. "Julio, Going to be gone for the weekend skiing with some friends. See ya, Sean" Underneath Sean's note was a stack of messages on pieces of paper he'd snatched at random.

Freda, the woman I was going with when I met Rosa—wonder what she wants? he thought, putting it at the top of the pile. The others are probably photo shoots, a couple of friends. There's no one I really feel like calling to tell them about Luzia. My little Luzia, and my grandmother's dead. "Luzia Ramona," Julio said out loud.

His heart no longer felt inexhaustible, but instead he felt a tired sense of finitude. A hollow, complete exhaustion. Like the dead, he thought. Something's died in me. Yes, I feel it, though I don't know what it is.

Freda's name floated up to him. Was I alive then? Julio asked himself. Will I be alive again?

He wandered into the kitchen and poured a glass of brandy, a good-sized one, and took it to his bed. He picked up the phone and tried Rosa's number. Finally, the operator came on the line telling him, "That area is not in service, sir." "When will it be in service?" "We can't predict that, sir." "And why not?" "You'll have to keep trying, sir." I'll just have to keep trying, he repeated to himself. That's all I needed to hear. That's all I fucking do is keep trying, Luzia Ramona. Rosa.

Then Julio became aware of the hot, salty tears that covered his face, and kept on flowing till he sobbed out loud as Rosa had over the buried placenta, that fleshy medium that had sustained a life. Once it had been indispensable. Now it was useless. Now Luzia struggled to breathe and eat without the gentle medium of the dark. The placenta.

And in that knowledge there was a death. "Take this gift, my sacred Earth. My daughter lives. Bless me, Mother. Bless my birth," were the words Rosa had spoken. And in that knowledge there was birth.

Men are chasing him. Shots ring out in the air above him. He is filled with fear, but it only makes him run faster, without a sound. There is no sound but the guns. His breath is easy, and the ground is so close, so close. Then he sees his feet. His paws. His great furry paws with claws inside. He feels his claws curled back, tense. The men have stopped and they shoot aimlessly in their anger. He is free as he stretches himself out, muscles working so perfectly he barely feels the ground. And the ground is alive with the smells of life.

Rosa managed to complete a watercolor for Rob—a rendering of the lilac sky painting—a sketch of the view outside her kitchen window for Rolf, and a watercolor of Luzia for Julio.

She'd called Julio when her phone finally had a dial tone one morning. They'd decided to wait a month before he came back up— he'd send three hundred instead of two hundred, he'd bring the photographs of the birth, he looked forward to the watercolor she was working on. They'd been calm, careful, delicate in their new peace.

Now Rosa bundled Luzia and, placing her in the basket, put her in the back of the car surrounded by blankets and pillows, and went out with her, for the first time, to mail them.

Ray greeted her curtly, telling her the store was open, "Not too much right now, but maybe there's somethin ya might need. I could order ya baby food. Heard ya had one." He weighed the packages, took the money, then followed Rosa into the grocery store.

She bought coffee, milk, bacon, eggs, bread, even wine. She didn't want to take Luzia out of the car, so she moved quickly.

"That should keep the wolf from the door," Ray said, ringing it up.

"Were there ever wolves up here?"

"We run em out way back, Roza. Nothin to be afraid of now. Killed a few myself. There were too damned many of em." Ray scowled.

Rosa drew in a sharp breath. "What a shame. They're so beautiful. Why did it happen?" She felt more sorrow than anger as she looked at Ray's unhappy face.

"They're killers is all." Ray turned away.

Rosa sighed. "Do you want to see the baby?"

"May as well." He walked out to the car and then told her, "Nah, don't bother er, I can see er from here." Ray peered in, briefly, saying, "Looks like ya got a baby there, Roza." Then, he actually smiled, and regretted it so quickly that he turned and left without another word.

She stood in the soft air for a moment, and then she drove away. Luzia began to stir in her basket. "They're killers," she muttered, rolling the window down a notch and drove straight home.

It was already May, and sometimes Luzia slept for two solid hours. In the last month Rosa'd wept from sheer exhaustion and joy by turns—but it was already May. May. Spring. Its very beginnings, at least in the air. The air was softer, infinitely softer, but there were no flowers visible to the eye, so the ground held no color. Rosa looked for color, a flower. The sign of spring.

She'd sketched a bright, yellow daffodil, ridiculously yellow, and hung it up by the kitchen window. Periodically, she'd take it down and add another, then another, till the drawing paper resembled a meadow erupting with flowers of every conceivable color.

Diana was coming in the afternoon, and she planned to do a watercolor portrait of her. Diana was also bringing some groceries for her, and then Rosa remembered the groceries she just bought at Ray's, so she called to tell her not to bring those items.

"I feel like I should've set my hair for this or something," Diana laughed.

"Come as you are. That's the point. My only suggestion woud be to wear beautiful earrings. I've seen some nice ones on you."

"What would you suggest?"

"Surprise me. Don't forget the chicken and vegetables, okay?"

"Got it all right here."

Luzia stirred searching for her mother's breast. She didn't cry. She was accustomed to the feel of arms at her first sounds of complaint. Rosa fed her, sitting in the rocking chair she'd placed in her studio, facing the final rainbow painting. All of these will have to be framed, she thought. I'll have to find someone in town.

The face was complete. She'd sketched the face the following morning. Quetzalpetlatl had stayed all day and receded, again, within her mystery during the night. But all day—all day—she had been there with Rosa, within the diamond, and Rosa had sketched her exactly as she'd seen her. Broad, high cheekbones, eyes almost closed, staring downward. Timeless. Now she wove the rainbow encircling the Earth from the spiral of her serenity, from the wisdom of her womb, from the spectrum of her sun.

People will see what they see in this painting, Rosa thought—of course. Luzia had fallen back to sleep, curled against Rosa's belly. Without the rainbow, without that protection, there would be no life, the thought came to her. Isn't she the invisible weaver of our world who loves the flaw in the lilac sky, even if I don't? "Yes, even if I don't," Rosa murmured.

She looked at the shawl, nearly complete, and she thought of Clara, long-dead now, and remembered something she'd almost forgotten about, entirely. It was as though Clara's cancer and death had wiped it from her memory: Rosa's visit when Clara was being hospitalized for a nervous breakdown, as they called it, about four years before the cancer. Yes, the nervous breakdown, Rosa remembered—the rage of being alone after she left her husband. When Clara had seen Rosa's serious face, she'd laughed and said, "You're safe, Rosa. We're all crazy here, you know."

"Well, Clara, the fold is not insanity. We weren't crazy, after all." Luzia stirred at the sound of Rosa's voice. "The ring of orchids will be for you, Luzia," she said, looking at her daughter. "But the fold will be yours someday," Rosa whispered.

"I decided not to bring Joel so I can relax," Diana said, carrying in the bags of groceries.

"Good idea. I'll put these away and then we can start. You look great, by the way."

"I'll open the bottle of wine I brought. It's kind of sweet, but I think you'll like it."

"Okay, well, just settle in. Just relax. Luzia should sleep for another hour or so. It was a good idea not to bring Joel so you can just sit. Anyway, a watercolor doesn't take that long, and I thought it'd be fun," Rosa said to Diana.

Diana sat directly in the light coming through the window. "The face is better than you could describe it. It's wonderful," Diana said, looking at the rainbow painting. "Would you sell it, Rosa?"

"You know, I don't know about this one. Not now, that's for sure. But I do want to show it, of course. I'll show you all three together later, if you want."

"A private showing, great. You've had some adventures here, haven't you?" Diana laughed.

"Whoever it was that slashed my tire, I could've lived without. If it hadn't been for Dale I'd have been up shit creek. He came out and changed it in two feet of mud. Imagine me standing on the porch with a gun in my hand yelling, 'Whoever you are, if you touch my car again I'm going to blow your ass away!' And poor old Zack sleeping outside every night for a while there. When I heard that low bark of his I knew they were coming back."

"Hey, I can imagine it. I'm glad you didn't have to do it, though. They caught the guy, didn't they?"

"So am I," Rosa said, almost to herself. "He broke into almost all the empty cabins, Dale said. But they caught him trying to sell some of the stuff," she said as she worked on the eyes.

"Why do you suppose he slashed your tires?" Diana asked.

"Boredom." Rosa laughed. "Did I tell you about that time I saw a huge footprint in the snow—but only one. I mean, it was big. I thought of Big Foot, of course."

"People have seen him, or her, up here, I've heard. I never have, myself. But I don't doubt it. My feeling is that they're gentle and shy creatures, though. Nothing to be afraid of."

Rosa thought of Ray and the wolves—his words, "Nothin to be afraid of now . . . They're killers." But they eat what they kill, and I am only afraid of men. Other human beings and their unpredictable cruelty. Rosa sighed, deeply. Mine included.

"In Tibet they call it the Yeti, and, supposedly, they recognize them as guardians of the Goddess. Why not, then, the guardian of women? After that—though I won't kid you, it scared me—I've come to think of it as a kind of ally."

"This summer I'm taking you camping somewhere very special. Do you think Julio might come up and take care of Luzia for a night or two?" Diana shifted in the rocking chair, getting comfortable again.

"We could probably work something out. Where're you thinking of going?" The mouth began to take shape.

"I want to keep it as a surprise. Are you interested in this Dale, by the way?" Diana smiled.

"Don't smile too much right now. Just try to keep the same expression pretty much. In other words, wipe that smile off your face." Rosa laughed. "No, but he's been a very nice guy, to say the least. Detouring the creek, changing the tire. I gave him a good bottle of brandy. He is a very interesting man, though."

Diana started laughing.

"Laughing's worse. Anyway, like when I brought the brandy over, he was listening to classical music. Mozart, no less. Maybe he's my Big Foot."

"But you're really not interested in him?" Diana persisted.

"Right now I'm not interested in anyone. Too much else going on. That's the truth."

"You will be," she said, smiling again.

"You're smiling again, A——. I'm going to end up making your face out of whack. I warn you," Rosa said, jokingly.

"Are you waiting to see what happens with you and Julio?"

"I don't know anymore. You know, I think it's worse between us when we make love. It aggravates our situation. Crazy but true." There was sorrow in her voice.

"So far that's what I've found to be true. It's hard to live with someone. My lover spends a night or two sometimes, but he always goes home. I guess that's the difference between having a lover and being in love."

"I guess. Do you have any men friends? I mean just friends like a woman."

Diana made a sound of exaggerated exasperation. "Maybe that comes later or something. But right now, no. Mostly, men just seem to want to test my mattress. Don't get me wrong. There are men that I like, but it never works out to a friendship, and I think it's more their fault than mine. For the time being I've got some pretty wonderful women friends, so no complaint."

"Maybe it is a matter of time or age or whatever. Like my friendship with Rob is very fine, and I keep thinking that's exactly what's lacking between Julio and I. A lot of passion with us. Not enough friendship." Rosa worked on the shadows on Diana's face.

"But sometimes I wonder if Rob and I became lovers, would that tug-of-war begin? I want both. I guess that's it. I want both. A friend and a lover, all in one. It's beginning to seem impossible, like asking for world peace." Rosa smiled to herself.

"But like world peace, you have to keep on asking for it." Diana shook her head and her right earring tumbled free from her long, dark hair.

"I asked you to wear some beautiful earrings and I just noticed them. What're they made from?" Rosa stepped forward and touched the long, beaded earring that nearly reached Diana's shoulders.

"They're porcupine quills. I bead these myself. Would you like some?"

"I'd love some. They're absolutely beautiful. Do you ever think of going back to where you grew up?" Rosa began the earrings, giving special attention to their design and color. They were rather like personal flags, like symbols of wholeness.

"I think when I killed my snake, I killed the part of myself that belonged there." Diana's voice was soft in the waning light, and for an instant her face held an unspeakable longing. Then, her face became firm, almost angry.

"You know, I dreamt a snake while I was pregnant. I dreamt that it entered me. That's what it felt like, and it did feel terrible."

"It's not an easy medicine. Some need none, some one, some many." Her voice sounded harsh and final, as though from the distance of old age.

"Rosa, do you mind if I take a break for a minute?"

"No, go ahead. In fact, I think I can finish from here. Just don't peek at it yet. You sounded very old just now, very wise."

"That was my grandmother." Diana flashed her a smile and went to the kitchen.

Rosa worked for twenty minutes more, and then the baby began to wake up.

"Do you want me to get Luzia for you?" Diana asked.

"Would you? I think I'm done. Walk her for a few minutes, okay?" Rosa could hear Diana talking to Luzia in the other room. She finished the coiled snake around Diana's neck. It hung, loosely, like a living necklace around her neck, its own head poised and alert, nearly parallel to Diana's face, so that it didn't appear to be merely an ornament, but the powerful presence of a snake. Her snake. The snake she'd killed.

Rosa realized she would've taken no pleasure in this depiction of the snake even a year ago. They'd always repulsed her since she was a child. She put down her brush. This lime-green snake with its coral head is beautiful, Rosa thought. Beautiful and dangerous. She'd almost painted the white dream snake Diana had told her about, but this was the one she saw instead.

"You can bring Luzia. I'm done, A———. Come and take a look."

Diana handed Luzia to Rosa, and just stood there, silently, for a while staring at her portrait. Tears rolled down her face.

Finally, she asked, "Do you see that?"

Rosa nodded her head. "Maybe that part of yourself had to die to become fully conscious. Maybe a better word would be transformation. You know, E equals MC squared. Like my friend, Rob, believes that the sun will never die. Only matter changing. I think he's right."

Rob was dead. Her package was returned, unopened, with an envelope taped to it. The letter read:

Dear Rosa,

I'm Rob's ex-wife. He mentioned you to me once as a good friend, and Jeff told me about the great time he had roller skating with you and Rob in Golden Gate Park. I'm sorry to have to tell you this, in fact I'm surprised you haven't seen it in the paper. Rob was shot and killed by a man demanding drugs right in the clinic. They tell me it happened before and Rob had the man arrested. Jeff's doing well, I think. Rob's been cremated, his ashes sent to his parents. Again, I'm sorry to have to tell you this.

Sincerely,

Norma

The orchids were nearly done. They hung in the lilac sky, in a circle. Each one was purple, a deep, rich purple; only their centers varied, from a spectrum of light yellow to a glowing gold. Sunrise to sunset. One was nearly white in its yellow light.

"Is that how you left, Rob? Through the center of my orchid? Who will imagine the sun now, Rob?" she asked out loud.

Rosa walked outside and looked up at the warming June sun and she looked for Rob's face, but she couldn't see it. She looked at the clearing, at the miles of valley between the trees, and it only looked empty. Not eternal. Empty.

"You know, my last visit was pretty peaceful. Wasn't it, Rosa?" Julio asked. Julio had arrived early that morning, and he was holding Luzia in his arms. She smiled at him with a wide, toothless smile, as though she knew that this were her father. It pleased Julio. Immensely.

"I think part of the secret to that success is that we weren't lovers. It doesn't work for us to be lovers, Julio. Don't you agree?" It has to be said and there's no other way to say it, Rosa thought.

She had no desire to make love to Julio, or anyone. Something was dying in her, and Rob's death clung to her like a ceaseless mourning. The violence of his death and the violence of her sorrow merged in that mourning.

Julio glared at her for a moment, but then he said, "You may be right. How long do you think this'll go on, not being lovers? I never was a good monk."

"Just because you and I aren't lovers doesn't mean you don't have to have a lover. That's up to you, Julio," Rosa said, softly.

"Then, needless to say, it's the same for you. Do you have a lover now?" he asked, raising his voice slightly.

"Obviously, it would go both ways, if and when, in the future. If you choose to have a lover, it'll be none of my business. Do I make myself clear?"

"So you have a lover now, is that it?" Julio demanded to know.

Luzia began to cry and suck her fist.

"She's hungry. Do you want to give her a bottle? She takes a bottle or the breast about equally." Rosa put the bottle on to warm.

"This is why it doesn't work, every time. What I'm trying to tell you is that you don't have to be celibate, and I'm not going to answer your question. Also, we might think about making it legal or whatever. Like divorce, if that's best."

Julio switched Luzia up to his chest and walked with her. Finally, he said, "Okay. Fair enough. Then, do you mind if I stay for a week or two?"

"If it works, fine. I want to go camping for a couple of nights with some friends. Well, tonight we'll see how you do with everything. I'm sure she'll be fine. You have to feed her about every three hours." Rosa handed Julio the bottle.

"Do you think it's safe to sleep out up there by yourself?"

"It's safer than the city, that's for sure. I've gotten to feel safer here than I've ever felt anywhere. I know I have to watch where I put my feet, but, if anything, wild animals run for it when people come around."

"What about that guy who slashed your tire?" There was a trace of satisfaction in his voice.

"He was the rarity, not the norm around here. There's no burglars or rapists pounding on my doors," Rosa laughed. "I can't explain it. I just feel safe. Protected. By the Yeti."

Julio watched Luzia as she sucked at her milk, recording her with his eyes in lieu of his camera. He looked up at Rosa. "The whatty?"

"The Tibetan Yeti. Big Foot, as they're more commonly known. Guardians of the Goddess. How's that?" Rosa's womb stirred as she watched Julio feed Luzia, but she told herself, firmly, No.

Julio smiled. "Why not? I figured you had something out of the ordinary going on up here, Ms. Luján. By the way, I love your paintings. The new ones. The orchids aren't done yet though, right?"

"I haven't been able to finish it, but I will. I'm almost done. I was supposed to lend that one to Rob for a while." Rosa got up to pour another cup of coffee. "Do you want some more?"

Julio nodded. "You can put in some extra work time while I'm here, you know," he said, looking at Rosa.

His eyes held an offer she couldn't accept, and she shifted her eyes to the pine tree in front. "I'll take you up on that. I could use some blocks of uninterrupted time. I want to finish these pieces before I start anything else."

The only sound in the room was Luzia's sucking, with occasional short pauses to catch her breath.

"Are you taking Zack with you tonight?" He held Luzia up and she burped, loudly.

"Good one," Rosa laughed. "Probably. I'm going to take a quick walk. Do you mind?"

"Go ahead. That's why I'm here. Maybe next time we can bundle her up and take her for a walk."

"I've taken her in the front pack. She likes it, in fact. I just want to take a walk by myself."

Julio took a deep breath and said, "I brought the birth photos. I think there's one you'll especially like. One of you."

"Why don't you show it to me when I get back?"

"Okay, take your time." Julio began feeding Luzia the rest of the bottle.

The wildflowers had finally appeared. There were clusters of purple lupine, bright-red Indian paintbrush, and the tiniest, white flowers, like a carpet of earthbound stars, that made the rocky soil look tender with light. The grass that grew close to the creek was young and green. Soft.

Rosa lay in it, turning her face down into it, feeling it, the fresh, young grass. It's wonderful to be alone, Rosa repeated to herself with pleasure. Then she got up and cupping the cold creek water, she cleansed her face and drank. It tasted clear and good. Like freedom, she thought.

The ranch was open again, but they only used this trail in the afternoon. There was fresh horse shit here and there, so she stepped off the trail. She visualized Julie riding by, spurs and horseshoe earrings glinting in the afternoon light. Her look of disdain for those on foot, real or imaginary. Rosa sighed. Julie hadn't called or been by, once, during the entire winter. Well, something goes, something comes, Rosa thought. I suppose. Rob came to mind and any wisdom that she had fled.

She sipped the water again and thought of Diana and Iris. She looked forward to the camping trip with them at the end of the week. And Sierra was coming up at the beginning of July. Nothing was resolved, but Sierra wanted to visit, and Rosa couldn't deny it—she longed to see her old friend. At the same time she dreaded it. There was anger on both sides. Distrust.

For an instant, Rosa doubted the wisdom of camping out on the peak by herself. Tonight, she thought, like a challenge. Tonight. You promised, she told herself.

Zack came running back up the creek and drank deeply from it while the water swirled around him.

"Do you want to sleep out with me tonight, old Zack? How about it?" Rosa smoothed his mask with her hands as he panted excitedly.

As Rosa circled the creek she noticed a car parked in front of one of the cabins. The summer people. She decided to cut through Forrest's property, and there he was measuring a piece of wood, in the silence, with his worn leather tool belt strapped to his waist. His chest was bare as he worked in the open, and Rosa responded to his beauty with an intensity that surprised her.

"Why, Ms. Luján! I hear you had a little one. A girl, is that right?" Forrest beamed a smile at her. A genuine one. "I was thinking of coming by, as a matter of fact, to see how you're doing. Looks like you saved me a trip."

"Well, didn't your wife have a boy? What's his name?"

"We called him Ethan." Forrest's face tightened. "We split up. I'm living here now. She just doesn't want to live here, and after all this work." He shrugged his shoulders. "So, I'm finishing up for the winter." He looked at Rosa. "What's your daughter's name?"

"Luzia. Well, I'm sorry to hear that. Maybe it's temporary. Maybe Cheryl will change her mind." Rosa could see he didn't want to talk about it. "Anyway, it looks like a great house from here. I like all the windows, and the stonework is pretty impressive."

"Haven't you seen it? No, you haven't, have you. Come on in and have a spot of tea with me," Forrest said, laughing with a sense of relief.

"Sounds good, but just for a minute." Rosa looked for Zack, but he was gone. "Zack!" she yelled. "Get over here, Zack!" Nothing. "Oh, well. Maybe he went home. Okay, how do you get up here?" Rosa gestured toward the porch about five feet off the ground.

"I have just the thing, Ms. van Gogh. Excuse me for a moment." Forrest brought a ladder from the side of the house and propped it up against the porch. "Usually I just vault it. Only use the ladder when I'm drunk."

"I didn't know Johnny Appleseed touched the hard stuff. I'm very dismayed," Rosa said with a laugh.

"You never give up, do you?"

"You called me Ms. van Gogh first, Johnny. What a beautiful old door. Where'd you get it?"

"From a house being torn down. Turn of the century, and absolutely free. Most of the wood and windows have been free. I'm a scrounger. Do you want tea or wine?"

"Wine sounds good, actually. Just a little. I like your house," Rosa said, walking room to room. "What's upstairs?" she asked, pointing to a ladder. "Do you plan to put stairs in, ever?"

"Maybe. It keeps me on my toes." Forrest poured the wine. "That's my bedroom and a loft area."

"Do you mind if I take a look?"

"Help yourself. It's a little gnarly up there though, I warn you." Forrest settled into a large, oak rocking chair.

"I like this room, by the way. It's like a greenhouse, all this light. Do you cook on that wood stove?"

"Ms. van Gogh, I even bake bread and biscuits in it." Forrest took a sip of his wine and watched her climb the ladder. "I see you've lost most of your p.g. weight."

"By jumping rope in the front room, leg lifts and shovelling snow seven feet high. A little yoga, too."

"Cheryl lost hers right away, too. Just naturally, I guess. Probably something to do with being twenty-one."

"Thanks a lot there, Johnny Asshole. I like your tree house. Very impressive." A clear skylight held a view of the tops of the tallest trees, and French windows opened next to his bed. There was a beautiful, old quilt on his bed, and small stacks of books were everywhere. A large jar of wildflowers caught her eye.

"No offense intended. Jesus, if you don't use the F word on me, you use the A word on me," Forrest said, laughing loudly. He began to tune his guitar in an aimless fashion.

Rosa came back down the ladder. "Is this a concert? I'll forgive your last remark if it is."

"What's the big deal about your being in your thirties? I'm going to be in my thirties, hopefully. You're going to be in your forties, hopefully. Right?" He stared at her, intently.

Rosa smiled at him. "You've got me there, McBride." She sat on a well-worn couch and took a sip of her wine. It was delicious. "What is this?"

"Good, isn't it? You are drinking a 1978 Petite Sirah, which I, personally, helped bottle."

"And how is that?" Rosa watched his fingers move, delicately, over the guitar. He was strumming the beginnings of a piece. A beautiful piece.

"After the work's over at the ranch, I take off for the harvest at a vineyard for a couple of months. It pays well, and I get cases of this good wine almost for free. Last year was the first year I've missed, but I'm going this year for sure. Cheryl being pregnant and all." His voice slackened for a few seconds, but he caught himself.

"Help yourself. The bottle's on the kitchen table." Forrest began to play.

"Hello!" a man yelled. "Anyone home?" He paused and yelled louder. "Hello!"

Forrest got up, putting his guitar carefully back in its case, and walked out to the porch. "What can I do for you?" he yelled back.

"There's been a dog fight! My dog's pretty badly mauled, and I was wondering if you owned a malamute? A big, furry wolf-looking dog?"

"Just a minute," Forrest answered him, and went back in to where Rosa still sat.

"I don't believe it, but it sounds like Zack. Goddamn him, anyway!" Rosa got up and walked to the porch. "I think that's my dog you're talking about."

"You should have that dog chained, lady! I'm taking my dog to the vet's, and I hope you're prepared to pay the bill!" he said, with more than a trace of nastiness.

"Look, I'm sorry. Of course, I'll pay your bill. I live in the cabin across this meadow. My name's Rosa Luján. Just bring me your bill. Is your dog all right?"

"He isn't moving. That dog of yours is vicious. Plain old vicious. Mine just barked and that devil was on him like flies on shit." He lowered his voice, but his anger was still audible.

"I don't think that's really necessary," Forrest interjected. "She said she'd pay your bill, and she said she's sorry about your dog."

"You either chain that dog or I'm calling the sheriff!" the man said, and, turning abruptly, he stalked away, kicking stones out of his way.

"I'd better go, Forrest. Save me a glass of that wine. And that

piece you were about to play. Goddamn it, this is the second time it's
happened," Rosa said, angrily and close to tears. "What in the hell's
getting into Zack?"

Forrest put his hand on her shoulder. "My dog used to get in his
share of fights, but, frankly, he was usually the casualty."

Rosa laughed. "I'd better get home and put him inside. Thanks
for the tour. Drop by my place sometime," Rosa said, without thinking of Julio.

Zack was on the front porch with blood on his fur. He crouched
low when he saw Rosa. She grabbed him by the collar saying, "What
is wrong with you, Zack? You're a bad dog! A bad dog!" She jerked
him to his feet and brought him into the house.

"What's wrong?" Julio asked.

"Zack's been in another dog fight. I guess he'll be staying here
tonight. Damn it!"

"Maybe you'd better skip it. It's up to you, of course," Julio
added, seeing the flash of irritation across her face. "So what happened?"

"I didn't see it, but I understand he jumped a dog because it
barked at him. Anyway, the owner will be by for a check for the vet's
bill. Shit! Look, I'll leave a signed check, just make it out. Tell him
I'll be by later to see how his dog's doing."

Rosa wiped the blood off Zack's fur and looked for cuts, but he
didn't seem to have any.

"Did he run off? Is that why you didn't see the fight?"

"Yeah. I'm going to have to keep an eye on him and put him on a
chain when we pass by any cabins, especially in the summer. I'm
going to have to keep him on a chain outside for a while as well.
Anyway, I thought he ran back here." Well, I'm not lying, Rosa
thought. I'd just rather not start the Forrest issue again. It'll start up
sure as shit and I don't need it.

"Then what I'll do is take him outside and wait for him to do his
business and bring him back in."

"Thanks, Julio. How's Luzia?"

"She's doing fine. Went right back to sleep after the bottle. I
changed her diaper and all. I enjoy feeding her, you know? It must be
something to be able to feed her from your breasts," Julio said,
smiling, but there was some sadness in it.

"It is. Almost like a privilege," Rosa said, looking away. "Luzia
should wake up in about an hour. I think I'll wait till she does and
breast feed her one more time before I go. I'd like to get up there by
three at the latest."

"Do you know where you're going to spend the night just in case we have to send in a search party?"

"Not really, Julio. Basically, I'll be up on that slope," Rosa said, pointing to it. "I'm sure there's a good place somewhere up there. I'm not going to make a fire, just some snack stuff will do it, so I'll be back for breakfast around noon."

Why does it feel like she's hiding something from me? Julio thought. Why does it always feel like she's hiding something from me? "Rosa, why are you going up there by yourself?"

This was the farthest she'd gone following the creek behind her house, which was now almost dry. Just a trickle reflected the sunlight. The pond beside the cabin was gone, leaving a deep bowl of fine sand. The lupine and paintbrush thinned out as she continued the climb. How strange it felt to be walking alone, without Luzia. Or even Zack.

The silence was profound, and the creaking of a tree in the wind, the occasional wind, made her stop to identify it. Rosa took off her pack and sat in the sun. The farthest peaks still had some snow at their tips. She took a sip of water and then a small dot of color caught her eye. She bent down and touched its leaves. Little thorns. It has little thorns, Rosa realized. Could these be roses? They must be. "Wild roses," she said to the air with sudden happiness.

There were more small bushes along the way, and then they were gone. A loud, shrill cry jerked her head upward. An eagle—a large, dark golden eagle—spiralled to her left and then flew out of sight. Automatically, Rosa turned and started up the steep, rocky incline, staying in the open to avoid the thick, stubborn manzanita brush, and possibly snakes.

The pack felt heavy now and sweat poured from her body. She took off her jacket, tying it at her waist, but it wasn't enough. No one's here, Rosa told herself, why not? She took off her top, exposing her breasts to the sun and wind. She could feel her milk gathering, and her breasts felt beautiful beyond any doubt.

Always too small, always too droopy, always covered as though there were something to be ashamed of. Here they were absolutely beautiful. Rosa could see that. She cupped her breasts in her hands and felt a strange new strength run through her body, almost like an orgasm, but everywhere at once and without the sudden violence of genital orgasm.

A slow, sliding movement made her heart explode. Close to the ground it moved, slowly, into the shadows of the manzanita—so smoothly, Rosa imagined a hiss like silk in its wake. A rattler. A huge rattler. Her body trembled with the indecision of wanting to break and run, stay glued to the spot, or go forward. It got out of the way, didn't it? she reasoned. It wants nothing to do with me. It got out of my way, didn't it?

She forced her feet to move further up the slope. It was beautiful, Rosa thought, involuntarily, as her body shuddered, once, with delight like she had as a girl when sexuality had been new to her. When its terrible secret invaded her. Yet how eagerly she'd walked toward it, toward the terrible, wonderful secret.

Clusters of lupine and wild iris covered the slope at the top. There was soft, new grass where it levelled off, creating the illusion of a meadow. This was it, and the view was magnificent. Peak after peak, in the distance, revealed themselves to her eyes, and the air was transparent, clear, as though she'd never seen so far.

A large piece of wood, shaped like a dragon with its head rearing up toward the distant peaks, held the most level ground of all. How many years of erosion and settling did it take to create this small patch of soft, level ground? And this tree, this once living tree, into this smooth dragon's form? Rosa asked herself, as she spread her sleeping bag out beside it and opened her pack.

Luzia came sharply to mind as her breasts reminded her they were full. She took out her breast pump and put it to one side. She slipped off the rest of her sweaty clothing and spread them out on the dragon to dry and freshen. No one comes up here, and she reminded herself, no one can hear me if I scream at the top of my lungs.

She climbed up on a rock, aware of the contact she felt with everything: the earth, the wind, the sun, the scratchy hardness of the giant stone. Rosa stared out at the vastness and a single note came out of her mouth. She sustained it for as long as her breath would allow. And then again, and again, varying tones until her head was full of that sound, and she felt full of that horizon.

Then, the word "Rob" came out of her in the same single, sustained note, softly, then harshly till it became a scream. A long, steady scream of pain and separation. A longing. A fierce, naked longing. She wept, but she continued her one note song. Sobbing, she stopped, and then began again until the harshness finally subsided and her voice became clear and even with the word "Rob."

The sun was warm wherever it touched her, and the vastness was not empty. It was eternal. As eternal as transformation. And whatever she'd become, or whatever Rob had become, was gathered by her longing. She accepted that. That's all she had, and she knew it.

The rock began to bite into her tender skin and the rising wind brought an edge of chill. Rosa climbed down, touching the dark, dry moss that covered the giant stone. Her feet felt the small stones and dried pine needles, distinctly, and all of it felt alive with pleasure. The silence was deep and unbroken. Even the common stellar jays didn't break the silence here. She looked up, scanning the sky for the eagle, but the sky was still.

Rosa reached into her pack and brought out the gun and its clip, wrapped and tied in a small towel. She unwrapped the gun and held it in her hand, shoved the clip into it with a snap. She felt the earth under the fallen tree and it was soft and yielding. Like flesh, the words came to her.

All the bullets were in the clip. Every one. She'd never fired it. Rosa went to the tail end of the dragon where its long tail came to rest. She kneeled down, laying the gun beside her. She dug her hands into the soft coolness of the ancient earth, and it gave way, without a struggle, to her surprise. She began to tremble, not from fear but anticipation.

Rosa picked up the German gun and pushed it into the earth, but at the same time she felt an unmistakable taking—a receiving. It was unbelievable, but it was true. The earth took the gun from her hands, and she let it go.

The little girl in her dream, dead—Clara, dead—Rob is dead—her desire to kill Julio, dead—to kill the enemy, dead—the German soldier, dead—the dark-skinned children, dead—an entire village, dead—all the children, dead—all the men, dead—all the women, dead—the desire to kill each other—dead. Naked and kneeling, she let it go. Let it go. Go. Into the ancient earth.

"Estoy juntando la noche, Mamacita," Rosa said aloud. She realized she was cold and her legs were stiff. The sun was setting. Thin pastels were layered on the horizon, exquisite and quickly changing.

As she dressed, she imagined a slash of magenta, and, as though the sky had read her mind, it was there spreading itself, briefly, then sinking into that pale lilac that never held or stayed. The lilac sky. She thought of the unfinished ring of orchids, and placing them in the twilight, they became complete. The last orchid's center so gold, it rivaled the sun.

After she ate her meal of bread, cheese and fruit, leaving enough for the morning, she poured the last of the white wine from the jar. The stars were all around her, fierce and close, and her cabin felt a million years away. She was utterly alone.

Rosa sipped her wine and felt herself blending into the darkness. If I had a fire, Rosa thought, I'd be a part of the fire, separate from the night, resisting it. It was frightening—the night, the silence, the solitude—but it continued to claim her. "Then I'd be human," she murmured, reassuringly.

The wind had stilled and the darkness was complete. Rosa slipped into her sleeping bag, stretching her legs into its warmth, lying on her back. The stars seemed to be falling from the sky, yet the familiar ones remained.

For the first time since Luzia's birth, Rosa made love to herself, and in the moment of her orgasm she became the fire.

He's the one. The one I could never face. The one I dread and desire, equally. Dark, dark he is, and lovely. His dark eyes don't let me go . . . He rushes toward her, and she faces him. Rosa forces herself not to turn away this time. She feels his entire body enter her. Completely. Her eyes do not let him go.

This was Luzia's second bottle in a row. She was restless and refused to go to sleep. Julio felt the plump little arms, remembering how frail she'd been at birth. Her eyes began to flutter and close, and her mouth fell away from the wet nipple.

He was afraid to move. She might wake up, he thought. Julio positioned himself carefully on the couch, with Luzia next to him— tiny, delicate, sleeping. He listened for her breath and closed his eyes, peacefully, with this evidence of his daughter.

The baby is crying, loudly, for milk. He looks for bottles, but there aren't any. The baby continues to cry, now with desperation. Julio opens his shirt and he sees that he has breasts. A wild joy fills him. "I have milk for you, Luzia. I have milk for you." As Julio places her to his breast and she finds his nipple and begins to suck, a feminine voice says, "Union."

A rainbow encircled the sun. The sun had a rainbow around it. It was clearly a rainbow. Not as vivid as those she'd seen during a rainfall, but it was there, gentle and distinct. As Rosa stared up at it, shielding her eyes from the early morning sun's intensity, the eagle flew into the circle of the rainbow. Rosa held her breath and then she was gone.

"Are you still alive?" Rosa asked, opening the door.

"I've got breakfast ready to go if you're hungry. Do you want some coffee? How was your trip?"

"Just what I needed. How's Luzia?"

"Well, she's asleep now. She was up every three hours last night. On the nose." Julio handed Rosa a cup of coffee. "By the way, those muffins are from your friend, Forrest." He put a snide emphasis on the words "your friend."

"Forrest came by?"

"Earlier this morning. They aren't bad." Julio looked at her piercingly.

"I'm going to take a look at Luzia."

"Do you want an omelette? I'll fix it for you, if you want."

"Well, if you're offering, I'll take it."

Julio began the omelette. He still couldn't get over the way Forrest had knocked on the door, with a plate of muffins in his hand, and just walked in when Julio told him Rosa wasn't there. "Do you have a cup of coffee to go with one of these? I'm all out of coffee at the place. Got to get some," Forrest had said, sitting down in a kitchen chair.

"She looks fine, like you did a good job." Rosa picked up a muffin. "Did this come with the muffins?" she asked, indicating an embroidered napkin.

"It sure did. Actually, the muffins were warm when he brought them. We had coffee together."

"You're kidding," Rosa laughed. "I assume he's won your heart."

"I don't know about that." Julio paused. "He seems to be a pretty nice guy, and either he's an excellent actor or he's never seen this place. He liked your work. Quite a bit."

Zack came up to Rosa and sniffed her hand for attention.

"Has he been out? Go on, Zack. Bad dog. Go on and lay down."

"He's been out and fed, and the guy didn't come by."

"It'll be a while before he gets a pet from me, damn it. Anyway, what did you two talk about, if you don't mind my asking?" Rosa continued to ignore Julio's innuendos.

"The ranch, mostly. Building his house. Rosa, what're we going to do about us?" Julio began to move toward her.

Rosa put her hand out to stop him. "I don't know. I really don't. All I know is that if we were lovers we'd be screaming about Forrest right now. I just can't do that again. I won't, Julio."

"Don't you think it might be different this time?"

There was a long silence between them, and then Rosa said, "I don't think so. That's what I really feel. To be honest with you, I've considered it, but I just can't. I just can't do it anymore. Everything goes wrong between us when we make love. Everything."

"So, it's different lovers, is that it?" Julio said, angrily.

"That's up to you. You know the gun you gave me?"

Julio's face registered alarm. "Yeah, what about it?"

"I buried it yesterday. Up on the peak. There was a rainbow around the sun today, this morning."

"You could've just given it back to me, you know. It was a perfectly good gun. Why did you bury it?"

"Because I had to."

Julio walked to the stove and flipped the omelette onto a plate, placing it on the kitchen table. He looked out the window and then back to Rosa. "Was there actually a rainbow around the sun?" His voice was soft with understanding.

"Yes."

Julio stayed for two weeks, and it'd worked because they hadn't been lovers. Almost one night. Almost, but Rosa stopped herself, cold.

He was patient with Luzia, spending endless time with her, taking her for walks, caring for her. But, periodically, Rosa had felt his glance on her, angry and hot.

The orchid ring was complete, yet the painting remained, in some sense, incomplete to her. The black, lace shawl was stunning in the center of the orchid ring, with each of their sun-centers full of light. Is it still the sky? The color of the sky? Rosa asked herself. "It's done as far as I'm concerned," she said out loud to no one. "The damned lilac sky."

Sierra would be arriving soon. She'd just called about a half-hour ago and she was only forty or so miles away.

Rosa looked at the photograph Julio'd given her. It still startled her to look at it. It was a full frontal of her crouching, about to give birth, in that lull when everyone froze. Julio hadn't. He'd caught it. The delivery room lights had created a glare of light on her back that resembled outstretched wings. Maybe I'll paint this, Rosa thought as she stared at it. Maybe.

It was a hot day. She wondered how Sierra was driving up in the heat with the baby. "Stop and take a swim," Rosa had told her.

Rosa poured a glass of French colombard, putting a slice of

orange in it, and went outside on the front porch to sit and catch the occasional breeze, thick with summer, as it drifted by. Clusters of butterflies were on the dark, wet earth where she'd just watered, opening and closing their wings in a kind of ritual ecstacy. The huge monarchs seemed almost tame.

One of the monarchs flitted lazily in the air and landed on her hand. Rosa kept absolutely still and watched it turn while it opened and closed its wings, tasting her with what appeared to be a slender, black tongue.

She thought of the lake where Diana and Iris had taken her. They'd spent two nights, and, except for brief journeys into silence, they'd talked and talked, laughed and swam, continuously.

The lake was a treasure. A jewel set in a rough, granite bowl. The water itself was like silk as it parted for the swimmer. The lake was snow-melt, and when Rosa swam to its center a chill ran through her. Not of temperature, but of what lay at its bottom.

A few people had hiked out during the day, but at night they'd had the lake to themselves. The second night they gathered enough wood for a small fire. Then they decided to go in for a swim in the moonlight. The wind was still as they passed a pipe between themselves. The sweet smell of grass floated in the air, and their naked bodies were warmed by the fire.

How beautiful they are, Rosa thought. Diana dark, Iris light.

All of them held hands, and then stood together facing a waning full moon. Then, Diana ran for the rock ledge, and as she stood, poised, in the darkness about to dive into the equally dark water, her body looked silver in the moon's light. The water rippled and splashed as she dove, and when she came up she screamed with delight.

Rosa imagined herself silver, like a fish, and dove deeply with shudders of pleasure. Each of them dove, again and again, unafraid of the fisherman. The lake was alive with a woman's magic. The moon's magic. The Goddess' magic.

Just as Iris began to dive, the last time, she yelled, "The Goddess is alive! Magic is afoot!" Then Diana, then Rosa.

"I must get a tattoo," Iris said, laughing. "But I don't know where exactly."

"You'd better figure that one out. It'll be on you forever," Diana answered her, laughing.

"I've got brandy. Would you like some, ladies?" Rosa asked.

They towelled off quickly, and lay in their sleeping bags facing the dwindling fire and the lake beyond was smooth with the moon's light.

"What an excellent idea. To bring brandy," Iris murmured.

"Is it always safe here, like this?" Rosa asked. "I've never felt so safe as a woman. Do you know how rare this is?" Tears filled her throat.

"We know, Rosa," Diana said. "That's why we brought you here."

Sierra's car turned up the road and Rosa jerked to attention. The butterfly flew away. Rosa opened the door a crack to see if Luzia was awake.

"So, this is it, at last. I took a couple of wrong turns back there. Your not having a street sign doesn't help," Sierra said with reproach.

"I told you it wasn't an easy drive. Anyway, you must be hot. Come on in." Rosa took some of Sierra's things in with her. "But wasn't it beautiful driving up through the canyon?"

"Toward the end there, I didn't notice anything. Well, you got remote, that's for sure." Her voice was strained.

Why did she come? Rosa asked herself. "Did you stop and swim? In this heat you should've."

"I stopped and sat by the river for a while, but decided to wait to swim. Where can I put Felipe down? I brought a portable crib."

"You can put the crib here in the front room. Why don't you put him on my bed? Luzia's still asleep," Rosa said, keeping her voice neutral. She felt the beginnings of anger. She went to the refrigerator and poured the wine coolers she'd prepared.

Sierra came into the kitchen, smiling for the first time. "Luzia looks so cute. And fat. You'd never know she was premature. I wonder how they're going to get along?"

I wonder how we're going to get along? Rosa thought, handing her the chilled glass. "Wine cooler. Some white wine, orange and lemon juice, and sparkling water. After they wake up we're going swimming. There's some places by the creek where you just drive into, and it's closer than the river."

They took turns swimming in the clear, chilly water. Immense fronds grew in the center of the creek in places, and a small waterfall was constant in their ears. The babies lay together in a shaded spot. Already Luzia was beginning to be tired, but Felipe crawled and rolled until he was off the blanket. Zack lay next to the babies, protectively, as he did with Luzia whenever she was placed on the floor.

"Bob will be moving out by September, and I'm seeing about getting a roommate," Sierra said in a depressed tone.

"Don't you think it'll be better? I mean, after everything he told you, it must be a bummer to see him every day." Rosa sipped her wine cooler.

"He's moving right in with her. Not going to skip a fucking beat. All that time, even when I was pregnant, he was seeing her. Son-of-a-bitch!"

"Have some more wine cooler. The worst that'll happen is that Felipe will get a little drunk with you."

"What the hell. Lay it on me. This place is so fucking beautiful it makes you realize how screwed up your life is, when it is. That fucking liar!" Sierra gulped her drink.

"It's a good thing I brought a gallon of it," Rosa laughed, gently. "He's going to give you child support, I assume?"

"He's going to give me more than that for a while till I work things out." Sierra poured herself another drink. "This stuff's pretty good. Delicious. Not that strong either. Just takes the edge off things. Is that what you've learned to do, Rosa? Take the edge off things?"

"I don't know about that. Not entirely, that's for damned sure. But I'm certainly not going to stop enjoying myself, or stop living, for anyone. Anyway, I think you'll be happier without him around, to say the least. You just have to get used to it. Things will change. I'm going to get in the water. Be right back."

Zack followed Rosa along the creek bank, sniffing excitedly, but he wouldn't go in the water.

Sierra watched Rosa dunk and swim, and she realized how true her words were, "Things will change." We've changed, Sierra thought. Felipe began to cry, so she picked him up and fed him. Feeding him, nowadays, made her want to cry as though everything vulnerable within her were being exposed.

"I see she fell asleep," Rosa said, dripping the cool, delicious water. She covered Luzia with a thin blanket. "Take a swim when you're done. I'll keep an eye on him." Rosa poured a fresh wine cooler, slicing an orange into it.

"Rosa, I'm sorry I wasn't at your birth. I wanted to be. I don't know what happened. I guess it had something to do about leaving Bob by himself," Sierra said, miserably. "It meant a lot to me to have you at my birth. I just want you to know that."

"Do you want another wine cooler?" Rosa poured Sierra another and sat down next to her, putting her arm around her.

They wept because they loved each other, and they wept because they'd changed.

Dale called the next morning. He wanted to know if Rosa would cover for the bartender for all the weekends in July. "It'll be about eighty to a hundred dollars a night, including tips. That's what Kate makes. I talked to a Mrs. Spencer, a summer person, and she said she'd be glad to watch your little one. So you might get in touch with her. Thought you might be able to use the money."

"I sure can. Thanks a lot. When does it start?"

"Tonight's Friday. Starts tonight. It'll be till Sunday. Seven till two, closing time for the bar. Simple bar. Beer and wine coolers. Some wine margaritas. The recipes are under the counter, Kate says."

"I'll call Mrs. Spencer. And, thanks, Dale. See you tonight."

"Dress up a little. Something off the shoulder. It helps the tips," Dale said, laughing.

"I'll see what I can dig up."

Rosa hung up the phone and turned toward Sierra. "Well, I just got an offer to do some fill-in bartending, starting tonight. I could make up to a hundred. I can really use it. The only thing is, it starts tonight. I have to be there at seven."

They'd just had breakfast and were sitting around with their third cup of coffee.

"I'll watch Luzia. That's no problem."

"Are you sure you don't mind?"

"Are you kidding? Go for it. I'll make a little fire and relax. Anyway, I'll be staying till Sunday morning."

"How about getting out to the creek early? I'll fix a snack real quick. You're getting pretty brown there, girl."

"I am, aren't I?" Sierra said, admiring her arms.

A band was setting up, plugging in their amplifiers and checking the lighting. Tony, the manager, was waiting for Rosa behind the bar. He smiled as she approached.

"You look right nice. Nothin to it. Here's the recipes," Tony said, pointing to them under the bar. "I'll be back to take care of the till. Just pocket your tips. I'll pay you then. Be payin you cash."

"Okay. Thanks, Tony. These are the prices, right?"

"That's right. Just give me a holler if you need any assistance. I'd love to give you a hand, you know." He looked at Rosa knowingly and she turned away to check the supplies.

The band started to play a country rock song, and an older couple got up to dance. People began to order drinks.

"Ah'll take one a yr wine mar-gar-eetas, ma'am." The exaggerated drawl sounded familiar. It was Forrest.

"What're you doing here? And with a cowboy hat? Jesus!" Rosa started to laugh.

"I could ask you the same thing, Ms. Luján. How bout that margarita?" He pushed his cowboy hat back, revealing his eyes.

"By the way, thanks for the muffins. They were delicious. I still have your plate and your cute little napkin."

"I believe the custom is to return freshly baked goods with the cute little napkin over them. I love brownies with walnuts." Forrest sipped his drink. "Not bad. If you keep this up, I'll tip you."

"How many more do you plan to have?" Rosa couldn't help smiling.

"Just enough so I have to use the ladder. Your friend, Julie's here." He indicated her approach with his eyes. "Excuse me while I become invisible," Forrest said, pulling his hat down and turning toward the band.

Rosa braced herself.

"So, you're filling for Kate. Jake and I'll take a couple of beers. Well, how are you, Rosa? I see you survived the winter." Everything Julie had on was tight. Especially her jeans.

Before Rosa could answer her, Julie shifted her attention towards Forrest as if Rosa had disappeared. "Well, Forrest, how about a dance tonight? Show me your stuff!" Julie said in a challenging tone.

Forrest half-turned on the bar stool and looked at her. "How you doin, Julie? I see you're in top form tonight. I'm just planning to sit here and get drunk, so go on ahead without me. Who knows? Maybe I'll get to know the bartender," he said, smiling at Rosa mischievously.

"Well, what was it? A boy or a girl?" Julie's face registered a slow burn.

"I had a girl, Julie." Rosa looked at her evenly.

"How nice. That is, if you didn't want a boy."

"I got exactly what I wanted."

"I see," Julie said, looking at Rosa, then Forrest. She picked up the beers and walked over to Jake.

"She sure has changed. It's hard to believe we used to be pretty good friends. Does she always come on to you that way, or was that strictly for my benefit?" Rosa looked at Forrest and burst out laughing. His eyes were crossed in a hilarious mockery of pain.

"Do you like me better this way? I'll keep it up. Another margarita, bartender."

"Didn't your mother ever tell you you might stay that way? Look, I'm supposed to be working. Uncross your eyes. I can't stand it," Rosa managed to say between bouts of laughter.

A man came up and ordered six margaritas and asked Rosa to deliver them to his table. "When you get a chance, Rosa honey," he said, reading the name tag all the employees and guests wore. His name was Dutch. Then he winked at her and walked away.

"Rosa honey," she muttered. "Fuck."

"Didn't your mother ever wash your mouth out with cleansing properties? You and that F word. You have an affection for it, don't you?"

"Here's your drink. Maybe you'd better cross your eyes again and cheer me up."

"Only if you promise me, in a solemn vow, to not use the F word. Rosa honey, it just doesn't become you." Forrest crossed his eyes and stuck his tongue out at her.

"I love the word *fuck*. It keeps me sane," she said, beginning to laugh again. "Drink your drink. I want you to fall off the ladder."

Almost everyone in the room was dancing to a slow tune. Julie was dancing with one of the young wranglers and, as Rosa passed, Julie ground herself right into his body. It looks good to me, Julie, but not on the dance floor, Rosa thought, and kept going.

Dutch tipped her a five, and he asked if she'd bring fresh ones in about twenty minutes. "Thank you much, Rosa honey," he said with a broad smile.

Rosa kept her distance and smiled politely. Three men and their wives. A little over middle age, a little overweight, and a little too white. Rosa's white people phobia loomed into view. I wonder if they're German or English, like me? she reminded herself. But unlike me, they aren't Mexican, or Yaqui. Her guard went back up.

The tips were gathering in her jeans pocket. Rosa was glad she'd worn the scooped Mexican blouse. Even with the open windows it was getting hot. It could go off the shoulder, she thought, if I loosened the ribbon. Maybe if Dale shows up I'll do it as a joke. She smiled and fixed a margarita for herself with extra chablis. Her first drink. She'd called Sierra and everything was fine.

Forrest came back with his hair wet. "Another margarita, Ms. van Gogh, por favor."

"Where've you been? Where's your cowboy hat?"

"I just jumped in that dinky little pool out back that looks so big in their brochures. I'll take your place if you want to follow suit. But, first, I have a surprise for you."

"Thanks, anyway, Johnny, but I'm being paid to be here. Is it open after the bar closes?"

"This here's for Ms. van Gogh," the guitarist said into the microphone. The band broke into a loud, funky rendition of "Brown Sugar." It'd been country music all night, so the Rolling Stones were a jolt.

Forrest grabbed Rosa's hand and pulled at her. "Come on! You have to dance this one with me. Special request and all."

"I can't, Forrest. What if someone wants a drink?"

He held onto her hand and looked at her. His eyes were on fire. "Fuck em!"

They're *his eyes*, Rosa remembered, suddenly. The Greek dancer's eyes. *That fire.* Forrest held onto her hand as they walked out to the dance floor.

"Fuck em?" Rosa laughed, moving toward Forrest.

"Yeah, fuck em," Forrest smiled at her. "Best possible curse that could befall anyone. Keeps you sane, you know?" Forrest danced as though he had no bones and he were trying to give away his spine and his hips. "Move it!" he yelled, egging Rosa on.

And she did. She moved it, feeling her body's urge. She didn't care that people were staring because she'd lost her bones, her spine, her hips. "You move it!" Rosa yelled back.

"That feels great. Just what I needed," Rosa said, towelling her hair. "I think I just woke up."

"If you come by my place I'll finish that piece on the guitar, and open a cabernet you won't believe."

"Are you trying to pick me up, Mr. Appleseed?"

"It all depends."

"On what?"

"On the fucking ladder."

Forrest lit a lantern. The house smelled of lupine. There were bunches, everywhere, in jars.

"It looks like we passed the first ladder test. Do you think you can pass the next one?" Forrest asked, without taking his eyes from hers. His red hair sparkled with fire, and his beard looked infinitely soft and inviting.

Rosa reached out and touched his beard, running her fingers through it, and, then, finding his neck, she pulled him close to her. His lips were soft, and, slowly, they opened to her.

He laughed deep in his throat and held her to him, moving his hands the length of her body until it became unbearable. Unbearable with heat.

They kissed again and their tongues moved and moaned into each other's mouth. Their knees began to buckle and sway.

"Are you ready for the second test?" Forrest asked, thickly.

"I think so."

A cooling wind blew through the open windows next to his bed, and the stars looked plastered against the skylight directly over it. A huge bunch of the sweet lupine were on an old oak night table, filling the room with its scent as though there were nothing else in the entire world but lupine. Sweet, purple, wild lupine.

"I've never made love to anyone with red hair," Rosa murmured.

"That's not my fault," Forrest answered, smiling. "No, let me do that, please."

He undressed her like a child and caressed her like a woman until she lay on the multi-colored quilt naked and wild.

"Take off your clothes, Forrest. Strip!" she commanded him in a husky voice.

"Only if you say the F word in my favorite way," he said, smiling, as he began to take off his shirt.

"Fuck you, Forrest," Rosa said, softly. "Fuck you."

"That's it. My favorite curse," he laughed, softly.

His body was lovely and brown from the sun, and his penis was even lovelier—curved and taut, like a snake, in front of him. He lay over her, holding himself up by his hands, letting his penis stroke her with its heat.

Rosa cupped his penis in her hands, gently. "Fuck me," she said. "Fuck me."

"Not quite yet," Forrest said, as he began to lick her breasts, and then further down into her belly—and then he found her, and he stayed there until she screamed with pleasure.

When he entered her, she thought there couldn't be more, there couldn't possibly be more; but there was. Much, much more . . . it felt like she was opening to light. To a great shaft of white light. From the moon, from the sun. From the sun, from the moon. Her body rippled in waves of white light, and Forrest followed her to where the light began, and ended.

"You're beautiful," Forrest said, trailing his hands down to the soft slope of her ass. "I also approve of your tattoo."

They were sticky with joy, and Rosa rested her head on his shoulder.

"You ain't ugly, McBride." Rosa laughed softly and the fresh breezes soothed her.

"Would you like some of that cabernet I promised you?"

"I'd love some."

He kissed the inside of her neck, inhaling her scent, and got up.

"Rosa! Would you take these?" Forrest held two glasses and the wine bottle out to her. He climbed up the ladder carrying his guitar, and sat down at the foot of the bed and began to play, so perfectly she wept.

"Why're you crying?" Forrest asked, alarmed.

"Because I feel like it." Rosa touched him with her feet.

"Then that's okay," he smiled.

They made love again, and when Rosa opened her eyes it was morning. Five-forty-five. She leaped up and reached for her clothes.

"Where're you going?" Forrest opened his eyes.

"I've got to get home. A friend's staying with Luzia."

"I'll come by later. Fix me some brownies," Forrest said, lazily.

"Okay, see you later on, but you're going to have to wait on those brownies till I get some chocolate. Bye."

"Kiss me, Rosa."

Everyone was asleep. Luzia lay on her stomach, breathing in and out. Her eyelids fluttered as if to open. Rosa stood absolutely still and then, without a sound, got into bed.

Luzia's cry woke her, and, with consciousness, Forrest's new presence came to her, vividly, with shivers of delight. "Forrest," she said his name out loud to make him real. He was.

Sierra was in the kitchen. "When did you get in, anyway?"

"Do you mind getting me a cup of that coffee?" Rosa asked, sitting down to feed Luzia. "How was she?"

"She was fine. Woke up twice, that's all. Here's your coffee. You take cream, right? Now, where've you been, mujer?" Sierra mimed exaggerated suspicion.

"It looks like I'm having an affair with my neighbor. He's lovely." Rosa smiled to herself. "Anyway, he may be coming by later, so you'll meet him."

Sierra's face darkened with disapproval. "Do you think it's fair to have an affair while you're still married to Julio? I mean, doesn't he think you two are getting back together?"

"We've talked about the possibility of other people. We haven't been lovers for a while, Sierra. So, it's not like I'm lying or sneaking around. Anyway, I certainly didn't plan this, but I'm sure not sorry. Not one bit. I tell you, the man's lovely," Rosa laughed.

"Sean and Julio called last night. Both of them said they'd call back today. Well, who is he?"

"His name's Forrest, believe it or not. He has red hair, green-gold eyes, he plays flamenco guitar, he's twenty-four."

"Twenty-four? Are you kidding? Aren't you asking for it?"

"For what?" Rosa flared up.

"To get hurt, I guess. He's almost Sean's age." Sierra's face looked hurt and tense. Angry.

"You know what? I'm not asking for anything. So whatever I get will be more than enough. Like last night." Rosa sipped her coffee.

"I see," Sierra drew in a deep breath. "Well, I guess you know what you're doing. I mean, I don't know what I'm doing right now." She smiled at Rosa. "He must be hot."

"He sure is. What do you want for breakfast? How's omelettes?"

"I'll chop. I don't want you to cut yourself or anything. Your eyes aren't exactly focused." Sierra laughed jaggedly. "Is that collage signed 'Rolf' from the Rolf in Germany?"

She indicated an almost poster-sized collage made from bits of tissue material and gold foil which he'd entitled "Skies." The gold foil looked like bits of sunlight in the blue-pink-red-purple mixture. To the left he'd glued a soft piece of black velvet, just a strip, by itself. The night.

"That's him. We've been writing for a while now. He might be visiting next summer again, he said."

"You might have your hands full, don't you think?" The disapproval returned to Sierra's face.

Rosa got up to put Luzia back in her crib.

"I came by earlier in the afternoon, but you weren't here," Forrest said. Ethan was on his back in a baby carrier.

"I'm sorry. We went to the creek for a couple of hours. Do you have Ethan for the day?" Rosa wanted to smooth his face with her hands, but she stopped herself.

Forrest leaned over and kissed her. "Can I put him down? I'm taking him back to Cheryl's in a couple of hours."

"Of course. Anywhere you want. Here, let me give you a hand." Rosa took Ethan out of the carrier and handed him to Forrest.

"Do you take care of your son often?" Sierra asked.

"He'll be going down to the bay area with his mother pretty soon, so I try to see him as much as I can." Forrest placed Ethan on a blanket spread out on the rug, and then stood next to Rosa, putting his arm around her waist.

"He's starting to crawl a little. Didn't get much done today," he said, looking at Rosa intimately.

Rosa had to look away. She couldn't stand it, and she was aware of Sierra's eyes. "We're having leftovers. Care to join us?"

"Do you have any wine? Look, let me go get a couple of bottles. Be right back." Forrest kissed her again, running his tongue along her lips and whispered, "Not bad." Then, he was out the door at a full run across the meadow.

"Well, it looks like we have three babies in the house," Rosa laughed. "You sure are a cute one, Ethan," she said, kneeling down next to him.

"And it looks like his daddy definitely has the hots for you," Sierra said, edgily.

The phone rang. It was Sean. He hadn't called in over a month, and he wanted to come up in a couple of weeks. Then Julio got on the phone, and he wanted to see about coming up at the end of August for a week.

"Looks like you've got your hands full right now," Sierra said, with satisfaction.

She could hear his guitar and his voice through the darkness. There was a lamp on his porch spraying a circle of light. Rosa stopped just before the brightness and listened to Forrest's low, soft voice. If I were a man I'd sing like that, Rosa thought. I'd sing softly.

As she walked into the room the lupine's scent was thicker and sweeter. Forrest stood up to greet her with a laugh. Rosa walked into his arms, without hesitation. Their mouths became wild with kisses as they prepared to devour each other like food: warm, sweet, human flesh.

Later, as they lay across the bed, heads pointed toward the open windows, they talked as their bodies became their own. Again.

"So, you're going to stay here even though Cheryl's going back to Berkeley?"

"That's what she wants to do. She doesn't like the mountains or the snow or the house. I guess she expected me to become civilized and get a full-time job, move to an apartment with a regular stove and a TV after the baby was born. I just can't do it."

"Do you still love her?"

"I suppose I do. Do you still love Julio?" He looked at her, closely.

"I really don't know, and that's the truth." Rosa got up on her elbow and looked at him. "Do you know there's fire in your eyes? Twin fires. That's what they are."

"If you say so," Forrest said, pulling her down with both hands.

The next morning Sierra was quiet and withdrawn as she prepared to leave. As she packed the last bag into her car, an excruciating sense of loneliness overtook her. She turned and faced Rosa's cabin, and the sun was warm on her face. "Summer," Sierra said to herself. "It's summer."

She reached into the poems she'd read by the creek the other day and pulled one out. "She Snake," she said out loud.

Rosa came out to the porch. "Are you taking off now?"

"This is for you," Sierra said, as they met on the patch of grass. "How many skins do you suppose we have?" She began to cry.

"As many as we need. You're the poet, tell me," Rosa said gently.

They hugged, briefly, and then stood apart.

"I liked Forrest. I really did," Sierra said, turning to leave. "Wish me luck with the dragon. One goddamned dragon after the other. I think I'm becoming fireproof." She half-smiled.

"I think the trick is to burn."

"Do you think so?"

Rosa laughed. "Absolutely! The goddamned dragons are trying to give you something, believe me."

"What if I don't want it?" Sierra asked in a weary voice.

As Sierra's car drove away, the dust and the silence settled, and Rosa read the poem out loud:

She Snake

There is a wisdom in a snake.
It sheds its skin and
grows a new one—they would
have us believe a snake is
evil & loathsome & treacherous & sneaky—

they would have us blame her for
her wisdom.

I shed my skin nightly.
I dream of a suppleness.
I dream without bones.

I leave my form as a decoy
for those that would
define me.

"Yes, you do, Sierra. You want it," Rosa said to the warm summer air. "Yes, you do."

"Do you want me to get some wood while I'm here?" Sean asked.

He was holding Luzia, and she could've been his daughter. She looked so much like him, and he was old enough to be her father.

"You and Luzia look a lot alike. She's a little darker. And cuter." Rosa laughed. "That'd be great. It'll be cold in another month, though I find it hard to believe. But first I want to take you to a lake close by. I've got a friend to watch Luzia for the day."

Sean hadn't met Rosa's eyes, once, since he'd come through the door.

"Forrest will be coming with us, if you don't mind. In fact, that's how we're going. He's taking us there."

"I know you and Julio are seeing other people now, but don't you think this guy's a little young for you, Mom?" Sean looked up at Rosa and their eyes met.

"If I were a man it'd be different. Have you thought of that? It's always been considered normal for men to be involved with younger women."

"Whatever," Sean said in exasperation. "I don't care if he comes. It's your business."

"He's going to take us to a string of lakes. I've been to the first one, and it's incredibly beautiful—but Forrest says there's a few more tucked back into the mountains. Smaller and a bit harder to get to."

Sean stood up and put Luzia down on the rug close to some toys. "Well, it looks like U.C. San Diego is where I'll be heading this fall. I'll be able to run year round. Did I tell you I had to register for the draft or not be eligible for my scholarship?"

"Well, you seem pretty calm about it. Have you considered what you'd do if they activated the draft?"

"They aren't, Mom. But if they did, I just wouldn't go. Period. I'm not dying to kill anyone, but I want to go to school and I need the money," Sean said in an impatient voice.

"I guess I don't blame you, Sean. It's the endless games with people's lives that I find so damned disgusting."

"They ain't gonna get my ass in a uniform, I can tell you that." Sean started to laugh, but the hint of intimacy between them stiffened him again.

"So, is Forrest staying here?" he asked, eyeing the guitar case propped in the corner.

"Sometimes he does," Rosa answered, evenly.

"Is he staying tonight?" Sean's voice was strained.

"No, I thought we'd go out to dinner, and kind of have the night to ourselves. Do you think you can stand it?" Rosa smiled.

"Can you afford it? You're only working part-time and all." His face was serious as he turned away from Rosa's gaze.

"I'm doing pretty well, actually. The grant takes care of the basic things, and this part-time job pays pretty well. In fact, I've got some money put away. It's a lot cheaper to live here, you know. Having one movie theatre definitely cuts down on unnecessary temptations."

"It looks like you've got it made here in the wilds," Sean said, cynically.

Anger rose up in Rosa. "Do you know how hard it's been for me, Sean? Do you suppose it's all been a tropical cruise here or something? Would you be happier if I'd fallen apart instead?"

Sean walked toward the door. "I'm going for a walk. When're we taking off for dinner?" He stopped at the door for a moment.

"Be back in an hour," Rosa said, flatly. Tears of hurt and anger gathered in her throat, but she refused to let them fall.

Sean ate with an appetite, but he refused to relax or talk, so their exchange was sad and awkward. Then they drove back to the cabin in silence, as Rosa refused to compromise to his sullenness by drawing him out as she might've once done. I refuse to mother him, Rosa thought angrily. Ungrateful, over-grown baby, she continued as she turned off the motor and the headlights.

She went to her bedroom without saying good night. Luzia had taken over a corner in the studio for her night schedule. Soon, she'll need the entire studio, Rosa knew. Well, I'll just make the front room my studio. The whole damn thing.

As Rosa got into bed she missed Forrest's body, his presence, intensely. His crazy red hair, his low, sweet laugh, his soft, thick beard. His warmth. And then she asked herself what she'd rather not think about—How long will this last, anyway? Be realistic. How long will it last?

Sorrow flowed through her, and with it, finally, tears. Coyotes called in the distance as they ran. They were running in packs and calling to one another in the warm, summer night.

Forrest's light had been on as they passed coming back. A small, pin-point of light through the dense trees. She imagined him listening to the coyotes.

A young red-haired man holds an enormous, orange glass, a curved piece of glass. He's surrounded by space, empty space, and only the glass is there. He points to the orange glass that holds a small, red heart and says, "This is the heart." And then he points further, tapping a glass that can't be seen, and says, "This is the Buddha."

Voices woke her and the image of the young man and his words, "This is the Buddha," were disturbingly clear. It filled her with a strange and powerful energy. No, it wasn't Forrest, Rosa thought, but close enough to be his brother.

"Morning there, Ms. van Gogh," Forrest said, smiling at her. "I thought I'd put together some supernatural walnut-honey pancakes. We've fed the child for you, and the coffee's on the stove."

"Well, thank you, Johnny."

"I think that deserves a kiss, don't you?"

Rosa glanced at Sean's face. He was looking out the window, intently.

"I think you're right," Rosa laughed, kissing him quickly on the lips. "Were you guys planning to eat this by yourselves or what?"

"I was just about to wake you up. Ask Sean." He smiled at Sean. "Okay, first batch and ladies first."

"I'll get the syrup," Rosa said, walking toward the cupboard.

"Not on these babies! There's warm honey here in the pan. Get back, woman! I'll dribble it on for you."

"What do you mean, get back? I can put my own honey on, McBride."

Sean walked out of the room to change the record. He was obviously embarrassed.

"May I serve you, Luján? I want to serve you, okay?" Forrest turned toward the stove and dribbled honey on the pancakes.

"How can I resist an offer like that?" Rosa sat down with her coffee.

As Forrest served her, he kissed the exposed portion of her neck, making her tremble.

Luzia began to cry.

"Do you want me to put her in this plastic chair?" Sean asked.

"That's probably what she wants. Thanks, Sean." Rosa took a bite of the pancake. Little bits of walnut melted on her tongue. "These are delicious, Forrest."

"I know they are. And don't ask me for my recipe, either. You're next, Sean."

"Jesus, you're an asshole!" Rosa laughed.

As Rosa cleared the table, handing the dishes to Sean, something hit the window. Hard. She ran outside and found a large hawk, stunned, on the ground.

"Keep Zack in, Sean! Don't let him out! It's a hawk! I can't believe it. It's a hawk." She kneeled down next to it.

"Don't touch it, Rosa!" Forrest shouted. "It'll rip you up!"

Almost involuntarily, Rosa reached out her hands and picked up the still stunned hawk.

"Mom! Put it down!" Sean yelled angrily.

At the touch of her hands the hawk quickened to consciousness, but it was still hurt and let her hold him. Then, he turned his head toward her at a sharp angle, showing her the fiercest eye she'd ever seen. Ever. It was blood-red.

His talons tightened on Rosa's palms, and she knew that if she panicked and tried to move away, he'd rip her palms wide open. She could already see the small, unnaturally white bones of her hand exposed to the morning light.

Instead, Rosa brought him close to her abdomen and talked to him in a soothing voice. Then, slowly, she walked to a blackened tree stump, and, placing her body against it first, she carefully placed the hawk in its scooped-out center.

They were all silent as they watched the hawk gather himself to a firm standing position. He stood there for a few minutes, and then, suddenly, he moved forward to the edge of the tree stump, and, flexing his muscles, flew away.

"That wasn't too swift, Mom. You're lucky that hawk didn't claw you up," Sean said, not knowing whether to follow his instinct to admire his mother, or resent her.

"Sean's right, you know," Forrest echoed.

For a moment they blurred in Rosa's eyes—son and lover. And then she started to giggle uncontrollaby. "Since I'm thirty-six going on thirty-seven, gentlemen, I think that choice is up to me," she managed to say.

Sean looked at Forrest. "When she's in this mood you may as well save your breath. Believe me."

At least Sean was talking. To Forrest. They talked all the way as Forrest drove to the trail head. Then as they began to walk they became silent. The morning was perfect—clear skies, sun falling like a gentle hand on the harsh landscape, and the wind was absolutely still so that the air seemed to pulse in the silence. Wherever the eye looked a translucent quality said without words: perfection.

Rosa shuddered with joy, and loved everything without reservation, though the hawk's talons still clutched her, and his red eye still held her.

Perfection.

Zack ran ahead of them, returning to circle them without a sound, except for his rhythmic panting.

Forrest led them off the trail over stones, small, dry creek beds, and then up a sharp, steep incline to a small, sheltered lake. It wasn't as stark with the depth and feminine presence as the one she'd gone to with Diana and Iris.

No, this is a lovely, but sheltered, lake of sons and lovers, Rosa thought with recognition. How beautiful they look here. She watched Forrest and Sean plunge into the sun-filled, glittering water, one after the other. "How fleetingly beautiful," she murmured.

That night as Forrest and Rosa lay together listening to their breathing even out in the silence, a feeling of culmination enveloped them. Not as a couple, but as a precious, separate knowledge.

They'd made love quietly, aware of Sean's presence in the house. Somehow, the lake had explained the situation to all of them, and it was only natural that Forrest spend the night. Sean had been reserved, tactful as they'd wandered off to bed, seeing his mother as a woman. Why was it so painful? was the thought that had occurred to him. He didn't know the answer, but he felt it, painfully. Because he was a man.

"Tell me, Rosa, is there anything you're afraid of? I wouldn't have picked up that hawk for anything." Forrest watched her face, carefully, in the darkness.

Rosa turned to face him. He looked smooth and beautiful. This is not *my* son, Rosa breathed out. "I'm afraid of love."

"What do you mean?" His head jerked in surprise.

"I was afraid of that hawk, but I had to pick him up anyway. You could rip me open like that hawk, don't you see?"

"Yes, I think I do," Forrest said, softly. He thought of Cheryl and Ethan and, for once, his pain was eased.

"Your son loves you very much. He just doesn't know it yet."

"Do you love your mother?" Rosa asked.

"Yes, I do. Very much." Forrest's voice wandered off. "Listen, before winter sets in, I want to take you camping somewhere. My treat. I want to buy all the stuff and cook it. I just want you to bring your sleeping bag. Understand?"

"Where is this place?"

"My only hint is that it's got a hot mineral bath. A natural one. Beyond that, I ain't tellin, Luján."

"Do you know whose bed you're sleeping in?"

"Don't tell me—it's the bed van Gogh slept in."

They began laughing, and Rosa tried to pin Forrest down but he was too strong for her.

"We'd better quiet down. Sean's in the next room, remember?"

"Isn't that a little convenient when you're losing?" Forrest laughed.

But they did quiet down. And then they slept.

The coyotes called to one another, loudly, in the distance, not so far away. Zack whined at the door as they took the summer with them.

Rosa was beginning to wean Luzia and the constant sensation of filling and emptying in her breasts was lessening and soon it'd be gone. She watched Julio carry Luzia in one arm as he made the omelettes.

"Do you want a hand? You could just put her down, you know. Morning's her best crawling time."

"No, I'm fine. I'll put her down in a minute." He was savoring his daughter's weight in his arms. "Why do babies smell so damned good?" he laughed.

"Except for when they smell like ca-ca, I think it's so we'll wait on them hand and foot. Are you going to miss Sean? He's taking off in a couple of weeks, right?" Rosa held a smile deep inside of her as she watched Julio's exposed tenderness.

They were in Julio's apartment, and Sean was out for his morning workout. Then he'd go to work. She'd hardly seen him.

"Oh, I'll miss him. We've gotten fairly close, but I guess I couldn't take your place. Not really. I think he actually missed having it out with you." Julio turned and smiled. "Anyway, it'll be nice to have my privacy again, I suppose. Do you want a tortilla with your omelette?"

"Yes, please." Rosa went to the plate glass window and stared out at the horizon. When the fog wasn't in, the sunsets were lush with color. The ocean seemed placid from this distance. She felt like she'd travelled such a long way, from the ocean to the mountains, and back to the ocean. Full circle, she thought.

"Your omelette's ready, Rosa." Before she could get up to get it, Julio brought it to her. "Maybe I miss having it out with you."

"Doesn't your lady friend give you a run for your money?" Rosa smiled at Julio, meeting his eyes.

"I can live without my privacy, Rosa, anytime you say." Tears gathered at the edges of Julio's eyes, and it struck Rosa with an unexpected force, like a blow to her stomach.

"I don't think I'm done living in Lupine Meadows. Not yet. And, really, do you really think we could live with one another again?" Just the thought of beginning where they'd left off repulsed her. Would we begin again? Rosa thought to herself.

Luzia began to squirm in Julio's arms.

"We could try, Rosa. I've changed, you know. Don't underestimate me."

Luzia began to cry.

"Well, I can smell the ca-ca," Julio laughed and held her up in the air, playfully. Luzia held her arms out, suddenly, like a bird, a little bird, in flight, and she didn't know whether to laugh or cry for a moment. As he brought her back to his chest she began to cry.

"She's hungry too, Julio." Rosa faced the window and ate in silence. Tomorrow she'd go back to Lupine Meadows. Forrest would be gone to the vineyard, and then he'd be going back to Montana for a while to see his family.

The gallery had been interested in new work, so Rosa had brought down the rainbow series, the painting of Dolores, and a couple of older ones. She'd decided not to bring the lilac sky painting, though it'd seemed silly. Yet, she just couldn't let go of it. Not yet. It just didn't seem complete, though there was nothing else she wanted to do with it.

The visit with Dolores had been slightly calmer, no doubt because of Luzia's presence. Louie had greeted her loudly, "Ya look like ya seen the elephant or somethin. Take a load off yr feet. So, this here's the kid, Luzia. Couldn't give er an easy handle, could ya?"

"Oh, shut up, Louie. You sound like you don't have a brain in your head. Well, she's as cute as they come, that's for sure," Dolores had said almost shyly.

Rosa had offered Luzia to Dolores to hold and Dolores had almost refused. "I don't know how to hold babies. I might drop her."

"Here, just put your arms out and I'll put her in your arms."

"Oh, she's squirming. You'd better take her," Dolores had said, but her face had revealed an intense pleasure.

"Give the kid here," Louie had said, taking her out to the backyard.

Then Rosa had brought in the painting of Dolores playing the piano years ago.

"Who is it? Wish I had a piano. I was thinking of getting a piano and pay on it every month. There's plenty of room here for one."

Rosa had interrupted her. "It's you."

They'd both stood there staring at the young, dark-haired woman in the deep purple dress bent over the piano keys, the half-moon of her face soft with dreams. Her hands on the piano keys were strong, determined. A spray of purple iris, with slashes of yellow, entered the painting to the right. To the left, a square of sunlight, a yellow similar to the center of the iris, lay on the worn, wooden floor.

"I don't remember ever looking like that," Dolores had said almost to herself.

"It's you," Rosa had repeated.

Then her visit with her aunt, and her uncle disapproving, as usual. But this time he didn't look like the Mexican Man to Rosa, but only a man who'd been cheated of his possibilities by the time he was ten years old—working in the fields when he was five until he left for the army, where he got his first pair of new shoes.

Her aunt had heated and re-heated the tortillas, and Rosa had thanked her, but she'd finally made her aunt sit down. Rosa had actually had to say, "If you don't sit down, I'm not eating. I mean it." Her aunt had sat down, nibbling at her own food like a nervous guest. Her uncle, uncomfortable, had asked for more hot coffee, and

Rosa had bitten her tongue and gotten up quickly, putting the pot in the middle of the table. Angrily, he'd poured his own, and Maria's eyes had met Rosa's for a moment, sparkling with silent laughter.

Then, as always, Rosa was glad to leave. She'd kissed them both, and, carrying Luzia, walked towards the car.

"Take care of Luzia for us," her aunt had called out. "Maybe a piece of mi mamá is in this one's soul." Tears fell from her aunt's eyes.

"That's why I named her Luzia, Tía," Rosa had said, waving goodbye to this woman she could never change.

All her visits, all the news, and with each a sense of loss followed Rosa. An inexplicable sense of loss, and yet she knew what once was could never be retrieved or recreated. But the sense of loss remained.

Erica was having a baby, and Carmen would be a grandmother soon. She'd almost driven to Rob's place after she'd visited Carmen. It was in the same neighborhood. And then she'd remembered, as though for the first time, that he wasn't there, in his house, waiting to answer her knock.

She'd pulled over and stopped the motor and sat there, stunned. It was as though everything were in a new light, and though the sun had remained constant, the seasons had changed on Earth, and, just as implacably, within Rosa.

Then, she'd turned the car around and driven to a nearby park. Rosa had taken the book she was reading out of her purse, and sitting on the thick, green grass, she'd opened it to the marked-off page. She'd read its message, again: "Resentment, the sense of betrayal, rose from resisting the knowledge that she must go, pretending she could keep what she loved. There was nothing to keep, except maybe the willingness to love. If she lost that she was lost, all right."

Across the way from her, a man and a woman began to dance, first stretching their bodies in the bright, full sun. It was still so warm in the bay area. They were young, in their early twenties. He was black, she was blonde, and when they began to dance, their contrasting bodies touching, swaying, turning, apart, together, it seemed to Rosa a beautiful, utterly graceful, dance of opposites, just for her. She tried to imagine the hate their dance might provoke in some, in her time, and she suddenly knew they were aware of it. That possibility. But they danced and they danced, anyway, without fear, for their audience of one.

"How was the omelette?" Julio was standing next to her, holding Luzia. "She ate everything. Bananas and the cereal."

"I ate everything, too." The image of the dancers still clung to her, so that the room seemed out of focus. Rosa looked down at her plate. "It was delicious, Julio."

Zack lay in a corner with an air of boredom, getting up to grunt, loudly and re-locate himself in another corner.

"I'd better take him out for a walk. A long one. We'll be taking off in the morning."

"Do you mind if I go? I'll carry Luzia in the pack."

They drove down the coast to an empty stretch of beach, and Rosa let Zack off the chain.

"I've had to keep a sharp eye on him with all these damned fights he's been having. Now that it's getting to be winter I'll be able to let him run up there, at least."

"Are you really staying another winter?" Julio's voice was thick with anger, and it was as though he'd forgotten their earlier exchange.

"I've got all my wood in." Rosa looked at him. "Didn't you think I was serious this morning? We talked about it, remember?"

"I guess I was hoping you weren't. I guess I was hoping we could find something together around here. I know you've been seeing someone, and, as you know, so have I. But it's not the same. Is it the same for you?"

"If you're asking me if it's going to last, I don't think so. No, I suppose it's not the same—the same expectations. We thought it was going to last, didn't we?"

"Thanks a lot," Julio said, angrily.

"I'm not trying to hurt you. Not really. I'm trying to answer you, and maybe myself, you know?"

"Well, the woman I'm seeing is my age, exactly. So, maybe we have a shot at it if I give it half a chance." Julio was furious.

"Sean told you, I take it."

"What do you expect, sleeping with this guy with Sean there?"

A woman and her dog came out of the dunes, and Zack had already spotted them. Rosa ran up, shouting, "Zack! Get over here, Zack!" But she was too late. The dog began barking at Zack, a small dog, and Zack leaped on it and began flinging it in the air.

The woman was screaming and her dog was spurting blood from an artery in its neck. Rosa grabbed Zack by the collar and he pulled away from her. For the first time Rosa was afraid of him. The woman stood still in utter horror. Zack lunged at the dog, and then the dog was still.

Rosa clutched Zack's thick fur and pulled at him, fully expecting him to turn on her. "Goddamn you, Zack! Let go! Let go! Damn you! Let go!" she screamed savagely.

Zack pulled back, panting as though he'd been chasing a shore bird that'd gotten away. Zack's fur was splattered with the bright, red blood. She chained him and handed him to Julio, who'd moved away because of Luzia.

The woman was standing over her dog, crying, "My baby. Oh, my poor baby." She looked at Rosa and said, "Would you hand him to me?" her eyes looked crushed with pain.

Rosa took off her sweat shirt and forced herself to pick up the small, bleeding dog. It was dead. She wrapped it in the sweat shirt.

"Can I take you somewhere?" Rosa asked the woman, handing her the dog.

The woman clutched the dog to her. "My car's down here." She began to walk away, woodenly.

"Do you want my name?" Rosa called after her.

"Just leave me alone. Just leave me alone," the woman said, tonelessly, as she walked away.

"I'm going to have to kill him," Rosa said, numbly.

"You mean put him to sleep, don't you?" Sean corrected her.

"Goddamn it, Sean! I mean, I'm going to have to take him to the fucking vet's and hold him while they kill my dog. So *I'm* going to kill him."

"Couldn't you let the vet do it for you? Plenty of people do it that way, you know."

Rosa got up from the table and went to the sink for a drink of water. She turned and looked at Sean, who'd gone over to Zack. He was petting him.

"I wish you wouldn't reward him, Sean," Rosa said, sharply.

Sean kept looking at Zack and said in a low voice, "I never told you this because it was so long ago and I didn't think it mattered anymore. When Zack was about a year old I used to take him in the back fields and make him fight my friend's dogs for money. Zack's signal was when the dog barked at him." Sean was close to tears. "Zack never lost. Did you boy?" Sean buried his head in Zack's neck like he used to when he was a little boy.

Julio looked at Rosa and he saw that her eyes were stunned with grief. He waited for her to speak, to be angry, to cry. The moment was unbelievably awful.

Finally, she said in a voice precariously balanced between murderous rage and naked sorrow, "You were just a boy, Sean. You were just a boy, that's all. But Zack's going to have to die now, Sean."

Danny dug the grave for her, in the woods, behind the cabin, and Iris had Luzia. Rosa clipped the chain to Zack's collar and led him into the front office.

The vet came out to meet her. "My assistant will be here in a minute if you'd rather not be present. In fact, Mrs. Luján, most folks leave their animals and, for a little extra, we dispose of the animal for them." He was an older man, with kind eyes, and at the same time they held a detached impatience. He'd saved animals for their owners, and he'd killed them at their request.

"No, I'm staying with Zack." Zack's head moved at the sound of his name and he panted, excitedly. "And I'll be burying him at home. Thanks, anyway."

"This way then. It's quick and painless, I can tell you that. Are you sure you want to stay now?"

"Yes."

The vet picked Zack up and placed him on the examining table. Zack became agitated and tried to leap down. Rosa held him by the collar and stroked him, saying, "It's okay, Zack. You're a good dog, Zack. You're a good old dog . . ."

He was dead before Rosa finished speaking. For an instant he looked perplexed that sleep would come to him in this strange place, and then he shuddered, once, and died without a sound or a trace of fear.

Zack was heavier than she'd expected. She carried him like a baby halfway, but her strength gave out. He'd been a large dog. Larger than she'd realized. Rosa thought of asking for help, but the idea repulsed her. She couldn't stop crying. It was impossible to stop crying.

Rosa ended up dragging Zack by the bag the vet had put him in. Then that tore apart over the rough stones. But she was almost there. The bag was in pieces, so she removed it. His fur was so soft, and his body was still warm as though he were only sleeping. She kept expecting him to wake up. He was such a strong dog, Rosa thought. He might just wake up. He was still.

She held him by the shoulders under his forelegs, and pulled him toward the grave. She was sweating and sobbing, and she tripped over a log, and then she picked Zack up again.

He fell into the soft earth. She arranged his body and tucked his paws under him. Then she placed a favorite stone she'd found on one of their walks around the creek by Zack's outthrust tongue. The many white lines crossing and re-crossing on the small, grey stone had reminded her of a map. A constellation.

"Go home, Zack. Go home, Sirius," she whispered. "Go home."

Rosa covered him with the dark, mountain earth, all the time fighting the urge to uncover him. That he might breathe—that he might breathe. She made a small circle of stones and placed a hawk feather, firmly, into its center.

Rosa showered. The brandy was in the cupboard. She opened it and poured it out. It was amber like honey with a taste of pure fire and it numbed her mouth, immediately, and that was good. And then it numbed her cheeks, her lips, the tips of her fingers, but something, something essential, would not be numbed.

So she dressed. It was dark and winter was coming. The cold made her reel for a moment. And then she began to run toward the creek. A waxing quarter moon was up, and the night was full of stars.

She followed the creek, listening to its voice in the darkness. She stopped looking down and just followed that voice until she had to stop. Her heart exploded with an ear-shattering howl as Sirius found her.

There was a light snow on the ground, and Julio had come to take Luzia to visit his aunts for Thanksgiving. They'd argued the night before, bitterly, and then something had compelled Rosa, in the middle of it, to cross the room, holding her palms up to touch his. How silly they'd both felt, till their palms touched.

Rosa lay in Julio's arms, watching the sky begin to lighten. Julio's chest felt broad and familiar, but she knew it was temporary—only temporary. She couldn't be sad. She smiled in the grey light and got up, without a sound, to shower.

As Julio prepared to board the plane, Rosa handed Luzia to him. Her baby smell pulled at her. *This is my daughter*, the words came to Rosa as her eyes took Luzia in.

"Take good care of her, Julio. I've never been away from her for more than a day, you know." Tears came to Rosa's eyes. "If she wakes up in a strange place at night, you might have to walk her, you know."

"I know." Julio held Luzia, closely.

"Don't pass her around if she doesn't want to be. I hate that when babies don't want to be held by strangers. Promise me, Julio. I don't want to think of her crying away from me. Do you promise? I mean it."

Julio smiled. "I promise."

"I mean it, Julio. I'm not kidding," Rosa said, beginning to feel her anger rise. "She's not used to being away from me. Take care of her, Julio."

Then the call for people with small children came on over the speaker.

Julio fixed his eyes on Rosa's and said, "I promise you, I'll take care of this Native Person just as you've said. I promise."

The last of the young children were being boarded, and a person in a wheelchair was being assisted down the ramp.

"I wouldn't have missed it, Rosa. Not even the pain."

"Do you mean that?"

"Yes, I mean it."

Rosa watched until the plane disappeared, entirely, into the twilight. The last of the sunset colors were gone. She's his daughter, too, Rosa admitted with a fierce reluctance, but she couldn't deny it, a curious sense of relief as well.

The drive home seemed longer by herself, and Luzia's baby seat looked depressingly empty. Up and down, Rosa thought. I certainly have enough of that just by myself. She gave out a loud, sustained sigh.

She turned on the radio, but nothing was on. Terrible music and static. She began to talk to herself: I'll begin the painting I dreamt of holding Luzia with my left hand, and Mamacita with my right hand. The sea in the background, and Mamacita standing on the floating, rickety steps. The first visit I've had, in dreams, from her since she died twenty-two years ago. Only love isn't temporary, the words came like an answer. And then Rosa remembered the feeling in the dream of holding her grandmother's hand, tightly, so that she wouldn't die again, and that Luzia's child's hand and her grand-mother's hand felt exactly the same.

"Gracias, Mamacita, por todo."

It was late by the time she got to Lupine Meadows, but she stopped to get her mail. Ray's lights were out. Rosa turned on the bare light bulb over the post office boxes and found her own. A letter from the gallery, the junior college, and one from Rolf. Still nothing from Sierra, though she'd written her over a month ago.

After the fire was secured, Rosa got into her sleeping bag on the couch. I'll sleep here just like I did when I was pregnant. With Luzia, Rosa thought. Suddenly, she felt very foolish and stupid and guilty for letting Luzia go with Julio for five days. "Five days," she groaned. Julio will forget his promise to not pass her around, she began, and then she stopped herself, remembering his words: "I wouldn't have missed it, Rosa. Not even the pain." "Why do we cause each other pain?" Rosa whispered.

She sipped her wine and opened Rolf's letter. It was short and funny, and as usual he cheered her up. But there was also an unmistakable tone of longing in his letter. He'd enclosed a bright, red balloon. "These can be filled with helium, and they will last for days. I would still rather live in the sky, Rosa, but I suppose you've convinced me I belong to the earth as well. A friend of mine, a poet, wrote this little poem, and I thought of you with your lilac sky dilemma. So this time instead of color I send you words. . . ."

Briefly, Rosa read the poem, but it made no sense to her. She was too exhausted to concentrate. She closed the fire screen, felt for her Buck Knife, and slept.

A red balloon is rising into a clear, blue sky. Rosa holds it by a thin string, and it begins to pull away. She tries to clutch the string tighter, but it begins to slip away. Away from her hand. Grief chokes her until a coin is flipped. As she looks up at the red balloon, she lets it go. She lets it go, freely, into joy. Joy, joy, joy, it tells her. Joy.

In the morning the sky was the clearest blue. In the dream the sky was this color, Rosa realized. The clearest blue.

After breakfast the sun began to warm the front porch—distant but persistant. Rosa picked up the mail and went outside, sitting in the pale sun.

The gallery was asking if she was interested in showing in their affiliate gallery in New York. Just two pieces, but it was exciting. She'd never shown in New York. And the junior college was confirming an interview in two weeks for a part-time position in spring. Spring, Rosa thought—a world away.

Then she opened Rolf's letter and read it again, smiling. She fingered the red balloon and thought of her dream, and she laughed out loud.

She unfolded the poem.

The Sky

I see now
why they colored
the sky blue
the tongue of the abyss
is a welcome color
to embrace the clouds,
again and again,
the words that fill the
air with blue bits,
blue bits of sky and
motion and blue, again
and again, the ultra violet
shadow, then purged
clean of its sorrow.

She read it again. Then it struck her. The words, "the ultra violet shadow," struck her dumb. That's the color of the lilac sky. That's why I can't *see* it. I'll never be able to see it. I can only witness what it does. The way it births us, the way it kills us, came to Rosa's mind. Yes, the way it births us, the way it kills us, *the ultraviolet light,* like love.

"Like Germany killed me, and a German birthed me," Rosa said to whomever was listening. "Like love. Like the ultraviolet sky that I fear so much, that I love so much. God-fucking-damnit!"

She wept, but the clearing that held the early morning light— that sacred light of earth and sky—remained eternal. *There is no inherent evil in the universe,* an exultant voice told her. A voice that rose from the center of her being. From her soul. Only humans *create* it, if they so choose.

"E equals MC squared," Rosa murmured, softly. It was like

saying I love you to all creation, for whatever it was worth. *And it was worth it*, she knew.

Sean would be coming tomorrow. She'd made him promise to go with her to a peace march being planned in town. A simple one from one end of Main Street to the other.

"Do I have to hold a candle? I mean, I'll walk with you, but I think it's kind of hokey to walk around carrying a candle."

"You're going to carry a candle, Sean. Don't you think you'll look more conspicuous not carrying a candle? Anyway, we'll talk when you get here."

Sean was silent, and then he laughed. "What're you turning into some kind of hippie, for God's sake?"

"For Goddess' sake." For Quetzalpetlatl's sake, Rosa thought, because she loves the flaw in the ultraviolet sky, and weaves her rainbow for us, endlessly.

After Rosa hangs up she begins to sing, but words feel clumsy to her, so she walks out back where her placenta and Zack are buried.

A single sound, a single note, comes out of her mouth, and she repeats it in varying tones until it lets her go.

It is longing. It is praise. It is hers.

ABOUT THE AUTHOR

Alma Luz Villanueva is well known for her feminist writing. She is the author of various poetry and fiction works, and has contributed to collections such as *Hispanics in the United States: An Anthology of Creative Literature, Women Poets of the World, She Rises Like the Sun: Invocations of the Goddess by Contemporary American Women Poets*, and *Ms.* magazine. Villanueva has given writing workshops and guest lectures at a number of colleges and universities. She has an MFA in writing and is currently teaching writing at the University of California at Santa Cruz.